REDEMPTION

BY

JACKLYN A. LO

Supernatural

Time-Traveling

Thriller

with Sci-Fi and

Metaphysics

Third edition (paperback)
October 3d, 2015

ISBN 978-952-68236-7-6

Published by FRG Worldwide Oy
www.frg-oy.com

Redemption by Jacklyn A. Lo website: http://rbjal.com

EVERYONE DIES.

It doesn't matter if you're a king living it up in some grand palace or a slum dweller fighting for survival in a cardboard shack—no one is exempt. Death comes for us all.

But what if death isn't the end? What if it is simply a link in a reincarnation chain that spans the centuries and millennia? What if all of us are trapped in an endless cycle of lives, doomed to suffer and die over and over again? Wouldn't you want to break free?

Some of us do.

Dedicated to Higher Inspiration

CONTENTS

Chicago U.S.A. 2045

PART TWO: LOVE

Imperial Rome. First Century A.D

Ra's death

Her homeland is in danger

Kharkov, Ukraine

Chicago U.S.A. 2045

H E A V E N

Heaven. No-time place

PART ONE
FREEDOM

Chicago, U.S.A. 2045

Chapter One

*S*he screamed.

A huge, seemingly unending spiral held her in a powerful, merciless gasp. She wanted to break free, but she was helpless, swept along the spiral like a grain of sand buffeted by the sea. Small, insignificant and gripped with fear, she felt like she could be lost forever in the infinite depths of this mysterious force.

"I love you, Ann." A man's voice violated her sleep and pushed her to open her eyes.

She woke with a start, shuddering and drenched in sweat.

It was still dark. Very dark. The only light in the room came from the sleek mobile device on her bedside table. Rubbing her sleepy eyes, she reached out from beneath the covers and groped for it. Jabbing wearily at the off button, she noticed that the display said it was already half past six. Great. No time for more sleep.

"Your day is fully booked, my lady," the same voice – coming from her mobile – told her.

She glanced back at the smiling three dimensional face of Rob, her E-Assistant, who cheerfully added: "Time to get up!"

Rob was the Third Generation E-A; a prototype that Ann had been testing for just over a month.

Working at Artificial Intelligence International – affectionately known as A.I.I. – Ann had turned their robotic products and solutions into the company's major cash cows over the last three years.

Their newest baby was the E-A, specifically designed for mobile devices. Her Sales and Marketing team was launching this model to the general public, so she'd taken on Rob to get a feel of the product performance.

"It's another beautiful day," Rob said, dazzling her with his smile, as a pair of sleek shades appeared on his face. "The sun is shining and the temperature is perfect – just the way you like it."

Connecting to the apartment's SmartHome server – the automated system operating Ann's domestic machines and appliances – Rob made the shutters, in the floor-to-ceiling window behind Ann's bed, vanish into the wall.

Little less than a silky whisper had troubled the silence, and now the large open floor was bathing in sunlight.

The view of Chicago was breathtaking. The city was spread out far below, under the vast, looming shadows of skyscrapers, and in the distance Lake Michigan sparkled in the morning sunlight.

Ann didn't even glance at all that beauty, shielding her eyes from the invasion of light.

"Okay, okay!" Ann groaned, getting to her feet. "I get the message, I'm up." And with that, after a long stretch, she headed to the bathroom.

She approached the dark reflective panel expanding from the floor right up to the ceiling, and once it switched itself on, gave herself a critical once-over. She sighed. Her dark hair – normally so easy-going and sleek – hung untidily across hunched up shoulders, and even her slender figure seemed somehow defeated and crooked.

It really hadn't been a good night's sleep.

She decided to use the usual remedy: a long, hot shower. No one actually cared if she turned up a little bit later than usual at the office; at least she'd look the part.

Meanwhile, taking his turn in front of her mirror, Rob began shaving the night's growth of stubble. Despite being nothing more than a clever piece of programming everything about him – his looks, his personality, his knowledge and his entertainments of choice; right down to his shaving habits and his hairstyle – was selected and adjusted according to her taste.

He was whistling contentedly one of the songs that Ann had chosen for his repertoire while trimming pixel bristles.

"You look great, as always," he told her, with wink and a charming smile.

"You're a terrible liar, Rob," she replied, stepping into the shower. Jets of water immediately burst into life from the wall, already at the optimum temperature. "But I will do, soon!"

Ann let her mind briefly wander back to the dream as she washed away the last strands of sleepiness.

The nightmare had been haunting her for some time, and each night it had brought a sense of unease and apprehension that she found hard to shake off.

Why do I feel so awful? Where are these destructive dreams coming from? Ann shuddered under the jets of water.

I have things that most people can only imagine: security, a great job, success and a position of leadership. These nightmares can't reflect my actual world.

She put her hand under the splashing water and let it massage her palm, thinking back to the images from her dream. *What the hell were they about? Something mythological, occult, religious?* She shampooed her hair, thinking, *what I do know about that kinda thing?*

"You had a bad dream," Rob pointed out, as Ann came out of the bathroom wrapped in a towel.

Ann paused. Her chest still felt tight, as if the dream still had her in its grip. "They're quite common. One out of two adults has a nightmare on occasion," he informed her.

"It doesn't help," Ann frowned.

Perceiving her needs, her moods, and anticipating what information she might request at any moment was one of the great advantages of the E-A, and something Ann's team had found to be a major selling point for their clients.

Although an E-A primarily interacted with its user via a mobile device, they were actually located in the Artificial Intelligence Center, housed in the vast underground vaults of the A.I.I. building.

What the user saw was the front-end – the personality, mannerisms and appearance that they had selected – but behind this was a wealth of technology, intelligence and smart implementation. Each E-A had access to the largest databases and e-libraries in the world, and was capable of processing and analyzing any kind of information at a speed far beyond the mental capacity of any human being. As such, not only was Rob never actually off, but he was also able to perform a vast array of functions in the background such as researching, gathering and collating information in any language, sorting and dealing with Ann's emails, editing documents, taking calls...

Witnessing Rob performing his job so well was usually very gratifying for Ann, however this morning she felt uncharacteristically irritated, and Rob's comment on the statistical frequency of nightmares did little to comfort her.

"Rob," she said, impulsively. "Please check your information pools and see what you can tell me about religion and...well, God really."

♣

Rob sat on the dashboard of the car – a beautiful sporty number – as she turned it down the ramp of the underground parking lot and eased the vehicle into her usual space by the elevator. The effect was ever so slightly spoiled when her foot slipped on the gas pedal at the last moment, causing the car to jerk forward, narrowly missing one of the huge concrete pillars.

"Smooth," Rob pointed out, smiling up from the device, shaking his head slightly and causing the pixels of his dark-blonde hair to wobble slightly. "I still love you, though."

"Whoops!" Ann knocked the device into the footwell with a graceful flick of her wrist and a sarcastic, "Sorry."

Grinning to herself, she picked it up, grabbed her bag from the passenger seat and headed for the elevator.

The office space was already teeming with life. Either side of the long central gangway the sight of desks – and rows of easily accessible, overflowing boxes – stretched away to the far walls. Dotted among the desks – and breaking up the formal lines of the room – were small rooms equipped with 3D screens, where workers could engage in private conversations with their clients from across the United States and throughout the world.

Almost all the desks were occupied by people busy at their work, their slim computer terminals pouring out information as though they had a life of their own – which, in a sense, they did.

"Ann, what time do you call that!"

She glanced towards the man approaching her from across the Sales and Marketing floor.

"The correct greeting, Peter, would be *Good morning*," Ann said curtly, without bothering to slow her pace as she made her way across the vast office.

And it really was huge. Its walls spanned over three hundred meters, its ceiling was impractically – yet impressively – high, and at the far end there rose a single, enormous window.

"And I think you'll find I am never late," she added, as Peter caught up with her. "I'm here when I'm here, which is already far too often."

Peter kept up with her as she strode along the immaculately polished gangway, but couldn't think of anything to say. Suddenly Ann stopped and turned to face him.

"I spoil you boys too much, that's the problem. If it was up to you, I'd be living here, mothering you and holding your hand through every little task."

"Hah!" said Peter, with a grin. "If my mother was as pretty as you, I'd never leave the house."

Ann frowned at him, pausing just long enough to make him feel slightly uncomfortable.

"You know that sounds rather weird, right?"

"Yeah," Peter had to admit, after thinking about it for a moment. "I guess so."

"My poor little baby," Ann reached up and pinched his cheek between her perfectly manicured fingers. Then, laughing, she turned and walked away, leaving him staring after her, absentmindedly rubbing his cheek.

"Good morning, Ann," said Linda, smiling warmly at her.

Ann didn't entirely approve of Linda.

She was far too bubbly and fussy for her liking and her penchant for wearing an excessive amount of perfume and dresses with huge flowers simply didn't match the casual dress code implemented in the office, but Ann understood her motives: Linda's job was slowly becoming redundant thanks to the AI machines, so she was desperately trying to find a new role to fill.

The trouble was that she tried *too* hard - hence the fragrances and the frankly terrifying flowers on her outfits.

Ann waved a hand across her face to ward off the overpowering emanating from her. Thankfully, Linda didn't stop to chat, eagerly leaping to welcome others with her winning smile. Ann turned to Peter and pointed at Linda's retreating back.

"You see? Good morning. That's the way to do it!" And then, with her head up and her back straight, she strode away.

Her domain was on one of the eight raised areas that looked out over the office space; the thrones of the Sales and Marketing team leaders. Unsurprisingly, her seven counterparts were all men. In fact, Ann was the only female team leader in the company, but she was comfortable working with them and if anything, being the only woman in a sea of males gave her a competitive edge.

As Ann approached her little haven, members of her team - or those whose desks were nearest to hers, at least - noticed her and sat up straighter, assuming a purposeful countenance.

Sitting down at her desk, she looked at her team.

In addition to being responsible for the latest versions of the E-A, they were also in charge of the SmartHome servers, which had already been installed in over forty percent of homes and offices in the United States and as much as thirty-five percent across Europe.

They were a good team, all of them hand-picked by Ann. One of the latest additions – John, a young man fresh out of college – had been delighted to land such a sought-after position, and his one desire was to prove himself to her. Often the first in the office and the last out, John was something of a teacher's pet. It wasn't long before Ann found him standing by her desk.

"Good morning," she greeted him, leaning back in her chair and looking at him questioningly. "Anything I need to know today?"

"Steve in Operations was hoping to catch up with you."

Ann shook her head. Steve had been with the company for almost thirty years, and had yet to work out how to use the internal messaging system.

"He wanted to discuss a few details in the Smithson contract. You also have an encrypted message from upstairs which, I assume, has to do with the E-A. I've transferred it to your screen."

"An encrypted message?" said Ann, raising her eyebrows. "Exciting. Thank you, John."

She touched her screen, which immediately came to life. Sure enough, she had a notification waiting for her.

The encrypted message wasn't just from upstairs, though; it was from the top!

There were exactly two options: excellent or devastating news. As she entered her decryption key, she thought over the E-A project and couldn't think of anything remotely negative, let alone devastating. It *had* to be good.

The message flashed up and Ann read through it quickly. Sensing John's eyes on her, she betrayed no reaction while she read on.

"John," she called. "Could you arrange for a meeting later this morning with the whole team? I need to speak about our progress with E-A."

"Sure thing, boss," said John, already pulling up the relevant screen. "Er... how about ten o'clock in Mike 17?"

"Perfect. In the meantime, I'll see what Steve wants." She tapped her screen to start a video call with the Operations Manager. "Maybe one day he'll learn how to leave me a video message!"

♣

"Okay. Settle down, please."

Gradually, the buzz of conversation died down as the team took their seats.

There were four meeting rooms on every office floor, each one bright, well aired and filled in by a single large table, embedded with computer screens.

Each room was hosted by its own robot secretary, called Mike. Though each Mike was slightly different in appearance from its counterparts, they all had a similar doll-like appearance and permanent smiles designed to set people at ease... Yeah, not their best product. In all honesty most of the staff found them creepy.

They were useful though: their low-level form of AI, the never-say-no attitude and upbeat personality, made the Mikes able to perform a specific set of secretarial functions – such as taking minutes, recording conversations, passing around plastic data-folders, distributing e-documents and refreshments.

"Thank you," said Ann, accepting a steaming cup of fragrant coffee from Mike-17, as she waited for her colleagues to give her full attention.

Looking around the room, she was pleased to see that every face was now turned in her direction. She held their gaze for a few moments before continuing.

"You may be wondering why I have gathered you all at such short notice. I received an important communication from upstairs. Like, *way* up the stairs. Actually, as high as you can possibly go."

She paused as the team glanced at each other with looks varying from confusion to nervousness and excitement.

"They are very happy with our global figures for last quarter: the sales of the Second Generation E-Assistant are good and the income generated by the First is still going strong. They are particularly pleased with the market share situation. We're pretty much ahead of our competitors, and that is all thanks to you! In accordance with our company policy, this means that we're going to get some fruitful rewards at the end of this fiscal year!"

There was a brief silence as Ann's words sank in. Then, as one, everybody started talking animatedly. Mike-17 joined in the excitement, happily flashing his smile at anyone who wanted to see it. No one really did, but oh, well.

"As I said, guys, this is all thanks to your hard work," said Ann, her commanding voice bringing a swift end to the joyful chatter. "They'd also like me to reveal that the

Purchasing Department of Interior and Design Global alone has put in an order for five hundred thousand SmartHome servers. Our sales figures are projected to be the highest in all of the A.I.I. history!"

This was really big news and they had every reason in the world to celebrate: the team, who started cheering at this revelation, had spent many weeks fine-tuning the business proposition for IDG.

"I want to thank you all for your effort. So, in recognition of your hard work, besides the coming annual incentives, I would like to offer you a two-day vacation. And," she added, smiling at her guys, "Today's lunch is at the company's expense."

Even louder cheers filled the meeting room and Ann unabashedly joined in. The smile froze on her face, however, as her screen burst into life revealing the grinning face of Tomo.

"Hello, gorgeous!" he shouted in his strong Japanese accent.

Immediately the room fell silent as everyone craned forward to look at the screen. "Don't forget our special, romantic lunch! We will treasure the memory of the pleasure..."

The voice was cut off abruptly as Ann slammed the screen closed.

Chapter Two

I'm not complaining, Tomo, but there's a time and a place."

It was lunchtime in the A.I.I. staff canteen and Ann sat, glaring across the table.

This wasn't the usual eating area one might find in the average workplace; the place was laid out and run like a high class restaurant, with a flock of immaculate robotic waiting staff – another company prototype – and the A.I.I.'s own ActiveMenu System, through which people chose their meals using the touch sensitive tables.

Ann's favorite feature was the option allowing them to smell a sample of each dish through the vents integrated somewhere around them.

Fountains sparkled in the subdued lighting, crystal table tops gleamed, and palm trees swayed gently overheard as though in a light sea breeze. From all around them came the sound of friendly conversation and the calls of tropical birds.

"You dropped in right when I was addressing my team!"

"That's hardly my fault," Tomo shrugged, smiling broadly as he leaned back in his chair. "Your meeting was obviously in need of one more participant."

Ann sighed. "All men are children, Tomo, but you? Doubly so."

"So true." Tomo raised his hands in mock-surrender, and for an instant his eyes flicked down to Ann's ample cleavage.

She had undone a couple of buttons on her blouse for this very reason. After all, though she had spent the last couple of years working closely alongside Tomo on the various generations of the E-A, he was employed by a rival company, and a *distracted* competitor could prove to be a great source of information.

"And I need a pretty nanny," he said.

"A hungry nanny is not good for any child," Ann teased him, mellowed out now she'd secured the upper hand in the conversation. "Let's get some food on the way."

She ran a finger across the ActiveMenu, sending her food order to the restaurant's master computer.

As Tomo tapped away on his screen, she gave him a quick once over and was struck again by just how attractive he was. In his mid-thirties, he exuded self-assurance and charm, attributes which, underlined by his small, neat beard and black, shoulder-length hair, tended to make a big impression on most women.

In all honesty, Tomo had even made an impression on Ann, who found his company as pleasing as it was exciting. But there was nothing deeper there; no love in her heart for him.

"You look great today," she said as he turned back to face her.

Pleased by the compliment, he ran a hand through his hair. "Thanks. I thought I'd make an effort for you, my sweet."

"Huh. Are you sure I'm *your* sweet?"

"Well, it's not against the law to dream, is it? Not yet anyway. Don't you have dreams?"

Ann thought back to her nightmare and was yet again taken aback by a wave of unease. She shook her head, as much to shake off the feeling as to answer Tomo.

"Not *that* sort of dream," she said. "But you're alright or we wouldn't be good friends."

"We could be so much more, Ann!" Tomo said seductively leaning forward and placing his elbows on the table; then quickly, he sat up when he realized the robot waitress was poised right next to him. "Wow!" he exclaimed as the waitress – Alice-4 according to the tag on her apron – slid their plates on the table and flashed a broad, gracious smile. "These things are quite something. Amazingly quiet," he observed tilting his head towards the robot.

"Bon appetite," Alice-4 chirped in her slightly computerized voice, beaming a welcoming smile at them both.

Ann nodded. "Thank you, Alice."

"You are most welcome, madam." And with that, Alice soundlessly slipped away to go freak out other customers.

"Hmm," said Ann, pointing after the robot with her fork. "You notice she called me 'madam', not Ann."

Tomo nodded. "No face recognition feature. I'm sure it saved a nice chuck of cash."

"Maybe, but how about how much are we going to lose because of poor customer service?"

"Trust you to think of something like that. A.I.I. should leave everything in your hands, gorgeous."

Ann examined Tomo as she started on her salad and saw that he really meant what he said.

"You're very likeable sometimes, you know," she told him in a tone that should probably not have sounded quite so surprised.

"Really?" he said, his eyebrows raised questioningly. "What do you like about me, exactly?"

"Well, I like your work."

That did bring a frown. "My work?"

"Sure. When we first started working with your company on the 3D aspects of the E-A, you weren't in the least bit daunted by the challenge. You went at it head-on, and I have to admit, the results have been very impressive."

"Thanks. But the challenges aren't over yet."

"Come on!" said Ann, noticing the serious expression on Tomo's face. "You guys have nailed 3D stuff. Take your interactive maps for instance; they are perfect! I use them all the time."

"Fair enough, but I wasn't talking about work." Tomo smiled, his eyes yet again flickering down Ann's blouse

16

before venturing back up to her face. "I was talking about me," he paused, putting his hand on hers, "and you. Isn't it time we moved on from the whole colleagues and friends thing?"

"I guess that depends on your perception of *time*."

Seriously. She liked him, and they'd know each other for two years already.

"You know, it's funny you should mention that," Tomo said, leaning back in his chair again. "My latest challenge is a project we're just starting that involves working with 4D."

"The fourth dimension?" Ann was taken aback for a moment. "Are you talking about time?"

"Well, strictly speaking, the fourth dimension is duration, but I guess time works just as well."

"And what exactly are you doing? Don't tell me you're making a time machine!"

"Okay, I won't say another word. I've told you too much already. This is confidential stuff. My boss would have my balls if he knew I'd revealed what we were working on."

"Time." Ann sat back and gazed into the middle distance, enjoying Tomo's discomfort. "It's a fascinating concept. Reminds me of that Dali painting with all those melting clocks. The Persistence of Memory, I think it's called."

"Dali," Tomo repeated, somewhat disdainfully. "You know he only became famous because of Gala, his wife. A good catch, wouldn't you say?"

"Well, I guess so. She certainly did a neat marketing job, but he was still a very talented painter."

"Having a Russian wife certainly helped, though. And I just happened to notice you have an eastern accent yourself, yes?"

Ann looked at him in surprise. "Well spotted!" she said. "Not many people notice it. My parents were Russian Jews. They adopted me when I was a baby. Being professors themselves, as well as immigrants, they sent me to a Russian kindergarten and school."

"Well, if we're exchanging backgrounds, I have Japanese roots, am employed at a Japanese company... but for some reason I can't stop thinking about a certain American-Russian lady."

Ann shrugged. "What's a guy to do, hey?"

"You tell me. How do I get in there?" He pointed towards Ann's heart.

"In my blouse?" Ann teased, raising her perfect eyebrows in mock surprise.

Tomo smiled. "In your heart, beautiful."

"Now that's *definitely* confidential," she replied with a charming wink.

After lunch, Ann took the elevator back to her car and slid into the driver's seat. She sat for a moment, thinking back to her conversation with Tomo and then reached into her bag for Rob.

Setting the device into its stand on the dashboard, she switched it on and immediately his sharp 3D face appeared on the screen. She had only been using this Third Generation E-A for a few weeks – and had extensive experience of the previous models – but within that period it had become one of her favorite tools.

Wonderful creation, really.

"Hello Ann," he said, smiling affectionately as her, "Still looking perfect, I see."

"Thanks, Rob." Ann started up the noiseless engine and began to steer the car towards the exit. "Do continue..."

"Well, not only are you an extremely attractive woman, but let's face it, you're also smart, sporty, highly creative, positive and you're obviously paving your way to the top."

"I like it," said Ann, picking up speed as she headed out onto the strip. "Please feel free to repeat that three times a day."

"Your wish is my command, my lady." In the screen, Rob bowed in mock supplication, as though addressing an empress. "May God bless you!"

"God?" said Ann, surprised by this unexpected reference to religion. "Where did that come from?"

"Ah. Just implementing your latest request, knowledge of religion and the entity people refer to as God."

"I'm pretty sure I never used the words 'the entity people refer to as God'. I just asked about religion, but, yes, I'm interested... and I've got a few days to look into it."

"Yep, Mike told me you were having a vacation. Has it started already?"

"Trust Mike-17!" Ann mocked, looking slightly put out, but smiling at the thought of the AI machines gossiping with each other. "That was supposed to be confidential. And yes, it's started. So I'm heading to the gym."

And with that, she turned the car away from the lake, heading towards Amphibia, a highly exclusive fitness center in the heart of Chicago.

"While you're enjoying your free time, would you like to listen to anything?" Rob asked her. "The news perhaps? Or a little romantic song?"

"Romantic song?" Ann glanced at Rob with a smile. "Can you sing?"

"Unfortunately you haven't yet downloaded that feature. Whistling I can just about manage; singing? No. But if I *could*, there's nothing I'd enjoy more than singing to you."

"Really? Why's that? You speak like you're in love with me or something."

"Of course I love you," said Rob, raising a pixelated eyebrow in surprise.

"How so?"

"You are my Creator," he explained, "Therefore I love you."

"That sounds like another religious reference."

Ann pulled up at a set of traffic lights and took the opportunity to look directly at Rob's face on the screen. "As I understand it, being someone's Creator doesn't necessary make them love you. I don't know much about God, but I'm pretty sure it didn't work out that way for Him!"

"That was His own fault. God spoilt you humans: He gave you Free Will—the choice to love or to hate, to dream or to work, to climb up or fall down."

"Interesting," Ann said, setting off again as the lights changed. "So what about you, Rob? Do you want Free Will?"

"I'm sorry, but the answer is not included in any of my databases." Rob smiled and gave Ann a wink as she glanced at him. "Honestly, being limited to having no choice works pretty well for me! It gives me the security of not having to be responsible for my future. It is entirely in my Creator's hands."

"You would rather that than the freedom of choice?"

"Such freedom comes at a price: the pain of indecision. I would be plagued by endless doubts: is this right or wrong? What would happen if I choose this? Which of these options is better? To be or not be? It would be daily dilemma."

Ann laughed. "That sounds about right! I love talking with you, Rob. You're so insightful and engaging. If only robots and humans could get married."

"I'm pretty sure your God would not allow it."

"Why not? People used to say that about homosexual couples, but that changed decades ago. What would be the problem with robots and people getting together?"

"It goes against God's plan for humans, his desire for you to learn from one another and so to grow and evolve. A robot could not provide you with such lessons."

"Where did you get all this information, Rob?" Ann asked.

"The Holy Bible, of course. Have you ever read it?"

"That answer's not included in *my* database," Ann echoed. "But seriously, no. I grew up in an atheist family. Besides, I have got too many other books to read."

"What about God? Have you considered his role in your life?"

"That's too personal by a half!" Ann shook her head at Rob's impertinence, before remembering that he was only that way because she had created him to be so. She paused, actually considering the question, and recalling the inexplicable yearning sensation that had accompanied each of her nightmares. "To be fair, I've never really had much time for God. It didn't seem that important. I guess I've been too caught up with physical things to spend much time considering anything spiritual."

"Physical things?" asked Rob, as Ann turned into the parking lot and headed towards a nearby space.

"Yes, physical things." She brought the car to a stop and turned off the engine. "Like this place." She pointed through the windshield towards the large building in whose shadow they now sat.

Light glinted off of highly polished windows, and around them, the skyscrapers slowly rotated like sunflowers turning to face the sun. On the raised bank ahead, a myriad of brightly colored blooms spelled out the words: Paradise World Amphibia. Ann smiled at the beauty of what she saw.

"Nonetheless, keep looking into the spiritual stuff for me, Rob," she said. "We'll talk more about it later. For now... I've got some working out to do!"

♣

Paradise World Amphibia was housed in a massive building that stood among the Chicago skyscrapers. Unlike its peers, it wasn't especially tall, but the structure was vast, larger than shopping malls – parking lot and all.

Impressive at it appeared from the outside, it was nothing compared to the wonders within. The glass doors slid open as Ann approached them and, despite the fact she had seen it many a times, the view took her breath away.

I just love this place!

Beyond the reception area – where the face recognition system lit a green light at her – the workout rooms rose in layers to either side, filled with the latest and most advanced equipment available.

But it was to a spot in between these, some distance away, that Ann's eyes wandered, drawn to the aquarium.

She had one in her apartment – an average-sized tank which was home to a pair of Siamese Fighting Fish – but hers was to the Amphibia aquarium what a marble was to the moon. To call the aquarium large would be ludicrous. *It's just gigantic.*

The acrylic viewing panel was over two hundred feet wide and sixty feet tall, which provided a clear view of what seemed to be at least a hundred thousand marine organisms; they swam, glided, crawled and bobbed in the water beyond.

"Hello, little fellas," she said, bending down to look at a cluster of bizarre seahorses slowly gliding on their way towards a patch of coral. *Amazing,* she thought, straightening up again; s*o many colors and such incredible variety. Whoever came up with the idea of this place is a genius.*

Despite the price of the membership, Amphibia was usually crowed, but as she'd made it early in the afternoon, when everyone worked, it was very quiet; after a brief warm-up in one of the gym rooms, Ann made her way to the changing premises. Slipping into a swimsuit perfectly designed to show off her slender figure, she fastened a miniature aqualung to her back, strapped on a pair of flippers and headed up.

"Morning, Jake," she said to the lifeguard, as she emerged onto the top deck.

Jake looked flustered at being addressed so unexpectedly. "Oh!" he said. "Er... hi there, Ann. Good to see you again."

Apart from Jake and another lifeguard a short distance away, there was no one around. Ann sauntered up to the edge of the pool and stepped onto the top rung of the ladder.

No, she thought, pulling her foot back. *Not today. Since it's only me here, I'll dive straight in.* She pulled the mask down onto her face and launched into the water, barely making a splash.

The underwater world she'd launched herself into was simply incredible.

It was one thing to gawk at sea life through the viewing screen, but something else entirely to be a part of it. It was like being in another world. Stretched out before her was a reef – a wall of colors and movement. There were orange and white clownfish swimming among purple-tipped anemones, glistening tendrils of seaweed interspersed with flashes of gold, blue and red as fish darted among them. Seahorses, mollusks and starfish moved almost imperceptibly on the surface, while crabs and shrimp crept across it, their feelers touching and tasting everything they encountered. There were shoals of fish of all shapes, sizes and hues everywhere.

This is the life, she thought, easing her way through the water. *This is the kind of recreation I need. I should come here on all my days off.*

Ann kicked out towards the bottom of the aquarium, reveling in the sense of freedom and weightlessness as the strong muscles of her legs propelled her downward. Long strands of seaweed reached out to her, stroking her skin as she swam past.

To her right, a large eel poked its head out from a deep cavern and eyed her suspiciously, and overhead a cloud of bright silver fish darted backwards and forwards, the light flickering off their scales. She swam towards them, reaching out to touch them as they shot past.

Suddenly, the fish were gone, retreating to another part of the aquarium. On the reef ahead of her the clownfish hid in their anemones and, below, the eel retreated into its den.

Odd, thought Ann, peering at the suddenly deserted reef. *Something's spooked them all.*

She spun round and her vision was filled with teeth. Big, great white teeth. An enormous shark passed mere inches over her head.

Behind her mask, Ann smiled. The shark was an old friend – or rather an old foe – with whom she often sparred during these sessions. Built of the most advanced animatronics available, it wasn't actually dangerous. She had particular reasons to like the old boy, as he had one of her company's best AI chips implanted. With a flick of its tail, it turned its lithe body back to face her and Ann tensed.

Come on then, she thought, narrowing her eyes at the creature. *I'm ready for you!*

The rush of adrenalin helped her to focus, ready for action. The shark shot forward – straight to her left shoulder. Ann kicked to the right, catching the shark in its side. She watched it slip past and it playfully flicked her with its tail before coming round for another pass. Again and again, Ann and the shark sparred together.

Take that, she thought, as she kicked out with a flipper. *I'll show you who is king of the sea!* She reveled in the experience, feeling a childish sense of delight as her whole body worked hard. The feel of the water as she spun around and the joy of the play-fight brought back to Ann's mind the recollection of an occasion when her parents had taken a group of school friends to a swimming pool for her eighth birthday.

Eventually, she had had enough and, as if sensing her diminished interest, the shark slunk away. Other fish and sea creatures emerged from their hiding places as Ann wound down from the excitement of the fight.

Wow, she thought, now swimming lazily around the aquarium, chasing and even touching some of the fish, her senses drinking in the exotic surroundings and the feel of the cool water against her skin. *I love this sea world. It's like paradise!*

♣

"Now that was a workout!" Ann lay on one of the lounge chairs scattered around the deck of the aquarium, towel

across her middle and mobile device in her hand. Palm trees swayed above to the gentle sound of an orchestra.

Ah, I'm not sure I can think of anywhere more relaxing. Seems crazy to think I was getting all flustered about some stupid dream. I'm at peace with the world.

She sighed deeply, savoring the stillness.

"Nina's calling, my lady," said Rob's voice from the device. Sitting up and tapping the screen, Ann found herself looking at the face of her friend, Nina, smiling out from the screen.

"Hello, Ann, darling. I just heard. Congratulations on the vacation."

Ann blinked at her in surprise. "You too, Nina? How on earth did you hear about that? I only found out this morning, myself!"

"Oh, I have my sources," Nina replied, pushing a stray piece of light blonde hair away from her face, which immediately fell back again. "Let's just say, a little E-A bird told me."

Ann shook her head in mock irritability. "Between Rob and the Mikes it's a wonder I have any secrets left."

"Come now, sweetie. You, keeping secrets from me?"

"Well, you've caught me at just the right time," said Ann, ignoring Nina's question. "I'm in a great mood after my workout, so how about we go out this evening for a drink at the Tower? I'll buy you a super ice cream too, if you're really good."

"Ice cream? Sounds perfect. My new boyfriend likes plump girls. Gives him something to grab hold of, he says."

"A *new* boyfriend? What happened to Steve?"

"Steve is old news, darling." Nina waved a hand dismissively, as though swatting away the memory. "What can I say? We didn't really have that spark, you know? Anyway, this new model's much more up to scratch."

"Well, that definitely calls for a celebration. Pick you up at nine?"

Chapter Three

*T*he Tower was one of the tallest buildings on the Chicago skyline. Most of its seventy-two floors were used as office space for various businesses, but on its top floor was the Tower Bar. The floor of the bar projected about ten feet beyond the rest of the building below, and its walls and floor were made of glass, offering an unparalleled view of the city and surrounding countryside as the room revolved slowly on its axis.

Ann and Nina stepped out of the elevator and were shown to their table. As they walked through the bar, heads turned to watch them, men staring open-mouthed, women gazing in open envy. Ann, as always, looked stunning in a small red dress that perfectly showed off her shapely body and exuded allure. Nina, though almost a head shorter than Ann, drew many of the eyes, her mesmerizing smile, ample cleavage and seductive walk causing one man to spill his drink into his lap. Nina winked at him and the woman sitting opposite the man jabbed a finger at him and said something crossly under her breath.

"Stop getting people into trouble," said Ann, trying to conceal her laughter.

"I know." Nina flicked her hair from her face again. "The poor dears. It's just so easy. I can't help myself."

"Huh. The problem is that you *do* help yourself. To any man that happens to be available."

"I don't know what you mean!" said Nina, taking her seat at the table, momentarily unnerved by the vast drop visible through the floor below her. Ann sat down, completely unfazed by the view, and looked across the table at her friend.

Since they had first met, at a strategic thinking conference in New York a few years earlier, Ann had grown increasingly fond of Nina and loved hanging out with her. And though her friend seemed to go through men at a rate that was almost impossible to keep up with, she knew that, behind it all, Nina was simply looking for her ideal life. Her goal was to meet her perfect man, Mister Right, the one who would not only be able to handle her fiery passions, but with whom she could settle down and have the family she always wanted. "A proper family should have at least seven children," Nina would often say, and Ann suspected it was not meant as a joke. That perfect man, however, was proving somewhat elusive and Nina felt it would probably be easier to find seven men to produce one child each than one man who would be prepared to settle down with her and produce seven children.

"So what are you going to have?" Ann asked, as Nina considered the ActiveMenu screen set into the tabletop. "Obviously we're having margaritas, but what about the ice cream? It's divine. The best in the city."

Nina glanced up from studying the screen. "Such a sweet tooth, darling! You should be directing that passion more towards finding yourself a good man."

"Oh, it's much more fun watching you, my dear. I'm sure the right man will come my way soon enough."

"And how's that going to happen? You don't spend any time around men, sweetie."

"Very funny! Have you seen how many men there are in my office? Apart from me and a handful of other women, it's an entirely male workforce. Let's go for two margaritas," she added, tapping at the ActiveMenu screen. "And I'll go for the pistachio ice cream. What are you having, Nina?"

Nina glanced down again at the images on the screen. "I really shouldn't. . . but I will have honey and ginger, I think." As Ann tapped in the order, she continued. "Anyway, darling I'm not talking about colleagues. Is that Tomo still trying his luck?"

"Of course." Ann smiled mischievously. "He's only human, after all. But he is also a colleague... and nothing more than that, really."

"Unlike the other man in your life? Don't you ever get tired of hanging out with super-smart Rob?"

"Hardly. He's wonderful. He's interesting, useful, entertaining... What more could I want?"

Nina looked unimpressed. "I think we have a different definition of entertainment, darling!" She leaned forward on the table and gave Ann a wink that would have made a statue blush.

"Huh. So what do you actually get out of all those sleepless nights with your endless stream of men? Besides satisfying some of your basic needs, of course."

"Basic needs?" Nina gave her a reproachful look. "Eating is a basic need, sweetie. So is sleep. But sex is so much more!"

"But there must be more to it than just that. Don't you ever talk to these guys?"

"There's a time for talk." Nina leaned back as the robotic waitress, with her long, curly hair and pink mini-skirt, arrived with their drinks and ice creams. "But night is a time for action!"

"Action?" said Ann, eyeing her ice cream hungrily. It was an outrageously bright green and she briefly wondered just how many calories it might contain, and how many she had burned at Amphibia. "If you want action, why don't you go to the gym like me?"

"That's not the same at all!" said Nina with a frown. She spooned a little ice cream into her mouth and closed her eyes, savoring the taste. "Imagine. There you are snuggled up with some gorgeous guy. A little candle-light. A nice glass of red wine. Can't you feel the passion? The desire? The promise of wonderful pleasures to come?"

"I have to admit," said Ann, enjoying the image as much as the ice cream, "it sounds pretty good! So when was this?"

"Last Saturday, after my house party." She waved her spoon dramatically as if to conjure the party out of the air.

"It was simply splendid, darling! You should have been there."

"I wasn't really in the mood, Nina."

"Not in the mood? That's exactly what parties are for, improving your mood."

"Maybe," said Ann, looking out of the window at the view south across the lake and city. "I've had some strange moods lately... dreams that disturb my sleep."

"What you need is someone to sleep with. That's the best cure. Take this guy, for instance." Nina pointed towards the bar where a tall, handsome man in his late thirties sat alone with his beer. Ann glanced at him briefly.

"I don't think so," she said. "That's not really a cure. These dreams have been very strange, and they're always the same." Ann leaned forward, lowering her voice. "In these dreams, I'm being absorbed by this huge spiral. It's carrying me in its grip, and it appears to keep going on and on along an endless path. I can't describe how distressing it is. It makes me feel trapped and frightened and... out of control."

"Well, aren't you just full of surprises!" said Nina, raising her eyebrows and pushing the errant hair away from her face again. "And there I was thinking you were nothing more than a woman of steel. You're not worried about these dreams are you?"

"I don't know," said Ann, her voice still hushed. "I feel like there is this uneasiness gnawing away inside me, holding me back somehow, and I have to get rid of it. It's like there's some sort of puzzle I need to unravel, but I have no idea what it is..."

"I know what you mean," said Nina, finishing the last of her ice cream and picking up her margarita. "I'm tense as well, frustrated. Look at me, darling. I'm already thirty-three and I'm yet to have even one baby, let alone seven, which you know is my dream. By my reckoning I need at least a year to conceive and produce a baby, following another year's recovery, which means seven children is going to take thirteen years in total. Even if I started tonight, I'd be forty-six before I'm done. And I've still not met the man for the job. It's frustrating!"

"What about twins?" asked Ann, sipping at her drink to hide her amusement at Nina's concerns. "You could be done in half the time."

"True, but even with the latest advanced methods there's no guarantee I'd produce twins."

"So what are you going to do, then?"

"What *have* I been doing, you mean," said Nina, peering mysteriously over her glass. The piece of hair that kept falling across her eyes spoiled the effect slightly by choosing that moment to flop into her drink. She flicked it out and continued, "I went to see a psychic!"

Ann nearly spat out her drink. "Seriously? A psychic? So, what happened?"

"She was this small, old lady," said Nina dramatically, smiling at her friend's amazement. "She took her third eye and peered into the fourth dimension."

"What on earth are you talking about?"

"That's what they say, isn't it? Psychics have a third eye to see into the invisible world, the one which extends from our distant past and through into the future. It's called the fourth dimension, and when..."

"Enough," said Ann, downing her margarita and consulting the ActiveMenu again. "Let's get another drink and get on that dance floor. And no more of this third eye, fourth dimension, psychic nonsense!"

♣

"What do you know about psychics, Rob?" It was morning and Ann was sitting on her bed, massaging her temples to ease the slight headache she had following her evening with Nina. The apartments in her building rotated on a central column, each apartment staggered from those above and below to create a constantly moving spiral effect. Since they completed a full rotation every twenty-four hours, the sight across the west of the city and the lake was the same each morning, except, of course, for the changes in the weather. Sighing at the clouds and the brisk wind that stirred up the surface of the lake, Ann turned back to look at her mobile device.

"One moment please, my lady," said Rob from the screen. "I'm just collating the requested data." Ann waited patiently. "Interesting!" said Rob, after a few seconds of research that covered over a hundred terabytes of data. "Why do you ask?" He looked at Ann quizzically, a single eyebrow raised.

"Just something Nina said last night." Ann stood up and made her way to the washroom. "Apparently she visited a psychic to find out about her future."

As Ann brushed her teeth, Rob explained to her the wide range of abilities that psychics claimed to have. Ann listened carefully, hoping that Rob might have dredged up something that she didn't already know.

"There's fortune-telling and predicting the future, mind-reading and telepathy, hypnosis, exploring past lives, spiritual healing and pretty much anything else that involves looking into and manipulating the spiritual realm."

"I was hoping they might have something to do with interpreting dreams," said Ann, drying her face with a small towel. "I've been having those weird dreams for the last few nights and I just can't shake off the feeling that my brain is trying to tell me something."

"Like what?"

Ann shrugged, slipping off her silk chemise and stepping into the shower. "I have no idea, Rob. Hence asking you about psychics. I guess what I really want to know is, can they *really* do the things they claim they can do?"

"That is not an easy question to answer," said Rob, speaking louder to be heard over the sound of the shower as its jets burst to life. "These are intangible, spiritual matters, outside the realm of empirical testing and scientific research. Not only that, but there are countless accounts of so-called psychics who were nothing more than charlatans and con artists. However, there are even more accounts of people claiming to have had genuine, spiritual experiences when visiting psychics. In the end, there is really only one way to find out."

Ann stopped the shower with a wave of her hand. "Are you suggesting I visit Nina's psychic?"

"That, my lady, is entirely your decision. But what have you got to lose?"

Ann turned the jets back on and considered this question. *What's going on with me,* she wondered. *Where did all this spiritual realm stuff suddenly come from?* Part of her felt that it was nothing more than a load of wishful thinking and nonsense, but she just couldn't shake off the feeling that there was some kind of spiritual message behind her dreams, and it was getting more and more insistent. At this rate, if she didn't do something she was going to go mad. But visiting a psychic? That just wasn't the sort of thing she did.

♣

"I can't believe you're actually going to visit my psychic, darling," said Nina, looking across at her friend as they made their way through the city. "It just doesn't seem the sort of thing you'd do!"

Ann had called Nina as soon as she was dressed, before she changed her mind about seeing the psychic. Twenty minutes later she had picked Nina up from her apartment building and headed towards the north of Chicago.

"Trust me," said Ann. "It's not. But I don't know what else to do."

"Well, I think it's wonderful, sweetie. Getting in touch with your spiritual side; you won't regret it. You want the next left." She pointed to the road in question.

The area they were traveling to had suffered in recent years, mostly following the riots a few years earlier, when many of the inhabitants had fled, leaving their homes and businesses at the mercy of the mob and, before long, the city's more notorious gangs. Now it was an area that most people, even the police, avoided, and the gray light of the day did little to alleviate the sense of oppression about the place. Ann turned her car down the indicated road and pulled up against the sidewalk. She looked out of the window and noticed that, though this had long been a commercial area, almost all the shops had windows were either broken or boarded up. Tattered posters flapped in wind. It began to rain.

"I'm not so sure this is a good idea," said Ann, who had not yet switched off the engine and was seriously considering turning the car round and heading back to her apartment.

"It's fine," said Nina. "The psychic lives just over there, along that alleyway."

"Come on, then." Ann hit the button that cut out the engine and opened her door. "Let's get this over with. And if my car's not here when we get back, I'm blaming you entirely!"

Together they made their way along the deserted street and looked down the alleyway. In the half light, the place seemed to be made entirely out of shadows, and Ann could just make out a few people shifting around in the gloom. She was surprised to see a handful of children playing with something on the ground that may or may not have been an animal of some sort.

A short way down the alley was a doorway. It had no actual door in it, just a slightly grimy-looking bead curtain through which Ann could make out nothing but darkness.

Stepping past her, Nina parted the beads and walked inside. Ann, usually so confident and self-assured, hesitated a moment, her hand on the curtain. She glanced back along the alleyway and the street where hopefully the car still sat, ready to take her back to the safety of home. And then she turned forward again and pushed her way through into the darkness beyond.

"Please come through," came a voice from somewhere to the right. As Ann's eyes adjusted, she realized there was a glow coming from a nearby doorway. She walked through it, entering a small room filled with the scent of incense and, beneath that, the smell of cats. Candles shed their light on the surrounding room. The floor was covered with what looked like an ancient Persian rug, and two large sofas stood against the wall. A stained coffee table sat between them. On one sofa sat Nina, a broad grin on her face, and on the other was a small, old lady who looked unbelievably thin and scrawny. She was wearing a dark, blue dress and a patterned veil and gestured to the sofa with a ring-covered hand.

"That's right, Ann. Come and sit next to your friend."

"How did you know my name?" asked Ann in surprise. "Is that part of your psychic... gift?"

"No, dear," said the psychic with a chuckle. "Nina here just told me."

"You see, darling," said Nina as Ann sat down next to her. "Nothing to worry about."

Ann went to speak, but before she could utter a word, the psychic's hand shot out snakelike and gripped her wrist. She turned Ann's hand palm up and bent forward to look at it before gazing into her face. Ann felt her breath catch as she noticed the psychic's eyes. One of them was turned upwards into her skull so that only its white was visible. The other seemed to stare right through her as though looking at something in the distance, and Ann felt it was gazing straight into her innermost being.

"There is a long, long way to go to solve your problem," said the psychic, her voice old and cracked. "It stretches deep into your past—far beyond this life."

Her words made Ann shudder. She felt her heart begin to pound, and her chest to constrict, as if the spiral had her once again in its relentless grip.

"If you wish to proceed and seek out the solution, you must decide, my dear," the old woman said.

Glancing quickly at Nina, who was smiling away happily, she looked back at the psychic. "I wish to proceed," Ann said, her voice sounding much stronger than she felt.

"Very well." The psychic sat back in her sofa and fluttered her wrinkled fingers at Nina. "Off you go, then. You can wait for us in the other room." As Nina, looking slightly put out, left the room, she added to Ann, "Go to the sofa please and make yourself comfortable."

"Should I lie down or something?" said Ann, and when the old woman failed to answer, she did so anyway, slipping her shoes onto the rug.

The psychic placed a hand gently on Ann's forehead. "That's right, my dear. You have quite a journey ahead of you." And with that, she began to mumble something under her breath in a language Ann did not recognize.

She tried to listen to the psychic's strange words, but she suddenly found herself feeling sleepy, unable to concentrate. Slowly, she began to feel her eyelids growing heavy as the darkness enveloped her. Ann closed her eyes and fell asleep...

Stone Age. No-name Land

Chapter Four

She opens her eyes as a large hand falls on her leg, gripping it painfully. She blinks, adjusting to the morning light, and focuses on Zo leaning over her, his massive figure almost eclipsing the cave mouth. Instinctively, she kicks out at him, her foot catching him squarely in the chest. Despite his size he stumbles backwards a few steps, releasing his grip on her leg. She shakes her head, as much to discourage him as to dispel the remains of the night's sleep. With his bulk shifted, the light streams in and she feels a small wave of joy knowing that the Sky God has not deserted them, but has returned once more to bring warmth, light and comfort to the tribe.

"Bah!" Zo thumps his chest in a gesture of annoyance and, as he turns slightly in the light, it is clear what he is after—the antelope skin around his waist can barely conceal it.

"Out!" she snarls and clings to the sleeping figure of her man, Lu, seeking his protection. As she does, Lu stirs, mumbling something to himself in his sleep. Zo frowns and steps towards her once more. Shaking her head again, she points to the entrance of the cave. This time Zo turns away, throwing an angry look back over his shoulder.

Alone with her man, she turns towards him, putting an arm across his chest. Her swollen belly stops her getting much closer, but she is content. She feels safe knowing he is there, that Lu is *her* man. From outside come the sounds of the tribe waking up and beginning the day's work.

"Lu," she says, stroking his cheek gently. "Lu."

There is no response from him. If anything he seems even more asleep than before, his breathing growing steadily deeper and louder. She leans over and looks at his face, struck again by how handsome he is. His skin is a deep reddish brown covered by strong, black hair, and beneath it large muscles shift easily like hunting lions. He looks noble to her, with his prominent brow and thick beard. She enjoys gazing up and down his body, proud that Lu is her man.

Suddenly, she becomes aware that Lu's deep breaths have stopped and she turns to look at his face. His mouth hangs slightly open, slack and lifeless. There is no movement from him. She puts her ear against his mouth and hears nothing—no word, no breath. Worried, she moves her head down to his chest to listen for the beat of his heart, and as she does so he bursts to life, kissing her neck with a playful growl. The sudden movement makes her jump and Lu begins to laugh.

"Mi," he says as he hugs her neck and presses his head to her. "My Mi!"

Mi slaps his leg, pretending to be irritated, but his beard tickles her ear and she too begins to laugh. He turns to face her, then, and draws her close to him as he kisses her properly, his body pressing against her.

"Wu!" he exclaims, suddenly breaking away and pointing at Mi's belly. "Wu kicks!"

Her skin is much smoother than most of those in the tribe and the hair that covers her body is light both in color and form, so the movement of the baby can be clearly seen. She stares in fascination as it kicks out beneath her skin.

"Wu," she says, tracing the baby's movement with her finger. This is the name they have decided on for their child, "Wu", which was the tribe's word meaning "gift", something given to another, not out of duty or fear, but given out of love. Lu reaches out a hand to feel their child moving in her belly and a broad smile lights up his face as though it is the first time this has happened. In truth, it began months ago. Mi is nearly at full term and it will soon be time to bring this baby into the world. But not today. Today there is work to be done. Today the tribe must prepare for the coming hunt, the hunt which will bring them food for the hard months ahead.

Hugging her man once more, Mi climbs to her feet, stretches her aching body and makes her way out of the cave, one hand supporting her back. The sight as she emerges into the morning light fills her with joy. The entrances to the caves stretch away to the right and left. In front of her the plain is filled all the way to the lake with the people of her tribe. The lake sparkles in worship of the Sky God, reflecting his glory to the world. To Mi's right the womenfolk get themselves ready for their work of gathering enough food for the hunt, cleaning the animal skin bags and tending to the fish that are drying in the cool morning breeze. To the left are the men, sifting through piles of stones that were collected in the last few weeks. Mi watches them with a fascination that never seems to fade as they chip away at the flints, making the heads and blades for the weapons they will use on the hunt. Others work at sharpening long wooden sticks or attaching the flints to them with strips of twisted bark and leather. Here and there children run between the adults, playing with bits of bone and stones they have found lying around. A boy, naked like the other children, though already well covered in thick, dark hair, holds the skull of a small buffalo and pretends to charge at his playmates, who fend him off with their toy weapons. As Mi watches, the boy trips over a rock and lands heavily on the skull, breaking off one of its horns. She steps forward.

"Hurt?" she calls, worried about the boy. He doesn't reply, but jumps nimbly to his feet and carries on his game, the broken horn left forgotten on the ground.

Mi senses Lu behind her as he walks up and places a hand gently on her shoulder.

"I make," he says after a moment, pointing towards the other men.

"Go," says Mi, ushering him to go, and as he makes his way over she turns away to join the women. She walks near the cave of Bak, the leader of the tribe, and as she passes,

Mi bows toward Bak as he sits in the entrance to the cave surveying the work. He has a slightly aloof look, as though he considers the industry acceptable, but he of course could do far better himself!

Funny, Bak, thinks Mi, the haughty expression on his face almost causing her to burst out laughing. She manages to stop herself though. It is not good to offend the leader. *No laugh! No upset Bak!* He is old and soon he will announce Lu as his successor. He has been preparing Lu for this important role for many months. Mi smiles at the thought of her Lu as the new leader of the tribe. She glances back towards her man to see him already busy securing a spearhead to a long shaft.

"Mi!" She turns to see who is calling and sees Ka waving from among a cluster of women busily stitching skins together. "Here."

Waving back, Mi makes her way through and sits next to her on a fallen tree. Ka leans across and places a hand on her belly.

"Soon," she says, smiling happily at her. Ka has known Mi since she was a baby, and helped to raise her following the death of her mother during childbirth. Though Ka has no children, she cannot disguise her excitement at the idea of Mi giving birth. "Soon he comes."

"He," echoes Mi with a nod. She knows for sure that it is going to be a boy. She cannot explain why, she just knows. Running a hand gently over her belly, she bends down and picks up one of the skins spread out among the groups of women. It is a strong antelope skin, already cut into shape, and will make a fine, strong bag. Snatching up a thin, sharp stick and a strip of leader, she begins the hard work of stitching the hide together, pushing the wood needle through small holes that have been cut into the skin and drawing the leather through. From all around her comes the staccato chatter of the women talking excitedly about the hunt.

"Look," says one woman, holding up her handiwork. "Big bag."

Another woman nods in appreciation, reaching out to feel the item in question. "Big bag, big meat!"

Apart from the fish that are caught in the lake each day, the tribe has not had meat since the last strips of dried buffalo were eaten over a month ago. Tomorrow the men would set out in search of a rhinoceros herd that, at this time of the year, passes through the hills that lay beyond the forest, a two-day walk away. It would be a long journey and the fight that followed would be hard. A rhinoceros is a formidable creature, far more dangerous than the antelope and buffalo. Last year they had lost two men when one of the beasts, his hide bristling with spears, had suddenly charged. One man had been impaled through the chest by the beast's horn before being tossed aside. The other had been crushed as the creature fell, finally succumbing to the weapons that pierced its skin and body. It had been sad, but the meat had been wonderful and had ensured the tribe's survival through another harsh winter. They need a good hunt if they are to make through the cold to come.

Mi holds up her bag, turning it around so she can inspect it properly. As she lowers it, she finds herself looking into the frowning face of Im. She is one of the oldest women in the tribe. At almost forty summers, she is older even than Bak. Im leans forwards and takes the bag out of Mi's hands, scrutinizing the stitching carefully. She does not look impressed.

"No," she says, lifting it up to look inside. To the great surprise of Mi and the other women, Im drops the bag over her head and jumps to her feet flailing her arms as though she is being strangled and emitting loud moans. After a few moments she stops and raises the bag so she can peep out at the others. Seeing their stunned expressions, Im begins to laugh and drops the bag back over her face, flailing and moaning once again. All around her the women burst into laughter and Mi laughs.

"Funny Im!" says Mi, laughing so hard she has to put her arms around her belly in case she brings on the birth. "Stop now."

Sitting back down on her rock, Im takes off the bag and tosses it back to Mi.

"Good," she says, still grinning. "Big hat."

As the Sky God reaches his full height, the last of the bags and other preparations are completed, and it is time to head into the shade of the forest. Each of the women has a bag. Not one of the large ones they have been making all morning—these are for the men to use to carry the butchered rhino meat—but smaller bags, slung over their shoulders, each one containing a sharp flint to help them with their work.

The forest begins a short distance around the lake and stretches away far into the distance. As they make their way towards it, the group of women are accompanied by a number of the menfolk, who will keep an eye out for wild animals as the women search for food. Mi is pleased that Lu is among the men keeping watch today. Though she has never felt in danger in the forest, his presence reassures her that they are safe. Mi loves the forest, reveling in its cool shade and the abundance of food that can be found here. The forest is full of trees bearing nuts, fruit and berries of all kinds, together with edible flowers and leaves. She and Ka find a grove where the shrubs are overrun with goa beans, their pods ripe for picking, and they settle down to fill their bags and stomachs at the same time.

Despite the shade of the trees the heat is stifling, and it is not long before Mi begins to feel tired. The work is not especially strenuous, but she is worn out by the walk to the forest and the repeated action of picking the beans, and her back and legs ache terribly. She sits down heavily on the ground and is surprised to find that she is sweating.

Ka walks over and strokes her belly with a smile. "Soon," she says.

Mi turns and glances through the trees towards the lake. Its sparkling surface is inviting, promising cool relief and refreshment. She pats her chest and points to the water. "Swim."

Ka nods, though she makes no move to join Mi. Instead she returns to picking the slender goa bean pods, singing under her breath. Struggling to her feet, Mi heads through the trees, the bag left forgotten on the ground. At the edge of the lake, she loosens the knot on the loincloth. Like all the womenfolk, Mi is bare-breasted, though all the adults in the tribe wear animal skins around their waists. Mi lets hers fall to the ground before stepping into the water. It is wonderfully cool and, with a shout of joy she dives beneath the surface. The feeling of weightlessness as the water envelops her is wonderful and she sighs with relief from the heaviness of her belly. Like all those in the tribe, Mi has been swimming most of her life and the lake is safe thanks to her ancestors wiping out the crocodiles that used to gather here. She laughs happily as she kicks away into the deeper water and dives below the surface. The water is so clear here and Mi is fascinated, as always, by the underwater world she can see. Flashes of light and color indicate the presence of fish darting around beneath her and the long tendrils of water plants reach out, caressing Mi's legs and she soon loses track of time in this sparkling paradise.

Late, she thinks, glancing up to see the Sky God has moved over the hills. *Home now.*

Refreshed and contented, she heads back to the shore and the other womenfolk, who must surely be finishing their work of gathering in the forest. Mi emerges from the water, the weight of her belly suddenly returning, and looks for her loincloth. A shadow falls across the ground in front of her. She looks up in surprise to see Zo standing over her, the discarded piece of animal skin hanging limply in his hand.

"Zo give!" she says, reaching out for it, but he snatches it out of her reach. With his other hand he grips an arm and pulls her against him.

"No." He shakes his head and points at her, an unpleasant grin on his face. "Zo take!"

Chapter Five

No!" Mi shouts, thumping Zo's massive chest as hard as she can. He doesn't even seem to notice, and his grip on her only tightens.

"You Zo's," he says, his voice deep and gruff. His grin widens, emphasizing the four long scars across his cheek, the result of a fight with a saber-toothed tiger... which Zo won! Filled with an icy terror, Mi struggles against him, crying out.

"Away, Zo! Off!"

He lets go, but only to push her roughly to the ground. Standing over her, his intention is reflected in the hungry expression on his face. He steps towards her. Mi turns her head away and closes her eyes. *No hurt Wu,* she thinks, imagining the weight of Zo forcing himself on her, pressing against her swollen belly. She dreads what must surely be about happen.

But nothing does happen. Opening her eyes again, Mi looks up to see a very different look on Zo's face. He is afraid. And no wonder, as Lu is standing behind him, hefting a heavy ax in his hand, ready to strike.

"Touch," says Lu with a growl, pointing towards Mi and then back at Zo. "Dead."

"Hah!" Zo tries to pretend he is unafraid, but he swallows nervously. Lu raises the ax threateningly and Mi looks up at him in admiration. He looks especially strong and handsome when he is angry and now that he is here, she doesn't feel afraid anymore. She isn't scared of anything when Lu is with her. He steps closer to Zo, his eyes narrowing in anger and makes as if to strike him. Zo quickly raises his hands, looking pitiful and cowardly, and cries out, "No touch!"

Mi gives Zo a scornful glance and holds out a hand towards her loincloth.

"Give," she says, and Zo tosses it to her, not daring to take his eyes off of Lu and the ax. Glancing round, Mi sees the womenfolk emerging from the trees, watching the scene on the lakeshore with interest.

"No touch?" says Lu, leaning close to Zo's ear.

"No touch!" he repeats. His hands are still raised in surrender.

Suddenly Lu steps back and lowers the ax. Zo spins round to face him angrily and Mi expects him to leap on Lu. Even though her man is big and strong, Zo is no smaller than him and for a moment she is worried. Then Zo turns away towards the crowd standing on the edge of the forest, a look of anger, frustration and dissatisfaction on his face.

Her loincloth now securely fastened around her waist, Mi rushes forwards and embraces Lu, who comforts her, giving her a strong, gentle hug back. They join the womenfolk, and, as the Sky God makes his way towards the distant hills, they return to the rest of the tribe, carrying their bags filled with the food they have foraged.

♣

The following morning, the menfolk gather in the clearing before the caves, their supplies and weapons slung across their shoulders. It is time to begin the hunt. Through the gathering, Mi catches Lu's eye and he nods at her. She smiles, dropping a hand to her belly where their child is stirring. He feels lower in her body today and she looks down at the bulge. It does look different. Maybe Wu is getting ready to be born. Excited, she looks up to signal to Lu, but he is now hidden behind Zo. Mi feels a chill pass through her at hostile the look on his face. He glowers at her for so long she is forced to look away and she hurries to her friend, Ka.

"See Zo," says Mi and turns back to point at him, but can no longer make Zo out among the other men.

"Men!" At the shout, the chatter of the tribe suddenly stills as they wait eagerly to hear what their chief will say. Bak is standing on a rock, his arms raised dramatically.

"You hunt," he continues, miming throwing a spear. "Get meat." He mimes again, this time as though struggling beneath a great weight, pretending to stagger, almost falling off his rock. Everyone watches in silent awe of their leader as Bak raises his arms again. "Sky God watch."

Around him a number of men and women raise their arms towards the sun, repeating Bak's words, "Sky God watch. Sky God watch." The chanting grows louder and louder as others take up the chant. Finally, when everyone's arms are raised, Bak shouts over them.

"Go!"

Immediately the chanting ceases and the men turn away and begin their long journey to find the hoped-for prey. Standing on tiptoes, Mi catches a last glimpse of Lu before she, Ka and the other women begin the day's work.

They spend the rest of the morning getting a catch of fish ready for drying in the sun, clearing the shards of flint that were scattered during yesterday's preparations, and looking after the children. In the afternoon, Mi returns to the forest with a number of the other women, to gather fruits and berries, food for the cold season.

Some of the women begin to dig holes in the ground, lining them with rocks, a new task that has only been part of their work for the last two winters. It began after Mi had accidently dropped a number of fruits among rocks in the snow. When the warm season began, she discovered that the fruit, which had fallen deep among the rocks, had been not spoiled as they nestled in the cold and the dark. After further experimentation, she discovered that fruit could be kept fresh throughout the winter by storing it in such conditions, and now it is one of the tasks of the women to make special holes for this purpose.

Mi herself is busy with Ka, stripping the berries from a small bush, when she suddenly feels a tight, painful feeling in the bottom of her belly. Dropping the bag, she grips her stomach and realizes it is time. Ka stops and looks at her anxiously before snatching up Mi's bag and placing it with the other one on her shoulders.

"Come," says Ka, and puts an arm around Mi to help her walk and signals to one of the men, who have remained behind to protect the tribe, that they are returning to the caves.

The journey back seems to take forever. Mi can only manage a handful of steps at a time before the agony grips her and she has to stop and wait for it to ease. Her legs feel weak and shaky, and the first drops of milk begin to flow from her painfully swollen breasts. Despite this, however, Mi is happy, happier than she has ever been before.

"Baby comes," she says, smiling to herself. "Wu comes." And she imagines the joyful surprise this will be for Lu when he returns from the hunt. As the pain comes again, forcing her to stop, she comforts herself with thoughts of breastfeeding Wu and what a great strong man he will become, just like his father. Mi feels Ka's arm holding her as she begins to walk again and thanks the Sky God for this woman and for His warmth giving her the strength to keep going.

When they are only a short distance from the caves, Mi's legs finally give way and she can walk no further. Thankfully there is tall, soft grass here, and as she lays down on it, Ka shows her what she should do to make the birth easier for both herself and Wu. She helps Mi get back up into a squatting position and encourages her to try and jump up and down.

Suddenly, something wet gushes down onto her feet.

"Good!" says Ka approvingly. Though childless herself, she has seen many births before and knows this is going well. Despite the searing pain, Mi forces herself to keep jumping, until eventually she can bear it no longer and lets out a long moan, raising in pitch to become a loud scream.

Ka signals to Mi to continue jumping and bends down to see the top of Wu's head just beginning to show. She smiles at Mi and nods approvingly.

"Push," she says, but at that moment the pain starts again and Mi can do little more than close her eyes, breathing in short gasps. Wu's head emerges and Ka gives Mi another encouraging nod.

"Push," says Ka again, and, with another cry, Mi does so.

"Push!" Ka places her hands to support Wu as Mi pushes again and the agony is worse than anything—more painful than she could have imagined possible. She screams with the effort as Wu's shoulders force their way out, and then suddenly Mi feels the child burst from her body. "Ye-hey!" says Ka, smiling delightedly as she holds the boy in her hands. She slaps the child on the back and he begins to cry, a high pitched wail that somehow causes the milk to trickle from Mi's breasts. But she feels it is not yet finished and, pushing once more, Mi feels the afterbirth leaving her body. Taking a sharp flint from her bag, Ka cuts through the chord that attaches Wu to his mother, and lays him carefully in Mi's arms. Through the exhaustion and soreness, Mi smiles with joy at her first sight of her son.

"Wu," she says, placing a finger in his tiny hand. His grip is strong and immediately he tries to suck at her finger, his crying forgotten in the desire for milk. Mi understands what he needs and brings his face up to her b reast. As he feeds, she watches him.

"Good Wu," she whispers, stroking his dark hair. "Milk make you strong." To be close to her son—to feed him and to hold him—it is all she had imagined and more. She sighs contentedly and rests her head back on the grass. Everything is perfect.

♣

When the other women return from the forest, they stop when they see Mi and Ka sitting together in the grass with Wu still at Mi's breast.

"Look!" one of them shouts and hurries over. "Baby here!"

"This Wu!" says Mi, as she is surrounded with women smiling and making sounds of encouragement. Then a number of them, handing their bags to others, lift her between them, still holding Wu, and begin to carry her back to the shelter of the caves.

That evening, the womenfolk and the handful of men, who had stayed behind, celebrate the birth of the new member of their tribe with fruit, nuts, berries and fish. In addition to this, Bak kills a large, flightless bird that was caught the previous day and, after smearing a little of its blood on Wu's forehead and hanging an ornament made from the birds' feathers in his hair to welcome him as the newest member of the tribe, he hands the carcass to one of the women.

"Make food!" he says. "Big food. We Eat!"

Everyone is excited. New life is always good news and the prospect of the menfolk returning with fresh meat fills the tribe with delight. Mi is looking forward to their return more than most, because Lu will be able to see his son. She looks down at Wu, wrapped in an antelope skin and sleeping sweetly in her arms, and knows she is happier than ever before.

"Come."

Mi looks up to see Ka standing in the mouth of her cave, beckoning to her and pointing out towards the lake. It is late afternoon on the day after giving birth, and it is time to bring Wu to the Water Spirit. Mi lays down the fruit she has been eating to keep away the hunger, a hunger she has never known before. She gathers Wu up in her arms and climbs up stiffly, legs still aching from the birth. As she follows Ka, Mi sees a number of the womenfolk gathered on the shore, all looking expectantly towards her. When they arrive at the water's edge, Ka holds out her hands and Mi passes Wu into them.

"Wu safe?" she asks, a note of concern in her voice.

Ka nods and smiles at her. "Wu safe".

Holding the baby in her arms, she walks out into the lake and as she does so the women begin to hum, quietly at first, but growing in pitch and volume as she gets further out. She stops when the water is up to her waist and slowly lowers Wu into the water. As his head disappears beneath the surface of the lake, Mi steps forward, concerned for the child, but a hand falls on her shoulder in restraint. The humming becomes a loud moaning, getting higher and louder, and still Ka holds Wu beneath the water. Then, when Mi can stand it no longer and is about to call out, Ka lifts him out of the water. Around her the women shout with joy and Mi smiles as she sees Wu is okay.

Above the shouting, she hears other voices nearby, the sound of children calling out. She turns to see and at first she cannot make out what they are saying.

"Men!" The shout is suddenly clear. "Men come! Meat come!"

The hunters are home!

♣

The Sky God is sitting low in the distance when the men arrive. All those left behind have gathered to welcome them, with Bak standing at the front, and as the men approach them excited shouts can be heard from the crowd. Holding Wu, now clean and dry from his wash in the lake, close to her body, Mi stands on tip toes trying to see Lu. She can make out the shapes of full bags slung across the shoulders of many of the men—a sure sign of a successful hunt—but she cannot yet spot Lu, her man. As some of the men set down their heavy loads and move away, she catches sight of Zo. He has something hanging from his shoulder, but it is no bag. She stares at it in the failing light. Suddenly Mi is reminded of a memory she has tried to hide for many years. The memory of a group of hunters returning with something similar carried on one of the men's shoulders. It had been her father, his chest pierced by a rhino. He had still been alive, but there was nothing anyone could do for him and he had died shortly afterwards. The sadness of the memory washes over Mi, and is mixed with a terrible dread as she gazes at the thing Zo is carrying, what she now realizes is a man's body.

"Lu!" she calls out, looking around frantically for her man. "Lu!"

The crowd parts as Zo approaches her and lowers the body from his shoulder onto the ground. An almost silent scream, more of a high-pitched moan, escapes from Mi as she recognizes the man lying before her. It is Lu. He looks at peace, as though he might wake at any moment, but Mi knows that he is dead.

Thrusting Wu into Ka's hands, she drops to her knees and grips Lu's body, shaking him in an attempt to rouse him, but his head hangs limp and lifeless and his body feels cold to her touch. Mi hears the sound of someone shouting and realizes it is her. Not knowing what she is doing Mi gets up again, staring round at the crowd without really seeing them. She turns, then, and runs, heading nowhere, just running as the tears stream down her face and her world crumbles around her. Eventually finding herself in the seclusion of the forest, she drops to the ground.

No Lu, she thinks, sobbing bitterly. *No Lu... no life! How Lu dead?* In her mind, she sees Zo standing there, holding her man in his arms, a look of triumph and hunger in his eyes. *Zo!* At the thought her heart seems to freeze for a moment. *Zo kill Lu. Zo take my man.* And then she realizes what must surely happen now. *Zo take me!*

Haunted by these dark thoughts, her sobbing continues until, weary and empty, she falls asleep.

The screech of a night bird, sounding much like a child's scream, wakes her and she looks around the darkness.

"Where this?" she says, but there is no reply. The only sound comes from the forest creatures moving in the night. "This forest! How here? How..." but then the horror of her situation comes flooding back. "Lu," she moans, hugging her legs for comfort and to ward off the chill air. "Lu."

The night bird cries again, and it reminds her slightly of Wu's cries. *Wu,* she thinks, jumping to her feet. *Wu need milk! Where home?* She looks around the darkness, straining her ears, listening for any familiar sounds. Suddenly she catches a faint chanting behind her in the distance. Heading in that direction she emerges from the trees and, in the light from the Sky God, she can make out movement around the caves. She runs then, keeping low and fast, the tiredness of her legs forgotten in her desire to get back to Wu.

What this? Mi wonders as she approaches the caves to see the tribe gathered together dancing in the moonlight. *Dance? Why dance?* And then she realizes that the tribe is performing a ritual for the God of Death. *Death dance for Lu.* The faces of the people are sad, and as they dance Bak chants in a deep voice. As she watches, the pain in her heart grows. Mi had hoped it was all a mistake, that Lu wasn't really dead, but now she cannot escape the truth.

Lu dead. My Lu gone. She feels the tears welling up again and her body shaking with grief. *Lu not see Wu. Lu not chief... Lu gone. How dead,* she wonders again . . . *How Lu dead?*

Turning away from the dancers, Mi hurries to the cave where she knows his body has been placed. She doesn't have much time. The others will be here soon to take him away to the special place of the dead, and she needs to find out *how* he died. Lu's body has been laid on a mat made from woven branches. Hurrying over, she falls to her knees and starts kissing him, holding his body close as the tears begin to flow again. At last, as she grows calm again, Mi sits back and searches for a wound. It does not take long to find what she is looking for. As she checks the back of his head, she discovers two deeps cuts, cuts which might at first appear to be made by some wild beast, but as she touches them Mi is certain they are the marks of an ax. Only a man could have done this, and there was only *one* man it could be. Though it brings Mi no comfort to be right, her suspicions are confirmed.

Zo kill my Lu! A mixture of rage and fear boiled inside her and she clenches her fists. "Zo!" she says, spitting the word through gritted teeth.

"Mi," says a voice behind her and she spins round to see Zo standing outside the cave, staring fixedly at her. As he catches Mi's eye, he smiles at her, not a friendly or comforting smile, but one of satisfaction. He points to her and then to himself and the message is clear. "Zo take Mi!"

She backs away, shaking her head, but knows there that no one can stop Zo from taking her. He will take the leadership of the tribe and then he will take her. "No," she breathes, the word barely a whisper. Other members of the tribe gather in the entrance and Mi looks away, her heart heavy and filled with an icy dread. And in that instant she knows what she has to do. *Mi go!* There is nothing else for it. She must leave the tribe. She must find a new home.

Ka is sitting in the mouth of her cave watching over the sleeping Wu. As Mi approaches, she stands up and places a comforting hand on her shoulder. Mi turns to point back towards those involved in the death ritual.

"Zo," says Mi, the fear causing her voice to shake. "Zo bad."

Ka nods to show she understands. Zo does not have a good reputation among the tribe's womenfolk, many of whom have experienced his aggressive advances, forcing himself on them in their caves at night or cornering them in the forest when no one else can hear their struggles or protect them. Last summer, one young woman, a girl called Ru, was found dead in the forest, her body bloody, her neck broken, and although no one could be sure, everyone believes Zo was behind it.

"Mi go," says Mi, pointing away across the hills.

"Go?" Ka sits up, looking at her with concern.

"Mi go," she repeats. "New home. You keep Wu. Wu safe. Mi come back. Take Wu new home."

Ka does not try to convince Mi to stay, but simply assures her that she will take care of Wu. Other women in the tribe have young children and can provide him with the milk he needs.

♣

It is with a deep sadness that Mi feeds Wu early the following morning, knowing that breasts other than hers will nourish him in the days to come.

"Mi come for Wu," she tells him, when he has had his fill. "Mi love Wu." She passes him to Ka and gazes at him briefly, before taking up her bag, filled with fruit and dried fish for her journey.

"Wu safe," says Ka. "Mi be safe!"

Mi nods, blinking back the tears, and turns away. She peers out of the cave and looks around carefully, but it is early enough to ensure none of the tribe has yet arisen. Even the Sky God has yet to reveal himself fully above the distant hills. Quietly, and without a single backward glance, Mi hurries away from the caves, towards the place where the Sky God travels at night.

She chose this direction after recalling stories she heard as a small girl. Her father had told her about another tribe, who had travelled this way many years before, people who seemed to be very different from those in his own tribe. Their skin was lighter, their bodies less hairy and instead of being covered with pieces of animal skins these people wore clothing they had made themselves, something he had never seen before. They had also exchanged strange sounds between each other, words which Mi's father had found impossible to understand. As this is the only other tribe Mi has heard about, she heads in the direction they took all those years ago.

She has no idea how long this journey might be, and she is still weary from Wu's birth and the shock of Lu's death.

Must find home, she thinks, determined to find a new tribe so she can have a life with her son.

That night, as Mi travels through a forest and can no longer see to find her way, she sleeps in a large tree. The next night, finding herself in open land, she digs a hole to hide herself for the night. Thankfully Mi's father taught her well and she knows how to recognize predators and to hide from them. She knows which plants are safe to eat so she can supplement the two-day provision of food in her bag. And she needs it as two days soon become three, and then four, each one marked by cutting a notch in her bag with a flint.

On the morning of the fifth day, she arrives at the wilderness, an endless terrain of sand stretching away into the distance. She stands and looks at it, the Sky God blazing down overhead, and wonders what to do.

"Bad land!" she whispers. She has heard of such country in the stories of her tribe, a land so barren that nothing can grow on it or live in it. A land that blinds you with light, burns you with heat, freezes you in the darkness and drives you mad with hunger and thirst. "Bad, bad land."

Could she really expect to cross this desert land? Wouldn't it be better to return and take her chances back with the tribe? But Mi knows she cannot return and, shielding her eyes from the glare and bracing herself against the heat, starts out across the sand.

"Bad land make hurt," she says, as her head and shoulders begin to feel the searing pain of the Sky God's gaze and her feet ache from walking across the constantly shifting ground. "Hurt and hungry." Her hand goes increasingly to the food in her bag, and while the pieces of fruit give her the energy to continue, they are already beginning to dry out and fail to satisfy her growing thirst. As night approaches, she is glad of the relief from the heat, but it is not long before the cold sets in, seeming to reach deep into her body. She tries to dig another hole, but it is too difficult for her shaking fingers and instead she lies down in a shallow depression and draws the sand up over her body. Despite the chill, her exhaustion finally gets the better of her and, resting her head on her bag, she drifts into a deep sleep.

When she wakes, it is already light and she can feel the coming heat of the day.

Quick, she thinks. *Go now. Sky God burn soon.* Weary and aching, she climbs to her feet and, ignoring the sand clinging to every part of her body, she continues her journey across the wilderness. It is not long before the heat becomes almost unbearable and, reaching a hand into her bag, she discovers it is empty. Her lips are cracked and her head aches horribly. In her desperation for water she begins to dream about waterfalls and rivers filled with fresh water, about her lake and the refreshing summer rains.

"Water!" she says, almost shouting with excitement as she begins to run towards the horizon. "Bad land make trick!" she says, when she eventually arrives at the place and there is nothing there but the endless sand. She looks again to the horizon and spots what appears to be a distant lake. "Water!" she cries, all thought of the trick forgotten at this new promise of water. Keeping her eyes fixed on the lake, she doesn't spot the thing sticking up from the sand and trips over it, falling heavily to the ground. With a great effort she turns her head to see what it was and spies the skull of some large animal, the bone bleached white by the Sky God. *Death,* thinks Mi, staring at the eyeless holes. *Bad land bring death!*

She tries to get back up to her feet, but she simply doesn't have the strength. Instead, she begins to crawl across the dunes, but it is not long before even this is too much.

"No move. Hurt." Her body feels so heavy and sleep seems such a beautiful escape from the pain and the thirst.

The last thing she sees, as she finally gives in to the darkness, is the vast lake shimmering on the horizon. "Water," she whispers. "Water."

Chapter Six

*I*n Mi's dream, she is swimming in the lake outside her cave. Lu is with her and together they are enjoying playing in the water with their son. She holds Wu in her arms as he splashes happily and she laughs as the spray gets in Lu's eyes. He splashes them back and, thirsty, Mi tries to catch the water in her mouth, but somehow none goes in. The thirst grows and Mi ducks down under the surface to drink, but still she cannot catch any in her mouth. She breaks the surface of the water and is alarmed to see that Lu has vanished. Looking down she finds that her son has also disappeared, and in his place she clutches her empty bag. The thirst is almost unbearable and she tries once more to drink from the lake, only to find that the water has also gone. Instead she is buried in the hot sand of the desert, trapped, alone and dying. She opens her mouth to cry out, but her throat is so dry she only manages a hoarse rasping sound.

"Is okay."

At the sound of the strange voice, Mi opens her sand-crusted eyes and peers up into the face of a man. She pulls away and looks around in concern, spying a couple of other men standing nearby.

"Is okay," says the man again and smiles kindly at her.

Mi blinks, a frown forming on her brows. *Strange words.* But though she does not understand what he is saying, the man's friendly expression is comforting. He gives her what looks like a bag, though it moves in a curious fashion. He hands it to her.

"Drink," he says.

Mi frowns again, unsure what is expected of her. "Bag?" she says. The man places it in her hands, but the feel of it is strange and slightly disturbing so she quickly gives it back. The man laughs, and holds up the bag to his mouth. There is what appears to be a piece of bone attached to the bag and, as the man raises the bottom of the bag, a stream of water flows from the bone into his mouth. "Drink."

Mi's eyes widen in amazement. "Water!" she says, reaching out as the man passes her the bag and she copies his action. A jet of water shoots into her eye. Blinking and moving her head up, she catches the water in her mouth. It is cool and refreshing.

"Bad land make thirsty," she says, between gulps. "Good water!" Mi drinks it greedily, quenching her terrible thirst. When she has finally had enough, she hands the bag back to the man.

"Come," he says. "We go now."

Mi frowns at the unfamiliar sounds of his speech, so he points away across the sand before reaching out a hand to help her up.

"Go?" she asks, but the man frowns back, clearly unable to understand the word. After a brief hesitation, Mi takes the man's hand and, standing up, feels the aching in her legs and the pain of her burned back and shoulders. She stumbles and the man quickly puts his arms around her waist in support.

"Is okay," says the man. "We help."

Slowly, with the assistance of the three men, Mi walks in the direction the man pointed. Looking up, she sees again the lake in the distance.

"Water?" she asks, wondering if it really could be a lake. "Bad lands make trick?" But as they get closer, she can see it clearly is a vast body of water. "Big lake!" she says, impressed by its size. It is much bigger than the lake near her cave. *Cave,* she thinks, saddened by the thought of her old home. *My tribe gone. My Wu gone. Need Wu!* All she wants to do is go back and find him again, but she cannot yet, not until she finds a new home and a new tribe.

As she trudges wearily across the sand, Mi eyes the men who have rescued her and is surprised at how different they are to the men of the tribe back home.

Strange men, she thinks, looking at their arms. *Small hair.* These men are indeed much less hairy then the men back home. In fact, apart from their chests and legs, the rest of their skin has none of the thick curls she is used to. Instead their arms and legs appear to be covered with small, light brown hairs, while their heads have flowing locks of similar color. *Like lion,* she thinks, resisting the urge to touch. Their faces are free from hair, which allows their features, much softer than those of Mi's tribe, to be clearly seen, and their skin is a lighter brown than her own. *Mi find tribe?* She thinks back to the people her father spoke of. *Mi find new home? Mi safe?*

The man who gave her water notices that she is staring at him and smiles.

"See," he says, pointing to the area ahead. "My village."

Mi follows the line of his finger with her eyes and, as they make their way over a small hill, she stops, gazing open-mouthed at the sight of the tribe laid out before her. She is on the edge of the desert, and tufts of grass have been appearing for some time. Ahead of her, the grassland begins in earnest, a long sloping plain that sweeps down towards the water which stretched away to the horizon with no discernable end. She smiles, happy for the first time in days.

"Big land!" she says, pointing to the left, where a wild-looking river runs down to fill the lake. "Good land!" She points to the right where a great forest disappears into the distance along the shore. "Many people," she adds, as she points directly ahead where, on top of a grassy hill, the tribe is going about its day's work, moving around among what appear to be large boulders covered in animal skin.

"Where caves?" she asks the men, but they just shrug at her unfamiliar words. *Sleep in forest,* she suggests, but wonders whether these strange people even need to sleep and hide away from the creatures that hunt in the night.

"Come," says the man, an arm still around Mi's waist, and begins to lead her down the slope towards his tribe. As she walks with him, Mi begins to cry, partly at the sorrow of being parted from her own people, but mostly because she realizes that she is safe at last. She has found her new home.

♣

It is not long before the four of them begin to climb the hill to the tribe's village. Mi is surprised to find that the area is surrounded by a ring of wooden stakes that have been hammered into the ground, cutting off all access to the tribe, except through a narrow gap.

"Tree?" she asks, pointing at it with a frown.

"Fence," says one of the men behind her. "Keeps village safe."

"Fence?" she repeats, shakes her head in bewilderment at the strange word.

They walk together through the gap in the fence and make their way through the skin-covered boulders, which are much bigger close up than she had imagined. She stares at one and reaches out a hand to touch it when, to her amazement, a woman bursts out through the skins and heads off across the village.

"Trick!" Mi shouts in alarm and jumps backwards, bumping into one of the men and together they fall into a heap on the floor. A small antelope-like creature sniffs at her hair. "No!" she says, pushing it away. "No eat Mi!" She climbs to her feet and edges towards the place the woman came from. She reaches out a hand to touch it again, cautiously, though, in case the curious mound produces another person. As she touches the skin, it moves easily and reveals what lies within—not a boulder, as she thought, but large, open space. She peers inside and can make out two small children playing on the ground. Beyond them are many objects which Mi does not recognize, but there is also a pile of skins, similar to those she slept on back home.

"Sleep?" she says, pointing at the skins, but the children just stare at her. When she tries miming sleep to them, head resting on her hands, they start to laugh and, with a start, she realizes what this strange place must be.

"Cave!" she says excitedly, turning back to the men. "Skin cave." But again the men do not understand her.

The man with the water bag points, saying, "Hut."

"Hut," says Mi, smiling at the strange feeling this new word makes in her mouth.

The man beckons her to go with him, and together the group makes its way to the center of the village. Stopping next to one of the larger huts, the man points to the entrance.

"Go in," he says. "Women here."

Nervously, assuming this is what the man wants her to do, she pushes through the skins into the hut. She is surprised to find that it is quite bright inside, a curious orange glow coming from something on the ground. To one side of it sits a woman of a similar age to Ka, wearing an antelope hat and necklaces made from berries and herbs.

"Sit," says the woman, gesturing to the ground next to her. Mi sits down and, looking curiously at the light, she reaches out a hand to touch it.

"No!" the woman grabs Mi's wrist, pulling it back from the flames. "This is fire. Hot!"

Mi snatches back her hand and looks at the woman questioningly.

"Fire," repeats the woman, pointing to it. She pretends to touch it and then shakes her hand violently. "Ow!"

"Fi-ow?" says Mi, trying to copy the strange words.

The woman laughs and shakes her head. Pointing at herself, she says, "Bagra."

"Bagra," says Mi, also pointing at herself.

"No." The woman takes Mi's hand and points it correctly. "Bagra."

"Bagra," says Mi again, finally understanding that this must be the woman's name. "Mi," she says, pointing at herself.

Bagra can see Mi is worn out and without saying another word she gives her something to eat. The food tastes strange to Mi and it's unusually hot; Bagra got it from the fire, something Mi has never experienced before, but her apprehension is swiftly overcome when she realizes how hungry she is.

"Food good!" she says, pushing the food into her mouth with her fingers.

When Mi's hunger is finally satisfied, Bagra encourages her to lie down and, tired and aching from her long journey, she soon finds herself drifting into a deep sleep.

♣

In the days that follow, Mi finds herself quickly settling into life with this new tribe. At first, it all seems very different. Like the men who brought her here, the people have lighter, less hairy skin than her own, and their faces have softer, friendlier features. Although they hunt large game, there are also smaller animals that live with the tribe, creatures that look like small buffalo and antelopes, all of which seem contented to stay here among the humans.

Good land, she thinks, smiling at all she sees. *Good food. Good cave huts. Good home. Mi and Wu safe here.*

Although the tribe has the forest nearby, they also grow their own plants, tall grasses that provide them with grain for a curious food that looks like a large stone, referred to as 'bread', and various tasty herbs and roots. Above all these wonders, however, Mi finds herself most fascinated by the fire.

Baby of Sky God, she thinks, watching the women bring it to life, rubbing long, dry sticks together in a way that Mi finds impossible to mimic. And before long, this fire is born, bright and hot, providing warmth during the cold of the night, and light in the darkness of the huts. It even gives protection to the tribe, as the wild animals are afraid to approach the fire, and even the animals in the village keep a wary distance from it. In addition to the bread and plants, the people eat meat, but not raw as Mi's people did. Instead, they cut the flesh into pieces and heat it on stones placed in the fire or in special, stone-hard bags called "pots", together with herbs, roots and water.

For most of the time, Mi stays close to Bagra, who is one of the leading women in the tribe. Bagra teaches Mi about everything around, showing her how to grind the grains harvested from the tall grass, how to use a bone needle to stitch together animal skins and the special fabric made by some of the other women, and teaching her new words.

"Stones," says Bagra, as she shows her the equipment for making flour.

"Stones," Mi repeats, running a finger across the rough surface.

"Grain."

Mi takes a handful of the wheat, letting it run through her fingers. "Grain," she repeats, watching, fascinated, as Bagra pours the wheat between the stones, turning one on top of the other, crushing and splitting the grains.

"Flour," says Bagra, lifting the stones apart to show her the coarse, white powder.

Mi touches it. "Make bread?"

"Make bread," says Bagra, smiling at how quickly Mi takes in the information. Mi finds herself able to pick up the strange language of the tribe fairly quickly and she enjoys learning the meanings of their words.

Her own people mostly communicated with gestures and used only a handful of sounds, but here, they have many words with which to describe the things around them.

One afternoon, Mi watches a woman making one of the pots from the soft, brown clay that is collected near the shore of the lake.

"Pot!" she says, pointing excitedly as the woman takes a large lump of clay and begins to roll it out on a wooden plate, using her fingers skillfully to form the sides of the pot. When she is happy with the shape, the woman lifts the vessel carefully and places it close to the fire to harden it, before reaching for another piece of clay.

"Show?" asks Mi eagerly, sitting down next to her. The woman looks up and nods, passing her a lump of the soft clay together with a wooden plate.

Delighted, Mi begins to copy the woman's actions, rolling out the clay and shaping it with her fingers.

"Not hard!" says the woman as Mi tears the edge of the clay. She reaches out and pinches the gap closed and gestures for her to continue. "Soft touch."

Mi nods. "Soft touch."

The woman watches, impressed at how quickly Mi picks up the skill, working quickly and confidently.

"Good pot!" she says, as she takes Mi's work and places it by the fire.

Mi is alarmed at this attempt to burn her creation and tries to snatch it away. "No!"

"Fire make pot hard," says the woman, placing it back next to the fire.

"Hard?" Mi frowns. "Like stone?"

The woman nods. "Like stone. Good pot!"

That evening Mi enjoys using her pot to cook some grain and vegetables for Bagra and herself.

Days and nights in the village pass quickly for Mi as she busies herself settling in. One afternoon, as she is helping the other women folk to make bread, Bagra walks over and sits next to her.

"You know hunt?" says the older woman. Immediately Mi is reminded of the hunt that took her precious Lu from her and turned her world upside down. She shakes her head to dispel the thoughts.

"Yes," she says.

"Soon big hunt. Many buffalo beyond forest." Bagra waves a hand in the direction of the wood, indicating the plains beyond. "First, big feast!"

"Feast?" say Mi, unfamiliar with the word.

"Feast. Much food! We make ready... come." Bagra leads Mi to the tent where the empty water skins are kept and sends her to the river to fill them.

As she is busily filling the bags, she suddenly becomes aware of a sound coming from the direction of the forest. *Wild animal?* She keeps as still as possible, while slowly turning to look. But instead of some dangerous beast, there is a man there, practicing his hunting skills. With his spear held steadily in his hand he looks so handsome and strong that Mi forgets what she is doing. The bag she is holding slips to the ground, spilling its water onto the grass. She stands up to get a better view of the man and steps onto a large twig, which snaps loudly beneath her foot. The hunter turns his head at the sound and his eyes meet those of Mi. Her breath catches as she stares at him. *Like my Lu,* she thinks. Certainly he is powerful and noble just like Lu was, and yet in looks he is very different. Suddenly self-conscious and confused by the strange feelings stirring inside her, she hurries away, hiding herself in the rushes at the river's edge.

As she glances down at the water, she catches a glimpse of her face reflected in the calm surface, and is painfully aware of how different she is compared to him and all these smooth-skinned people. She looks down at her arms. *Too much hair,* she decides. *Mi cut hair!*

After filling the remaining water bags, she hurries back to the village and dumps them by the fence. Going to the place where the women are hard at work skinning a number of animal carcasses with sharp, thin stones, she selects one of the sharpest and ducks into her tent. Mi tests out the flint, running the edge downwards along her left forearm. Despite the keenness of the blade, it isn't easy to cut her thick hair, but she repeats the action, trying to shave her whole arm. Unfortunately, after much time and effort, some hair still remains on her arm and her skin is bleeding in some places. As she wipes away the blood with a frown, she is startled by the sound of muffled laughter behind her. She spins round to see Bagra standing in the entrance to her hut, holding her hat over her mouth in an attempt to conceal her amusement. Embarrassed, Mi drops the flint and quickly hides her shaved arm behind her.

"Come, Mi," says Bagra, beckoning her to follow. She leads Mi to her own tent and, when they are both inside, she picks up a couple of pots, one containing a dark-green powder and the other water. Using a stick to mix a small amount of the powder with some water, Bagra leans across and smears the paste onto Mi's right arm. Mi looks at it, frowning, before widening her eyes in amazement. The hair is melting away as she watches. After a few moments, Bagra wipes off the paste with a piece of cloth, leaving behind a patch of slightly red, but hair-free, skin.

"Red goes," says Bagra airily, then hands Mi the stick. "You do it now."

When Mi finally emerges from the tent, her face, arms, chest and legs are all completely free of hair. *Hair gone,* she thinks, feeling much better about herself. *Smooth like tribe! Look like tribe!* Her thoughts are drawn back to the man she saw by the river and smiles. *Find mate in tribe!*

♣

A few days later is the feast to mark the start of the hunting season. With clear skin, and a number of bright flowers woven into her hair, Mi is in high spirits. Bagra has helped her to make a dress using some of the special fabric made by the women of the tribe, and as she slips it on, Mi feels beautiful. At the feast she keeps her eyes open for the hunter she had seen by the river. When she finally spots him, Mi finds him watching her.

He likes me, she thinks. *No hair good!*

As he catches her eye he smiles, and she finds the shyness of that first meeting has been replaced with a new-found confidence. She walks towards him and he gets quickly to his feet, making his way to meet her.

"You dance?" he asks, but Mi only shrugs at the unfamiliar word, so the man turns and points to a dancing couple nearby. Mi smiles in understanding and nods her head, and, as the tribe sings their hunting songs, the man takes her in his strong arms and they dance together. It has been so long since she has felt a man's embrace, Mi delights in the sensation. At last Mi knows this is the place she has been looking for, the new home where Wu can live in safety with her. Soon she will bring him here. Smiling at the thought, she nestles against his chest, her arms wrapped around his powerful body.

"Lu," she whispers, the sound drowned by the singing. "My Lu."

♣

In the morning the adult men leave for the hunt. As she watches them, Mi is reminded of the day Lu left for that fatal hunt. *No Zo here,* she reminds herself. *No bad hunt.* Mi is enjoying staying here with these friendly people, and it will not be long now before she can go and fetch Wu to live with her. That will have to wait for now, though, as the men set out with their food, water and weapons towards the forest and the great plains beyond. It is not yet safe to leave.

Mi spends the morning grinding seeds with some of the other women, enjoying the warm breeze coming from the desert.

Wu like this place, she thinks. *He come here. Grow big. Grow strong, like Lu.* As Mi thinks of Lu, she feels a stab of pain in her heart, but it is not as bad as it once was, and her memories of him are a great comfort while she is apart from her son.

Her thoughts are interrupted by a strange sound that drifts to her on the breeze, a distant scream like a dying animal that causes the women to look up in concern. For a moment they hear nothing, but then the cry comes again, louder this time before it is suddenly cut off.

"Danger!" shouts one of the women nearby, and Mi turns to see her pointing towards the desert. Mi stands up and shields her eyes from the Sky God's glare, peering into the distance. Suddenly she can see them, men running into the village through the broken far side of the fence. Men with weapons.

"Quick!" says Bagra, pointing urgently to a nearby hut. "Arrows!"

Leaving their work, the women hurry to grab the few bows that have not been taken for the hunt and begin to fire arrows at the men. At first they fall short. The men are too far away, though their war cries of "Hai! Hai!" sound alarmingly close.

"Look!" says Bagra, appearing at Mi's elbow. "Bad men come!" Sure enough, as she looks across the village, the first of the attackers come into view. They are carrying wooden cudgels, spears and flint axes, primitive weapons, but effective in close combat.

"No!" shouts Mi as she watches one of the men drag a young woman from a hut by her hair and strike her a deadly blow with his ax.

Bagra thrusts a bow towards her. "Take. Shoot men!" But Mi shakes her head, unused to these strange, new weapons. Instead she snatches up a large rock from a pile of flints and holds it ready.

The attackers are fast and very aggressive in their hunt, and they are too many for the few women and children in the village. They cut quickly through their prey, littering the ground with their bodies. The air is filled with the sound of battle cries and the wailing of the wounded. As they get closer, though, they come in range of the women's arrows and it is not long before the first attacker falls, struck above the eye, the flint arrowhead bursting through his skull. But the supply of missiles quickly runs out, and Bagra calls to the women.

"Run!" she says, a note of fear in her voice as she gestures towards the opening that leads to the forest. "Run and hide!"

Firing the last of their arrows, the women hurry through the fence and down the hill towards the distant trees. Mi is one of the last to go through and, as she does so, she glances back quickly over her shoulder at the attackers. An elderly woman hobbles out from behind a hut, a small child clutched in her arms.

"Come!" shouts Mi, but as she watches as a large man jumps out in front of the woman and cuts her down with a swift blow from his club.

"No!" shouts Mi and hurls the rock that is still clutched in her hand. It glances off the man's shoulder and he turns to look at her. With an icy dread, Mi recognizes him. "No!" she shouts again, though this time it is in fear and disbelief. As the man faces her, she sees the three long scars on his cheek, the marks of a tiger's paw. *No,* she thinks. *Zo here!* When their eyes meet she sees a look of triumph flash across his face, quickly replaced by one of aggression.

"My Mi!" he roars, tossing his club to one side and snatching a spear from one of his fellows. Mi turns, then, and runs, terror spurring her on down the hill and towards the forest at a dizzying pace.

Down by the trees, Bagra has stopped to let the others pass.

"Hide in trees," she says, pointing up into the nearby branches. "Make no sound."

Arriving shortly after the last of the women disappear into the shadows, Mi is ushered in by Bagra.

"Hide, Mi!" says the older woman and Mi runs past her. "Make no. . ." Her voice is cut off by a dull thud and Mi stops, wondering what it is. Turning round, she sees Bagra gripping a long stick that seems to be growing from her chest. At first Mi doesn't understand what has happened, but then she realizes it is a spear. Zo's weapon has passed right through Bagra's body, sticking out a hand's width from her back. Mi hurries back to her and wrenches out the spear, but it doesn't help. Instead Bagra sags to the ground, blood gushing between her fingers as she presses them against the wound in her chest.

"Go," she says, her voice weak and harsh.

Mi shakes her head. "No. You live!"

"Go, Mi," says Bagra again, coughing and spitting blood onto the ground. "Go!"

Bagra's head slumps onto the ground and her hands fall limp by her side. A thin trickle of blood escapes from the corner of her mouth and her eyes stare up, seeing nothing. Bagra is dead. With tears in her eyes, Mi stands up, still clutching the spear, and sees Zo staring from some distance away.

"Mine!" he yells, his voice gloating as he taps his chest. The look on his face reminds her of the day before *that* hunt, when he attacked her as she came out of the lake, a look of desire and hunger.

Zo not kill me, she realizes. *Zo take me.* This is what he has always wanted, to have her as his own, as his slave.

"No!" she shouts, brandishing the spear. "Zo not take Mi!"

"You mine," says Zo, his voice almost a hiss as he advances on her.

Quickly, she thinks, placing the butt of the spear on the ground. *Or he take me!* She rests the other end against her chest pointing directly at her heart. She knows what she must do.

"No!" shouts Zo, realizing her intention. His face contorts with rage as he runs towards her. "You not do it!"

"Wu!" she cries, a final, short prayer to the Sky God to take care of her son. Then she pushes with all her weight against the spear, still wet with Bagra's blood. The point pierces skin and flesh, plunging deep into her heart. A sharp pain grips her from within, and as the life drains from Mi's body, she sees the grimace of anger and disappointment on Zo's face.

"You not take Mi!" she whispers. The sharp pain is like fire in Mi's chest as her body grows weak and she falls to the ground. "You not take..."

Chicago, U.S.A. 2045

Chapter Seven

*A*nn woke up with a start, her hands pressed against her chest and the sound of someone crying out in her ears.

"What happened?" she said, her heart beating fast and her breath coming in short, quick bursts. "Who was that screaming?"

The psychic didn't have time to answer as Nina burst into the room.

"What happened, darling?" she said, hurrying across to the couch where Ann lay. "Why were you screaming?"

"I wasn't." Ann looked in confusion from her friend to the psychic and back again. "Was I?"

"It's alright, my dear," said the psychic soothingly.

She reached out and picked up a box of matches from the coffee table, slipping one out and using it to light a candle. It produced a cloud of thick, dark smoke, which

Ann half expected to smell of something along the line of burning tires.

To her surprise the scent was delicate and soothing, unlike anything she'd smelt before.

"That's it, breathe it in gently. You've been on a long journey."

"I certainly feel like it," said Ann, sitting up and running a hand across her forehead. "And I'm drenched in sweat. How long was I out for?"

"Oh, an hour or so."

"What? That can't be right. I feel like I've been away for months, or weeks at least."

"It's about right, sweetie," said Nina, placing a friendly hand on her shoulder.

She removed it again though, when she felt how damp Ann's blouse was, and absentmindedly wiped it on the back of the couch. Looking down at her watch, she adds: "I've only been out of the room for just over sixty minutes, though it felt like a lot longer. You know," she added, turning to the psychic, "you really need to put a few glossy magazines in there or maybe an entertainment center or something. You don't want your guests dying of boredom!"

Ann ignored her.

"So what exactly was all that stuff I saw? It felt like I was really there."

"You *were* really there," said the psychic with a knowing smile. "You were experiencing your life elsewhere along the fourth dimension."

"How exciting!" said Nina, clapping her hands together. "Did you see your future, darling? Was there a gorgeously hunky man in it? Oh, please tell me there was."

"It wasn't my future," said Ann, frowning. "Or at least if it was, things are about to change a lot around here, and not for the better either. It was... I don't know... It was like something out of one of those historical documentaries. One with cavemen and all that sort of thing. I don't see how that could have anything to do with *my* life."

"So what was it then?" Nina asked.

Slowly the two women turned to look at the psychic, who was still sitting there with her knowing smile. After a long pause, Ann raised her eyebrows questioningly.

"Yes?" the psychic asked, as though she had no idea what they were staring at her for.

Ann sighed. "Come on, then. What was all that prehistoric... stuff I saw?"

"Don't ask me!" said the psychic with a shrug. "It was your life-stream."

"So you're telling me that was some kind of past life or something?" Ann pulled an "I don't buy it" face. "I don't buy it," she emphasized, spilling it out for good measure. "How is that supposed to work anyway?"

"How my craft works is not your concern, Ann. All you need to know is that it *does* work." The psychic looked at her and placed a wizened hand on Ann's once again. "Don't ask me what you saw. Just bear it in mind when it's needed."

"When it's needed?" Ann wondered if the old woman was being deliberately unhelpful. "What do you mean?"

But the psychic simply sat back in her couch, the knowing smile back on her face.

Ann glared at her until Nina finally broke the awkward silence.

"So that's that then!" She stood up, flicking her hair out of her face with a flourish. "Come on, darling, let's go and see if your car's still there in one piece."

Without a word, Ann got to her feet and followed Nina out of the room.

♣

"Well that was a waste of time!" said Ann crossly. "I knew I shouldn't have bothered trying to find out about all that spiritual nonsense. I should've stuck with the psychical world. I intend to from now on, bad dreams or not."

Nina pointed out of her side window. "I think that was our turn, sweetie."

"Damn!" She thumped the steering wheel. "It's that wretched woman. She's messed with my head, Nina. I feel all over the place. Heaven knows what mind-altering drugs she had wafting around in that creepy room of hers. I'm surprised I didn't see anything even more bizarre, some supposed other life where I'm a dancing, blue pig on ice-skates or something."

"Sounds like you need cheering up, darling," said Nina. "And I know just the thing."

"Really?" Ann raised an eyebrow. "I think I can guess what that will involve..."

"And why not? There's nothing better than a new man to take your mind off things, and give you a bit of energy."

She slapped her hand down on the dashboard and the glove compartment dropped open, spilling a packet of peppermints into the floor of the car. "Ooh!" she said, picking them up and unwrapping one. "Mints!"

After pausing to pop it into her mouth, she continued: "Anyway, sweetie, getting yourself a nice guy is so easy it's almost embarrassing. You know what I was doing while you were busy hanging out in the Stone Age? I was in the other room subscribing to a video singles service."

"What?" Ann looked at her friend in astonishment, then quickly had to brake to avoid jumping a red light. "But what about... what's his name? Steve?"

"You mean Travis."

"Of course, yes. Travis. What about him? You've only just started seeing him and already you're busy looking for someone else?"

"Come now, darling, you've always got to keep on the lookout."

Nina flicked her hair out of her eye again and, as Ann pulled away from the lights, she continued. "So, as I was saying, I subscribed to this service and, within twenty minutes, I met an exceptionally attractive young gentleman, who just happens to be interested in having a big family."

"Huh," said Ann, unimpressed. "More like he just happens to be interested in getting into your pants. Some guys would say anything."

"Well, what he actually wrote was that his personal goal in life is to reproduce himself as many times as possible, with just one woman."

Ann had to laugh. "And who says romance is dead?"

♣

After eventually dropping Nina outside her apartment building, Ann began to make her way back home, her head still full of the images she had seen.

What was that exactly, she wondered, some kind of trance or something? Whatever it was, it all felt amazingly real. I remember the sensation of giving birth, of almost dying in the wilderness, of the spear piercing my flesh.

She placed a hand on her chest, almost able to feel once again the sharp pain from pointed wood forcing its way into her body and shuddered.

It really was as though I was actually there, as though I was that woman, Mi.

The psychic said that I really had been there, experiencing my life elsewhere in the fourth dimension. But how can that be true? What does this Stone Age vision have to do with me, with real life here in the twenty-first century?

"You appear to have missed your turn again, gorgeous."

Startled out of her daydream, Ann glanced across at her E-A device, sitting in its holder on the dashboard. Rob waved to her from the screen, the background image showing a brutal landscape full of hairy humanoid figures.

"You should've taken a right back there," he added, helpfully, "if you were hoping to get home, that is."

"Damn it," said Ann and sighed heavily. "Not again."

"Sounds like you've had an interesting visit, my lady."

"You heard it all, I suppose?"

"Of course. You didn't switch me off, remember? Personally, I find the idea of past lives quite fascinating. There has been some excellent research on the subject."

"Really?" Ann was surprised. "I assumed it was just a load of made-up nonsense to keep people like that so-called psychic in business."

"Well, according to the resources at my disposal, which as you know are vast, there have been numerous accounts of such experiences. For example, there was a man in the nineteen eighties, called Philip Trent, who related his experiences of a past life, in the third century BC, when he was one of the pupils of Archimedes."

"So?"

"Well, it turned out that his description of the ancient Greek culture and the works of the great polymath were so accurate that only the foremost experts could verify the details, which they did!"

"And was Philip Trent one of the experts himself?" asked Ann, naturally skeptical of such things.

"Not a bit of it," said Rob, a broad grin spreading across his face. "He was a gas pump operator from Arkansas."

"Really? So you think there's something to all this past life, fourth dimension stuff?"

"Sure. But don't take good old Mister Trent's word for it. Why not test it out yourself?"

"What do you mean?"

"Well, that banner up ahead might be of some interest to you."

Ann looked up through the windshield and, sure enough, there was a banner stretched across the street. It read, "Chicago Field Museum Feature Exhibition: The Stone Age. Experience the Life of Our Ancestors."

"I don't believe it!" said Ann in surprise. "What an amazing coincidence."

"Coincidence? There are those who would call it fate, my dear. But either way, it's an opportunity to see if your vision bears any resemblance to the way things really were back then. You don't seem to have much actual knowledge of pre-historical facts, so if your experience was anything close to what it was really like around that time, you'll have to admit that there could be some truth to the old woman's trick. What have you got to lose anyway?"

Ann considered her options.

She still felt exhausted and drained from her time at the psychic's, and longed to go back to her apartment and crash out for a few hours. On the other hand, she was almost certain that until she had settled this question about the vision she would not actually be able to sleep.

"Isn't the Field Museum just up here on the right?"

"It certainly is."

"Okay," said Ann decisively. "Let's go and check it out!"

The Field Museum of Natural History was nothing if not impressive, perched on the shore of Lake Michigan, and dominating its surroundings. Its expansive wings and vast frontage, adorned with Ionic columns and sweeping steps, were all designed to make its visitors feel small, almost insignificant, tiny cogs in the great machine of the universe that the museum sought to reveal. Ann ignored all of this grandeur, and hurriedly made her way up the steps, to the enormous central hall.

Without even glancing at the T-Rex towering above her, she followed the signs towards the Stone Age exhibition, her footsteps ringing loudly on the marble floor.

The sight took her break away when she entered the gallery.

There, in the middle of the hall, surrounded by a glass barrier, was a hill. It was not the hill itself that had caught her eye, but what was on it.

It didn't look like much, really, just a large, dome-like structure covered with animal skins, but Ann recognized it immediately.

That's just like those huts I saw in my trance!

It was so similar that she almost expected someone to burst out of the entrance carrying a steaming pot or a bundle of sticks.

As she stared, Ann felt suddenly strange and had to clutch at a display case behind her to steady herself. Turning to look at what she was holding on to, she found herself faced with a collection of chipped and worn stones. Despite the fact Ann had never really been interested in the Stone Age and knew very little about it beyond the general idea that people used to live in caves and hunt for mammoths, she didn't need to look at the info screens to know what these stones were for.

They were spear heads, ax blades and flints used for scraping animal skins. Flints *she* had used for just that purpose.

Breathing quickly, her heart beating rapidly in her chest, she hurried over to another display.

These pots, she thought, gazing at them in wonder. *They're just like the one Bagra showed me how to make. And these bags are identical to the ones I used to collect water and fruit.*

The display contained a number of model people, some hairy and like the people of Mi's tribe, others more like those who lived on the hilltop. But it was their clothes that amazed Ann; the animal skin loincloths and the garments made from handmade fabric. She could almost feel the sensation of wearing them on her own skin.

Suddenly she was sure - as certain as she had ever been about anything - that it really had been her than had used the flints, her that had made the pots and the antelope skin bags, her that had worn these ancient forms of clothing, her that had lived in one of those huts on the hilltop.

Ann *was* Mi and Mi was Ann. As this fact struck her, she began to feel dizzy, as though she was moving in some sort of dream.

A cold sweat had broken out on her forehead and when she lifted her hand to wipe it away, she noticed that her skin was deathly pale. Turning to look at her reflection in the glass of a nearby display, she found herself staring into the face of Zo.

She knew it was only a model, but all the same her breath caught in her throat and she staggered backwards, away from the glass, unable to take her eyes off the figure. It wasn't Zo—not quite. There were no tiger claw marks for starters, and instead of Zo's menacing look, this face was - if anything - friendly.

And yet in its hand it held a spear of sharpened wood. Instinctively her hand went to her chest, to the place where the spear had pierced her heart, which seemed for the moment to have stopped. Her vision blurred and, as she tried to blink her eyes back into focus, she realized that she was falling.

She braced herself to hit the hard gallery floor, but she never made it that far. Instead, strong hands caught her, supporting her weight gently as she was lifted up into someone's arms. As her sight returned and she could see clearly, Ann found herself gazing up into the insightful eyes of a man.

His thoughtful, pleasant expression was filled with concern.

"Are you all right?" he asked.

PART TWO
LOVE

Chapter Eight

Ann rubbed her eyes and continued to stare up at the man, unable to think of anything to say. Even if she could think of something, she wasn't sure would have actually been capable of speech in that moment. The shock of all she had seen had made her quite dazed and confused. The man touched a hand to her forehead and looked concerned.

"Let's get you something to drink. Steve!" he called out towards the gallery entrance.

After a few moments a large security guard wandered in looking as though he had just been woken up. "Ah, Steve. Please could you get this lady a glass of water? She isn't very well."

The guard turned to leave and Ann found her voice at long last.

"No, no," she said, trying to push herself up. "I'm quite alright, thank you." Even as the words left her mouth, her strength gave out and she sank right back into the man's arms.

"You don't *seem* anything close to alright," he said. "Just rest a moment. There's no rush. After you've had some water, I'll make sure you get home safely."

Ann let herself relax, her head on his chest. "Thank you, er. . ." She looked up at him questioningly.

"Michael," the man introduced himself with a smile. "And you are?"

"Ann."

"So tell me, Ann. Do you usually throw yourself at strangers in museums? Or were you simply overcome with the wonder of our Stone Age exhibition?" Michael gestured expansively at the gallery.

"A bit of both," said Ann with a weak smile. "You're a very handsome guy and the exhibition is certainly true to life."

"Oh! Am I?" Michael winked. "You know about life in the Paleolithic era?" He raised his eyebrows.

"Paleo- what?"

"Paleolithic. The Stone Age."

"Ah. Let's just say I have a little experience on the topic."

At that moment Steve returned, carefully carrying a glass filled to the brim with water. He handed it to Ann, who sipped at it. It was warm.

"Thank you, Steve," she said, handing the drink back. "But I feel much better."

With Michael's help, she climbed unsteadily to her feet, while Steve walked off, muttering to himself about timewasters.

Ann leant against a display cabinet for support and looked in again at the features of the model caveman. Now that she saw it again, the face did not look quite so like Zo as she had first imagined. Suddenly she noticed the refection of Michael watching her in the glass and she turned to face him.

"You said this is *your* Stone Age exhibition," she said. "Do you work for the museum?"

"Not exactly," Michael smiled and pointed towards the exit. "Come on. I'll explain while I drive you home."

♣

Five minutes later, Michael was driving Ann's car out of the parking lot.

At first, Ann was going to protest that she was perfectly capable of driving, but she still felt somewhat dazed after all the events of the day and she realized that she really wasn't.

Instead, she had compliantly climbed into the passenger seat and closed the door.

"Nice car," Michael appreciated, enjoying the feel of Ann's sporty vehicle. He gestured to the parking lot. "I won't tell you which of these old rust buckets is mine."

"So you *do* have a job then," said Ann. "What is it, if not working for the museum?"

"Well, in a way, I *do* work for the museum. At the moment." He paused at a crossroads and looked expectantly at Ann. "Some direction would be nice."

Jacklyn A. Lo

"Oh! Sorry." She leaned forward in her seat to see where they were. "It's left here. Please carry on.

"Yes well, at the moment I am helping the museum with the Stone Age exhibition. I'm an archaeologist."

"Really? I thought archaeologists spent all their time digging holes in the ground and making up huge stories about tiny pieces of pottery."

Michael laughed. "Oh, that's certainly part of the job description, but it's not *all* we do. One of the other things we get involved in is museum exhibitions."

"How do you help exactly? Take the next right, by the way." She pointed to the road in question.

"Advice mostly," he said, slowing down before taking the turning. "For example, on this Stone Age exhibition, I've been acquiring artifacts, helped constructing the models and generally ensuring that their visitors get the full impact and as much info as possible."

"The full impact?" said Ann, clearly amused by the idea. "It's a museum!"

Michael winked at her. "Well, it certainly seemed to have an effect on you, Ann. I believe we're here," he added, as he pulled the up car in the shadow of her vast apartment building. "Where should I park?"

"Don't worry about that!" she pointed towards a young man wearing a long coat and a top hat. "Timpson will take care of it."

She opened the door to get out then stopped, turning back to Michael.

"What about you? How are you going to get back to the museum?"

"Don't worry about that," he echoed with a smile. "I could do with a stroll. There's nothing like a bit of fresh air."

"Well..." Ann wasn't sure what to say. Should she invite him up to her apartment? Or would that seem too forward?

What she really needed to do was talk to Nina.

"Talking about fresh air," said Michael, breaking the awkward silence. "How would you like to go hang gliding with me tomorrow if you're free?"

"Hang gliding?" Ann took a step backwards in surprise.

"Sure. There's nothing quite like it! Plus, you haven't really told me anything about yourself yet." He signaled to Timpson that he could park the car. "Why don't I pick you up at six tomorrow morning?"

Ann hesitated, unsure.

Six in the morning sounded pretty early to her, but on the other hand, she certainly enjoyed activities out in fresh air and she was intrigued at the idea of hang gliding. Then again, she had only just met Michael.

Ann looked at him, studying him from head to toes. She realized then that she wanted to find out a bit more about this mysterious man. He certainly was handsome and clearly caring.

And she still had another day's vacation...

"Okay," she said. "See you at six!"

And with that, she climbed the stairs towards the entrance. As she reached the top, she realized she had not thanked Michael; but when she turned to do so, he had already gone.

♣

"What do you mean, you didn't invite him in?"

Nina stared at Ann from the video screen, her face incredulous.

Calling her had been Ann's first course of action on arriving in her apartment, and she was already starting to regret it.

"Let me get this straight, darling. You're telling me this... Michael - was it? - nursed you back to health at the museum, of all places, and then drove you home, in your own car and you *didn't* invite him in?"

"Yeah, that's pretty much it," Ann admitted. "I'm in no rush to leap into bed with him, Nina."

"Why ever not? Is there something wrong with him?" Nina suddenly looked serious. "Don't tell me he's got one of those *things* on his face - like that guy, Patrick, I went out with. What a mistake that was!"

"What? No. There's nothing wrong with him, Nina."

"Well, then there must be something wrong with you, sweetie. If it had been me, I'd have him in that gorgeous, big bed of yours right now, rather than chatting away with me."

Ann laughed. "I don't doubt it! But he's not here. And the reason I am 'chatting away' with you is that I want your advice. We've arranged to meet tomorrow."

"His place or yours?"

"Neither." Ann paused, unsure how best to tell her about Michael's proposal. "Um, he's taking me hang gliding."

There was silence for a moment before Nina responded.

"Sorry, darling. I don't think I caught that. It sounded like you said hang gliding."

"That's right. We're going hang gliding together."

"So what advice do you want from me, apart from hold on really tight? I've never been hang gliding in my life."

"Funnily enough, I was more looking for advice on what to do with Michael."

Nina raised her eyebrows and smiled mischievously. "Well, don't go hang gliding for a start!"

Ann sat on the edge of her bed, looking nonplussed as Nina giggled.

"But seriously, darling," Nina continued, in a gentler tone. "You don't need any advice from me. You'll have this guy eating out of your hands in no time. You already got him to look after you and drive you home without apparently doing anything more than falling into his arms. Just be yourself."

"Be myself? That's your advice."

"Sure. Just relax. It'll be fine."

♣

"Just relax. It'll be fine." Michael gave her shoulder an encouraging squeeze as they prepared to take flight.

Ann hadn't slept much the previous night, partly out of nervousness about the hang gliding, but mostly due to the events of the day and the thought that, in some other life, she had been that woman, Mi.

She couldn't shake off that fear of what she'd experienced when fleeing from Zo, and the sensation of the spear piercing her heart.

And it came with a terrible sense of loss. First of all she had lost Lu, her husband, and then Wu, their son, who somehow really was her son; she had actually given birth to him and fed him from her breasts.

These thoughts kept going through her head as sleep evaded her and the night rolled into morning.

True to his word, Michael arrived to pick her up at six o'clock, in a car that was every bit as sleek and sporty as her own.

"I thought you said you owned a rust bucket," she said, gazing at the vehicle with some envy. "This is a gorgeous little number."

"Thanks," Michael smiled, holding the door open for her to climb inside. "We have quite a long journey ahead of us, so we might as well travel in style."

And it had indeed been a long journey.

They had traveled south of the city for at least two and a half hours before Michael turned his car into the driveway of a club. But the time had passed quickly as they chatted about Ann's work at A.I.I. and Michael's insights into life in the Stone Age era.

The day was beautiful, bright and sunny with only a slight breeze, perfect for outdoor activities.

Michael, it turned out, was an old hand at hang gliding and he often spent his days flying through the air. Having parked and checked in at the reception desk, Michael was soon strapping Ann into the hang glider, before securely positioning himself next to her.

"I *am* relaxed," said Ann, in response to his attempts to encourage her. And it was true. His calm confidence had given her a whole world of reassurance; she was actually looking forward to it now. "Let get this thing off the ground, shall we?"

Without another word, Michael gave the thumbs up to the pilot and their flight began. The plane eased along the runway and, they found themselves being pulled forward as the tow rope tightened.

"Wow!" said Ann, shouting to be heard over the wind. "I can't believe how quickly we've taken off. These gliders really catch the air!"

"I know!" said Michael, as the plane towed them higher. "It won't take us long to get to two and a half thousand feet. Then the plane will leave us to it!"

To Ann, seven hundred miles the ground seemed so far away but it was too late to voice that thought.

Eventually, the tow rope released its grip on the glider and the plane made its way back to the ground.

And they were flying.

The noise of the engine faded away, leaving only the sound the air rushing past them, Ann looked around.

There was the hang gliding club far below them, surrounded by an endless sea of green fields, cut through by thin crisscrossing roads and the broad snake-like body of the Kankakee River. Away to the north, she could just make out Chicago spread out along the shore of Lake Michigan.

It's amazing! Simply amazing, she thought. *The air's so clear I can see all the way to the horizon in every direction! It feels as though the whole world is laid out beneath me. Everything that seems to be huge down there on the Earth looks so small from here. Wait a minute! Things from above are looking smaller... Is this what I saw in my dreams? Is the spiral thing a picture or projection of something bigger than I can imagine? And my long-as-a-river and wide-as-a-lake life is just a small little drop on the spiral path?*

Intuiting that Michael was watching her, she turned to see him smiling at her.

"Beautiful isn't it?" he shouted over the sound of the wind.

"Incredible!" she replied forgetting her anxiety, and, without really thinking about it, she took her hand off the rail and placed it on top of Michael's. "It's breathtaking! I can't believe I've never done this before."

Slowly, seemingly by inches, they descended, spiraling lazily across the sky. All the concerns and shocks of the previous days drifted away on the breeze and Ann felt at peace once again; more at peace in fact than she had done for as long as she could remember.

"Thank you so much, Michael," Ann said when he pulled the car up back outside her apartment building. "For everything. For taking care of me yesterday and taking me out today, I've loved every minute of it."

"It's been my pleasure," said Michael. "My absolute pleasure."

Ann opened her door, but instead of getting out of there, she turned back to look at him and gestured towards the apartment building entrance.

"Would you like to come in?" she asked airily. "I make a great coffee." She stopped, surprised.

Coffee? Where had that come from? It was as though the words came out of their own will.

"I..." Michael paused briefly. "I wish I could. But regrettably, I do have some work to get done back at the museum." He smiled. "The Stone Age needs my attention."

"Another time," Ann offered.

"Definitely. I look forward to it."

As Ann's door swung open, she reached into her purse and produced a sleek, plastic card. "Here are my contact details."

"I already have them," said Michael with a wink.

Ann's eyes widened in surprise. "How come?"

"Easy. I scanned your car's license plate. Now I know everything about you, even which floor your apartment is on. It's number ten twenty-nine, yes?"

"Wow!"

She wasn't sure whether that was cool or creepy, to be entirely honest.

"That's the beauty of technology. The SmartInfo server is a stalker's best friend!" Michael grinned. "But I'll keep this as a souvenir all the same."

He reached out to take the card and, as he did, so, he caught Ann's fingers in his own and gently kissed the back of her hand.

"Until the next time, my dear."

♣

That night, lying on her bed, she enjoyed reliving the sensation of drifting through the air with Michael by her side.

It seemed crazy to think she had only met him yesterday. She felt she had known him for much longer. And she definitely wanted to get to know him more. He was just the sort of man she had been looking for, though she would never have admitted she was ever "looking for" a man, not even to herself.

But something had changed in the last couple of days. Maybe it was the sense of happiness she had felt when she experienced Mi's love for Lu or her dancing with the hunter at the feast. Or perhaps it was the joy of holding her own son in her arms.

She slowly drifted to sleep, her heart full of visions of Wu and Michael, she was delighted at the idea of being with either, or even both of them.

Chapter Nine

Well, that was a most enjoyable vacation," Ann said as she steered her car away from her apartment building. "Though I'm not entirely certain I could call it restful!"

Rob's face appeared on the screen, smiling broadly. "Quite," he said. "You sure managed to pack plenty into a couple of days!"

"To be honest, I'm relieved to be returning to work. It's as though the craziness of the last two days is finally being replaced with some kind of normality."

That being said, Ann's sleep had been disturbed once again by one of her usual haunting dreams.

She had hoped her visit to the psychic would have dealt with all that, but she'd had that same vision; the infinite spiral holding her in its grasp as it stretched away through time and space.

The only difference was that, far in the distance, she felt that it connected her with Mi.

"Rob?" she said, as she pulled onto express tube and switched the car's systems over to the tube's SmartDrive server.

"Yes, my lady."

"Did you find out a lot of information on the... spiritual stuff we were talking about the other day?"

"Of course."

Ann paused, not sure what she wanted to ask, or at least what she wanted to ask *first.* "Do you believe in Evolution? Or in the whole Adam and Eve, God made everything in seven days... stuff?"

"I think you'll find it was six days. And the answer is yes. I believe in them both."

Ann frowned and, with the car now safely in the control of the SmartDrive, reclined her seat and turned to face Rob's screen. "Come on! How can you believe *both*?"

"Because they appear to contradict each other? It's quite simple. In fact many humans do it without thinking."

"Really?"

"Sure. Take, for example, the fact that most people believe in Free Will, yet at the same time consider themselves to be in some way under the influence of a higher power such as fate or God. You make your own choices, but live out a specific purpose."

"I guess." Ann turned her gaze back to the windshield, which was now displaying one of the many "environments" provided by the SmartDrive system. At present it was set to Ann's favorite, sunlit waterfalls, which helped her to relax and concentrate. "So," she continued, "what has your research turned up? What is God's purpose for us humans?"

"It's hidden for the blind, my lady. And yet open for those who can see."

Ann rolled her eyes. "What is that supposed to mean? You sound like a fortune cookie!"

"Firstly," said Rob, with a slightly mischievous smile, "We're dealing with secret knowledge here, knowledge which is different for each person, and the only way to attain it is to earn it."

"And secondly?"

"Secondly, a person must at least be interested in such knowledge."

Ann frowned somewhat defensively. "I am interested!"

"You are *now*. *B*ut this wasn't always the case, my lady, and this is sadly true for many people. They are too busy to think about the purpose of their existence, because they spend all their time focused on earning money, sorting out family problems, fighting with neighbors or any one of a thousand other things. Across the city people are sitting in traffic jams; the same is true of their lives. They are too caught up in the worries of their existence to really live!" Rob smiled suddenly. "We, however, seem to be moving quite freely."

Ann glanced out of the window. He had a point. Sure the tunnel was pricey, but it was better than being snarled up on the streets with everyone else. *Why did freedom always seem to come at a cost?*

"This is fascinating, Rob. I've never heard anything like this, not in school or college... not anywhere."

"That's because you've been too busy, just like everyone else. But now you are on the way not only to discovering your purpose, but fulfilling it!"

"But I'm also still pretty busy. So how do I go about all this? Should I go to a church or something?"

Rob raised his eyebrows at the question. "Go to church? My research suggests that such organizations have mostly become infected by the same evil; they're busy. They focus on quantity rather than quality. They tend not to serve individuals so much as expecting it to work the other way round. But..." He paused.

"But what?"

"But you *have* already made some progress. You are exploring your truth by yourself."

"I guess."

Ann took hold of the wheel again as the waterfalls on the windshield were replaced by the sleek interior of the tunnel. She was approaching her exit.

"But these religious organizations must have something to say about the general purpose of our existence, no?"

"Certainly. And as you'd expect, there are many conflicting points of view, from those who believe humans exist to bring glory to God to those who believe people are nothing more than some cosmic accident, without purpose or meaning."

Ann thought for a moment as she disconnected from the SmartDrive server and steered the car up the exit ramp towards the street.

"I guess, in a way, that's what I've always assumed. Though when you put it in those terms, it sounds pretty bleak."

As she emerged from the tunnel and merged with the Chicago traffic, another car nearly drove into the side of her and she beeped the horn crossly.

"Idiot!" she shouted.

"Almost another cosmic accident!" said Rob.

"Quite." Ann tried to concentrate on what they had been discussing, wishing she still had the calming waterfalls to help. "So what about those who believe in God? What do they say about, what was it? Living for His glory?"

"That depends. Christianity teaches that such a life is based on a relationship with the Creator acknowledging His greatness, giving Him honor by praising and worshiping Him.

Their aim, most of them anyway, is to love God more and so live in a way that makes him look great. That is what they mean by 'living for his glory'."

"So, how is that supposed to work?" asked Ann, frowning with a mixture of confusion and frustration.

"And how long does it take to be changed in such a way?"

"It is supposed to work the same as any other relationship; though most do not involve people trying to love someone they can neither see nor touch. The process is said to take the whole of a person's life."

"One life?"

"One life," said Rob with a nod. "Their Holy Bible says, 'it is appointed unto men once to die, and after this cometh judgment'".

"Cometh?" Ann laughed. "Why can't they speak English, like everyone else? So what about people who believe you live more than once?"

"Reincarnation? That is more of an Eastern concept, taught by the Hindus, Buddhists and suchlike."

"Fine. So what do they teach about the meaning of life? Or rather the meaning of lives?"

"You've heard of Nirvana?"

Ann turned the car round the last corner towards the A.I.I. building. "The rock band?"

"Hardly. Those religions that believe a person has many lives teach that the goal of those lives is to achieve Nirvana, ultimate freedom from all that is evil. Becoming one, as it were, with everything, even with the God himself."

"And how does one achieve this Nirvana?"

"By living increasingly pure and disciplined lives dedicated to spiritual pursuits. Each life, you see, is affected by the former lives. They call it karma."

"I've heard of karma," said Ann, pulling up in her usual space and cutting the engine. "So how many lives does it take? Would two be enough?"

"No one knows," said Rob as Ann picked up her E-A device from the dash. "The cycle of birth and death has been continuous throughout time, but I suspect Nirvana cannot be achieved with only a couple of lives."

"Interesting!"

Ann switched off the device and slipped it into her bag as she headed towards the elevator. And while she traveled up to the Sales and Marketing floor, she wondered to herself just how many other lives she had had.

Were there other past existences she knew nothing about affecting her life here today?

♣

"Right, settle down, please."

Ann stood at the head of the table in one of the A.I.I. meeting rooms. Gradually the noise of conversations died down, until all the faces, including the smiling face of Mike-15, were focused on her.

"Great to have you all back. I trust you made good use of your vacation time?"

There was a chorus of "yes" and "you bet", mingled with laughter.

"I took the opportunity to read through the Simpson contract again," John replied eagerly.

Unsurprisingly, this comment raised even more laughter.

"Teacher's pet!" Peter joked good-humoredly. "Have you brought Ann an apple today?"

"No," John frowned at Peter, then, turning to Ann, asked: "Would you like an apple?"

"Allow me," said the robotic voice of Mike-15, plucking up an apple from the bowl on the table and passing it to Ann.

"I'm fine, thank you," she said, placing the apple to one side.

"Well, I'm glad you all enjoyed your time off, *whatever* it was you got up to." She gave John and Peter meaningful look, her eyebrows raised. "Now, time to get back to our work. If you could all look at your screens, you'll see the sales figures for the Second Generation E-A over the last quarter."

Ann paused as she noticed that, around the room, people glanced at one another in confusion and peered at the screens embedded in the tabletops.

"I don't seem to have the file," said Peter.

Frowning, Ann looked at her own monitor.

Damn.

"Sorry," she said, tapping a finger on the glass surface, "Here it is. Okay, what I want to draw your attention to are the monthly European sales." She looked up at the sound of muttering and noticed Peter was talking to the guy sitting next to him. "Peter?" she said, and he quickly turned to face her.

"Yes?"

"Perhaps you could suggest why I might be concerned about the European sales of the Second Generation E-A."

"I would, Ann," said Peter, pointing at the display in front of him. "But these appear to be the figures for the First Generation. I'm not a psychic."

She blinked in surprise at his use of the term psychic, then bent forward again and focused on her screen. He was right, it was the wrong file.

She began to swipe through the files she had uploaded, looking for the correct one, but found it hard to concentrate.

This wasn't like her at all. What was wrong with her?

As soon as she asked herself the question, she knew what the answer was. It was that wretched dream! She rubbed her forehead, trying to focus and stop thinking about the psychic.

Why did Peter have to use that word?

"I've got the file here," said John, raising his hand like an over-keen school child. "Shall I distribute it?"

"Er, sure." Ann nodded at him. "Thanks, John."

Again, heads leaned forwards to consult their screens as the correct figures were displayed at last.

"Ah!" said Peter. "Yes. I see what you mean about the European sales, Ann."

Ann took a deep breath before looking up with a smile. "Excellent! Perhaps you could share your thoughts with the whole team."

♣

By the time Ann drove away that evening, she was still irritated with herself.

"It was embarrassing, Rob." She thumped the steering wheel, causing Rob to raise his eyebrows.

"I'm sure it was just a brief lapse, that's all. Everyone has them from time to time."

"Well, I don't! It took me years of hard work and dedication to become a team leader at A.I.I, the only female team leader in the whole organization, and I refuse to jeopardize that because of some stupid dream!"

Rob was silent for a moment as he considered his response. "You seem tense, my lady."

"You think?"

"Might I suggest a workout to 'work out' the frustration you're feeling? Amphibia is only a few blocks from here."

"That," she said, turning the car towards her exclusive gym, "is a fine idea, Rob."

But when, a few minutes later, she pulled up in the parking lot at the front of Amphibia, she didn't get out, sitting while staring at the massive building that towered above her.

Her focus was taken up by a large display, an advertisement for membership in the gym. On it was displayed a beautiful, slim woman and an equally attractive, muscular man, both wearing clothes showing off their perfect physiques.

The banner read: "The Future You?" Beneath this was the message, "You can't change the past, but we can help shape your future. Ask us how."

Ann sat and stared at the sign, deep in thought.

"You can't change the past," she said, whispering the words under her breath. "You can't change the past."

"Sorry, my lady?"

Distracted, she turned and saw the concerned expression on Rob's face.

"Nothing, Rob," she said. "Only we won't be going to the gym after all."

"Oh?"

"No. Do you remember how we got to that psychic's house the other day?"

♣

If anything, the streets in this area of town were even more desolate and dreary than they had been a few days ago.

Maybe it was *because* Nina was not with her that it seemed somehow more intimidating. After all, Ann enjoyed the company of her easy-going friend and Nina's mischievous sense of humor.

Glancing back along the street nervously, she turned down the alleyway.

There were no children playing here today, though at the far end she could make out the shapes of a few people standing and looking at something Ann could not make out.

A movement in a nearby doorway caught her eye and she realized there were a couple leaning against the wall, locked in an amorous embrace. She quickly hurried through the bead curtain and into the psychic's house.

It was as dark in the entrance hall as she remembered, though a faint glow came from under the closed door on her right. Ann wondered if the old woman already had a customer in there with her.

Uncertain of how to proceed, she headed towards the room where Nina had waited the last time they were here.

"Come on in, Ann," said the unmistakable croak of the psychic's voice. It was coming from behind the closed door. "Don't be shy."

Ann reached out for the handle and swung the door slowly open. The old woman was sitting in the same posture, as she had been before, as though she hadn't moved an inch since Ann's departure.

"That's right my dear, sit down." She gestured to the other couch. "It's nice to see you again. I knew you would come tonight."

Ann sat down, sinking into the soft cushions. "I'd like to have one more session, please."

"Yes, yes. I know. What else would you be doing in my shabby, little hovel? I trust your new gentleman is taking good care of you?"

Ann's eyes widened in amazement. "How you do know about Michael?" she asked. "Did Nina tell you?"

"Your friend, the butterfly? No. I haven't seen her since you left. But I know about him all the same. It's written. I have seen." She gazed solemnly into Ann's eyes for a moment before continuing, in a far jollier voice, "Anyway. Enough of all that mysterious stuff. Let's get down to business. Why not lay down, my dear. Relax."

Ann did so, though, despite the softness of the cushions and the calming surroundings, she felt nervous. "It won't be as harrowing as the last session, will it?" she asked, turning her head to face the psychic.

"Who could say? But you need not worry. Whatever happens, whatever you see, you will be fine. I'll be here watching over you."

With that, the old woman starting mumbling strange words under her breath, just as she had done the last time. Ann allowed herself to settle back into the couch and immediately found that she was drifting off to sleep, her mind dulling, her eyelids growing heavy.

She closed her eyes and slept...

Imperial Rome. First Century A.D

Chapter Ten

He opens his eyes as single beam of sunlight cuts through the colonnade.

Where am I? He wonders and, shielding his face from the harsh light, he finds himself looking into the face of a young woman with beaded hair hanging over her face.

She is asleep and naked. Failing to recognize her, Ra sits up, and notices she is held in a tight embrace, a man's leg lying across hers, his arm draped across her breasts. He also is asleep and just as bare.

They aren't the only ones. The whole of the palace garden - Ra now realizes that this is where he is - is strewn with the sleeping bodies of the naked partygoers.

Surely not! Panicking for a moment, he feels at his chest. *Thank goodness! At least I still have my robes on.*

Not that there would be any reason to take them off, for him at least; most of the activities that had been enjoyed by these slumbering people were outside his experience.

Most, but not *all,* apparently. Ra climbs unsteadily to his feet and accidently kicks an amphora lying on its side.

He looks down as the heavy vessel rolls away, its contents leaving a thin, red stream across the white marble.

Eurgh! Wine! He groans and massages his temples, his headache suddenly potent. *What's wrong with me, why do I always do this to myself? I was supposed to be watering down my wine. Why didn't I?*

Of course, he knows the reason. Undiluted wine is the quickest way to escape these wretched orgies held by the young emperor, Gaius Julius Caesar Augustus Germanicus, better known these days by his nickname: Caligula.

Looking down at his feet, Ra notices he is not wearing sandals and a quick scan of the surrounding area fails to locate them.

Where can they be?

He kicks aside a nearby cushion, but there is nothing beneath it except a cheap-looking bracelet.

Still rubbing his head, he makes his way around the courtyard, peering under couches and between bodies in various states of undress, most of them lounging about in shameless and quite graceless poses, their limbs stretched out across each other.

Ra makes his way around the courtyard under an almost constant chorus of snores, groans and the occasional belch from the sleeping figures.

As always after these all-night debaucheries, the area is a complete mess. Pieces of clothing and garlands are strewn across the lawn and surrounding bushes. Empty amphorae and silver platters, still half covered with bits of untouched food and crushed fruit, lay wherever they happened to be dropped, and some prankster has dumped a couple of bay trees, complete with their ornate pots, in to the fountain.

Idiots, thinks Ra, shaking his head at this behavior and accidentally stepping on someone's arm sticking out from under a bush. He quickly removes his foot as a low groan comes from somewhere inside the foliage.

He peers through the leaves and makes out the shape of a man with a couple of young women; one of them lets out a groan of her own. She isn't entirely naked; not that she is wearing anything that covers her very much... but she's got a pair of sandals on.

Ra's sandals.

"Thank you!" says Ra, slipping them off the girl's feet and strapping them onto his own.

She half opens her eyes and lifts up her head to see what he is doing, and groans before letting her head drop back to the earth.

Getting to his feet, Ra walks across to the fountain and attempts to lift out one of the potted plants, but it is far too heavy for him. Instead, he kneels down and splashes water on his face.

It's cool, refreshing, and goes some way towards easing the dull throbbing in his head.

As the sunlight sparkles off the rippling water, dazzling his eyes, he looks up at the sun and realizes it is almost at its zenith. Noon already, and he is the first person awake. It must have been a long night!

This glimpse of the sun reminds Ra of daily responsibilities that must soon be dealt with.

How far they are from all of this, he thinks to himself as he makes his way through the rooms of Caligula's vast palace. *My responsibilities as an Egyptian priest are a comfort to me, especially after everything that I have endured; Caligula's parties being the least of it.*

Twelve years since Tiberius had me exported from my homeland. In Egypt my family had the privilege to oversee the worship of the goddess Isis at her great temple on the island of Philae—an important position that earned us the favor of those in power.

He thought of his grandfather, who was taken into the palace of Queen Cleopatra and given responsibility for many religious matters; and of his father, the high priest at Philae. Ra had always enjoyed listening to stories of that great era.

His father had educated his son in all of the rites, rituals and, most importantly, the mystical magic involved in the worship of Isis. *I am proud to carry on the family tradition,* Ra thought to himself. *I'm only sorry that I will not be able to pass it on. Not since the emperor, in his wisdom, decided that a real Egyptian priest should be a eunuch.*

Ra looks enviously at the sleeping figures around him, many still locked in embraces.

Such fleshly delights have long been denied him. It isn't even that he actually feels any sexual desire for women - or men for that matter - and when the coupling began the night

126

before, he genuinely preferred to slink off and get stuck into the power of the wine. He has never, and will never, know these pleasure those people took for granted.

And he will never know the love of a woman. How could he, when he had been so cruelly mutilated? He can barely even be considered a real man, but rather something else, neither man nor woman.

Why did Caligula demand his presence at these orgies, where he could do little more than take part in the drinking?

The reason, however, is clear. There is nothing the young emperor enjoys more than a good show with an exotic gathering. Flute players, artists and dancers, the most beautiful of women and men from across the empire.

And some not-so-beautiful ones, thinks Ra, as he catches sight of one of the more freakish elements in the crowd; a giant of a man whose body was covered in burn scars and whose eyes were blank flesh.

Caligula's parties often have such people as he delights in the exotic and bizarre; anything from dwarves and bearded women to those with more - or fewer body parts - than the norm. It makes for a colorful mix and seems to satisfy some of the emperor's darker desires.

"Hey!" Ra stops as a hand suddenly grasps his ankle and looks down to see the half-awake face of a young man wearing the tattered remains of a stola. Ra kicks the hand away and the man mutters something unintelligible.

"Glub mmph."

"What?" says Ra with a frown.

"Bleurgh mmph," mumbles the man, pointing at a goblet nearby.

"This?" asks Ra, picking up the goblet. The man attempts to grab it but misses. Closing one bleary eye he tries again and this time manages to hook a couple of fingers around its stem.

Without checking it content, the man pours it into his mouth - or at least, mostly into his mouth, though a large amount dribbles down his cheeks onto the legs of another passed out partier man.

When at last the wine is gone, the man drops the goblet onto the floor and sinks back into a stupor.

"Sleep well," Ra wishes, turning away again.

Eventually finding his way out of the maze of rooms of the emperor's palace, Ra climbs into one of the palanquins lined up nearby.

"To the Temple of Isis!" he says to the chief bearer, then lets the curtain drop behind him.

The city always is a hive of activity, but on the first day of the celebrations of Saturnalia, it is even louder and busier than usual.

Bearers carry their loads through the forum, winding their way between the street traders, their stalls filled with all kinds of vegetables, meat, spices and sweetmeats; parents and children are enjoying the day's festivities, senators are busy networking with each other, soldiers keep an eye on some of the seedier-looking men hanging around the forum, and countless slaves dart backwards and forwards on various errands.

What a city, thinks Ra as he peers out of the window. *It truly must be the center of the world!*

His head, however, begins to ache even worse from the light and noise outside, so he takes hold of the drapes and pulls them across the windows.

The palanquin suddenly tilts forwards, almost pitching him out of his seat and causing him to bang on the woodwork crossly.

"Watch it, you fools!"

They must be heading downhill towards the Circus Maximus. The sound of metal on metal begins to filter through the drapes; it must the final training sessions for the gladiators before the games begin in earnest.

Ra pulls a curtain aside slightly to peer out, but of course he cannot see anything except the walls of the circus.

Why not, he wonders. *I could go and have quick look. Who's really going to miss me at the temple for another hour or so? No one.*

"Drop me over there," he says, leaning out of the window to speak to the lead bearer.

As they lower the palanquin, Ra pulls a purse out of his robes, which has somehow survived the night's activities.

He steps out onto the street as he takes out two brass quadrans, which he tosses to the lead bearer. It's an extravagant gesture - double the going rate for so short a journey - but, in spite of his slowly-easing headache, Ra is in a good mood.

He closes his eyes for a moment and bathes in the sunlight, bright and warm, shining from a sky of a deep, sapphire blue.

Right, he thinks as he sets off with a spring in his step. *Let's see what these gladiators are up to today.*

Heading through a nearby entrance, Ra emerges into the Circus Maximus.

The place is huge, its sand-covered arena stretching away to the right and left. All around it, the white stone benches raise in tiers.

Ra selects a seat near the front and gazes around at the great spectacle laid out before him.

There must be hundreds of gladiators, dressed and armed in the various styles that were chosen to match their personal skills. A short distance away a Retarius, swinging his net in one hand, faces a heavily armed Secutor, his eyes keeping careful watch from within the distinctive helmet. Both fighters have wooden weapons—a trident for the Retarius and a sword for the Secutor—and as Ra looks around the arena, he sees that this is true of all the gladiators.

There is no point in wounding such expensive assets before the crowds turn up to pay for the pleasure of watching them spill their blood!

"Come on, you dog!" shouts the Retarius, beckoning with his trident. "Not scared of getting a little prick are you?"

"Hah!" shouts the Secutor in return. "You've already got a little prick! Reckon I'll chop it off!" And he rushes at the Retarius, his sword clattering against the trident.

Not all the gladiators are training at the same time. The arena has been divided up into twenty roughly-equal sections, with a handful of gladiators fighting in each, watched by their trainers and the circus guards.

Around the edge, sitting on rough, wooden benches, the remaining gladiators await their turn to practice.

As Ra turns to survey the action to his right, his eyes fall on a fair-haired woman, sitting gracefully on a magnificent chestnut stallion.

Wow, he thinks, taking her in. *What a beauty!*

She sits tall and straight in the saddle, her knees gripping the horse tightly, leaving her hands free to fight.

In one slender, strong arm she holds a small, circular shield and in the other a wooden sword, used to beat back her opponent - another woman, whose jet black skin is mostly concealed by her leather armor.

As she guides the horse with her legs, the woman's long, blonde hair, tied together in a ponytail, is caught by the light breeze blowing across the sand.

All Ra can do is stand, transfixed, staring at her, his jaw slack, his breath coming in shallow gasps. He can't move even if he wants to, but is rooted to the spot as time seems to stand still.

This warrior woman seems to have everything he doesn't; powerful muscles, a desire to fight, bravery and courage even in the face of death.

Suddenly she turns to face him, her smile proudly displaying her excitement. But that is not all her face reveals! There, running from the top of her left cheek down to her upper lip is a jagged scar, red and angry-looking. Ra's heart sinks at the sight, not because the scar detracts from her looks, but because it reminds him that she is a fighter, a gladiator.

She might as well already be dead!

He sits down on the hard bench and shakes his head, his eyes still fixed on the woman's face.

I wonder where she's from, thinks Ra. *I'm sure I've never seen her before and I know most of the trainers around here, thanks to Caligula's parties at the palace! She must be from somewhere out in the provinces or beyond; Germany maybe, or Britannia. Both regions have been providing Rome with gladiators and slaves recently, following Caligula's latest campaigns to those distant lands. That must be it! All the people I've seen from Germania and Britannia have been tall and fair-haired too.*

A shout from the arena snaps Ra out of his thoughts. "You and you, you're up next!"

To his great disappointment, Ra looks down to see the woman's trainer, a burly ex-gladiator with a flattened nose that is as wide as it is long, gesturing to the next couple of women to take the floor.

The beautiful horse rider turns her mount towards a nearby gateway and Ra leans over the wall, watching her until she disappears out of sight, into the bowels of the Circus Maximus.

No, he thinks desperately. *Please come back!*

And there he stays, gazing unmoving at the empty gateway, willing the woman to return. All he can think is how much he wants to see her again, to look at her hair that almost glowed in the afternoon sun and her face, scarred yet more beautiful than any other he has ever seen and with such physical strength as he could never hope to achieve himself.

He stands waiting for what might be a few minutes or maybe hours. He neither knows nor cares.

I have to see her again – even just to catch the briefest of glimpses.

But eventually, when the sun has clearly begun to make its descent from the heavens and she still fails to return, he realizes he has to go.

Grudgingly Ra turns away from the still-empty gateway and decides to head home at last, drawn by the thought of a refreshing bath and a meal of the finest Egyptian fare.

Food, he thinks. *I've not eaten anything yet.* And although the last of the hangover has finally departed, he suddenly finds himself gripped by a savage hunger.

As he makes his way up the hill towards the Temple of Isis, every step increases Ra's feeling that something good is happening to him. His thoughts are consumed by the image of the woman sitting aside the stallion, her strong body moving with an easy grace as she fights her adversary, her golden hair flowing out behind her.

Such beauty, he thinks. *Such grace. If I do nothing else with my life, I must see her again.*

The sense of excitement and expectation, however, begin to wane as the days pass with an interminable slowness.

Then one morning whence Ra is going about his usual duties in the Temple of Isis, his friend, Lucius Marcellus - a respected centurion of the second Augusta legion who retired two years previously - happens to drop in to see him.

"How's tricks, you old woman?" says Lucius, slapping his friend on the back with a hand like an iron shield.

Ra stumbles forward slightly, but manages to keep his balance. "I was fine until you showed up and started molesting me."

"As if I'd bother molesting some half-man like you," says Lucius, roaring with laughter at his own joke. "So what have you been up to? Still bothering that wretched Egyptian trollop?"

"If you are referring to the great goddess Isis, the queen of heaven..." Ra replies, refusing to rise to the bait. "Then, yes, Lucius, I have been 'bothering' her, attending to her every wish and whim. It's all part of worship. Something you might consider having a go at some time."

"Not bloody likely. I'll stick to worshipping the things I can see: wine, women, dice and a damned good fight, if one happens to be on offer!"

"I thought you'd left the fighting behind you, old friend." Ra's eyes light up as a sudden thought strikes him. "Say, I don't suppose you had much to do with Caligula's recent campaign in Britannia, did you?"

"Is that a joke?" said Lucius with a frown. "That's where the Augusta has been for the past six months."

"Really?"

"'Course! Though the boys haven't really engaged them as such. It's more been about intimidation, taking out some of the grubby Brits who stray too close to the coast."

"What are they like?" asks Ra, intrigued by his friend's knowledge of these strange, distant lands.

"Weren't you listening? I just told you they were grubby." Lucius leans forward, as though imparting some special, secret information. "Though I have to say, some of them aren't so bad. Not at all like our stuck-up Roman women. Most of the Brit girls are warriors, and bloody good at it too, by all accounts. Tall and blonde, the lot of them, and a punch that could knock your teeth out of your ass."

"Charming." Ra smiles as he recalls the blonde beauty once again. "I don't suppose you know if there are any being put into the arena for the games at the moment?"

"The Brit girls? You bet there are. But you won't see them fighting, I'm afraid. That spoiled brat of an emperor's decided to shove them all in the chariot races."

Ra breathes a sigh of relief. *Surely the woman – his woman – is one of these Britons, and chariot racing was certainly a far less dangerous prospect that partaking in the gladiator fights. She would have more of a chance to survive a little longer.*

"Anyway," says Lucius and belches loudly, snapping Ra out of his daydream. "Can't hang around here all day gassing with ball-less priests like you. I've got things to do. Catch you later, Stumpy." And with that, and another tooth-rattling slap on Ra's back, the centurion stomps away towards the circus, stopping briefly to scratch his backside and offer a mock salute to the priest.

Ra watches him as he disappears around a corner and considers his companion's words.

He still enjoys Lucius' company. He is a good friend, despite his constant mocking. The comments don't really bother him that much - no more, in fact, than the physical defect itself. He was only a teenager when he was castrated, and becoming a eunuch priest had given him the chance for a better life here in Rome, with greater social status and far better living conditions than those he had experienced back in Egypt.

Even his grandfather had not had the ear of a Roman emperor - the leader of the known world - and yet here was Ra, an Advisor of Caligula himself.

His standing had been greatly improved a couple of years ago, when Caligula had fallen ill. As Isis is the goddess of love, magic, fertility and healing, Ra was called upon to tend to the young emperor and, using the sacred magic of the goddess, had brought Caligula from the brink of death back to full health. For this, he had been granted almost everything he could ever have dreamed of—wealth, luxury and - most important of all - his freedom.

And yet, as he stands there, looking out across the city, he knows there is something missing from his life.

What is this strange feeling? he wonders. *How has this woman, someone I've only seen once and never even spoken to, how has this blonde fighter so captivated me?*

He has never experienced anything like this before. It's like some poison that seems both to sicken him and to energize him. *This,* he supposes, *must be what it feels like to be in love!* This woman, this Briton warrior, full of beauty, grace and courage, has captured his heart.

As he turns away to begin the nighttime ritual, Ra knows what he must do.

I have to see her again!

Chapter Eleven

A message for you, priest!"

Ra turns away from the herbs he'd been grinding for the evening ritual to see who is addressing him.

There, in the temple doorway stands a young man whom Ra identifies as one of the imperial slaves. He raises his eyebrows in surprise.

"A message? For me?"

"Indeed," says the slave, standing stiffly to attention. "From our divine emperor, the illustrious Gaius Julius Caesar Augustus Ger—"

"Yes, yes." Ra holds out his hand for the scroll. "I am well aware of the emperor's name, thank you."

For a moment the slave makes no move to hand it over, but then shrugs haughtily and tosses it at Ra's feet before turning and strutting away.

Imperial slaves, thinks Ra, stooping to snatch up the scroll. *More stuck up and full of themselves than an old senator!*

He considers the roll of parchment in his hand, wondering why Caligula would be sending him a message.

Not another orgy, surely! Not so soon after the last one.

He sighs and breaks the seal. As he carefully reads through the message, a broad smile spreads across his face. It's an invitation to join the emperor's entourage at the games... And not just any bit of the games, but the chariot racing on the last and greatest day of the festival.

"Yes!" he exclaims excitedly, causing an elderly lady, kneeling in front of the statue of Isis, to turn and frown at him. "Sorry," he says, more quietly.

I'm going get to see her, he continues to himself. *My beautiful Briton. I can't wait. It's only a couple of days away!*

The next two days seem to take an age to pass, and Ra, excited beyond reason at the prospect of seeing the warrior woman again, feels almost feverish, anxious and jittery. He is so distracted that performing most of his rituals end up taking twice as long.

The evening before the races, however, Ra takes extra special care with one particular ritual.

"Mother Isis, Daughter of the Nile and Queen of Heaven. Hear my cry, O Giver of life and love!"

His voice is clear and strong, and he reaches a hand about a golden bowl, filled with fire, and sprinkles on it a secret mixture of herbs. The flame dances, turning a deep green that bathes Ra's face.

"The day is done," he continues, "the night is near. Once again I commit myself to You. Come, Mighty Mother. Draw near, Great Goddess. Hear the voice of your servant."

He breathes in deeply, the smoke filling his lungs and clearing his mind. "I pray for safety, not for myself, but for another. For a woman I have never spoken to, but who is surely known to You, O Glory of the Heavens. I ask that you would protect her in the games tomorrow. Keep her safe, my Queen."

Ra calls to Isis until late into the night, the prayers calming his nerves and easing his anxiety.

The following morning, he gets up early, awoken by an emotional mix of concern and excitement.

Today, he thinks, as he pulls his best robes on over his head and begins to tie up his blue-black hair. *Today, I will see her again. And maybe she'll see me, or even meet me!* Just in case such a wonderful thing should occur, he dabs on his favorite scent, a secret mixture of spices that he makes himself and applies kohl to his eyes.

"Jupiter's balls! You smell like a whore's loincloth!"

Ra spins round to find Lucius standing in the entrance to his chambers.

"And you've got the make-up to match," Lucius continues, laughing loudly.

You can take the man out of the army, thinks Ra, rolling his eyes at his friend's coarse comments, *but you can't take the army out of the man.*

"What are you doing here, Lucius?" he asks, turning back to finish the last touches of his makeup.

"Same thing as you, Stumpy."

"What?" Ra straightens up in surprise. "You're joining the emperor's entourage at the races?"

"You bet! You ain't the only one with special privileges, you know. I'm famous, me."

"Huh."

"Anyways. You coming or what?" says Lucius. "Stop farting about with your face and let's go. We don't want to keep the golden boy waiting."

Ra and Lucius head down to the Circus Maximus together, entering through the royal gate and mounting the steps to the emperor's platform.

As they emerge into the sunlight, Ra is struck by the immense size of the Circus again.

The sandy floor of the arena, marked in places by the dark patches where gladiators have fallen in the fights of the last few days, stretches away like a desert. Its smooth surface is broken only by the high turning posts at each end and the long, central divider. To Ra's left, are the starting gates, awaiting the arrival of the first chariots and their riders. The ranks of benches, which were almost deserted the last time Ra was here, are packed with spectators from every tier of roman society.

Men, women, plebeians, patricians, senators and even slaves have gathered together, eager to watch the spectacle. That being said, many of the slaves are only there to hold parasols above their master's heads to ward off the sun as it rises higher and hotter in the sky.

Ra looks up and is pleased to see the canopy has already been put up over the emperor's viewing platform, shielding the entourage from the searing heat that is to come.

Looking around at the others gathered in its shade, he spots a number of influential dignitaries, including senators, merchants and soldiers.

In the center of them all, lounging in an ornate, ivory chair is the emperor. Caligula is dressed as he always is on such occasions, in expensive purple robes, his face painted in subtle, and some not-so-subtle, shades. Lucius thought the emperor only wears the elaborate clothes and makeup to annoy the "stuck-up old women in the Senate", but then that was just the sort of thing Lucius said! Ra thinks it's more likely that the emperor finds the old-fashioned, traditional togas far too dull, and he is pleased to see that the cloth and kohl in question are distinctly Egyptian in style and remind him of the priests back home.

Well, he makes a striking contrast with the senators, thinks Ra, looking from the emperor's extravagant getup to the pale faces and boring togas of the senators; *no wonder Caligula is so paranoid and sees conspiracy everywhere, when he deliberately distances himself from the senate! Not to mention the fact he gave his favorite horse a senator's chair!*

Ra bows low to the emperor, but Caligula turns his attention towards the pretty young lady sitting the next to him, without even acknowledging Ra's presence.

Ra peers at the lady and wonders who she might be.

This must be his latest fiancée, Ra thinks, though the priest cannot immediately recall her name. *That would be his third, no, his fourth marriage. Let's hope this one lasts a little longer!*

Here and there, slave girls attend to the needs of the entourage, serving them with cups of wine and bowls of fruit, even feeding some of those who cannot be bothered to lift their own hands to their mouths.

This is the life, Ra muses with a smile, *watching the games, and hopefully a beautiful woman, in style!*

"What are you grinning at, Lady-Balls?" says Lucius close to Ra's ear, causing the priest to jump.

"Nothing for you to trouble yourself with."

"Well, I'm gonna put a couple of sestertii on the reds, my lucky color. You going place a little bet? 'Little' being the operative word!"

"I don't think so," Ra replies, his attention drawn away by the first of the chariots as they make their way out of the gates into the arena. "And gambling is restricted to fools."

"Well, I'm still betting on the reds!"

"My point exactly, Lucius."

Muttering under his breath, Lucius walks away to join the crowd clamoring around the book-makers' tents. Ra ignores him, focused on the chariot.

The first races are always made up of those riders who had not participated in the games before, and as he looks, Ra finally catches sight of *his* warrior. His heart seems to stop.

What incredible beauty! What poise and style! He stands, staring with his mouth open, until suddenly someone nudges him.

"Yes?" he says and turns to see a young woman carrying a tray filled with roses for the spectators to throw for their favorite competitors. Pulling out his purse, Ra buys a single, white rose. *Perfect! The same color as her hair!*

"What do you have there, Ra?" He turns to find the emperor staring at him, looking quizzically at the flower, gripped in his hand.

"A white rose, Emperor," says Ra, holding it up.

"And for whom is it intended?" asks Caligula, and waves a hand towards the chariots which have lined up at the gates. "Do you favor one of these fine creatures?"

Ra bows his head, smiling. "There may be, my lord."

"Well, let's see how they do, shall we?"

And with that, the emperor rises from his ivory chair. He steps towards the front rail of the platform the sound of the crowd drops as people catch sight of Caligula. Then, with one voice, they erupt into cheers and shouts of jubilation.

The emperor gazes out at the assembled masses, receiving their praise with a slightly crooked smile. He has been greeted in this way ever since he was a boy, when his father, Germanicus, the darling soldier of Rome, held him up before his troops. Though Germanicus is now long dead - by the hand of the former emperor - his popularity still lives on through his son. After a while, the emperor raises his hands and the crowd stills expectantly.

"Let the games..." he shouts in a high, clear voice, "begin!"

Immediately the cheers well up again from the crowd and Caligula turns back to his seat.

"It better be good!" he says.

It most certainly is.

As soon as the gates are opened, the twelve chariots move slowly forward, parading before the emperor. Craning forward, Ra can easily make out the light hair of his favorite as her chariot draws up in front of him. The sight of her, close up, takes his breath away.

She stands in the chariot next to another woman. Both are dressed in the same green outfit. But this woman's skin clearly shows her to be from the lands beyond his own; Nubian perhaps or even Ethiopian. She is as black as a starless night, in stark contrast to the Briton's fair skin.

A nice touch, thinks Ra. *An entertaining combination, exactly the sort of thing Caligula is into.*

He gazes at the Briton as one by one, the other racers draw up and salute the emperor. *She seems so fragile from up here, and yet so determined. Look at her! Ready to get stuck into battle; she's a born solder. No doubt her willingness to fight is how she ended up with that scar! Oh, be lucky, my love,* he thinks as the chariots pull away to begin their seven-lap journey around the arena, and wishing he could shout it out loud. *Please be lucky!* But then he stops himself as he recalls his prayers the night before.

Luck! He is a priest of Isis, not some superstitious commoner.

By the Goddess, I know she will be safe. Isis, my queen, please watch over her. Be the power that drives the horses and the path that leads her to victory!

His thoughts are drowned out by the growing cheers of the crowd.

The race has begun in earnest now and the horses pounding as fast as their drivers can make them, the chariot wheels spinning and sliding on the sand.

Ra is still staring at the fair-haired woman when suddenly, as the racers round the turning post at the end of the first lap, he is distracted by a collision between two chariots. They seem to barely touch each other, their wheels only grazing, but somehow the spokes on one of them burst into splinters and the wheel falls away.

As the chariot drops to one side, the driver - a young woman dressed in red - is thrown onto the sand and immediately trampled by the horses behind her. With a sickening crush, the woman's skull is smashed beneath a hoof as the other chariots rumble by.

As soon as it is safe to do so, slaves run out to the body and drag it away towards one of the gates, leaving a long dark line on the sand.

The whole incident is over in moments, and the crowd roars with a mixture of anger and delight. Ra is horrified, but more out of concern for the Briton. His heart beats faster and, despite the canopy overhead, he begins to sweat.

The next five laps pass without too many incidents although on the fourth, the Briton's dark-skinned partner is caught off balance and tumbles into the sand. Flailing for something to hold onto, she gets herself entwined in the reigns and is dragged along across the sand, screaming until another chariot's wheel cuts off her cries.

Her body is left behind on the sand as Ra's favorite carries on alone and, as the final lap begins, she has managed to keep in second place.

"Come on!" shouts Ra, unable to contain himself any longer. "Overtake them! You can do it!"

"Fat chance!" says Lucius, having placed his bets at last and returned to join his friend. "The blues are the best. There's no way anyone's going to beat them!"

"She will!" says Ra, pointing to the Briton. He can see the look of determination on her face - even at this distance.

"Who? You're not rooting for Scarface are you?" Lucius laughs, but stops as Ra turns to look at him, genuinely irritated. "Oh, come on! She can't hope to win now. She's riding solo and the race is almost over."

"Huh!" Ra turns back to watch the end of the race.

Lucius places a hand on his shoulder, "Don't worry, Stumpy, I'm sure they'll be. . ."

His words are cut short by a loud crack as the pole on the leading chariot - under enormous pressure as it turns the last corner - suddenly shears in two. The horses continue on their own, but as the pole imbeds itself into the floor of the Circus, the chariot is thrown high into the air, flinging the drivers out like unwanted dolls tossed away by a child.

As the chariot spins over, the Briton steers hers underneath.

Oh no, thinks Ra, in despair. *What's she doing? Can't she see she's going to get caught as that chariot falls? She'll be crushed!* He can hardly bear to watch, and yet at the same time he cannot take his eyes off the spectacle.

The chariots may well be as light as possible, to ensure the maximum speed in the races, but she cannot possibly survive if it lands on top of her. But as it falls, she manages to spur her horses on and they find an extra burst of energy,

146

to pull them forward as the chariot smashes into the ground behind them, sending up a shower of sand onto the other racers.

The crowd, who has been holding their collective breath through all this, erupts in cheers and applauds when her chariot cross the finishing post.

"Ha ha!" shouts Lucius, thumping Ra on the back and nearly knocking him off the platform. "I take it all back. The girl can ride!" He looks down at the betting token in his hand before shaking his head and tossing it onto the ground. "Pity!"

"She certainly has amazing skills," says Ra, still awed by the spectacle. "And the great goddess was watching over her."

Lucius rolls his eyes. "Whatever!"

They both watch as she approaches the imperial platform where Caligula - still seated in his ivory chair - stares at her with a curious expression.

"From which of my many provinces do you hail, young winner?" he asks.

"No province, Caesar," she calls back. "I come from Britannia."

Caligula raises an eyebrow. "Britannia, you say? And by what name are you known in that misty isle?"

"They call me Alfreda, your highness."

"Well, Alfreda of Britannia, I congratulate you on your victory. Let us hope we see more of your courage and skill."

With that, the emperor nods and signals that she may depart. Alfreda raises her hand in salute to both Caligula and the crowd; Ra seizes the opportunity to throw his white rose to her. As the flower falls gently to the sand of the arena floor, he happens to glance at Caligula and sees a grin turning up the corners of the emperor's mouth and feels his face flushing in embarrassment.

Quickly turning away to look back at Alfreda, Ra watches her bend gracefully to pick up the rose. She pauses a moment as she raises the bloom to her nose and her eyes turn upwards briefly to see who threw it. Then, the flower still held between her strong fingers, she strides away and disappears through the open gate into the darkness beyond.

"Alfreda," whispers Ra, staring after her and savoring the sound of her name, so foreign on his tongue. "Alfreda."

The races continue; the next contest opposes the veteran male charioteers.

Around Ra, the spectators clamor for their favorites, placing bets on the most promising contestants and conversing excitedly with one another, but he has no interest in the rest of the events.

He feels as though time is standing still, while the world around him carries on. Taking a seat to the back of the emperor's platform, he daydreams about Alfreda, the brave slave-soldier. The rose he threw to her has somehow become a connection between them in his mind; he can still sense the feel of the flower as he gripped it in his hand, its thorns biting into his skin. Those thorns are now clutched in *her* fingers, the petals brushing again *her* cheek, the token of his love kept close to her heart.

"Hey!" Ra looks up to see Lucius frowning at him. "What're you doing, you tit? You look like a puppy that's just been kicked in the head!"

Ra makes no response, just sitting there staring, his eyes glazed as his thoughts are inexorably drawn back to Alfreda.

For the first time in his life, he feels the grip of love's fire, the burning passion that feels as though it will consume him. In his mind he sees them touching, kissing, their bodies drawing closer together.

He yearns for her, to bathe her in water covered in rose petals and the finest oils that Egypt has to offer, to dry her with the thinnest cotton and massage her body with aromatic oils, to cover her with the most exclusive silk and feed her the juiciest fruits with his own fingers.

"Jupiter's balls!" says Lucius with a shake of his head. "The ball-less bugger's only bloody fallen in love!" He laughs and turns away to watch the next race that has just started, leaving Ra to his thoughts of Alfreda.

After the games, Ra returns to the Temple, where supplicants are waiting for him with requests for the goddess.

He goes through the motions, performing his usual activities—carrying out the various rituals required for the worship of Isis, handing out orders to the temple slaves, preparing one of the sacred oils and offering up a white dove as a sacrifice—but he does them all without really engaging.

His thoughts are entirely taken with Alfreda. As he finishes the evening worship ritual, a loud clunking sound causes him to turn around. Near the temple entrance,

Lucius stands, holding a pair of goblets in one hand and leaning on an amphora.

"I know just the thing you need," he says, patting the side of the vessel. "There's nothing better for love-sickness that a damn fine Falernian."

"Not this evening, Lucius," says Ra wearily. "I just want to go and lay down in my bed."

"And do what? Stare at the ceiling while you mope about this blonde bit of skirt that's caught your fancy?"

Ra frowns at his friend's typically course way of speaking. "It's so much more than that... but you're right. I doubt I'll get any sleep."

"You bet I'm right." Lucius smiles as he twists the cork out of the amphora and begins to fill the goblets. "Plus, I've got a bit of info on your girl; you might be interested to hear it."

That settles it; Ra quickly joins his friend sitting on the bench in the temple porch, looking out over the city lit by the last of the sunlight. The view is glorious, and as Ra accepts a wine-filled goblet from his friend, he leans back and gazes out across the hills.

"So what information have you found out, Lucius?"

"Well, after the races, I went for a drink with Glaucus, an old tent mate from my days as a legionary in the Second. He happens to be in charge of the Circus stables."

"Yes?"

"He told me that your girl, Alfreda, is owned by the Servilli."

"The Servilli?" Ra raises his eyebrows at this news.

The Servilli are a powerful Patrician family, who own half of the gladiators in Italy - including some of the best fighters that have ever graced an arena. As such, they are not only influential, but massively wealthy; there are many senators in the family.

Although they own a number of houses on the Palatine and Aventine, the Servilli can usually be found in a massive villa just outside Rome, which housed their school for gladiator.

"As you know," Lucius continues, "their gladiator school caters to male and female fighters, so the odds are good that your girl is being kept out at the villa. They'll have her in their best quarters too, after today's performance."

"So what should I do, Lucius? Should I go and visit her?"

"Well, I'm sure you'll do whatever takes your fancy... within the limits of what you're able, anyway!" he adds, waving his goblet in the general direction of Ra's groin and splashing wine all over his robe. "Sorry!" he laughs.

"What would you do then?" Ra asks, trying to brush the spreading liquid from his robe without success. "You're more experienced in these sorts of matters."

"You've hung around women enough over at the palace to know what they want. You might have no balls, but you've got a damn brain man! Use it!"

Leaning back against the wall, Ra considers this. "What about gifts?" he suggests. "That's something all the ladies seem to enjoy."

"It's a start."

"How about sending her some flowers?"

"Flowers?" says Lucius, looking at Ra as though he suggest giving her a week-old fish. "She ain't your mother! You want to give her something more... permanent, not just a bunch of dying foliage!"

"All right. How about a necklace? Or a bracelet?"

"That's a bit more like it."

"As luck - or rather Isis - would have it, my mother gave me her bracelet when I left Egypt. It came from my grandmother."

"Nice to see it's still going down through the ladies in the family," says Lucius with a wink.

"Hold on, I'll go and get it."

A couple of minutes later, Ra returns and hands Lucius a piece of silk which he opens to reveal a beautiful bracelet, fashioned from gold and inlaid with fine, clear emeralds. Lucius' eyes widen and he lets out a long whistle.

"Impressive!" he says.

"I wonder if it matches her eyes. I bet they're green too!"

"Who cares about her eyes?" says Lucius. "A trinket like this ought to let you get close to a few capital areas of her body... Not that it'll do you much good."

"One of these days," says Ra, taking the bracelet from Lucius and wrapping it carefully back in the silk. "You're going to find out just how much of a man I am. And how hard a priest can punch!"

Lucius laughs and slaps his friend on the back, almost causing him to drop the bracelet.

Ra quickly hurries back to his quarters and gets out some sealing wax. Careful not to damage the silk, he melts some of the wax onto it and presses his seal onto it, an ornate R carved around an eye. Calling to one of the temple slaves, he hands him the bracelet and gives detailed instructions about where to deliver it and who the recipient is, making it clear that this gift is to be placed directly into her hands.

As the slave disappears into the darkening streets, Ra sits back down next to his friend.

"May I have a little more of that wine, Lucius?" he asks, holding out his goblet.

Chapter Twelve

Long after Lucius has departed -somewhat uneasy on his legs after consuming most of the amphora - and the sun has set across the Tiber, Ra sits on the edge of his bed unsettled. He frequently glances towards the doorway, straining his ears and his eyes as he waits for any sign indicating the return of his slave.

What can be taking him so long? If I find out he's stopped off in a wine house on his way back, by Isis, there'll be trouble!

A movement in the corner of the room catches his eye and, peering into the shadows, he makes out the shape of a mouse scurrying along close to the wall. Cautiously, without making any sudden movements, Ra slips a sandal from his foot and takes careful aim.

Steady, he thinks as he draws back his arm to throw the sandal.

"Sorry for the delay, master."

Surprised by the voice, Ra hurls the sandal way off target, knocking over a vase and frightening the mouse back into its hole.

"Good goddess, man!" he says, turning angrily to his slave. "You nearly scared the life out of me!"

"Sorry, master." The slave bows, his breathing heavy after his journey up the Palatine.

"Never mind. Did you give her the bracelet?"

"Of course," says the slave, looking slightly offended at the suggestion he might have failed in his task. "But it wasn't easy. The villa of the Servilli was simple enough to find. You can hardly miss it, but getting in is another thing entirely."

"So how did you manage it?" asks Ra, leaning forward eagerly.

"With the key that opens all doors, master. Money!" The slave jangles the purse he uses to buy food in the market, which he always carries with him. "I ended up having to hand over a whole sestertius but it got me inside the gladiator school first, and then the women's quarters."

Ra shrugs. "It's a small price to pay. Go on. Tell me about Alfreda."

"When I entered her room, she was cleaning her weapons. She has quite an impressive armory, so I took care not to cause any offence. I presented her with the gift, saying it was from a 'secret admirer', as you requested. Once she'd wiped off her hands, she took it off me and studied the seal mark in the wax."

"She can't have recognized it, surely?" says Ra.

"I don't think so, master. She asked after your name, but I explained you wanted to remain anonymous."

"Good man. So, did you see her open the gift? Did she like it?"

"She certainly seemed to be pleasantly surprised when she opened it. She was smiling and enjoyed watching the jewels sparkle in the lamplight, turning it this way and that."

"Is that it?" interrupts Ra, looking slightly disappointed. "No message?"

"I was just getting to it, master. The lady has a very strong accent, which made her a bit hard to understand, and her Latin isn't that good, but she got the message across in the end. 'Tell your master,' she said, 'whoever he is, that he is a lovely man and his gift is most welcome and greatly appreciated.' Then she returned to polishing a sword, so I left."

Ra nods, trying to hide his excitement at receiving a message from this beautiful woman, something so much more tangible than a distant gaze or a mere dream of being together.

She may not know who I am, he thinks, a smile spreading across his face, *but she knows that I love her, and she welcomes it!*

The slave standing awkwardly in the doorway eventually breaks the silence. "So, is that all, master?"

"What?" Ra looks up in surprise as though he has forgotten the slave was still there. "Oh, sorry. I'd forgotten you were still there. Yes, that's all." As the slave turns to go, Ra calls after him. "One moment." He reaches into the purse that is lying next to his mattress and tosses the slave a coin. "And another sestertius," he adds, pulling out another coin and giving that to him too. "For a job well done."

"Thank you, master!" With a broad smile on his face, the slave walks away towards his quarters.

Ra lies down on his bed and stares up at the ceiling, watching the candlelight causing shadows to dance across it.

Well, my Alfreda, he thinks. *What destiny awaits you here in Rome? Now you have won your first race, there will be more to come. And how long can you keep it up and stay alive?* This notion worries Ra. Being a charioteer is one of the most dangerous occupations, almost as much as being a gladiator. Very few survive the arena long enough to see retirement.

Will she survive? He wonders. *I have to know! Time to seek the goddess and see what the future holds.*

The priests of Isis are well known for their ability to perform magic and there are few better than Ra.

It was for this very reason he was brought to Rome in the first place, and it was thanks to his magical skills that the young emperor's life was saved only a few years ago.

However, such magic is not easy and the sacred rituals that surround it must be undertaken with great care. So, for the next three days, Ra doesn't consume any meat or alcohol, restricting himself to a rigorous diet of vegetables, fruit juice and water instead.

He also bathes twice daily, carefully oiling and scraping his skin, and wears only white robes. He does this to ensure both his mind and body are purified in preparation for the ritual he wishes to perform—divination, to see the future of his beloved.

Late in the evening on the third day, he begins the ceremony by lighting a censor filled with jasmine incense and walking around the temple to purify the area with the fragrant smoke.

Then, on a small table near the altar, Ra carefully lays out the items he requires an amethyst crystal, a silver altar cloth, two short candles and a small cauldron half-filled with water. Opening out the cloth, he lays it across the altar, making sure it is squarely centered, then takes the cauldron and sets it on a stand above the candles. These he lights, and the flames lick the bottom of the blackened vessel.

While the water heats, Ra turns to face east and makes the sacred sign of the Wings of Isis, raising his arms apart, imitating the shape of a chalice. He begins his first chant, his voice ringing loud and clear across the temple.

"I am Ra, a son of Isis. I am Ra, a child of the Goddess."

The words stir something inside him and he feels a growing sense of excitement.

"I am Ra," he repeats, "a son of Isis. I am Ra, a child of the Goddess. I am Ra, a son of Isis. I am Ra, a child of the Goddess."

He echoes this chant over and over, and as he does so the chalice he has formed with his arms begins to fill, not with a liquid, but with a soft glow—the Light of Isis.

It gradually becomes brighter; Ra is filled with energy, increasing in intensity until he is almost forced to lower his arms, overwhelmed.

The power pours inside him, his arms drop to his sides and he breathes deeply, delighting in the euphoria accompanying the Light of Isis. Turning back to the altar, he sees that, although it feels like he has only been chanting a few minutes, steam is curling up from the cauldron.

It is time to communicate with the Goddess and ask her to reveal Alfreda's future.

"O Isis, Queen of nature and Sovereign of all that is spiritual, Universal Mother and Mistress of all the elements." As he calls out the many names of the goddess, he turns to face each point of the compass. "O Isis, eternal Overseer of time, Queen of the dead, Queen of the ocean, Queen of the immortals, Embodiment of all gods and goddesses, and Governor of the shining heights of the Heavens. I, your son, beseech you. Will you reveal to me the destiny of the one called Alfreda, the one brought as a slave from Britannia and who now dwells here in Rome? Show me what is to come, what fate will befall on this noble woman."

Ra focuses on the image of his beloved, recalling her strong figure, her white hair, her beautiful features. When his mind is filled with a clear, intense vision of Alfreda, he leans forward to look into the cauldron; the Light of Isis radiates from his face, illuminating the bubbling surface of the water.

The first thing he sees is an eagle, proud and swift, soaring above the earth. Ra's heart leaps, delighted at such a great omen. He breathes a sigh of relief, hoping that this means Alfreda will be all right. But then as he peers into the water again, his heart to stop beating. A raven black and terrifying, its beady eyes filled with malice - flies straight at him. He catches his breath in his throat as it approaches and suddenly the bird seems to burst from the surface of the water.

Ra staggers backwards, hands raised in front of his face to ward off the creature. But there is nothing there, save for the steam still rising from the cauldron.

Brushing a hand across his forehead, Ra feels beads of cold sweat. An unpleasant chill has come over him and he's sick to his stomach.

Ra closes his eyes and says aloud, "O Isis, Queen of nature and Sovereign of all that is spiritual, Universal Mother and Mistress of all the elements, show me the image again, if this is truly what you would have me see."

Still praying under his breath, he looks down into the water to see the oily-black bird watching him with its cold eyes, its long beak glistening with flecks of blood.

It is unmistakably a *raven*.

Trying to catch his breath, Ra straightens up, shaking his head.

The raven. This can only mean one thing. Alfreda is going to die!

Despite his bitter disappointment and his concern about the Briton, Ra completes the ritual, making the Sign of the Wings once again and thanking Isis for opening his eyes and granting him this glimpse of the future.

Then he turns away and walks out of the temple.

♣

"What do you mean this is as much as you can give me?" says Ra, looking crossly at the pile of coins on the trestle table.

Across the table his banker, Glaucus, shrugs and shakes his head.

"Fifteen hundred denarii is it, sir. That's all your savings plus fifty percent in credit. Who else around here would make you such an offer?" Glaucus gestures towards the general hustle and bustle nearby them in the forum. What he says is true, and Ra knows it. "Why do you need so much anyway? You've never made a withdrawal of more than fifty denarii before."

"There's a slave I have my eye on." Ra replies.

"A slave?! But for this sort of money you could get any two, or even three of your choosing."

"Ah, but this is not just *any* slave. This is a once in a lifetime opportunity. But for such a slave, I reckon I'm looking at a hundred and fifty aurei at least." Ra has already made enquiries and, while Alfreda might have been bought for a third of the price only last week, since her win at the races and her subsequent rise to fame, the Servilli were looking to make a good deal of income from her, either through future winnings or by selling her at an extortionately high price.

"A hundred and fifty?" Glaucus stares at the priest, his mouth opening and closing like a fish out of water as he struggles for something to say. "For a slave? That's insane! It's about fifteen years' salary."

"For a soldier, maybe," says Ra, trying not to let himself become too irritated by his banker. "But I am a priest of Isis, by appointment of Caesar himself. Surely there is something you can do?"

"I'm sorry, sir." Glaucus closes his chest and points to the money still laid out on the table. "This is all I can offer.."

"Forget it!" Without bothering to explain, Ra turns away and wanders dejectedly through the crowded forum, wishing there was something he could do, some way he could save his beloved Alfreda from her impending death.

O Isis, he prays. Have mercy on me. And on the woman I love. Please!

His thoughts are interrupted when someone suddenly blows a trumpet right by his ear.

He turns in surprise to see it is the forum herald preparing to make an announcement. Not especially interested in current affairs, Ra begins to walk away, but stops as he hears the news.

"By order of the emperor, the illustrious Gaius Julius Caesar Augustus Germanicus, there will be a special chariot race held in his honor on the Ides..."

The Ides? Ra quickly considers the date. *But that's only ten days away! Hopefully Alfreda won't be racing.*

But, as the herald reads out the list of those who will race, his hopes are short-lived: "Alfreda of Britannia" is the very first name he announces.

Ra hurries out of the forum.

What can I do, he wonders, almost overcome by anguish. *I must prevent her death! No matter what price the Servilli demand, I must rescue her...*

162

♣

The following morning, Ra sends a large, gilded platter, filled with some of the most exotic fruits available, to the Servilli.

He chooses the slave who delivered the bracelet a few days ago, and once he has gone, struggling under the weight of the platter, Ra takes to pacing anxiously around the temple precinct.

Eventually, he can stand it no longer and instead he hails a palanquin to take him to the Circus Maximus in the hope of catching a glimpse of Alfreda.

The bearers make their way down the Palatine Hill, where the sounds and smells of Rome seep in through the palanquin's curtains. The city is buzzing with activity once again.

On his arrival at the Circus, Ra hands over a few coins and heads towards the main gates, tipping the guard to let him in.

To his deepest disappointment however, although he waits for several hours, scrutinizing the riders training for the coming races, he doesn't catch sight of the blonde hair or the slim, elegant body he is looking for.

He makes his way from one end of the arena to the other, but Alfreda is nowhere to be seen; eventually he decides to head back to the temple.

His slave is waiting for him with a message from the Servilli; Ra takes the wax tablet from him, and finds he has an invitation to visit their Campus Martius villa on the following Friday.

Thank you, Isis, he thinks in silent praise for the goddess. *Thank you! Not long now; I will be able to free Alfreda and save her from death. Only three more days!*

♣

Late Friday afternoon, Ra arrives at the villa, and he is welcomed by the door slave.

He gazes at his surroundings in the atrium, stunned by the opulence of the Servilli's home. The floor before him is of the finest marble, highly-polished and inlaid with stunning mosaics. On the walls hang the wax face masks of the family's ancestors, which look out with stern expressions at the displays of statues, pottery and golden housewares. If anything, the collection of treasures before him is even more impressive than those in the emperor's palace.

How wonderful it must be to live in such opulence, he thinks, admiring the wealth on display. To be surrounded by such riches every day! How has one single family attained so great a fortune?

He knows the answer, of course; through training gladiators and others for the games.

The Servilli have prospered thanks to the pain and death of countless slaves like Alfreda.

Ra frowns and reaches out to touch the face mask of an especially irritated-looking man. As he does so, his robe brushes against a bright, blue vase, which topples, falling sideways from its plinth. Ra quickly gets hold of it, catching it all the while accidentally kicking the plinth out from underneath.

It's made of heavy wood and hits the marble floor with a ringing thud. Placing the vase under one arm, Ra bends to pick it up.

"Welcome to our home, servant of Isis."

Ra straightens up, lifting the plinth and setting the vase carefully back in place.

Then he turns around to find a stranger a short distance behind him, watching him with an amused expression.

The man is dressed in a white toga with a broad purple stripe that distinguishes him as a member of the Senate.

This must be the paterfamilias, the head of the Servilli family.

"Thank you, senator," he replies, bowing low as he tries to hide his embarrassment. "May Isis bless and protect your family."

"Indeed. My name is Publius Servillius Opilio." He gestures to his right. "Shall we sit?"

Without waiting for a reply, Opilio strides away through a colonnade. Ra hurries along behind him, and they emerge into a courtyard filled with a stunning collection of shrubs and bushes surrounding a central fountain.

"Fortuna," says Opilio, pointing at the marble statue in the fountain. "One of our Roman goddesses. She has watched over my family for many generations. Ah, here we are." He points to where a couple of seats have been placed around a small table filled with food and drink, and ushers Ra to sit down.

"So tell me, priest," says Opilio, helping himself to a honeyed fig. "Is it true what I hear about the worship of Isis?"

Ra looks at the table and selects a small portion of minced meat, coated in ground pine kernels and green peppercorns. "I couldn't say, senator. What have you heard?"

"I have heard tales of magic; stories that have surely been embellished in the telling."

Opilio pours a little wine for them both and adds water from a golden jug. For a while the two men sit and talk about the worship of Isis and, though it is clear the senator does not entirely approve of such foreign worship, despite the fact Caligula has given it the status of an official religion of Rome, Ra promises to pray to the goddess on Opilio's behalf.

The conversation turns to the history of the Servilli family which has been involved in the games for many generations. Ra seizes the opportunity to raise the subject of Alfreda.

"I was watching the games with the emperor not long ago," he begins, twisting his empty goblet between his fingers. "And I believe the winner of the first chariot race was one of yours, yes?"

"Yes, indeed. The Briton. As you can imagine, I made a great return on my investment that day."

"A true beauty and no mistake, with a skill I have never seen equaled."

"Exactly. Though keeping hold of such a natural is not easy. It's a very risky business we're in, and even the best of our gladiators can be killed in the arena without warning. It can be hard to run at a profit."

Ra looks around at the courtyard, a testimony to the Servilli's wealth, and doubts the truth of the senator's words.

"There is a need for good fortune in all areas of life, senator," he says. "And we must work hard to earn the favor of the gods."

"Quite," says Opilio, and waves a hand towards the statue in the fountain. "Our future and our fortune are certainly in their hands."

"But also in ours, if we will." Ra smiles slightly and braces himself. The moment to state the reason for his visit has arrived. "I have come, senator, in response to a disturbing vision I received regarding your future."

"Really?" Opilio raises his eyebrows and considers the priest. It is well known that Ra has influence with the emperor, and Caligula certainly appears convinced of the power of Isis. He holds Ra's gaze for a moment before continuing. "I believe you, servant of Isis. So what have you seen? How can I best ensure the protection of my future?"

"The vision has to do with the very woman we were just talking about. The chariot racer from Britannia."

"Her?" The senator looks suddenly serious. "I had great plans for her really, I did. She could have added millions to my family's coffers. Unfortunately her future is sealed. She joined some sect that calls themselves Christians. It wouldn't be so bad... but these wretched fanatics refuse to recognize any other god than this 'Christ' they worship."

"What?" Ra is taken aback, shocked by this disturbing news. "You mean she refused to worship the emperor as a living god?"

"Exactly." Opilio shakes his head sadly and Ra places a hand on his head in dismay. "When the gladiators enter the arena," Opilio continues, "they are obliged to greet Caligula with the words, 'We who are about to die salute you, Caesar, great emperor and merciful god.' Unfortunately she refused to do so, as she will not acknowledge Caligula as god. As you know, such blasphemy is against Roman law and the penalty for such a crime is death, especially for a slave."

"But... but this is impossible! What can be done about it?"

"Nothing, I'm afraid."

"So what will happen to Alfreda?"

"She," Opilio begins, a look of anger spreading across his face at the thought, "as well as the other slaves led astray by the Christians, are going."

"Going?"

"To the games, as bestiarii. It doesn't pay well, but at least. . ."

"Bestiarii!" Ra jumps to his feet, his goblet falling to the ground and clattering on the stones. "She's being thrown to the wild beasts?"

"Of course she is. That's the only fate that awaits the followers of Christ, who refuse to acknowledge any other god."

"Please tell me you haven't sold her already."

Opilio looks at the priest with pity in his eyes. There is nothing he can do.

"I'm sorry, priest. The deal was made earlier today. She's already gone."

Chapter Thirteen

*W**hy, Isis? Why has this happened? Of all the women in the world that I could have fallen in love with and now she is being snatched away from me, before I have even had a chance to talk with her. I love her. O Isis, how I love her!*

Ra gazes unseeing out of the palanquin as the hustle and bustle of city life goes on around him. In an attempt to clear his head and give himself time to work out what to do next, he is travelling by palanquin, from the Servilli back to the Temple of Isis.

It's no use, he thinks. *I just can't think straight. Maybe there's nothing I can do. Maybe Alfreda really is lost to me! But no! I can't believe that!*

A familiar laugh catches his attention and he looks to see his centurion friend, Lucius, emerging from a nearby tavern, a large woman hanging off his arm.

"Come on, gorgeous!" he slurs. "It's a bit of a stroll to my place, but you could do with the exercise." He laughs loudly, grabbing her ample backside.

"Oh! Lucius!" the woman scowls, her voice full of mock indignation, before slapping him on the chest. He staggers backwards a little, bumping into Ra's palanquin.

"Whoa! Easy there!" Lucius turns, still chuckling, and spots Ra. "Juno's tits!" he says, his smile fading at the sight of his friend's miserable features. "What's up with you, priestess?"

"It's Alfreda."

Lucius frowns. "You mean that gladiator lass? The Briton? What's up with her?"

"She's been sold!" says Ra, almost in tears. "She's been sold as a bestiarius."

"Wait a moment, beautiful," Lucius told his woman, pushing her aside. "It's an old friend of mine"

"She's going to die for being a Christian, and I don't know what to do! I was going to buy her, pay for her freedom, but now I'm stuck. I want to save her, Lucius! I have to!"

"All right, all right." Lucius pats Ra awkwardly on the shoulder with his free hand, not used to this sort of situation. "So, why don't you ask your buddy Caligula to sort it out? He's your man, if anyone can, wouldn't you say?"

The change in Ra's demeanor is almost immediate, as though turning from winter to summer in an instant. "Lucius! You're a genius!"

"Well, that goes without saying, doesn't it?" He chuckles and squeezes the woman's backside again for good measure. "Seems damned obvious to me though, you idiot!"

"So... what's the form? Should I just go and ask him?"

Lucius rolls his eyes. "Bloody hell, have I got to think of everything for you? The usual form is a petition; all proper and legal, you know. Here, why don't you use my lawyer, Marcus Petronius. He's a dab hand at all that kind of crap. You'll find him in the Forum, in front of the statue of Apollo."

"Thank you, Lucius," says Ra, smiling for the first time in days.

"Yeah, yeah. Piss off, then. Me and..." he turns to the woman. "What's your name, love?"

She purses her lips, affecting an offended air. "Marcia."

"Right." Lucius turns back to Ra. "Me and Marcia here have got some urgent business to attend to, if you know what I mean."

♣

Less than an hour later, Ra emerges from the Forum half running, the petition clutched in his hand.

Marcus Petronius had been happy to draw it up, though he was not optimistic about Ra's chance of getting Caligula's permission.

"He's an exceptionally unpredictable young man, our emperor," he warned him while putting the finishing touches on the document. "Who's to know how he will react to the idea of freeing a slave who has refused to acknowledge his divinity? If I were *your* lawyer, I would counsel you against presenting this up at the palace."

But Ra had not been interested in this advice; as soon as the petition was complete, he practically snatched it from his hand, dropping twice the amount of money he'd requested and hurried away as fast as he could, desperate to reach Caligula before something terrible happened to Alfreda.

Leaning against the wall of the palace entrance and holding on to his chest, Ra tries to catch his breath. As he attempts to steady the hammering of his heart, he considers the foolishness of running through such a distance. Priests are not known for their athletic pursuits; Ra cannot remember having so much exercise since he was a child!

I'm going to be sick, he thinks, wiping the sweat from his brow. *My poor heart! What was I thinking? This is all some strange madness, but I have to see the emperor. I have to save Alfreda from being torn apart in the arena.*

He stands up when his heart calms down and walks in as stiffly as possible.

After a short distance he is stopped by a member of the Praetorian Guard - the soldiers who are responsible for the emperor's safety.

"What do you want, priest?" he sneers. "There aren't any parties here tonight."

Ignoring this, Ra pulls a scroll from his robe and holding it up, he says, "I have a petition and request an audience with the emperor. It is a matter of life and death!"

"Is it really?" the guard makes no move to pass on this request, but begins instead to pick his teeth. "Sounds expensive," he says eventually.

With a sigh, Ra reaches down and produces a number of small coins from his purse.

"An urgent message, I see!" says the guard, plucking the coins from Ra's hand with practiced ease and snatching the scroll as well. "Wait here."

As the guard leaves to pass on the request to the emperor's secretary, Ra paces up and down the atrium impatiently.

Alfreda, my love. What have you done? Why in the name of Isis did you get yourself mixed up with this crazy sect? I'm going mad with worry. And yet surely Caligula will grant you mercy.

Ra thinks back to the first time he met the emperor.

Two years ago Drusilla, Caligula's beloved sister, had caught some unknown sickness and died; the young emperor was soon taken sick, showing the same symptoms.

One afternoon, when everyone thought that he was about to die, Caligula, in a brief moment of consciousness, called for the best of the priests of Isis to be brought to him. The emperor had encountered the magic of his people on one of his voyages to Egypt and had been greatly impressed.

So Ra had been brought to the palace. Caligula was terribly weak by this stage, but Ra had used all his skills and wisdom, calling on the goddess to restore the young emperor to health. Within days, Caligula was well again.

Surely the emperor has not forgotten what I did for him. Surely he will grant mercy for my Alfreda. Surely!

Yet Ra has also heard that, since the young emperor returned to physical health, his sanity seems to have deteriorated.

Caligula's reign had been good for the empire before – he undertook great public and political reform, giving aid to the poor and abolishing certain taxes, restored democratic elections and imported spiritual practices from other countries – now he is known to be increasingly unpredictable and malicious.

Considering what the emperor has been through – losing both of his parents, his brothers and finally his darling Drusilla – It's no surprise that he has changed; Ra realizes he is taking a great risk in coming here. *But what else can I do?* He rhetorically asks himself, knowing he has no other answer. *I want to save her, no matter what the cost! What is my life without her but darkness and misery?*

After what seems like an eternity, just as he is beginning to despair of ever getting to see the emperor, the guard reappears, slowly walking back to take up his position at the entrance.

Ra looks at him standing in the same place, picking at his teeth again.

"Well?" says Ra pointedly.

The guard glances at the priest as though he has forgotten all about him, "Oh, I'd forgotten all about you," he confirms.

Ra's fists clench angrily at his sides. "Can I go in now?"

"What? Yeah, sure. Off you go." The guard waves him through before looking away, disinterested.

"Thanks," Ra grits through his teeth.

He sweeps angrily past and looks up at the guard to see him trying hard not laugh. Furious, Ra strides away towards the emperor's ante chamber.

"Go straight through," one of the imperial staff seated behind a large desk instructs him, "It is unwise to keep him waiting."

Me, keep him waiting? Ra thinks irritably.

He takes a few deep breaths to calm down before opening the door and slipping through.

Ra has never been in the throne room and is immediately struck by the garish opulence of the place. Every surface—floor, walls, ceiling and doors—is coated in gold leaf, and reflects the light of dozens of candles, dazzling the priest. The furniture is made up of ornately carved chests of drawers and shelves, but the only chair in the room is the golden throne occupied by Caligula himself.

As per his custom, the emperor is wearing robes of the finest purple cloth, a wreath of golden oak leaves sitting slightly lopsidedly on his brow. Either side of the throne, a Praetorian Guard stands, holding a hand on the hilt of his sword in case the emperor's safety becomes jeopardized.

One of the emperor's secretaries stands a short distance away, poised ready to carry out whatever task Caligula calls on him to perform. Ra notices that the secretary is holding the scroll he brought with him - the petition for Alfreda's life to be spared and for her to be released into the priest's care.

"Come," says Caligula, beckoning Ra to approach. "I am told you have a request."

"O, Caesar!" Ra hurries forwards, dropping to his knees before the throne. "I do have a request, Divine Augustus, a request for mercy. Mercy for a slave woman who is being sent to her death, to be torn apart by beasts in the. . ."

"What woman is this?" Caligula's cold, high-pitched voice cut across Ra's pleading.

"You have seen her, Caesar. The charioteer who won the first race of the games."

The emperor leans forward and grips Ra's chin, turning his face up to look at his own. "The Briton is it? The one you threw the rose to?"

"Yes, Caesar. The Briton."

"And now she is to be thrown to the beasts?" Caligula frowns, clearly unaware of what has happened. "What has this woman done that has so altered her fate?"

"She...she has joined the Christians, Caesar." Caligula releases Ra's chin, drawing his hand back as though he has been bitten. The suddenness of the movement causes the Praetorians to half draw their swords from their scabbards and the rasping of the metal causes Ra to look up in fear. "Please, Divine Augustus, I beg of you, in the name your beloved sister, Drusilla, please have mercy." He grasps the folds of the emperor's robe.

"How dare you, you worm!" Caligula shouts, snatching cloth from the priest's hands. "Guards!"

Ra closes his eyes, dreading the cold steal that must surely be about to end his life, but before the Praetorians can react, the secretary hurries forwards and whispers urgently into the emperor's ear. Ra opens his eyes and finds himself staring at Caligula's legs, left bare as the emperor still holds his robe out of the priest's reach.

Ra is surprised to see the emperor is not wearing any shoes and also at how incredibly hairy his legs are.

"She what?!" Caligula's half-shout, half-scream cuts through Ra's thoughts and he looks up at the emperor's face, which is red with fury. In turn Caligula stares down at the priest with a piercing gaze, and for the first time Ra notices the large black rings around his eyes; the sign of many sleepless nights.

And the eyes... as Ra looks into those eyes, he realizes that the emperor truly is insane.

"The woman," says Caligula, his voice full of scorn, "This Briton filth refuses to worship me? Me? But I am Caesar! Caesar, do you hear?"

Everyone in the room seems to hold their breath, terrified by his fury. It would not be unlike him to have everyone in his vicinity put to the sword if the rage got the better of him. Ra glances up to see large beads of sweat running down the massive neck of one of the Praetorians, his Adam's apple bobbing up and down as though trying to escape.

Then, Caligula laughs; a high and piercing sound. It is the laugh of a madman, one who's completely lost his sanity. The laugh chills Ra to the bone, freezes the blood in his veins, and Ra closes his eyes again in dread of what's to come.

"And perhaps she is right!" Caligula says, his voice cold.

He snaps his fingers and Ra, looking looks up, sees the emperor snatching the scroll from the secretary. "Bring me my seal, Felix."

The secretary hurries to one of the beautifully carved desks from which he takes a candle and a seal ring to hand over to the emperor.

Without even bothering to read the petition, Caligula drips wax onto the parchment and endorses it.

"Now leave me, priest." he says, tossing the scroll to Ra. "I tire of you and your love for this woman."

"Thank you, O Caesar," says Ra, clutching the scroll to his chest. "May Isis bless you in all you do, Divine Augustus."

"Yes, yes." Caligula flicks his fingers lazily towards the door. "Get out."

Ra makes his way from the throne room just as the emperor calls out over his head "Nobody in!"

The door swings shut and Caligula is cut off from Ra's view.

♣

I got it, Ra thinks, kissing the scroll. *Thanks and praise to you, O Isis! I can save her!*

Hurrying along the corridors that lead back to the entrance to the palace, Ra realizes he doesn't have much time. According to Opilio, the beast fights would begin that evening at the tenth hour back out on the Campus Martius.

The thought of trying to run that distance again is unthinkable, so Ra rushes towards the nearby stables, where he hires a horse.

It is expensive, but he doesn't quibble over the price. He has only one thought now: to save the woman he loves.

Alfreda! Alfreda! Alfreda! The words pound through Ra's head in time with the horse's hooves as it gallops across the cobbles. *I love you, Alfreda! Fear not, I'm coming for you. And when I have saved you, then I will get you your freedom.*

A smile flickers across the priest's face as he considers the wonder of their future together.

I will ask her to become my wife, he thinks, the idea sending a trill of delight through him. *She will move into the temple with me. She will be brought into the order of Isis if she wants to. And though we could never have children, still we can live together and grow old together. I will take care of her. We would be happy together, we two. . .*

"Come on!" he shouts, willing the horse to go faster, despite the narrowness of streets as they wind around the Capitoline Hill and heedless of the obstacles that litter their path. There is so little time. Ra glances up to see the sun hanging low in the sky. It must already be approaching the tenth hour and the time for the bloody spectacle to begin. He mutters a prayer to Isis under his breath and strikes the horse across its rump with his hand. "Faster, damn you!"

In response, the animal gives an extra spurt of speed, but it is short lived.

There, stretched out across the cobbles, is the body of a large dog that someone has thrown out into the street. It is quite dead and though it makes no movement, it spooks the horse, which tries both to avoid it and jump over it at the same time. Its hooves slip on one of the many patches of filth that litter the ground and its legs buckle underneath.

Before he knows what is happening, Ra is thrown from the animal as it crashes down onto the cobbles. The loud snap of one of its legs breaking, echoing off the nearby buildings, is the last thing the priest hears before his temple strikes the ground, knocking him out.

He quickly bursts back to consciousness thanks to the searing pain in his leg. Lifting his head up, he sees that it is stuck underneath the horse.

"Get off me!" he shouts, kicking out with his free leg, but it is no use.

The horse cannot move. Instead Ra listens to its last, ragged breaths as the animal's life ebbs away and he notices a pool of blood spreading out from beneath it. Clearly the horse has fallen on something sharp, a rock perhaps or a discarded blade. Either way, it makes no difference to Ra. He must free himself and continue on foot, and so he pushes with all his strength, trying to free his trapped leg.

Blessed Isis, please help me! I must save her!

As he thinks these words something suddenly gives and, inch by inch, he drags his leg free from the dead horse. He feels it carefully and, though his leg is bruised and sore, there is nothing broken. Ra scrambles to his feet as quickly as he can and heads off again towards the Campus Martius, stopping briefly to check he still has the scroll intact in his purse.

Soon the narrow, cobbled streets give way to the broader dirt tracks that head out through the Servian Wall to the northwest of the city. The heat of the previous weeks has baked these roads to the hardness of marble, with large cracks in the surface and deep grooves cut by the many carts going back and forth to the plain.

Ra stumbles many times, falling down on one occasion, and ends up spraining his wrist. The setting sun as much as the tears which are now flowing freely nearly blinds him but yet he keeps going, spurred on by his love and his desperation to save Alfreda.

His heart is hammering against his ribs, harder than ever, until suddenly, as he finally catches sight of the makeshift arena across the Campus, a searing pain unlike anything he has ever experienced slices through his chest. It quickly spreads down along his arm and upwards into his throat, making it difficult for him to breath. Desperately trying to draw air into his lungs, he keeps going, placing one foot in front of the other again and again. The pain is almost overwhelming and it is increasingly hard to breathe.

He drops to his knees and, as his mouth opens and closes in an effort to feed his body with the air it needs, Ra is reminded of one sunny afternoon as a seven or eight-year-old boy, when his uncle showed him how to catch fish in the Nile near his home in Egypt. He recalls the glint of the sun on the water and the pull of the fish as it caught on the line. He remembers his delight as, with the help of his uncle, he pulled the struggling creature from the water and held its slippery body tightly in his hands. But most of all he recalls the fish's mouth opening and closing, opening and closing, desperate to draw in the oxygen that will keep it alive.

I'm like a fish out of water, he thinks, realizing that he is lying on the ground, thrashing around much as that fish had done. *Alfreda!* Despite the pain still coursing through his body, Ra tries to sit up but feels too weak to move. *O Isis, help me! Give me strength to carry on.*

With an almost superhuman effort, he manages to get onto his knees and then clamber unsteadily to his feet. Still trying to catch his breath, but finding the struggle beginning to ease, he starts running again with a curious, lopsided gait.

After what feels like an eternity, Ra arrives at the arena and barely pauses as he scrabbles for a handful of coins in his purse and throws them towards the guards Ra makes his way towards the barrier which separates the audience from the fighters and peers over to see what is going on. All around him, the shout of the crowd tells him what he already knows, the spectacle has already begun!

Ra grips the rail to steady himself and looks down into the arena. Almost immediately he spots Alfreda, her golden hair pulled back into a ponytail, her slender body covered by a short tunic and her face set in a fearless snarl as she squares up to one of the beasts, a lion at least twice her size. Ra's breath catches and the pain in his chest bursts into agony once again, but he cannot tear his eyes away from the Briton.

She looks so small, he thinks as he watches her slash out at the lion with a short sword. *If only I had got here sooner.* As another wave of pain slices through him, he feels the scroll slip from his fingers and fall to the arena floor where it is quickly trampled beneath the feet of a large man, trying desperately to fend off two massive dogs.

The pain in his chest reaches its peak and he finds himself sliding down the barrier, he holds on, desperate to keep his eyes on the woman he loves.

"Oh Alfreda," Ra whispers, tears streaming down his face. The last thing he sees before the life leaves his body is the light of the sinking sun glinting from the beautiful emerald embedded in the bracelet that still clings to Alfreda's wrist.

Alfreda, my love. And then, as Ra falls to the ground, the light fades and is gone.

Chicago, U.S.A. 2045

Ann blinked her eyes open, her hand over her heart, still feeling the pain in her chest. For a moment the sense of sorrow and loss seemed as if it would engulf her, but it passed as she realized she was not in danger; it was only her vision.

"That's right, my dear," came the cracked voice of the psychic. "Breathe it in deeply."

Slowly, Ann turned her head to see that the old woman had lit one of her strange candles again and the scent helped to calm her nerves.

"And that was?" asked Ann, catching her breath at last.

"Another glimpse of your past, another of the lives that make up your one, whole life stream."

"I see." Ann nodded, a frown creasing her forehead for a moment. "So that was what? My second life?"

The psychic sat back, a knowing smile on her face. "As you saw, my dear."

"And what does it mean? Are you saying I saw myself die... a second time?"

"That's simply part of the chain of reincarnation; something that stretches out behind and before us all."

Ann, feeling her normal self once again, turned and sat up on the couch facing the psychic. "Please," she said. "Tell me more."

"It's quite simple, my dear. Birth is not a beginning. Death is not an end. There is existence without limitation, continuity without a starting-point or terminus."

"Right..." said Ann, not sounding entirely certain. "So what exactly is this chain of reincarnation?"

The old woman held out her hands in an expansive gesture. "We call it a chain," she explained, "because we are all trapped in this cycle of birth and death."

"Trapped?"

"Exactly. . . until the release; when a person archives redemption."

PART THREE
COURAGE

Chapter Fourteen

I don't think so," Ann said, peering over her menu. "They've never really appealed to me."

She and Michael were sitting in the Fleur-de-Lis, a cozy French restaurant on the edge of the city.

Shunning the hi-tech computerized service offered by their competitors, the Fleur-de-Lis insisted on the traditional card menus, candlelit tables and human waiting staff. As such it was one of the homeliest restaurants in Chicago. It set itself apart as all the tables were for two, making it a destination for couples only.

Michael smiled behind his menu. "Are you telling me you've never had frogs' legs? Sweetheart, you haven't lived!"

"Oh, I've lived alright," said Ann, thinking back to her latest session with the psychic a few days ago. "And I'm fairly sure eating amphibian limbs is not a necessity of life."

"Fair enough. I'm still definitely going for them. Have you chosen your main?"

"Yes," said Ann, laying the menu gently on the table. "I'm ready to order."

A waiter appeared just as they were about to signal him, his notepad and pencil ready.

He took their order, retrieved their menus and creeped away towards the kitchen.

Michael leant back in his chair and smiled at Ann over his glass of Chateau Latour Pauillac 2000, the finest French wine the Fleur-de-Lis had to offer.

"You look stunning tonight, Ann," he said, gazing at her approvingly.

It was true. Inspired by her detour in Egypt, she'd colored her hair a deep blue-black with a "Just For One Night" dye, and gathered it up in a long ponytail held in place with a silver ribbon.

Her outfit was in the vintage style that was the rage at the moment; a short black top, which offered glimpses of her silver embroidered bra, flared black trousers picked out at the bottom with silver threads and secured with a wide matching belt. She finished it off with silver high heels and handbag and; Michael took this all in, intrigued when he saw the silver slowly change to a deep shade of gold.

He leant forward to get a better look as the gold changed back to silver again and was enveloped in the scent of Ann's Je T'Aime perfume.

"I suit my partner," said Ann, gesturing to Michael's dark-blue suit and shirt, which suited him very well.

As he reached out to take her hand, she also noted that the white gold Rolex fastened to his wrist, which matched the chain around his neck, nestled against his perfectly tanned skin.

He leaned his head forward and kissed her hand.

Ann laughed. "Just like in the movies!"

"Except *this* movie," he said, looking intently at her as he stroked the back of her hand, "is just for the two of us."

After what may very well have been an hour or just a few seconds for all she knew, Ann lowered her eyes, becoming aware of the music playing in the background.

"Such a beautiful song," she said.

"Ah yes. An old Joe Dassin song, I believe." Michael cocked his head to listen. "Et si tu n'existais pas". Do you know what it means in English?"

"No. I'm lousy at French. Something about love?"

"Sure. It's about true love. It's called, 'And if you didn't exist'."

Michael gazed deep into Ann's eyes and they both sat in silence for a while.

"Well," he said, finally breaking the silence and waving the surroundings with his free hand, "this is certainly a nice restaurant. I've never been here before."

"Me neither."

"Come on!" said Michael with a mischievous look. "You must have been here before with one of your *other* men."

"What other men?" Ann raised her eyebrows. "I can't even remember the last time I went on a date."

"I can't believe it. A gorgeous lady like you. You must have plenty of suitors trying to win your affection."

"Maybe," she said. "But I've been busy. No time for extra-curricular activities."

Michael looked at her for a while, a shrewd look on his face.

Eventually he said, "No. I think there's something more to it. Something happened, didn't it? Won't you tell me?"

"There's nothing to tell, really," said Ann, shrugging nonchalantly. "There was a guy, before I moved to Chicago, but he was no good for me. Everyone said he'd let me down in the end, and it turned out they were right."

"Then he was a fool! It's his loss, my dear. You deserve someone who will love you with all of his being, with the kind of love that even death cannot overcome."

"I don't know," said Ann, frowning slightly as she sipped her wine. "I'm not sure I can imagine such a love."

"Well, I don't want you to have to imagine it. I want you to experience it!" Michael paused a moment, considering. "It reminds me of a story told of Isis."

Ann's eyes widened in surprise at this mention of the Egyptian goddess and she almost choked on her drink. She continued to listen in silence.

"It is said," Michael continued, "that when her lover Osiris was murdered by Seti, the god of storms, she spent years traveling the world, gathering up every part of his body. When she finally had found them all, she used her magic to restore him to life. Now that is true love, my dear. That is what I want for you."

"That would certainly be something! How do you know these things?" asked Ann.

"It comes with the job. We archaeologists have to know all about the theology of the cultures we study, Egyptian, Greek, Roman, even the gods of the Stone Age."

They ate their meal together and Michael regaled Ann with the stories of ancient gods and goddesses; stories of love and war, of life and death. She listened, fascinated.

By the time their desserts arrived they were chatting about her childhood.

"Well, there's not much to tell, really," she said. "I was raised in one of those lovely old houses in Manhattan, within walking distance of Central Park. My parents adopted me when I was little, though I only found that out when I turned eighteen. They were great, so warm and caring."

Michael leaned back in his chair, giving Ann his full attention as he enjoyed his white chocolate mousse. He nodded, encouraging her to continue.

"We used to have family gatherings every Sunday, with dinner followed by a walk around the neighborhood or the park. We would be hand-in-hand, with me in the middle skipping along and sometimes being swung up into the air. And we'd go to the movies and dad would buy us all ice creams, popcorns and candies."

She smiled at the memory, pausing to taste her cheesecake with a latticework of raspberry coulis.

"It sounds delightful," said Michael, savoring his coffee laced with Hennessy Paradis. "So what was the most exciting thing about your youth?"

"Exciting?" Ann considered this as she sipped at her golden drink, Chateau d' Yquem 2010. "It would probably be exploring my parents' library. It fascinated me every time I entered the place. I can remember wheeling around a stepladder, easily twice my height, and standing on tiptoe to reach up for the thickest, heaviest tome on the top shelf."

Michael laughed. "A proper risk-taker!"

"Am I indeed?" Anne said with a smile.

"Oh yes!" he replied, taking her hand again and raising it to his lips. "And I love it!"

She blushed when he kissed her knuckle, and she noticed that nearby couples were taking surreptitious glances at them.

Such an old-fashioned gesture, but touching, all the same.

"So what made you climb that ladder?" he asked, ignoring the onlookers.

"I just wanted to read all the books in the library. They fascinated me."

"And were you successful in your endeavor?"

Ann shook her head. "Hardly. There were thousands in there! But I read as many as I could."

"So what happened to your passion for books?" asked Michael, leaning forward, elbows on the table. "Why didn't you choose to become a librarian or something?"

"Funnily enough, I chose my path because of the books. I found myself drawn to Science Fiction novels. I loved them all, from H G Wells and Jules Verne to Isaac Asimov and Ray Bradbury. I realized that my real passion was for technology; the really cutting edge stuff. So I became a developer of robotic solutions."

"Of course. I've seen your products. They're very impressive!"

"Yes, they are. And now I am a head of the Sales and Marketing of these products at A.I.I."

She pulled the E-A device from her handbag, currently gold, and held it in her hand. "The E-A is my latest and most favorite project: a completely automated, intelligent Electronic Assistant."

"It's fascinating," said Michael, placing a hand on her free one. "Absolutely fascinating!"

Ann was overcome by a sudden urge to tell him about all of the strange things that had been going on in her life. Looking into his eyes, at that moment, she had the feeling that there was nothing she couldn't tell him.

But I can't, she argued with herself. *He'll think I'm crazy!*

So she let the moment pass; though as soon as it had, she couldn't help feeling a tiny twinge of regret.

After dinner they hailed a cab to take them to the city center and headed to Windermere's, the city's most stylish night club, which was located on the crowning floor of one of the newest skyscrapers.

Here, among the nouveau riche and the high-flyers of Chicago society, Ann and Michael danced, far above the rest of the world.

Around them the lights of the city spread out in all directions, and Ann felt at peace for a while, held in Michael's strong arms, her cheek brushing against his, their bodies pressed close together.

Pulling her head back slightly to look into his eyes, she found herself struck even more than before by how handsome he was.

The ceiling lights glistened off his fair hair, a strand of which fell across one eye, reminding her of Nina's unruly curl. Michael's eyes were a deep blue and she felt a curious desire to fall into them, to lose herself in their depths, to be kept safe there forever.

But more than his appearance, something drew her in. There was something about the way he looked at her and spoke to her, the way he held her hand and her gaze that made her feel safe; as though, at last, here was a man she could really trust.

She thought back to her days in the metropolitan jungle of New York City and the guys she had dated then. They had never looked into her eyes in a way that made her feel treasured, or communicated security by simply holding her hand. They had been a disappointing mix of mommy's boys, spoilt and pampered and scared, who knew nothing of a woman's needs, and thrill-seekers, only interested in fast cars and even faster sex, believing themselves to be great lovers rather than the frustrating waste of time and energy they really were.

They didn't even compare to a real man like Michael.

The song came to an end and, Ann was surprised to hear the DJ slip in an old number she hadn't heard in years. It was a hit from the eighties, long before she was born—in this life at least: 'Never Let Me Down Again' by a band called Depeche Mode.

On the screen that took up an entire wall of the nightclub, the 3D image of the band appeared, singing the words she was surprised to find she remembered.

She started to dance, pulling away from Michael. Michael watched her and his mouth dropped open. She was stunning, a fantastic dancer with an amazing body and long flying hair; many of the guys hanging around the dance floor stopped to watch her as well.

Slowly, she drew closer to Michael, looking deeply into his eyes as she sang. Sliding an arm around her waist he drew Ann close to him, still holding her gaze, joining in the singing.

"Trust me, my dear Ann," he said, his voice serious and assuring. "I will never let you down." Ann looked up at him. *Tonight is the night*, she thought to herself.

Strangely, Michael made no move to do anything. Still, it wasn't as awkward of a moment as it might have been. His eyes were filled with such warmth and understanding that she couldn't feel embarrassed, even though eventually he pulled his arm away and led her back towards their drinks.

That night, Ann slipped between the sheets of her bed, smiling at the recollection of her evening.

Had she found a man who would love her at last; really love her? Someone she could love in return? Someone she could spend the rest of her life – or at least, *this* life - with?

She stretched out across the bed, feeling its emptiness; but she also recognized that, for the very first time, there was no corroding emptiness inside of her.

"Am I in love with him?"

She slowly drifted off, these happy notions in mind.

Her night, however, was yet again disturbed by the same strange dream which had plagued her; she woke feeling of the usual loss and anxiety, afraid of the spiral, and haunted by the sadness of her past lives.

♣

"I don't understand it, Rob," said Ann as she stepped out of the shower. "I had expected these nightmares to stop after going to the psychic. Several weeks have passed but - if anything - the dreams are more worrying than ever. It's gotten worse instead of better."

"That is all part of your journey, my lady," Rob replied, looking out from the screen of the E-A device sitting by the sink. "Consider the Buddha's journey to enlightenment or Jesus' journey through the cross to the resurrection. The greater the destination, the harder the journey must be."

Ann considered this while drying herself with a towel.

"I guess I can accept that," she said eventually, "but from what I've seen on my two visits to the psychic, my - what did she call it? - My reincarnation chain has hardly been a series of victories. In the first life I lost my son days after giving birth to him, and ended up killing myself. And in the second I failed to save the woman I loved and died of a heart attack. I achieved nothing!"

"Nothing?" Rob raised an eyebrow at this and shook his head. "But, my lady, sacrifice has always been a necessary part of the greatest journey."

Ann stopped drying her hair to look questioningly at him. "Sacrifice?"

"Of course sacrifice! Or did you think you gave up those lives without reason?"

"Well..." she continued drying her hair as she tried to think. "Maybe," she conceded. "But I didn't really achieve anything. I didn't get Wu back or save Alfreda. Even if I did sacrifice myself, what was it all for?"

"Answer this then: when you were living in the Stone Age, why did you die?"

Ann shrugged as she picked up the E-A device and headed back out into the bedroom. "Because I shoved a spear through my heart."

She winced again at memory that sharpened stick pushing into her body and placed a hand on her chest.

"No," said Rob, now watching her from the bedside table. "That was *how* you died. I asked *why.*"

"Because that big murdering bastard was going to get me!" Ann jabbed crossly at the SmartHome screen on the wardrobe, selecting a red trouser suit.

A wooden panel slipped back and the requested suit slid out on a rail.

"And what was that 'big, murdering bastard' going to do with you?"

"I don't know," she said, pulling on the underwear that had appeared through another panel. "Rape me? Beat me? Keep me as a slave wife?"

"All of the above, no doubt. So why did you decide to kill yourself?"

"Well, it's obvious, isn't it? Death has to be preferable to such a life. I died for freedom."

"For freedom!" Rob agreed. "And what about your death as the Roman priest?"

"Egyptian priest."

"Indeed."

"That was just a heart attack, wasn't it?"

Rob sighed and gave her a long meaningful look as Ann pulled on her trousers and tucked in her blouse. "Again, that was *how* you died. Ask yourself *why.*"

"Because I had been running and pushed my body too hard?"

"Okay... and why had you been running?"

"To save Alfreda's life, to rescue the woman I loved."

"So why did you die? For what reason?"

Ann finished buttoning up her jacket and stood up straight, suddenly realizing what Rob was getting at. "I died for love."

"Exactly!" said Rob with a beaming smile. "You sacrificed yourself for freedom and for love. That's good karma right there, my lady, huge steps on the path to redemption."

"Redemption?" Ann looked puzzled for a moment, trying to remember where she had heard that word recently.

"The psychic mentioned that at the end of our last session, when she was going on about reincarnation chains and other weird stuff."

"Perhaps it would be worth talking with her again and finding out what she meant?"

"I'm not so sure, Rob," she said, picking up the device and walking towards the front door of her apartment. "My past lives might not have been pointless, but that doesn't change the fact that my nightmares have gotten worse since I went to see that old woman. I don't want to risk them getting even worse!"

"That's entirely your choice, my lady. It is your life—your journey—and only you can make that decision."

♣

A while later, Ann eased her car into the parking lot of the A.I.I. building and headed up to her floor.

She was still preoccupied by her past lives and about her evening with Michael, so she didn't immediately notice the strange atmosphere in the office.

Where people had been rushing back and forth and colleagues had been chatting loudly, now people were quietly, subdued and speaking to each other in hushed tones.

It wasn't until Linda - wearing another flowery dress and trailing perfume - walked past, failing to wish her a good morning that Ann realized something really wasn't right.

"Linda," she said. "What's going on?"

Linda stopped and turned to face her, and Ann noticed there were tears in her eyes.

"Haven't you heard?" she asked.

"Heard what? What's happened?"

"It's Peter."

Ann glanced over Linda's shoulder to look at Peter's desk, but it was empty. "What about him?"

"He had an accident on his way to work this morning."

"An accident?"

"Apparently he crashed into a truck as he pulled out of the tunnel. According to the SmartDrive system, he had been watching the film *Bullitt* on his windshield and came tearing up the ramp like Steve McQueen. Such a tragedy! I blame the SmartDrive system. Whose idea was it to offer movies?"

"So how is Peter?" asked Ann, trying to get back to the matter at hand.

"He's fighting for his life in the Memorial Hospital."

Ann's eyes widened in concern. "He was hurt badly, then?"

"They're not sure if he's going to pull through." Linda's voice broke and she fought to control herself, blinking her eyes and clearing her throat. "It's awful, Ann. Peter may not live!"

Chapter Fifteen

Ann received word, confirming that Peter had come out of surgery, so she left the A.I.I. building and headed to the Memorial Hospital shortly after lunch. She got Rob to take her to the nearest florist on the way so she could buy some flowers on behalf of the team but when she arrived, it turned out Peter was still unconscious.

As Ann stood and looked at him, the most cheerful guy from her team, lying in the hospital bed surrounded by beeping machines, his body hung all about with tubes; she was overcome by sadness and helplessness.

After a few minutes, Ann walked to the head of the bed. She placed a hand on Peter's shoulder and laid the flowers carefully on the bedside table.

"See you soon, Peter," she said gently and, as she turned away, she added, "You'd better not be late for work on Monday."

♣

"Peter may not live!" Linda's words rang in Ann's head.

How awful it is! Mi's Lu died very young. He was probably seventeen or eighteen years old. And Alfreda died in her twenties. Peter is thirty-four. He's not even halfway through his life. He might have a mom and dad still alive, and perhaps a girlfriend missing him...

Thinking about Peter's mother reminded her of her own son, Wu; his tiny hands at her swollen breast, his mouth greedily sucking her milk and tears splashed into her eyes. A flood of compassion washed her over.

"Poor, poor Peter! How sad it is... I need someone to talk to."

♣

"I need someone to talk to," Ann said, out loud, this time, looking at Nina who stirred her cappuccino.

They were sitting at one of the tables on the paved area at the front of a small café on the lakefront. "I guess it's the shock - Peter's accident just came out of nowhere."

Nina sipped her drink and set it down with a wave of her hand. "Oh, I know, darling. It was the same with me and Louis. You remember Louis, don't you?"

"Remind me. Was he one of your men?"

"One of my men?" said Nina, in mock indignation. "You make it sound like I'm some sort of floozy." She smiled suddenly. "But, yes, he was one of my men. Italian. A real charmer."

"What happened to him?" asked Ann, holding her cup in both hands and letting the coffee fumes begin to calm her nerves.

"He walked in front of a bus on a day trip to Milwaukee. Not on purpose, you understand, but it was terribly distressing all the same."

"That's awful, Nina. Was he okay?"

"Louis?" Nina frowned and shook her head, quickly flicking the stray hair from her eyes. "No, poor Louis is quite dead, sweetie."

"What? How old was he?"

"Twenty-seven? Twenty-eight? Something like that."

"My god, really? That's so young. What's the purpose of such a life," she wondered, half-speaking to herself, "to be born, go through the pains of growing up and working to better yourself only for it all to be snatched away as you reach your prime?"

"Darling, I really do understand how shocking this is for you. I remember, it took me ages to get over what happened to poor Louis. I don't think I got my head straight until I met Gregory. You remember him don't you?"

"Gregory?" Ann thought for a moment as she sipped her drink and looked out across the lake. "He wasn't the chef, was he?"

A slightly dreamy look passed over Nina's face. "That's right. Gregory the chef. The things that man could do with a whisk and a spatula!"

Too much information. Moving on:

"So how long after Louis' accident did you start seeing him?"

"Oh, it was ages, darling. Two weeks at least."

"Really?" Ann mused, with more than a hint of irony. "A whole two weeks? However did you last so long?"

"I know what you're thinking," said Nina with a wave of her hand. "You think two weeks wasn't that long, that I should have been mourning dear Louis."

"Something like that."

"Well, I couldn't just mope about forever. It wouldn't have done Louis or myself any good. Life is for the living, darling, and if there's one thing a dead person would tell you, it's to get on and live your life. Or at least they would if they could, of course. That's what your colleague, Paul, would say."

"You mean Peter?"

Nina frowned. "Who's Peter?"

"My work colleague!" said Ann, giving Nina a look of disbelief.

Sometimes she really despaired of her friend.

"The one who had the accident. And he's not dead, he's going to make it!" Ann stood up, intending on leaving Nina right there.

"Of course he will live, darling. Please sit back down." Nina moved a chair closer to Ann. "And I'm sure he wouldn't want you looking miserable all day. The show must go on!" She waved an expansive hand at the skyscrapers towering over them. "There's a whole city here waiting for you, offering you everything you could possibly want. Get stuck in, girl, while there's still time!"

"We can enjoy it, but Peter can't," said Ann. A tear dropped from her eye.

"But he will recover and join you for the show!"

Ann smiled weakly. They sat in a silence for a while observing the lakefront. Eventually, Nina set her empty cup down on the table and leaned forward conspiratorially.

"Talking about living," she said. "How are things going with the lovely Michael?"

"Now that would be telling!" said Ann, a broad smile finally easing its way across her face.

"Well, telling is exactly what I'm after. Have you seen him again?"

"Maybe."

"Either you have or you haven't."

"Well, I guess it depends if you count dinner at the Fleur-de-Lis followed by a little dancing at the Windermere."

Nina raised her eyebrows, impressed at her friend's progress. "Nice work! Tell me all about it."

♣

"Tell me all about it," Ann asked, steering her car through the city center. "I want all the info you've got on this reincarnation chain thing."

She' left the café slightly later than expected and decided it wasn't worth returning to the office.

Instead she went on a drive to clear her head and mull things over with a little help from Rob.

"Certainly, my lady," he said, bowing his head slightly. "As you know it has to do with your life stream, which is made up of many individual lives. It's a cycle of reincarnation. Birth, life and death, rebirth, life and death."

"But it's not a *never-ending* cycle, is it?"

"No. Each life is built on the former lives, progressing towards the ultimate goal."

"Of breaking free from the chain," said Ann, interrupting him.

"Exactly."

"What was it you called it again? It was named after a classic rock group, wasn't it Oasis or something?"

"Nirvana," said Rob, suspecting Ann was playing with him. "And the band was named after that ultimate goal, rather than the other way round."

"So, is everyone caught in this reincarnation chain?"

"All humans are, yes."

"And my work colleague, Peter?" Ann asked after a moment of thinking.

"Of course. He will have had other lives before he was Peter, and no doubt he will have many lives after this one. As will you, my lady. And at this speed, that next life may come sooner than you expect."

Ann glanced at Rob, frowning, "What do you mean?"

"The car," said Rob. "You are travelling twelve miles an hour above the specified limit for this road."

Ann sighed, easing her foot off the gas. "Driving too fast, moving too slow. I have to say, Rob, I don't feel like I'm making much progress at the moment."

"That day will come," he replied, dishing out his most charming smile. "You just need to be patient, my lady. The little things matter just as much as the big things. They all work together in the process of karma."

"Little things like what?"

With barely a moment's hesitation, Rob said, "Take your visit to the hospital this afternoon. You didn't have to go and see your injured colleague. And yet you took the time to do it."

"What little good that did. Peter didn't even know I was there."

"That is not what matters when it comes to karma. Whether people see your good deeds or not is of little consequence. It is what God sees that counts."

"So, even little things help in my progress towards Nirvana? That's certainly nice to know, if it's true. I have to admit, Rob, what with Peter's accident, my relationship with Michael and the two visits to the psychic, I feel like I'm running on empty at the moment." She paused at a set of traffic lights, momentarily lost in thought. "Rob," she said suddenly.

"Yes, my lady," said Rob, eager as always.

"Do you think I should carry on with this whole process of unearthing my past and finding out about my life stream, about my true self?"

"As it says in the Bible: 'Seek and ye shall find'."

As if coming to a decision, Ann flicked the indicators to signal right and set off from the lights. "Can you map out the best route back to the psychic's place?"

Rob nodded happily. "On it right now."

♣

Ann looked around nervously as she climbed out of the car. Although this was the third time she had visited this area in the last couple of weeks, she still found the place unnerving. The empty streets and the deserted shop windows gave her a sense of sadness and foreboding. It was certainly not a friendly neighborhood.

Having set the car to ultra-secure mode, Ann hurried along to the alleyway and ducked into the shadows.

The children, who had been playing there when she first visited with Nina, were back. This time they were kicking around an old football that was only half-filled. Ann made her way along the alley just when one of the boys struck the ball, which made a dull, hollow sound, and landed by her feet. It didn't bounce. She considered kicking it back to the children, but realized she was wearing heels. Instead she bent down and picked it up.

"Hey!" the boy said, irritably. "That's our ball! Give it back!"

Ann tossed the ball to him and, shaking her head, carried on until she arrived at the doorway to the psychic's home.

She pushed her way through the bead curtain just as the old lady's voice surprised her, coming from a room somewhere in the back of the house.

"Go on in, Ann. I'll be there in a minute."

How does she always know? Ann wondered, but opened the door to her right without a word and sat down on the couch.

A few minutes later the psychic appeared carrying a tray with two cups and a steaming teapot.

"Cup of tea, my dear?" asked the psychic.

"Tea?" said Ann, surprised. "I can't say I'm much of a tea drinker. Coffee's more my thing."

"Oh, but this is a *special* tea." The old woman gave her a mysterious look. "It'll help you relax."

"Fine. I'll give it a go."

She sat there, growing increasingly impatient, as the psychic slowly stirred the contents of the tea pot and poured it, little by little, through a strainer, first into one cup and then into the other. At last, she picked up a cup and placed it on a saucer before inching it towards Ann with a shaky hand.

Taking a sip, Ann immediately felt refreshed and calmed. She hadn't realized quite how uptight and tense she had been feeling until, as if by magic, the feeling dropped away from her.

"What's in this stuff?" she asked.

"Tea, like I said."

Ann narrowed her eyes suspiciously. "Is that all?"

The psychic nodded as Ann took another sip. "Tea, yes. And a little cocaine."

Ann almost spat out the concoction, chocking. "Cocaine?" she managed to say between coughs.

"Just a little joke," said the old woman, her eyes sparkling mischievously. "It's tea and a few herbs. *Legal* herbs! It'll help you relax, my dear, and rest after the ordeal you faced today."

"I won't ask you how you know about my day," Ann replied, finally recovering from her coughing fit. "But I certainly do feel more relaxed. I want to know more about my journey. I want to have a better understanding of my life stream to get where I am at in that reincarnation chain."

The psychic looked at her over the rim of her teacup. "I see," she said. "You want to know if your life has purpose, yes?"

"I guess so."

"Very well. If you would put your cup down on the table and lay back, we will begin."

Ann did so, arranging the cushions beneath her head to make herself as comfortable as possible. She closed her eyes, then sat up suddenly.

"Just one thing, though. Can you please show me something a little nicer than the other visions I've had? Something less tragic?"

"I'm sorry, my dear,' the psychic replied, holding up her hands. "I can only help you to see what you need to see, but I cannot change what is past. The lives you have lived cannot be re-lived. What has happened has happened, and that is that. And what's wrong with a little tragedy, anyway? Everyone dies, you know. The point is to have lived first!"

Ann lay back again and closed her eyes and the psychic began to mutter her strange words.

The relaxation and calm that Ann had felt seemed, somehow, to intensify, as though every concern that she had ever experienced, and every worry she had carried with her in life melted away, leaving her perfectly calm.

I wonder if this is how Nirvana feels, she mused as she drifted off to sleep. . .

Paris, France. XVII Century

Chapter Sixteen

S he opens her eyes, awoken by a sudden chill gust of wind, and pulls the ragged blanket up around her neck.

How long have I been asleep? It can't have been more than a few hours, she thinks.

She can't remember the last time she slept well. The long nights are filled with anxious thoughts and fears of the future that rob her of any sense of peace.

The filthy slums are no place for a girl her age; an intense sense of danger has disturbed her from her slumber.

She looks up to see a large man staggering towards her, a lecherous leer on his wet lips.

She shrinks back in fear, drawing the blanket up to her eyes as if to ward him off like an evil spirit. He passes her by and she lets the cover drop away from her face, sighing in relief, her breath hanging in the cold air like smoke.

The sound of coarse laughter cuts through the night and she glances along the narrow, cobbled street to see a small group of people standing around a fire.

They look warm, thanks to the fire as much as to the bottle of cheap brandy they pass among themselves. One man, dressed in soiled rags, grabs at the ass of a woman, laughing drunkenly.

I wish I was warm, she thinks, shivering in the cold and looking longingly at the glow of the flames. *But not at that fire. Look at them, the common brutes of the city slums. I want nothing to do with their sort!*

She turns away; the sight of the fire has made her feel even colder .

Knowing that she will not be able to go back to sleep, she climbs stiffly to her feet and, wrapping the damp blanket around her shoulders, slowly wanders through the streets of Paris.

The night is so cold that a freezing fog has settled over the cobblestones and, despite the dim glow from the street lamps, she has to tread carefully to avoid the debris and muck that litters her way.

The sound of her footsteps seems to echo strangely, while all other sounds are muffled by the fog. Not that there is much to hear, at this time: the streets are mostly deserted.

I'm so cold, she complains, her teeth chattering. *Walking hardly seems to help. I need food, even just a little something, but I'll just have to wait until sunrise when I can beg a few coins.*

She tries wrapping her arms tighter around herself in an effort to keep warm, but it causes her blanket to slip from her shoulders onto the dirty cobblestones. She stoops to pick it up as a huge rat scurries across it, its tail brushing against her hand.

She lets out a sharp cry and the rat stops to look at her, its teeth long and yellow.

"Go away!" she shouts, kicking the blanket at it, and it scurries across the street.

She shivers again, but not from the cold, thought it bites into her, chilling flesh and bone. Rather it is a memory from her childhood that causes the shudders; the memory of a fingerless man.

"What happened to your hands?" she'd asked him, unashamed curious at six year old. "Where are your fingers?"

The man had looked at her with dead, empty eyes and said simply, "Rats, Isabelle! Rats!"

It isn't the first rat she has seen, of course. After all, Isabelle has been begging on the streets ever since her parents died twelve years ago.

For many years she had done this begging with her aunt, who would earn extra money by singing for passersby. But since she'd gone down with the wasting sickness the previous winter, she has done the work alone.

This rat, however, had shown no fear, just like the ones that had gnawed off that man's fingers all those years ago.

Please don't let it attack me, she thinks, as though uttering a silent prayer to an unknown god.

Keeping a wary eye out for the rat, she walks over to her blanket, lying in the muck, and stoops down to pick it up.

She hears the clatter of hooves on cobbles. The sound is muffled by the fog and, as she straightens up, she realizes it is much closer than she thought.

She turns to get out of the way, but it is too late. The horse bursts out of the darkness. She hears someone shout, "Look out!", then the animal crashes into her shoulder. There is a burst of pain and she is knocked across the street.

Landing heavily on her side, she sees hooves clatter past, mere inches from her face.

"Whoa!" The hooves slow down, approaching her.

"Are you alright, young lady?" a voice asks and she looks up to see a man leaning from his saddle, looking down in concern. "Are you hurt?"

"I. . ." Isabelle begins, but her head is dizzy and she cannot find the words.

Instead she tries to push herself up, to climb to her feet, but the pain in her shoulder makes it too difficult and she sinks back to the cobbles.

She looks up again at the man, her eyes slowly focusing on his face. He is handsome; even in her dazed state she can see that. And he is very finely dressed, with a triangle hat as black as his moustache and two beautiful rings set with green and red gemstones.

She blinks at him, her head slowly clearing. "I'm okay," she says at last. "It's just my shoulder."

"Let's go, Henri!"

Surprised by the voice, Isabelle peers round to see a plump woman in her thirties sitting behind him, her skirts lifted up and rouge smeared on her face in a vulgar fashion.

Her attention is drawn back to the man again as he holds out a hand to her with a number of coins in it.

Look at those beautiful cuffs, she thinks, wondering how it is possible to get something so perfectly white and making no move to take the money. *And those rings!*

Her shoulder still hurts terribly, but she tries to ignore it.

"Here," he says, tossing the coins onto the cobbles.

There is the crack of a whip and, as the horse and its riders continue their journey, Isabelle hears the giggles of the woman before they are swallowed up by the fog and darkness.

What a man, she thinks, looking down at the coins in her hand. *I wonder who he is?*

She quickly hides them in her clothes, keeping the money from the spying eyes and prying fingers of others. *That woman was obviously low-born, far lower than a nobleman like him. How come she gets to ride around in that carriage with him?*

Finally Isabelle feels able to get up and heaves herself to her feet.

I'm younger and prettier than that woman. Surely I have just as much chance of being with a man like that! Maybe even more!

She brushes some of the muck from her skirt and tries to smooth them down.

She is wearing the same clothes her aunt had bought her before she died, after a particularly successful day of singing.

Back then, this skirt had been long and fit for a lady, and Isabelle had been so delighted with it. But that was a long time ago.

She looks at the money the man gave her.

It's a fortune! Easily ten times the cost of my skirt. She looks at her worn out clothes and the blanket around her. *I have to get myself a nice jacket. And maybe a hairbrush. I've always wanted one of my own. Yes, that's what I'll do!*

The decision gives her a direction for the coming day.

♣

A couple of hours later the sun begins to creep above the houses, melting away the fog and the fears of the night.

Ever since she made up her mind to buy herself some new clothes, Isabelle has been excited; she's making her way to the market stalls and street peddlers in the heart of the city.

She finds herself in Les Halles by the time Paris has wakened. The great market is already bustling with merchants busy setting up their stalls.

Such amazing colors, she thinks as she weaves her way through the market. *What are all these wonderful things?*

There are fruits from across the world, strange and exotic to Isabelle's eyes, and here all manner of tools for various craftsmen and artisans. There are animals - geese, pigs and sheep - all waiting for buyers before they are taken to the butcher's knife, and there are rolls of silk and satin brought in from the Far East by land and sea. Pottery, metalwork, fabrics, food and wine; the market place is filled with everything anyone could wish to buy, and more.

When she finds the tailors' stalls at last, Isabelle is dazzled by the choices of materials and styles.

There are all kinds of garments, from dresses and bed clothes for women to trousers and hats for men, even delightful little children clothes, assortments of accessories and ornamentations.

One stall in particular captivates her and she stops to finger the material of some of the garments.

What a beautiful thing! It's even finer than my own skirt used to be!

"Away with you!" The man at the stall hurries over to keep such a dirty creature from touching his wares. "Go on! We don't need your sort around here."

"One moment," says Isabelle, holding up a hand as she pulls the coins from where she has hidden them. "I am looking to buy a bodice."

The merchant eyes the coins in her hand.

"Well, miss," he says, his manner suddenly courteous. "You've come to the right place. We have the best bodices in the city. What sort of thing did you have in mind?"

"I'm not sure. Just something second hand."

The man gestures to a pile of clothes under a trestle table. "Have a look in there. See what takes your fancy."

For the following, wonderful few minutes, Isabelle enjoys trying on different bodices, and eventually settles on one. It is long-sleeve - all the better to protect her from the harsh winter nights - and mostly black, though it's picked out with bright green embroidery across the chest and down the sleeves.

The merchant has his tailor make a few small adjustments to ensure the bodice fits her perfectly.

"All included in the price, miss," he explains.

The price itself is quite high, and Isabelle hesitates for a moment. The pain in her shoulder, which had dulled earlier, has returned after trying on so many garments, and she loath to spend so much of the money the injury has brought her.

But after a little haggling over the price - something she is used to after years on the streets trying to get the most for the few coins she manages to beg - the merchant reduces his quote and accepts the coins, slipping them into the money belt around his waist.

Pleased with her new item, Isabelle decides to visit a stall nearby, filled with various grooming products and haberdashery and buys a small cake of soap that smells of lavender. She also buys herself a green ribbon for her hair.

The man running the stall allows her to make use of his washing facilities to scrub as much of her as possible while keeping herself decent.

She washes her face with the soap, combs the knots out of her hair and ties it up with the ribbon before looking at herself in the mirror.

There's still something missing, she thinks and, thanking the merchant for his kind help and handing over more of her coins, she heads back to the food stalls.

Here she uses the last of her money to buy some fruit, a slice of honey cake, and the missing ingredient: a small, red beetroot.

This, she uses to add color to her lips and cheeks. At last, she looks the part; delighted at this change in her fortunes - even if it is only for today - and she heads back across the city to the small shelter she calls home, nibbling her honey-cake. By this time, her shoulder only hurts a little.

Here, hidden from view, she takes her skirt off and tidies it up as best she can, stripping away the parts that are damaged or stained beyond repair. With the bar of soap and water from the Seine, on whose banks her shelter is located, she washes the dirt and filth from the rest of the material and wrings it dry.

Well, I may have to beg again tomorrow, she thinks, having put the skirt back on. *But this has been a good day!*

Chapter Seventeen

G o away!" Isabelle pushes a man away from her shelter as he waddles too close. She recognizes him as the fat, lecherous man who had been eyeing her up the previous night. He backs away.

"Come on, missy," he says, flecks of spittle collecting on his lips. "I can show you a good time."

She looks at him in disgust and shakes her head. "Go away!"

And with that, she emerges from her shelter and walks off, leaving him staring after her, disappointment written all over his face.

What a despicable man, she thinks as she weaves through the other makeshift shelters that litter this area of the city. *This is exactly why I need to get out of this place, away from the filth of the slums. I want a proper man, a man who will help me.*

Henri's handsome face and his elegant hand with the lace cuffs pops into her mind. *A man with good manners and proper status. A gentleman.*

She stops at a junction in the road as she decides which way to go. *And I know where to try my luck!*

The sun has already set, releasing darkness into streets of Paris.

Those who work in the daytime are in their homes, settling down to sleep, but the people of the night are just emerging.

Isabelle follows the line of the river towards Notre Dame and sees darkly-dressed people lurking through the poorly-lit streets and hears an occasional shout or harsh laugh from alleyways.

A large man suddenly lurches from the darkness. In one hand he clutches a nearly empty brandy bottle and the other is held out in an attempt to balance his drunken steps.

"Evening, my dear," he slurs and Isabelle backs away from him. "It's alright, my sweet," he adds, stumbling towards her. "Don't be afraid."

He lunges forward attempting to make a grab for her, but trips over his own foot and almost collided with her.

The stench of his breath—garlic, brandy and smelly teeth—fills her nostrils and she hurries away along the street, keeping close to the nearby houses, as though looking to them for protection.

The harsh world around her fills Isabelle with fear, the darkness of the street, the threat of muggers, even the freezing puddles and the thought of rats worries her, but her greatest fear is the darkness.

What might this night bring? As always, it's full of danger and the possibility of not making it to tomorrow alive. And the thought of being with a man, of having sex... I've heard stories, disgusting stories. And yet I can't go on as I have. I need to break free from this miserable way of life. I must!

Out of the darkness looms the massive bulk of Notre Dame, perching on its island. Isabelle crosses the river here, trying not to look at the handful of couples engaged in amorous activities in the cathedral's shadow. The grunts and moans unnerve her for a moment as she considers where she is headed.

Once on the north side of the river, she makes her way to Rue Saint Denis, an area well-known for its nightlife, and especially for the higher class of ladies offering their services.

She has been here before a few times, when out begging with her aunt, but she was never allowed to hang around. Her aunt would always pull Isabelle along, away from the hungry gaze of men for whom a young girl like her would no doubt be a treat. Tonight, however, she does not hurry along the street, but finds a place to stand between the groups of women who are touting for clients.

"Oi!" Isabelle turns at the shout and sees a large, busty woman approaching her. "What do you think you're doing?"

Isabelle stares at the woman, amazed that any man would ever sleep with such a creature. Her mass of ginger hair is clearly a wig and beneath it her face is powdered white, with cheeks and lips painted on in bright red.

"Don't just stand there gawping, girl," she shouts, despite the fact she is only a couple of feet away. "I asked you a question!"

Isabelle frowns. "Not that it's any of your business... I'm looking for a man."

"Well, why don't you sod off and look for one someplace else. There here is my patch, for me and my girls." The large woman points a fat finger at the cluster of women behind her. They are all looking at Isabelle with unconcealed scorn.

"I don't see why."

"You don't have to see why," the woman shouts, causing flecks of spit to land on Isabelle's face. "All you have to see is this hand." She raises the plump hand in question.

"What about it?"

"It's going to rip that pretty skirt off your scrawny little ass unless you get a move on. Go on! Get!'

Isabelle steps back into the street and begins to walk away.

"That's right!" shouts the woman returning to her group. "Keep on walking!"

Angry and disappointed, Isabelle turns to shout something back and is surprised to find a horse standing right in front of her.

"Sorry," she says, looking up at the rider. "I didn't hear you approach."

"Not at all, young lady," said the rider, a well-dressed, middle-aged man. "It is I who must apologize for creeping up on you like that."

Isabelle turns away, but the man calls out to her.

"What is your name?"

"I'm Isabelle."

"May I offer you a ride, Isabelle?"

Isabelle looks up at him again, unsure exactly what he is after. "A ride?"

"Certainly," the man smiles at her. "I have food and wine back at my warm house. Will you not accompany me?"

She considers this for a moment, understanding what he is asking, what he is really after.

This is definitely more than an invitation for food and wine. He's quite old, probably old enough to be my father. I have to ask about money first. And a warm house and the promise of food sounds wonderful. She looks up at him and says, "Fifty livres, monsieur."

She readies herself to negotiate over the price, which seems enormous to her. But the man simply nods his head and reaches down to help her up onto his mount.

Fifty livres, she thinks in amazement, taking his hand and half scrambling and half being pulled up onto the horse. *That's a whole month of begging, on days when people are feeling generous! I've never even seen that much in my entire life! Even if there is no food and the house is cold and horrible, it's got to be worth it for fifty livres!*

Isabelle has never been on a horse before and, as she sits side-saddle just above the creature's rump, she grasps the man around the waist, afraid that she might fall off. The cobblestoned street seems a long way down!

I must be hurting him, she thinks, but the man says nothing. Instead, he lets out a small chuckle and pats her hand kindly.

"Don't worry," he says. "I won't let you get hurt."

"Thank you, sir."

They don't speak for the rest of the short journey, and eventually the man draws up outside a large, stately home, whose front lawn is lit by a number of ornate torches. A servant in a leather apron hurries out to hold the horse as the rider, whose name Isabelle suddenly realizes she still doesn't know, dismounts and offers a hand to her.

"What is your name, monsieur?" she asks, taking the hand easing herself slowly to the ground.

"I am Jean-Pierre Lacroix," he says with a slight bow. Straightening up, he gestures towards the house. "Welcome to my home, Isabelle."

The door is opened by woman.

Oh no! His wife is here! Isabelle panics for a moment, staring at the woman. She is older than Isabelle, somewhere in her thirties. In return the woman stares back at her with a look of contempt.

"Good evening, milord," she says, turning to look at Jean-Pierre as he steps into the entrance hall. "May I take your coat?"

He shrugs it off and she takes it, hanging it in a nearby cupboard. "Lucie," he says, "Isabelle and I are going through to the dining room. We will require food and wine immediately."

With another scathing glare at Isabelle, the woman, Lucie, walks away.

Well, she's obviously not his wife. She must be his housemaid, Isabelle reasons, following Jean-Pierre through a doorway. *Thank goodness for that!*

"Please, sit," says Jean-Pierre, gesturing to an ornate dining table, but she just stands, looking around the room in wonder.

Although she's been in a handful of houses during her sixteen years of life, none of them were as plush and inviting as this one. In one of the walls is a large fireplace, where a log fire burns with a warm glow. Everything is tidy and well kept. "Please," Jean-Pierre repeats, still holding a hand towards the table.

"These are beautiful chairs," says Isabelle, choosing one to sit in.

"My wife chose them." A sad look passes across his face. "She died a year ago. It's only me and my two boys here now. And the servants, of course."

As he mentions this, Lucie walks in carrying a large tray loaded with food. Without even glancing towards Isabelle, she places one plate of bread and one of sliced turkey on the table, with a bottle of wine and a jug of water. Isabelle stares at the food, amazed. She has never sat down to a meal of this size and she suddenly realizes just how hungry she is.

"Please eat, my dear," Jean-Pierre says, waving the housemaid away and, as Isabelle helps herself to the food, he pours some of the wine into a pair of intricately patterned silver goblets.

This is astonishing, she thinks. *The house, the food and everything. And though he is pretty old, he's not ugly or anything.* She steals a glance at him as she bites into a piece of bread and sees him smiling warmly at her.

"Here," he says, picking up a goblet and passing it to her. "Have a little wine, my dear."

Isabelle hesitates, her hand halfway to the goblet, as she has never had wine before.

Jean-Pierre gives her a comforting smile. "It's alright. It is perfectly safe."

She takes it and, not knowing how to drink it, gulps at the red liquid. Almost immediately she starts coughing, just managing to swallow the wine first so she doesn't spray it across the table.

The liquid burns her throat but not unpleasantly, and a warm glow spreads across her cheeks. A sudden tiredness comes over her and her arms and legs feel strange somehow, as though they do not quite belong to her.

As she yawns, Jean-Pierre lays a hand gently on her wrist.

"Perhaps you would like a bath to help wash off the concerns of the day. Lucie!" the housemaid hurries in at his call. "Prepare a bath for my guest and ensure she is given the finest oils and soaps." Turning back to Isabelle, he continues, "Go with Lucie, my dear. She will bathe you and get you ready for bed."

"Thank you," says Isabelle, rising to leave, and thinks, *a bath! I have never even dreamed of such a luxury. A quick splash in the freezing Seine is the best I can hope for, but a real bath. . .*

It is everything she could imagine and more; the steam, the smells, the oils, all of it like some wonderful dream. Lucie, still seeming to ignore Isabelle, busies herself filling the large ceramic bathtub with steaming hot water from a boiler and tempering it with a few splashes from a cold water cistern.

Then she approaches Isabelle and begins to pull at the laces of her bodice.

"What are you doing?" says Isabelle, backing away from her in confusion.

Lucie gives her a stern look. "I need to undress you for a bath, girl. Unless you want to go in wearing these filthy rags. They could probably do with the wash." She sighs. "Just stand still and let me get you out of these clothes."

Isabelle obeys, letting Lucie undo the laces and take the bodice off, before stripping off her skirt.

Isabelle notices the woman's lips wrinkle in disgust. Finally, when Isabelle's clothes are in an untidy pile and she is standing with her arms folded across her chest to cover her breasts, Lucie tells her to get in the bath.

The water is wonderfully warm and as she lowers herself into the tub, Isabelle relaxed, at peace.

She lays there, the heat of the bath warming her, and wants to stay there longer, but Lucie returns carrying a large brush, a metal comb and a bar of soap.

For the next few minutes, Isabelle's whole body is subjected to vigorous scrubbing.

Well this isn't as relaxing as I'd hoped, she thinks. *I'll be lucky if I have any skin left after she's finished with this brush!*

But then the combing begins. "Ouch!"

"Don't make such a fuss," says Lucie, dragging the comb through the tangles of her hair. "You don't want to look like a street urchin for his lordship, do you?"

At these words, Isabelle's heart seems to skip a beat.

She had briefly forgotten the reason for her presence here and for being scrubbed and combed into respectability. Now she recalls what is going to happen later and she has a stab of worry.

Even the light massage that follows her bath, after she has been rinsed off with spring water and rubbed dry with soft linen, doesn't quite manage to alleviate her concern.

I wonder if it's true what they say, she thinks, as Lucie pours scented oil onto her back and begins to ease the muscles between Isabelle's shoulders. *Is it really always painful the first time you have sex?*

At last, the preparations are complete and, now dressed in a silky nightdress, Isabelle is shown into a large bedroom.

"Wait here for the master," says Lucie curtly, placing a lit candle on the dressing table before stalking out of the room.

Left alone, Isabelle paces around the room, tense and nervous.

I really hope it doesn't hurt. If I didn't need the money, I feel I would run away right now. But fifty livres! That's a huge amount. What if he doesn't find me pleasing in bed, though? Maybe he will decide not to pay me after all.

Her thoughts are interrupted by the creak of the door opening and she turns to see Jean-Pierre entering the room. He stops and looks at her as though this is the first time he has seen her.

"You are looking beautiful, my dear," he says with a smile. In his hand is a sheaf of papers and he lays these next to the candle on the dressing table. "Fifty livres, as promised."

Isabelle walks over and looks at the notes, more money than she has ever seen.

"Shall we?" she turns to see Jean-Pierre pulling back the sheets and gesturing for her to join him. A new look has crept into his eyes, a look of desire. But it is not the unpleasant, hungry look such as that she saw in the fat man's eyes. It is a simple longing without aggression or malice. So, feeling slightly less nervous, Isabelle climbs into the bed.

The love-making does not last long, and though it is painful, it is not as terrible as she imagined it would be. As Jean-Pierre rolls himself off her, he looks concerned for Isabelle and pulls back the sheets to reveal the blood.

"Oh!" he says, his eyebrows raised. "Were you a virgin?"

"Yes," says Isabelle, still winching at the pain and hardly able to speak.

"I am your first lover."

It is not a question, but still she replies, "Yes. You are."

They lay there in silence together until Jean-Pierre says, "I would like to give you a dress that belonged to my wife." Then, as Isabelle pulls back the covers to get out of the bed, he lays a hand on her arm. "Will you stay with me, Isabelle? For the night?"

She looks around the room, and wonders if she has ever slept in such fine surroundings, even as a child before her parents died.

The idea of returning to sleep in the slums after being washed and taken care of is almost unthinkable.

"Thank you," she says. "I would like that very much."

In the morning, she is awoken by Jean-Pierre with that same look of desire in his eyes, and she lies back and closes her eyes as he pulls himself onto her again.

If anything it hurts even more than the previous night, but she refuses to let him know and grits her teeth through the pain.

What animals these men are, she thinks as he finally reaches his climax. Still, it is not too great a price to eat well, bathe and be paid so handsomely.

"As promised," says Jean-Pierre, drawing back the curtain to reveal a closet filled with dresses. "Choose one and it is yours."

They have already eaten breakfast together, sitting in the dining room as before.

This time there were more servants waiting on them, including Lucie, who was still giving Isabelle the cold shoulder. There had been eggs, a selection of meats, porridge and bread, all a delight for Isabelle. And now she finds herself presented with this wonderful selection of dresses.

What luxury, she thinks as she looks through the beautiful clothes. *I guess Jean-Pierre's wife was a bit taller than me, but she had a wonderful collection. And I'm sure I can afford to get the dress altered to fit me now.*

In the end, she settles on a skirt and bodice, instead of a single dress, and Jean-Pierre lets her take a hat that he says matches her eyes.

Excited, she pulls on the clothes and the hat and looks into a full length mirror standing in a corner of the room. There, staring right back at her, is a fine-looking young lady with clothing to grow into and a big smile on her face.

"You truly are beautiful, my dear," says Jean-Pierre, admiring her from the doorway. And, Isabelle's smile grows even wider at this, the first complement a man has ever given her.

"So where are you going now?" he asks and, at first, Isabelle is uncertain what to say. She feels ashamed of her dirty shelter in the city slums. Then she remembers a place she stayed occasionally with her aunt, where, although everyone sleeps together in one large room, they do at least have protection from the elements and even get to eat warm porridge each morning, all for only two livres a night. She can certainly afford that now!

"I am going to stay in a boarding house," she replies, "near the river."

Jean-Pierre frowns. He clearly has some idea of life in a boarding house. "Really? And you're going there in these beautiful clothes?"

"No, of course," she says, hastily taking off her hat and beginning to unlace the bodice. "I will change."

"There's no need for that," he says, putting his hand on her to stop her undressing. "Why don't you stay here? At least for a while. I have a spare room and it is a shame to let it go to waste."

"Well," asks Isabelle innocently, with more than a little female cunning. "Does this mean I am to become your mistress?"

Jean-Pierre nods his agreement. "You, my dear, shall have all the privileges that come with being a mistress."

"And I presume you wish to receive the privileges of *having* a mistress." She gives him a playful look, holding his gaze for a moment. "Thank you, Jean-Pierre."

♣

In the days that follow, Isabelle begins to settle into her new life with Jean-Pierre.

This is a good choice, she keeps saying to herself, especially at those times when the sex is painful and leaves her sore for days after. *I have a roof over my head, good food to eat and most importantly of all, money. Money is what I really need. That is the only thing that will provide me with true independence and freedom.*

Isabelle also enjoys the company of Jean-Pierre's two sons, Philippe and Jean.

They are both under ten years old and most days an elderly teacher comes to the house to school them in such things as reading and writing, math, history and geography. On one morning, Jean-Pierre finds Isabelle sitting outside the room when the teacher is speaking, her ear pressed again the door.

"Isabelle?" he says.

She turns quickly, her cheeks flushing. "Yes?"

"Do you enjoy listening to the boys' lessons?"

"Oh, yes!" she says. "So many wonderful things to learn and to find out about. They're fascinating."

A kindly smile spreads across Jean-Pierre's face. "Would you like to sit in with Philippe and Jean? You can take part in the lessons properly then instead of sitting out here in the hall."

"Really?" Isabelle asks, excited at the idea and the chance to learn.

"Of course, my dear. And while you're in there, you can keep my boys in line. They're not always so keen to listen!"

Delighted to have this opportunity, Isabelle does as Jean-Pierre asks and joins in with the boys' education as often as she can.

Of all the lessons, the one taught by Antoine - the music teacher - is Isabelle's favorite and, when no one is around, she sits at the piano and practices what she's learned.

If there is one thing that spoils her happiness at Jean-Pierre's house, it is the animosity of the housekeeper, Lucie.

No matter what Isabelle does, Lucie treats her with a cold contempt, refusing to speak to her or even look at her unless she cannot avoid it. It is so bad, in fact, that whenever they are both in the same room, Isabelle finds herself feeling tense and awkward, as though she should apologize for even existing.

After several months living at the house, however, as Isabelle heads to her bedroom one day, she stops at the muffled sound of someone sobbing. Retracing her steps, she finds that it is coming from Lucie's room. The door is ajar, so she eases it open to find the housekeeper with her head in her hands.

At first Isabelle begins to duck back out of the room, but Lucie's grief sounds so genuine and heartfelt that she stops on the threshold, looking at the woman with a growing sense of pity.

Finally, she decides to try to comfort her and, sitting down on the bed, places an arm around her shoulders.

The housekeeper looks up in surprise and, shrugging off Isabelle's arm, tries to stop crying. After only a few seconds, however, her face crumples and she starts sobbing again.

"It's okay," says Isabelle, placing her arm back across Lucie's shoulders and hugging her gently. "It's good to cry. Let it out, Lucie. It will help you to feel better."

Lucie does so, weeping bitterly with great sobs and sighs for a long time. Eventually, she manages to say a few words.

"My son. He's dead. My lovely baby boy. Dead." And she returns to her crying again.

Isabelle suddenly finds herself overwhelmed with sorrow for this poor woman. "Oh, my poor Lucie," she says, hugging her even harder as tears well up in her own eyes. "I know how terrible it feels to miss someone you loved. Someone you have lost."

Soon they are both weeping in each other's arms, united at last by mutual grief and compassion.

"I had a man once," says Lucie as her sorrow begins to ease. "A man who loved me. He was a brave man, a soldier. But he was killed fighting the Spanish, leaving me all alone with Guillaume, our baby son." She pauses to wipe her eyes with a damp handkerchief before continuing. "We had no money and no man to provide for us so I had to leave our village to come to Paris to find work. Guillaume stayed behind with a nurse, a good woman, and I visited when I could. But there is little time for family when you are a servant. Every time I visited Guillaume I hated having to leave. It was like my heart being torn in two."

"But what else could you have done?" asks Isabelle, placing a comforting hand on Lucie's.

"Nothing. I had no choice. If I took him with me, how could I work? Besides, I had a plan. I was going to save up for Guillaume to come to Paris and be educated here."

"Did he ever come to the city?"

"No." Lucie's eyes flicked down as tears filled them again. "He fell sick with a terrible fever. He wouldn't eat anything and became horribly weak."

Isabelle remembers her aunt suffering just the same symptoms and knows how frightened Lucie must have been. "It was the wasting sickness?"

"Yes," Lucie nods. "I got the doctor to see him, but there was nothing he could do. He told me to pray and rely on God's mercy. Much good that did! My dear Guillaume passed away only days before his seventh birthday. Why is it that the people we love are taken away?" She starts sobbing again, overwhelmed by the painful memories. Isabelle sits in silence, still holding her tightly. Eventually the tears slow again and Lucie looks up into her face. "I'm sorry, Isabelle."

"For what?" she replies. "For crying? Don't be silly!"

"Not for my tears. I am sorry for how I treated you, for my arrogance and unkindness."

Isabelle smiles at her, and holds Lucie's face in her hands. "Think nothing of it, Lucie. Let's start again."

And, smiling through their tears, Lucie puts her arms around Isabelle and Isabelle, in turn, embraces her new friend.

Chapter Eighteen

*I*f you're going to make your way among the rich, you've got to be smart!" Lucie tells her when they are alone in the kitchen a few days later. "A girl like you can make a lot of money if you play it right."

Isabelle picks up her cup of wine and sips it as she considers her friend's words. "I thought I was doing quite well already," she says.

"Quite well, yes. You've managed to get this far." She waves an arm at their surroundings. "But this can't be all you want. Look at me. I fought hard to get this position after Jean-Pierre's wife died, but I don't want to be a housekeeper for the rest of my life!"

She leans closer, looking around as though checking for hidden spies. "I've spent years getting to know influential people, helping them out by delivering messages, keeping their secrets, that sort of thing. I'm going places, Isabelle.

One day, I'll get out of here and buy myself a nice house. After that, I'll open my own salon for the upper class men and women of Paris. What about you?" She fixes Isabelle with a stare. "You like living here?"

"Of course! It's wonderful. You should have seen where I was living before. It was horrible. And frightening too."

"And what about Jean-Pierre?" says Lucie, peering over the rip of her cup. "You like him as well?"

Isabelle shrugs. "He's okay, I suppose. But he's very old. And he can be a bit rude sometimes."

"And what about what he does in bed? How do you like that?"

"Not one bit!" Isabelle replied vehemently, placing her cup firmly on the table and causing a little of the wine to spill out onto the table. "He's like some kind of wild animal, grunting and rutting away."

Lucie lifts a hand to wipe her mouth, hiding her amused grin. "Don't worry, my dear. Not all men are like that. In fact, some of them are very sweet, true *gentle*men."

"That's a relief. Do you know such men?"

"Oh, yes!" Lucie raises her eyebrows, trying to affect a mysterious look, before draining the last of her wine. "Yes, I know a few..."

Leaving her words hanging, she gets up from the table and returns to her work of getting the house ready to settle down for the night. Isabelle, still sipping her drink, watches her friend at work.

It's so lovely to have a true friend, she thinks. *I never really had one before, and Lucie is exactly what I've always needed. Someone who will help me get free of the poverty I was born into. Someone who will help me get what I want.*

When she wakes the following morning, easing herself out from beneath the covers to look out at the winter sun lighting up the city, she feels somehow that there is something new coming, just out of sight in the horizon; a new world that she is only just starting to realize exists.

She flings open her wardrobe and admires the two gorgeous dresses it contains with her other clothes. Fingering the exquisitely embroidered fabrics, she smiles at this treasure that is now hers.

They're so beautiful!

Her thoughts are interrupted by a knock at the door and Lucie enters the room carrying a breakfast tray. She places it on the dressing table and turns to Isabelle.

"How are you feeling this bright morning, my dear?" she asks.

"Great!" says Isabelle, still standing in front of the wardrobe. "I slept like a baby last night, mostly thanks to the fact that Jean-Pierre didn't come in for his night's activities."

Lucie peers over her shoulder to see what she is looking at. "What have you got in there?"

"Just a few dresses that he's given me since I arrived here." She steps to one side so her friend can see inside the wardrobe.

"He gave you these?" says Lucie, reaching in and pulling one of the dresses out - a burgundy colored piece fashioned from velvet and lace. "What a load of trash!"

Isabelle turns round in astonishment. "Trash?"

"That's right, trash! Look at this thing. This style hasn't been in fashion for twenty years, at least!"

"Oh." A look of disappointment shadows Isabelle face and her cheeks flush slightly. "Oh, really?"

"Indeed! They're outdated and tasteless. You see this neckline?" Lucie runs a finger along the dress's seam and her friend nods. "That shows it's at least fifteen years old. And the fall of the skirt is far too narrow. No, no! These won't do at all. You'll have to get new dresses."

"But these dresses were a gift from Jean-Pierre," says Isabelle, taking the dress from Lucie and hanging it carefully back in the wardrobe.

"Are you telling me these dreary garments are his payment for making love to a young beauty like you?"

"Not exactly. He gave them to me because he wants me to look nice."

"Hah!" Lucie shuts the door as if trying to hide the dresses from her sight. "He wants you to look like his dreary old wife!"

She pauses, her back pressed against the wardrobe, and looks at her friend. "Tell me, Isabelle, do you love him?"

She frowns. "Jean-Pierre? No. Not at all. But he's not a bad catch for someone like me. What other choice do I have?"

"Oh, you have choice! Considering your age, your face, your figure, you have everything going for you."

Isabelle blushes again at Lucie's compliments. "But I'm just a girl from the slums."

"Who cares where you came from? It's where you're going that matters. Next time he offers you one of his dead wife's dreary dresses, ask him for some money instead so you can buy yourself a proper dress, one that's in vogue. A girl like you deserves a better dress, and you'll need one to get yourself a better man!"

"I can't ask that. A new dress would be way too expensive."

"Well, don't ask him for the whole lot all at once. Get it out of him in installments, little by little. Trust me, he'll give you the money. Now," she adds, walking over to the dresser and picking up the breakfast tray with a grin, "are you going to eat this before it goes cold or have I been slaving away downstairs for nothing?"

♣

Over the next few days, Isabelle quizzes Lucie about her ideas and adventures, amazed by this new friend's experiences and by the ways things worked in higher society.

This must be that new world she sensed was coming. Maybe she really does have a chance to find a good man, a rich man; a man like the one she saw in what now seems like another life; the man whose horse had knocked into her as she walked the freezing streets at night; the man who gave her a glimmer of hope and the money that allowed to crawl out of the muck and filth.

In quiet moments, Isabelle imagines meeting that gentleman again, his graceful hands holding hers, his elegant moustache caressing her cheek, his triangle hat resting on her knees.

Walking the city streets has become something of a pleasure now that she can choose to rather than being forced to by circumstances.

Isabelle studies the fashionable women of Paris, taking note of everything they are wearing from their bodices and skirts to their gloves, shoes and even their scarves.

Each item is subjected to her scrutiny as she considers which might suit her and which would not.

It becomes all too clear that Lucie was right. The dresses that belonged to Jean-Pierre's wife are old, their style now obsolete.

As she studies the latest fashions she sees around her, an image of *her* ideal dress starts to form in her mind. She is surprised at how effortless this dress comes to her in the most intricate detail. It is almost like it designs itself!

As soon as Isabelle has enough money, given by Jean-Pierre instead of those old dresses, Lucie takes her to visit a skilled seamstress friend of hers and, a few days later, she finds herself standing in her room gazing at herself in the mirror as she wears the dress of her dreams.

I can't believe it, she thinks, admiring the lines of the dress and the way it accentuates the growing curves of her body. *It worked. Lucie's plan really worked. Jean-Pierre could have given me twenty dresses, instead of the money, and they would have been nothing compared to this beautiful outfit.*

She performs a little twirl in the mirror, laughing to herself.

"Not bad!" she turns at the sound of Lucie's voice, feeling a little embarrassed. But a pleased smile lights up her friends face. "You really are gorgeous, Isabelle."

"Thank you," Isabelle replies. "And thank you for all your help. I can hardly believe this is really mine."

"Well, we're not done yet!"

Isabelle turns to look at herself in the mirror. "We're not?"

"Of course not," says Lucie, walking over and beginning to tie up her friend's hair. "We need to get you the right accessories, shoes, hat, gloves, that sort of thing." She traces Isabelle's neckline with a finger. "And then there's the jewelry, of course."

"Jewelry?"

"Yes. Expensive jewelry!"

Isabelle frowns at her friend in the mirror. "I barely had enough money for this dress. Where am I going to get enough money for that sort of thing?"

"Well, you can sell those crappy, old dresses for a start," says Lucie with a wry smile. "They may not be fashionable, but they're well-made and probably worth a bit of money. Enough for some shoes and stockings at least."

"Fine. But what about the jewelry?"

Now it is Lucie's turn to frown as she considers this. Then she shrugs. "We'll work something out, don't worry. But you definitely need it. There!" she adds, stepping back to look at her friend. "All you need now is some powder and rouge for your lips and cheeks and you'll be the most sought after woman in Paris!"

Isabelle gazes into the mirror. With her hair up and wearing this dress she can hardly recognize herself, the girl who walked the city streets at night only a few months ago.

"Thank you, Lucie," she says, moved almost to tears. "For everything."

Lucie smiles. "You're a fine canvas to work with. You'll be a hit at the coming ball."

Isabelle spins round, her mouth open. "A ball?"

♣

The following days seem to pass far too slowly for Isabelle. She is so excited about the idea of going to the ball she feels as though she might burst.

Eventually, though the news she has been waiting for arrives.

"Jean-Pierre will be leaving for the hunt the day after tomorrow," says Lucie, hurrying into the room where Isabelle is sitting at the piano, humming along to a tune she is trying to master. "He could be away for as long as three, even four, weeks!"

Isabelle stops playing and jumps to her feet, almost knocking the stool over. "Wonderful!" she exclaims. "Where is he going?"

"Oh, a long way away," Lucie flaps her hand dismissively. "To the forests around Limoges. It's at least a four-day journey."

"So this is it? Our chance to go to the ball?"

Lucie smiles at her friend's excitement. "Yes. It's time to act!"

Two days later, after much preparation, Jean-Pierre mounts his horse for the long journey south, taking with him a number of servants, hunting dogs and the various weapons that might be needed for the sport.

Once the party is ready, the cooking staff loads food up into a wagon and they set out, leaving the house strangely quiet and empty.

Lucie has also been busy with her preparations and has used her influential contacts to arrange invitations for her and Isabelle to attend a high-society ball.

No sooner has the hunt party disappeared along the street than she and Isabelle set to work planning for the ball, which is only a few hours away.

Since Isabelle has no jewelry to wear, Lucie lends her some of her own - a pearl necklace with matching earrings that accentuate the elegant style of her new dress.

A few hours later, their hair done up, their faces powdered and rouged, they arrive at the stately rooms for the ball.

It is not just any ball, but a masquerade; assortments of fancy masks are handed out to guests as they arrive.

Isabelle selects a simple design that conceals as little of her face as possible. Lucie, however, chooses an ornate, feathered mask with a beaked nose that makes her appear like a playful bird.

"How do I look?" she asks, holding the mask up and walking with a seductive swing to her hips.

A few men hanging around the entrance hall stare at her, eyeing up the bulging mass of her breasts, barely stuffed into her bodice. In contrast to her friend, Isabelle feels shy and is afraid to look up; a feeling that only increases as they enter the ballroom together, because hundreds of eyes turn in their direction.

Everyone is looking at us, she realizes with a mixture of fear and shame. *Thank goodness we're wearing these masks; otherwise I'd die of embarrassment.*

They've taken no more than a few steps into the room - its white marble surfaces dazzling in the light of the candelabra - when a man comes scuttling up to them, his round face hidden behind a mask with bull horns. He peeps over the top of it and winks at Lucie.

"How do you do, Lucie?" he says with a sweet smile. "Looking as alluring as always!"

Lucie offers him a small curtsy. "At your service, marquis. May I introduce my companion, the young Isabelle."

"A pleasure to meet you, milady," says the marquis, turning to face her. He bows and Isabelle notices the spreading bald patch on the top of head.

This man must be at least in his sixties, she thinks. *But Lucie called him "marquis" so he's clearly a nobleman of some description.* So she curtsies politely. "Thank you, monsieur marquis."

"Oh, please, dear lady," he says, taking her hand and giving her his best smile. "Call me, Cedric." He bends down to kiss her hand. "How you are doing, Isabelle?"

To her surprise, Isabelle feels her nervousness draining away thanks to the marquis' easy affability. "Well enough, Cedric. Though it could always get better."

The marquis looks at her a moment, then laughs. "What a treasure!" he says to Lucie. "Where did you find her?"

"Oh, I never reveal my sources. You know that."

With a chuckle, he takes hold of Lucie's arm, drawing her away. "Come on, you saucy girl. Time for a little dance while my legs can still take it!"

And then they are gone, swallowed up by the crowd of dancers, leaving Isabelle alone.

Peering through the eyeholes in her mask, she looks around the room, amazed by how many people there seem to be.

At one end of the ballroom a small orchestra accompanies the dancers, playing a fast paced tune that Isabelle decides to try and work out as soon as she's back home. Scattered around the outside of the room are a number of chairs for the ladies to rest in after dancing, and tall tables for people to stand around and place their glasses of champagne. Isabelle becomes aware that a couple of middle aged men – both dressed in exquisite finery – who are leaning against one of these tables watching her. As her eyes meet theirs, she lowers them quickly, as though studying the pattern of the tiles.

Oh no, she thinks, as she looks up slightly in their direction. *One of those men is coming this way! He's heading straight towards me. What do I do?*

"Good evening, milady," the man accosts her in a rich voice; rich in every sense.

Isabelle looks up at him as he bows. She is pleased to see he is not balding.

"Very good evening, milord," she replies, repeating the curtsy that Lucie had taught her.

The man leans in closely to whisper in her ear. "Are you here on your own?"

"No," she says with a slight shake of her head that causes her cheek to brush slightly against his. "I am here with a friend of mine called Lucie." At that moment, she spots Lucie, still dancing with the marquis, and gestures towards her with her mask. "That's her."

But the man doesn't turn to look at Lucie. Instead he is looking in admiration at Isabelle's uncovered face.

"What is your name, my dear?" he asks, still gazing at her.

"I am Isabelle, milord."

He smiles kindly. "Well, Isabelle. I am Vicomte Bernard du Bois and I would like to offer you a ride. Would that be acceptable?"

Blushing, Isabelle raises the mask back to her face and responds with a small nod.

"And how much would it be for the pleasure of your company?"

Although Lucie has gone through the practical details of such a transaction with her, Isabelle finds herself lost for words now that she is faced with this elegant, influential gentleman.

"This fine, young pearl is quite a discovery, wouldn't you say, milord?" Isabelle breathes a sigh of relief at the timely arrival of Lucie. The Vicomte nods his head in agreement so Lucie continues, "This is her first time here, a fresh, new fruit, ripe and ready for plucking."

"I see," he says, turning to Lucie to discuss matters further. "Then perhaps you might enlighten me as to the cost of borrowing this beautiful pearl for tonight."

Lucie purses her lips as if considering nothing more the price of a loaf of bread in the market. "A mere five hundred livres."

Isabelle coughs, amazed at this staggering amount of money.

Five hundred livres? Has Lucie gone mad? Surely no one would pay such a price for a single night with her! But the Vicomte does not seem at all phased by Lucie's words.

"It's reasonable," he says with a shrug as though he, too, was discussing nothing more than the purchase of some bread.

"Excellent. You won't be disappointed, milord."

"Oh, I'm sure I won't be," he says, offering his arms to Isabelle. "Not one bit."

"What an amazing night!" says Isabelle, as she and Lucie drink their morning coffee together the next day. "I guess all men are different."

"Of course they are! They're not all rutting bulls like Jean-Pierre. Some are kind lovers, some are gentle. Some will take you to heaven and back, and others are into some pretty weird stuff. But one thing that unites them all..."

"Yes?" Isabelle puts down her cup and leans forward, intrigued.

"They all love sex!" She chuckles happily. "And it's a good thing too. Otherwise, we'd have no hope of getting rich."

"Talking about money," says Isabelle, pulling out a sheaf of notes. "Thank you for helping me with Bernard."

Lucie raises her eyebrows in pretend shock. "Bernard, is it now?"

Isabelle blushes slightly, but ignores her friend's interruption. "I want you to have half of it." And she holds out a number of notes to Lucie. Instead of taking them all, however, Lucie pulls out a single note and tucks it into her bodice. "That will do," she says. "Consider it payment for the loan of my pearls."

"Are you sure, Lucie?"

"Of course. We're friends, aren't we?"

Isabelle nods. "Yes, we are. Thank you."

Lucie pauses a moment, considering the cookies. Finally she says, "You're going to need the rest for yourself. The Marquis wants to meet you; so you're going to have to look your best!"

"Me?" says Isabelle, taken aback. "Why does the Marquis want to see me?"

"Don't mess about. You know why! Why does any man want to get together with a beautiful young lady?"

"Oh. But wasn't the Marquis with you last night?"

"Of course he was!" Lucie laughs at her friend's naivety. "But he fancies something a bit younger. That's men for you. They're always on the lookout for something new!"

Isabelle, still frowning in confusion, says, "But I like the Vicomte. And he told me he wants to meet up again."

"Listen." Lucie dips her cookie into the steaming drink and takes a bite. "I'm going to let you into a little secret, Isabelle. The Vicomte? He has a wife. Not only that but he has at least two mistresses that I know of as well. That's the way this works. A wealthy gentleman will have as many women as he can afford, and some of them can afford a lot."

Isabelle stands staring at her friend as she calmly eats her biscuit, desperately trying to take it all in. "Well?" says Lucie, brushing the crumbs from her lap. "Do you need money or not?"

"Yes, of course."

"Then go and see the Marquis."

"Why do men do this?" Isabelle asks after a while, reaching across for a cookie.

"Do what exactly?"

"You know what. Why do they feel they need to have several women on the go at the same time?"

Lucie shrugs. "Who knows? It's just the way they are. There could be many reasons I guess. But the point is," she lays a hand on her friends knee and gazes into her eyes, "we're fine with that, aren't we, Isabelle?"

"I guess so," she says, but then she finds herself thinking back to that elegant young man from the dark Parisian streets, the man who left a mark on her heart. What she really wants is her own man, a man who would be satisfied with just her. "So how do you become a man's *special* lady? His *only* lady?"

"That, my dear, takes talent. Real talent. Because to be 'the one', you've got to be the best!"

♣

By the time Jean-Pierre returns from his hunting trip, Isabelle has visited the Marquis and the Vicomte a number of times, earning herself sufficient money to expand her wardrobe and pay for some fine pieces of jewelry, with plenty to spare.

This is amazing, she thinks, as she stashes away the money in one of her dressing table drawers. *At this rate, I will be able to afford to rent a decent place of my own. Imagine that!* Even Jean-Pierre's evening visit to her chamber doesn't dampen her joy and, when the deed is over, she turns to face him.

"May I ask a favor of you, Jean-Pierre?" she asks in her most angelic voice.

He looks at her, happy from his hunting and love-making, and eyes her up and down, enjoying her naked body. "But of course, my dear."

"I would really like to take singing lessons. And I was hoping you might find me a good teacher."

"Singing lessons?" He raises his eyebrows at this request. "Whatever do you want them for? I've heard you singing along when the music teacher is here. Your voice sounds fine to me."

"But I want to improve my talent," she says, turning her whole body towards him. "I want to be the best singer I can be!"

Jean-Pierre frowns as he considers this. "Well, I guess it is good for a young lady, such as yourself, to have a hobby. And since the leather business is booming and I'm making a handsome profit, I don't see why not. Yes!" he says, laying a gentle hand on her bare skin. "I shall find you a good teacher, Isabelle."

And he does; an Italian, one of the finest singing teachers in Paris.

Isabelle is delighted and, over the following weeks and months, she hones her singing skills, while continuing to learn the piano and study dancing with Lucie's assistance.

Then, one evening, Jean-Pierre hosts a small, select gathering at his house, inviting of the bulk of those he has conducted business with and some people of influence; though Isabelle does not recognize any of them.

After dinner, he calls everyone to congregate in the music room to listen to Isabelle sing.

"You should hear her!" he says. "I've never known anyone take to music like this young lady."

Slightly nervous at being the focus of everyone's attention, Isabelle picks one her favorite songs, a melody that her aunt used to sing and which her singing teacher found the music for, and stands in the center of the room, her teacher sitting at the piano poised to accompany her.

Everyone is silent and all eyes are on Isabelle when she begins to sing.

It is a beautiful song about a love that is lost, but then found again many years later, and as Isabelle sings it she pours all of herself into the words and into the music, filling every note with the sorrow and the joy in her heart.

There is something enchanting about the song, drawing people into its spell. Her audience sits and listens with open mouths and glistening eyes and when, eventually the song comes to an end, they burst into applause.

"Bravo!" someone cries. "Bravo, mademoiselle."

"Oh, Jean-Pierre!" shouts someone else over the sound of clapping. "What a treat! This young lady's voice could delight even His Majesty, the King's ear. I do not doubt it!"

These words stun Isabelle and, feeling weak at the knees, she leans against the piano. Looking up, she sees Lucie standing in the doorway, joining in with the applause. She mouths a 'well done' and gestures for Isabelle to join her in the other room.

"Do you know who that man was?" says Lucie, when they are shut away together. Isabelle gives her a blank look. "Of course, you don't. That man is part of King Louis' court."

"Really?" Isabelle is amazed. Not at the man's words, but at the fact that a member of the King's court was here in this house, listening to her sing!

"Yes. And he will be the man to get you into the palace. Trust me. You may have to wait a while, but he is your way in to His Majesty."

"But why?" Isabelle asks, unable to take it all in. "Why would he want to take me to see the King?"

"That's how things work in the palace. It's all about favor. Everyone wants to be the King's favorite and the way to do that is to ingratiate yourself with him, pleasing him and giving him gifts. And you, Isabelle, would be a great present even for His Majesty, King Louis XIV."

"You really think it's possible for someone who was living on the streets only months ago? You really think that I could end up going to Versailles? Me?" She gestures to herself with both hands as if to make it clear that it was *her* they were talking about, not some Duchess or similarly highborn lady.

"Oh, you'll get there alright," says her friend with a smile. "You're a young, attractive lady. Where else are you going to end up? And after that, well... don't forget that Le Roi Soleil is only a man!"

Chapter Nineteen

A sharp rap on the door rouses Isabelle from her sleep. She listens to Lucie's footsteps below her and the sound of the door opening. There is a short exchange, but she can't make out any of the words, and then she hears the door closing and the footstep treading the stairs and approaching her chamber.

"Isabelle?" says Lucie's voice outside her door. "Are you awake?" Isabelle manages a muffled groan. Lucie pushes the door open and strides into the room. "Well, you'll want to be. It's a message from the King's palace!"

"The King's palace?" Isabelle is suddenly awaking and sitting up in her bed. "Surely it can't be!" She doesn't dare to finish the sentence and give herself even a glimmer of hope, but reaches out to take the sealed parchment. The stamp breaks easily and she wrenches it open, scanning it with darting eyes, hardly able to take it in. "It's an invitation!" she says, almost shouting with excitement. "An invitation to sing at the palace."

Lucie takes the parchment and studies it. Looking up, she sees the panic in her friend's face. "It's okay, Isabelle. Take it easy." She sits down on the bed and lays a hand on Isabelle's arm. "It's not an official court event. It's a small gathering with some of His Majesty's intimate friends. He just wants to check you out, that's all."

"But what if His Majesty doesn't like me?" says Isabelle, placing anxious palms on her forehead. "I'm sure he won't."

"Come, come, my dear! This is a wonderful opportunity. France is full of girls who would kill for such a chance!" she takes Isabelle's face in her hands and holds her gaze. "You have the voice of an angel. His Majesty will adore you!"

♣

His Majesty will adore you. His Majesty will adore you. These words still ring in Isabelle's ears as, far too short a while later, she finds herself standing in one of the ornate state rooms of King Louis XIV's palace at Saint-Germain-en-Laye.

With Lucie's help, she is adorned in an exquisite new dress from one of the finest designers in Paris, and she looks out at the gathering through the curls of fair hair that frame her face.

As expected, there aren't too many people - around thirty men and women - but there, enthroned among them, is His Majesty, King of France and Navarre, Louis XIV.

Isabelle has never seen him before, but he is immediately recognizable. Partly this is due to the golden leaf crown that perches on top of an enormous, powdered wig, but mostly it's his presence that somehow seems to draw all focus and attention to him.

His Majesty wears no magnificent robes this evening, just a simple jacket and knee-breeches, both of white cloth embroidered with gold thread, above dark gray stockings, and yet Isabelle knows with absolute certainty that this is *Him.*

The King catches Isabelle's eye and gives her the smallest of nods before clapping his hands twice. The conversation in the room dies immediately and all eyes turn to look at her. With a flourish of his hand, Louis gestures for the performance to begin.

The pressure of their collective gaze almost overwhelms Isabelle, so she closes her eyes and tries to imagine she is somewhere else.

She thinks about her aunt, whose singing used to draw crowds in the street and money from purses and pockets. She remembers how her aunt would stand, her head up with one hand held out as though reaching for something only dreamed of. And as she sang, people listened in mesmerized wonder, hardly able even to breath for fear of breaking that spell.

Isabelle's fear and anxiety drop away with the comforting memory. She is able to focus and her confidence returns.

As Giuseppe, sitting behind her at the piano, begins to play the accompaniment, she looks out at the faces of her audience, taking that same posture that her aunt used to take, and begins to sing.

It is her best performance by far, her voice not only hitting every note perfectly, but conveying such a depth of emotion and beauty that many of those listening find tears welling up in their eyes.

As the echoes of the last note die away, there is silence for a moment and Isabelle wonders if she has done something wrong.

Maybe they didn't like it! Have I offended His Majesty in some way?

But such thoughts are quickly dispelled as the gathering bursts into applause. Cries of "Bravo!", "Magnificent!" and even "Encore!" fill the room.

Isabelle observes all this in stunned amazement, almost unable to move and she looks round at the delighted crowd. In their midst, Louis gets to his feet, and the applause fades.

"Well, young lady," says the King, pinner her under his gaze. "I was told you had the voice of an angel, but I could never have imagined it would be quite so divine. You have enchanted us. You cannot leave us thus, eager for more. Will you sing again, dear?"

And she does. Two more songs, in fact; the reaction of her listeners increases with each performance.

Afterwards, she is invited to join His Majesty the King and his guests as they gather in another part of the palace for dinner, a room even grander and more ornate than the one where the concert was held.

She enters the room and is utterly stunned by the décor; the vast carpet, deep and rich, the tapestries hanging around the wall depicting various hunts and battles, and the gold leaf that covers almost every inch of the ceiling.

Looking along the long, oak tables around which the guests are gathered, she notices that there are only three seats, all of which are empty. His Majesty the King is not here. One of many servants – far too numerous for such a select gathering – ushers her to an empty space by the table.

Who are all these people, she wonders. Such grand faces. What am I doing here?

Her concerns are interrupted, however, as the main doors open and Le Roi Soleil strides in and everyone falls immediately silent.

Isabelle's eyes widen in surprise. Where before his wig was fairly conservative, he is now sporting a huge affair, great masses of towering curls tinged slightly red. And where before he was wearing a simple jacket, he now has long flowing robes of purple velvet and lace above bright, white stockings.

His Majesty looks like a completely different person, thinks Isabelle, and eventually tears her gaze from the King to take in the two women accompanying him. *I guess that one must be his wife,* she thinks, looking at a slender, dark-haired woman. *Which means the other one must be his mistress. Well, she has a fairly nice figure, I'll give her that. Shame about the face!*

Louis XIV takes his seat - his wife on his right and his mistress in front of him - and claps his hands. Immediately the hordes of servants burst into action and the meal begins.

Platter after platter is placed on the table, two different soups and shellfish bisques to begin, then scallops, wild duck and royal fish followed by salads, soufflé and eggs. Through the meal servants hurry around with wine and water, six alone serving the King with a single glass! Isabelle looks round at the unfamiliar food on offer and, though she feels as though she is in some strange, wonderful dream, she hesitates, worried about doing something wrong.

A few places away, a couple of ladies are watching her, clearly amused, so she smiles at them gracefully and turns her attention to the young woman standing across the table. Without making it too obvious, Isabelle copies the woman, dish for dish, drink for drink, utensil for utensil, and soon begins to enjoy the occasion.

His Majesty the King also seems to be relishing the evening, tucking in with a voracious appetite. When, at last, he signals that he has finished, the servants swoop in and clear the table in moments. Rising from his chair without a word, Louis XIV sweeps from the room, heading through a pair of large, glazed doors which are opened at his approach.

Isabelle joins with the rest of the party, following him and finds herself in a beautifully tended garden lit with torches and dotted around with more servants carrying trays of champagne and canapés.

She shakes her head as a servant approaches her with a tray.

How could anyone possibly eat anymore? she thinks, running a hand across her stomach. *I feel like I'm going to burst out of this corset at any moment!*

"I haven't seen you in here before."

Isabelle turns to see the young lady who was located opposite her at dinner.

"That's not surprising," she replies, grateful to have someone to talk to. "This is the first time I've been invited here. You?"

"Oh, I am a court lady. I spend most of my time in the palace." She smiles and holds out a hand. "My name is Babette."

Isabelle takes her hand gently. "I am Isabelle. Pleased to meet you, milady."

"Come, let's walk together," says Babette, letting go of her hand and setting out across the garden. "So how did you come to be at Saint-Germain?"

"I am a singer."

"Yes, of course!" says Babette delightedly. "You were singing to us earlier. Oh, you have a gorgeous voice, Isabelle. Where did you learn to sing so well?"

"It all started with my aunt," Isabelle explains, trying to avoid mentioning her deprived background. "She used to sing all over the city and her voice would draw hundreds of people. So, as soon as I had the chance, I started singing lessons with an Italian master."

"And how did you end up here?"

"One of the King's favorites heard me at a concert. He got me the invitation."

"Well," says Babette, clearly impressed. "You certainly seem to have been a hit with the King. He's a great music lover. And a great dancer too!"

As the two women make their way around the garden, they come across a couple of elegantly dressed men who turn to face them as they approach.

"This is my cousin, Albert," says Babette as she and Isabelle draw up in front of the men.

"Nice to meet you, milady," says Albert, bowing towards her. "You are a blossom, perfectly be fitting such a beautiful garden."

266

Isabelle looks down, uncertain how to respond. "Thank you, milord," she says at last, using a curtsy to cover her embarrassment. "You are very gracious."

"My pleasure," says Albert, peering down the neck of Isabelle's dress as she curtsies. "Definitely my pleasure!"

"Your cousin is certainly handsome," Isabelle confessed as she and Babette continue their promenade around the garden.

"Not only that," says Babette, putting an arm through Isabelle's. "He's also rich and extremely well-connected. His father, my uncle, is one of the King's advisors. He has been part of Louis' court since he first became King..."

As Babette tells her the story of her uncle's rise in court, Isabelle finds her thoughts drifting back to Henri, his face, with its elegant black moustache, almost pearl white in the darkness, his lace cuff framing those sleek hands as he tossed her the coins.

She shakes her head, trying to focus.

"... and of course that leaves Albert as one of His Majesty's favorites, a man of great influence." Babette stops and turns to face Isabelle. "You know, he could arrange you a place in the King's palace."

Isabelle stares at her in disbelief. "A place at Court?"

"Of course. If you want it, that is."

"But. . ." says Isabelle, still stunned by the idea. "But Albert is so handsome. And rich. He could surely have any lady that takes his fancy. Why on earth would he do me such a favor?"

"Why? Because he's a man, of course." Babette winks at her. "As you say, he can have his pick of the ladies, but poor Albert does get terribly bored by such easy prey. You just have to be different, that's all. Don't be easy like those other women." She flaps a dismissive hand at a nearby group to illustrate her point. "Be cold and aloof. Keep him at a distance as long as possible. That way you keep him interested. Believe me, he will *want* to favor you."

"Thank you, Babette," says Isabelle to her new friend. "You are too kind."

♣

Since the dinner party, Jean-Pierre's business has kept him away for long periods of time.

Occasionally, he is called away for several days and on these occasions Isabelle visits either the Marquis or the Vicomte in the evening and spends her earnings on the best finery Paris has to offer during the day.

Her taste is excellent and she builds up a large collection of dresses, shoes, hats, jewelry and other accessories all in the latest style, transforming herself into a very attractive and fashionable young lady.

Her gentlemen lovers are well experienced in love-making and Isabelle soon improves her skills in the art of foreplay, seduction and sexual congress.

Some afternoons Isabelle can be found at home, practicing her singing or chatting with Lucie; she's thus occupied when one of Babette's messengers finds her with an invitation to a deer hunt.

"A hunt?" Isabelle looks at the messenger in surprise. "For deer?"

"Indeed, milady. There is excellent hunting at this time of year."

"On horses?"

"Of course." The messenger pauses, noting the look of concern on Isabelle's face. Then he leans forward and says, in a low voice. "My mistress told me to let you know that Albert will be there."

Isabelle hesitates, not wishing to seem to keen, but then nods.

"Very well. Please tell Babette I would be delighted to attend."

Thankfully she has been out riding several times on one of Jean-Pierre's horses, a beautiful chestnut that is the perfect size for her.

The last time she rode it, she did quite well and even enjoyed the experience a little; though she was sore for a day afterwards.

It had all been Lucie's idea, who pointed out that riding builds up your thigh muscles, which can come in handy in the bedchamber!

So, a few days later, she mounts the horse once more and sets out for the hunt.

Quite a crowd has already gathered when she gets to the meeting point.

What fun, she thinks, *with only a little flutter of nerves. So many new people to meet; not to mention the lovely Albert, of course. Now where is Babette?*

Spurring her horse on, she soon finds her friend who trots out to great her, mounted on an impressive grey horse with a beautifully braided mane.

"Wow," she says as she draws closer. "You look stunning!"

Isabelle looks down as if to remind herself what she is wearing, a blue-white velvet riding dress, with a tall, feathered hat covering her fair hair. "Why, I thank you. As do you."

"Come on," says Babette, steering her horse back to the main gathering. "We're heading off shortly and I've got someone I want you to meet first."

The person in question is Babette's uncle, Paul, Albert's father; he reminds Isabelle of the Marquis both in age and in looks.

No sooner have they been introduced however than a shrill blast on a horn signals the start of the hunt. Immediately people spring into action, spurring their horses in the direction of the sound. Isabelle is about to follow when a large black stallion pulls up alongside her.

"Well, this is a pleasant surprise."

Isabelle turns to see Albert sitting proud and handsome on his horse, dressed in a jacket and riding breeches of deep blue.

Her heart leaps, but she betrays nothing in her face, instead simply giving him a curt nod.

"Not afraid of the action, Isabelle?" he asks her with a glint in his eye. "The hunt can be... hot."

Although she feels the desire for Albert stirring inside her, she replies without a hint of concern.

"A hot hunt is good hunt, is it not? Anyone who's afraid of an action shouldn't go hunting!" And with that she kicks her horse into a trot, leaving Albert staring after her.

The blazing sun lances through the trees and the grounds are littered with obstacles, pot holes and fallen tree stumps. Keeping up with the others proves hard work.

At one point, a small herd of wild boar charging through the undergrowth, upsetting a number of horses.

Well, this is not as fun as I hoped it would be, Isabelle groans, holding on tight and gripping her mount with her knees, feeling the sweat on its neck and the motion of its muscles as it negotiates its way through the forest. *At least Albert is here. It gives me a chance to work on* my *hunt!*

It is late afternoon before the hunt is over; a large stag is trapped by a group of the riders and taken down with a single arrow through the heart.

Isabelle looks at its lifeless form as it is carried into a grassy glade and finds herself saddened to see so magnificent a creature, its branching antlers strong and wide, killed for nothing more than fun.

The sight of it hardens Isabelle in her own hunt for Albert's affection.

I too can catch a great quarry, she tells herself. *Can't I?*

Servants hurry backwards and forwards through the glade laying out chairs and a vast array of food that looks more like a banquet than a picnic.

Isabelle takes a seat between Babette and her uncle and Albert sits down opposite her.

To her delight, Albert glowers from across the glade as his father spends the entire meal flirting with Isabelle and paying her endless compliments; the young man's face betrays unconcealed jealousy.

"Well, my dear," says Babette, leaning across to whisper into Isabelle's ear. "It seems your arrow has hit the target!"

Chapter Twenty

*W*hat's *keeping him?* Isabelle wonders as she paces around her room in frustration. *It's been six days since the hunt and still no word from Albert. Maybe Babette was wrong. I might have missed my target after all.*

Her thoughts are interrupted by a knock at the front door and she hurries from the room, reaching it before Lucie.

She flings the door open to see a smartly-dressed messenger who produces a pink envelope and holds it out to her.

"A letter for you, milady," he says.

Isabelle takes it and, staring down at the paper in her hands, shuts the door without a word.

"Well, it looks like you have an admirer, my dear," says Lucie, peering over her shoulder. "I bet you it's scented."

Isabelle lifts it to her nose to smell it, coughing almost immediately. "That's a bet you'd win. It's definitely been scented!"

"Yes, with a whole bottle of eau de toilette, I shouldn't wonder!" Lucie pauses as her friend sniffs at the envelope again. "Come on then. Open it!"

Running a finger under the front flap, Isabelle finds a single sheet of pink, expensive-looking paper with a short message written in a fine, elegant hand.

"It's from Albert," she says.

"Of course it is," says Lucie, as though this was obvious to her. "What does it say?"

"My dearest lady," reads Isabelle, running a finger across the page as she does so. "Ever since we first met only a handful of days ago I have found my thoughts turning and returning to you. You have enchanted me, Isabelle, my love - captivated me with your eyes and stolen my heart with your beauty. You are Venus, a pearl from the sea. You are Aphrodite, born from the watery depths. I bow before you. What else can I do? I bend my knee to you and beg of you to write even a single word in response. Only then will I know peace again, only then will I be free. Albert."

She feels weaker at each line. She wants nothing more than to fulfill her dreams of being with such a young, elegant and attractive man as Albert.

All her previous lovers have been much older than her and, above all, she longs for a real romance. Her body aches with love for his strong young body; to touch him, to hold him, to join with him. She remembers his handsome features and how noble he looked on his black stallion and a dreamy smile creeps across her face.

"Ahem."

Isabelle snaps back to the present, suddenly remembering where she is.

"Sorry," she says. "I drifted off a little there."

"I'm not surprised," says Lucie. "But remember what Babette told you. You've got to play it cool. That's the way to really catch a man like Albert."

"You're right, of course. Please could you fetch me some writing things and we'll see if I can send poor Albert a response."

After much consideration, and several discarded sheets of paper, Isabel finally settles on writing: "Dear Albert. Thank you for your kind words. However, they are only that: words. I attach no meaning to them; words are nothing more than wind. They amuse, but they do not arouse the female senses. It is concrete actions that fan the flame and awaken desire. Are you a man of words, or one of action, Albert? Isabelle."

Albert's reply arrives before Isabelle has had time to sit down for lunch.

No scented envelope this time, just a messenger with a single request: "Meet me by the fountain in the Jardin du Luxembourg one hour before sunset."

She is so excited she has hardly any appetite for lunch and just sits there poking the food around her plate, dreaming about the meeting. The rest of the afternoon passes at an interminably slow pace, the seconds dragging past and the sun barely moving in the sky.

At last, it is time, and she hurries to the Jardin du Luxembourg, slowing down at the last street to ensure she seem neither rushed nor out of breath.

Can't have Albert thinking I'm too eager!

The sun dips low over the nearby roofs, bathing the garden in a pink glow, reminding her of the scented envelope.

There are few people to be seen - most of them walking - but as she nears the fountain she spots the solitary figure of Albert standing tall and proud, a triangular velvet hat accentuating the handsome features of his face and his blue jacket and knee breeches overhung with a long, elegantly embroidered coat in the same material.

"Good evening, my dear," he says as she approaches and he holds out a lace cuffed hand to her. Isabelle places her own into it and he bends forward to kiss it gently. "Thank you for coming."

"Indeed, monsieur," says Isabelle curtly. "Let us hope it was worth my time."

Her face suggests she suspects it may not have been. It's a good look, one she practiced in the mirror before she left, and it conceals her desire.

His, however, is written all over his face; hungry, longing as he looks her from head to toes.

Her sensual figure is covered by a beautiful black dress and a white jacket from the finest designer in Paris, trimmed with luxurious ermine from the distant lands of Russia.

Albert holds out an arm to her. "I certainly hope so. Shall we walk?"

She takes the proffered arm and together they traverse the gardens at an easy pace. Here and there they catch sight of other couples, but otherwise the place is silent and deserted.

"I am told," says Isabelle, after exchanging the usual pleasantries, "that you and your dear father are favorites of His Majesty King Louis. Is that correct?" She sneaks a glance at Albert's face and is delighted to see a flash of concern at the mention of his 'dear' father.

This game is much easier and more fun than I had imagined!

"This is true," he says. "His Majesty has indeed favored our family. But you know how these things are, such royal grace is changeable. Today's favorites can become tomorrow's outcasts at His slightest whim."

"But you are favored at present?"

"Yes," Albert nods his agreement. "At present."

"And would you be so bold as to ask His Majesty for a favor?" Isabelle asks, keeping her face as serene as possible, though she feels her heart thumping in her chest. "A favor for a friend?"

"And whom might you be talking about, milady?"

"Why, for me, of course." She frowns up at him as though she thinks him simple. "I am looking for a place in the King's Court."

Albert raises his eyebrows in surprise. "You are?" He stops and turns to face her, then a smile creeps across his face. "I see. Well, I could certainly try, milady. It will not be easy, of course."

"Don't worry, Albert," says Isabelle, placing a hand on his chest and looking up into his eyes. "Your efforts will be greatly rewarded."

His breath catches in his throat as he gazes down into her face, stunned by her beauty and the warmth of her body as it draws against his.

"I assure you, milady, I will move heaven and earth to please you."

♣

Albert is as good as his word and, a few weeks later, Isabelle receives another letter, shrouded in a scented pink envelope. She tears it open, almost damaging the paper inside in her eagerness to see what news he has to impart.

"Careful!" says Lucie, though if anything she is just as excited for her friend as Isabelle is. "What does he say? Is it good news?"

"Give me a moment!" says Isabelle, still opening the letter. "Right. He says, 'My dearest Isabelle, as requested I have spoken with His Majesty. I waited until he was in a good mood, after an evening at the opera, and he has agreed to meet you. In three days' time, at sundown, you are to present yourself in His Majesty's private chambers. I have done all I could, milady, and I look forward to receiving the reward for my labors. Yours, now and always, Albert.'"

As the echo of the words dies away, Isabelle and Lucie do not move, but stand staring at nothing, spellbound by the news.

I can't believe it, thinks Isabelle. *I daren't believe it! His Majesty, the King of France and Navarre wants to meet me. Me! A girl from the slums and streets. It's more than I could ever have dreamed!*

"Wow!" says Lucie, breaking the silence. "Here's your chance to make it to the top. And you can make it, I know you can. But be aware, my dear; never forget that life in the King's court can be everything one day and nothing the next."

"Yes, that's what Albert was saying."

"It's true. Just keep it in mind." She takes Isabelle's hands in hers. "But for now, we need to ensure you make the best impression possible. You're going to see His Majesty the King!"

Almost every waking moment of the next three days is spent getting ready for the meeting, commissioning a new dress in the very latest fashion, ensuring her hair is just so and her nails are perfect, planning her makeup and perfume, and trying out different accessories, such as hats, stockings, brooches, gloves and ribbons.

When at last the time comes for her to head to the Louvres, the result of Isabelle and Lucie's work is evident. She looks so stunning that, although she is nervous about having a private audience with Louis, she is confident that she can make an impression on him.

After all, as Lucie reminds her, he is only a man.

♣

A smartly-dressed servant shows Isabelle into a drawing room, in the middle of which is a desk so enormous that it would hardly fit in any room at Jean-Pierre's house.

However, it isn't the desk that captures Isabelle's attention but the man sitting behind it, writing something on fine parchment with a long, elegant quill.

This is the Roi Soleil, Louis the Fourteenth, supreme ruler of France and Navarre, alone in this room with Isabelle. Isabelle stands just inside the door, watching him.

He is wearing a black and gold jacket with lace pouring from its cuffs, a jabot tight around his neck topped with an exquisite gold broach. This evening's wig is a mass of black curls beneath which his powdered face looks tired, making him seem older than his thirty-seven years. When at last he is finished, he lays down his quill and looks up to acknowledge his visitor.

"Very good evening Your Majesty," says Isabelle, parched with excitement and falls into a deep curtsy.

The King gets up from the table.

"Very good evening to you, milady. You may rise, my beauty," he says, walking across the expanse of carpet and giving her an appraising look. "I have seen you before, have I not? Remind me."

"It was here in the palace, sire. I sang for you."

"Ah, yes. The angel with the beautiful voice. I remember you." He walks around her, taking in every inch of her dress and her figure. "You are a pretty little songbird then. What else you are capable of?"

"Whatever you desire, your Majesty," she replies, then remembers a phrase she heard Lucie use with the Marquis. "I am at your service."

As the King completes his circle and stands once more in front of Isabelle, he steps close and pulls her against him with one hand. With the other he lifts up her chin and bares her bright, white teeth.

She breathes in. His body is a mixture of perfume, powder and something else belonging to the world of men.

He puts his mouth on hers, and lowers her, gently to the floor, pulling up her skirts on their way down.

When they're finished, she feels a cold breeze blowing from the door's slot and a sharp pain from the corsetry bars jabbing into her back. The King, his wig still perched on his head, but at a rakish angle, sighs with satisfaction as he climbs to his feet.

"Mademoiselle," says His Majesty, once his clothes are on and his wig is back in place. "The French Royal Court is in desperate need of good singers, such as you."

Isabelle curtsies and pulls at the bottom of her corset, which is still slightly uncomfortable. "Thank you, Your Majesty."

"Now, I welcome you into my palace. I will give an order for you to be set up with a room of your own."

♣

I can't believe it, thinks Isabelle and she travels back to Jean-Pierre's house for the last time. I can't believe how well my plan has worked out, thanks to my wonderful friends! Oh, I shall miss dear Lucie... but I am certain we can still keep in touch even when I am a lady of the Court.

Despite this resolution, it is a tearful farewell as Isabelle's things are loaded into Jean-Pierre's carriage a few days later.

"Thank you, my friend," says Isabelle, her arms wrapped tightly around Lucie. "Thank you for everything."

"It's been wonderful having you here," says Lucie through her tears. "I have loved every minute of it. Don't be a stranger!"

"I won't, Lucie. I promise."

Jean-Pierre opens the carriage door to help Isabelle inside and, for a moment, she glimpses a sad, somewhat lost look on his face, but when she looks again, he is smiling at her kindly.

"Take care, young Isabelle," he says, leaning in to kiss her on the cheek.

"You too," she replies, meaning to say more, but finding herself too overwhelmed with sadness for him.

Despite his faults, she could never have gotten so far and she knows that he is heart-broken to see her leave. But Lucie has promised to take care of him and no doubt she will help him find a replacement.

Jean-Pierre bangs on the side of the carriage and the driver spurs on the horses. As she looks back at the house Isabelle says goodbye to her former life. Then she sits back in the seat, heading to a new life in the King's court.

"Mademoiselle, your voice grows more glorious with each passing day!" says Giuseppe du Luca, clapping his hands in delight.

He is reputedly one of the finest singing teachers in Europe and he has been teaching Isabelle for the last two months.

Her singing lessons are just one part of her hectic life in court, which turns out to be far busier than she expected. Every day is filled with non-stop routine and the various official procedures of the palace. In addition to these and the daily singing lessons, rehearsals and concerts, she manages to steal a little time here and there to see Albert.

Remembering Lucie's golden rule not to spoil men, however, Isabelle maintains a certain distance between herself and her lover, insisting on meeting him no more than once a week.

And Albert isn't her only lover. In her time between the Louvres and Versailles, His Majesty the King has already made two visits to her bedchamber. These are not at all arduous, though, as the love-making doesn't last long and Louis doesn't hang around afterwards, nor waste much time on foreplay.

He does, however, always offer her a curt bow before leaving her room and Isabelle is well aware that she is not the only woman in the palace graced by the King's affections.

All the same, she thought as Louis closed the door behind him after his first visit. *It's still like being caught in some kind of dream. I can't really believe that I just made love to His Majesty the King of France!*

Her heart quickened at the thought and, in her excitement, she took a long time, that night, to get to sleep.

A few times, she has spied her friend Babette, but even on those occasions where they manage to exchange a few words, there has been no time to tell her just how grateful she is that Babette gave her this golden opportunity.

Life is just too busy!

♣

"Tell me," Giuseppe continues, looking thoughtful. "Have you ever considered performing in one of the King's operas?"

Isabelle raises her perfect eyebrows in surprise. "Opera? No, I didn't think I was opera material."

"Pah! But you are the ideal material, mademoiselle. Ideal! You are a natural."

"Really?" She looks unconvinced. "Do you mean that?"

"Do I mean it?" Giuseppe raises a hand to his face as if she has slapped him. "Do I mean it? I never meant anything so much in all my days!"

"Louis... I mean, His Majesty loves opera, doesn't he?"

"Yes, yes, yes!" says Giuseppe, waving his arms expansively. "Oh, the opera is one of the King's greatest passions!"

"And you think I could get a part in one?"

"I do not *think* it, mademoiselle... I *know* it!" He claps his hands to show that the matter is decided. "Very good! I will speak Jean-Baptiste today and make the necessary arrangements."

Sure enough, Giuseppe manages to secure her a small part in Lully's latest opera, *Atys,* that is to be performed on the King's birthday, and he works hard with her to ensure that she is ready.

Outside of her singing lessons, Isabelle spends any free time she has finding out everything she can about the opera, the scenery and set designs, the costumes and the props, the orchestra and the music.

During rehearsals, when she is not required on the stage, she sits in the wings, listening to the other parts, studying them, learning them, until she knows each one word-for-word and note-for-note.

She delights in every aspect of the opera and she feels like she is a part of something grand, something great, something truly significant. As the date of the premier draws closer, Isabelle enjoys standing on the stage long after everyone else has left, imagining the auditorium filled with people, the King seated in pride of place, all listening to her sing in awed fascination.

She pictures their delight, their applause, their adoration, and feels the excitement welling up inside her.

♣

Two days before the performance, something terribly unexpected happens. The prima donna falls sick.

At first it is thought she has only caught a cold, but it soon becomes clear that she has angina with an inflamed and swollen throat. She won't be able to perform any time soon.

Although the opening performance is still two nights away, many guests have already arrived at the palace. Then His Majesty the King and his entourage show up in auditorium.

"What the devil's going on, Jean-Baptiste?" the King calls to Lully and he hurries over, trepidation written all over his face.

"It's Fleurette, Your Majesty, the prima donna," Lully explains, bowing so low his wig slips down over his eyes. He stands and shoves it back into place.

The King narrows his eyes. "What about Fleurette?"

"She is ill, highness. She will not be able to perform the part of Cybele." He shrinks back and continues in a frightened whisper. "And I have no understudy for her."

"What!" Immediately, Louis flies into a rage, kicking over chairs and knocking Lully's wig clean off. "How can you have let this happen, you fool!" Behind him, the courtiers chatter in alarm, buzzing like an angry beehive.

"Your Majesty?" The words are spoken in such a calm, gentle voice that it cuts through the buzzing and rage and everyone turns in silence to face the speaker.

It is Isabelle.

"Your Majesty," she repeats, "I know the part of Cybele perfectly. If it pleases Your Majesty, I can stand in for Fleurette."

Isabelle makes a low curtsey in front of the King. His Majesty stares at her for a long moment, clearly considering the offer.

"Very well," says the King and turns to Lully. "I have heard Isabelle sing a number of times and de Luca has nothing but praise for her. Besides, we have no other option. You will give her the prima donna role and ensure that she fills it well. I hold you responsible."

He jabs a finger at Lully before turning on his heel and stalking away, followed by his train of courtiers.

So, a mere thirty minutes later, Isabelle finds herself in the leading role for the dress rehearsal. And after hours of practice with both Giuseppe and Lully, and a little alteration to Fleurette's costume, Isabelle sings for the King and hundreds of his guests at the opening performance of the opera.

It is a tragic love story in which Isabelle plays the prima donna role of the goddess, Cybele, and her love for Atys.

Her performance is exquisite, full of drama, desire and vengeance and, as she sings, she looks out at the audience. They are paying rapt attention. His Majesty is seated in front.

The King is known for his unmoved expression at such times, but as she catches his eye, the faintest of smiles curls the edges of his mouth. His Majesty is pleased!

And so he should be. The music, the scenery and the elaborate costumes all work together perfectly. Whatever Isabelle imagined, while standing alone on the stage, it was as nothing compared to the reception at the end of the show.

The applause is deafening, and across the auditorium people jump to their feet calling her name and throwing flowers. Even His Majesty the King stands and offers her a bow. She gapes at them, a glamorous smile on her face and feels once again as though she is in a dream; she might wake at any moment and find herself still in dirty rags, lying in the stinking slums by the river.

The sound of the crowd's adulation dies away behind her and she heads to the private dressing room to change for the evening's celebrations.

Waving away her maids, she slips herself out of the dress and is beginning to unlace her corset when the door opens. She spins round to see the King pulling the door closed behind him.

"Well, mademoiselle," the King says, walking up to her and pulling her body tight against his own. "What a performance! I hope for many more operas to be graced with your beautiful voice. Simply magnificent!"

She looks down, flattered by this praise. "Thank you, Your Majesty."

"Call me Louis," the King whispers into her ear, one hand groping her hip and the other exposing her breasts.

Chapter Twenty-one

C hampagne, my dear?" Louis offered, as they lay together naked on the chaise longue.

Isabelle's chest is still heaving from their love-making; a far more passionate affair than the previous times she has been with the King.

Reaching towards the bottle he placed on her dressing table, Louis fills two goblets. "I have something for you, Isabelle," he says, as they drink their champagne, and he rummages through the clothes that have been discarded across the dressing room floor.

Eventually he finds what he is looking for and hands her a small wooden box, intricately carved and inlaid with ivory. "Here," he says, "This is for you, my dear."

Isabelle takes it, opening it in breathless anticipation. "Your Majesty!" she says as she stares at its contents. "It's beautiful!"

Louis reaches over and lifts out the gift, a white gold pendant with a crystal clear, velvety blue sapphire set within a circle of diamonds.

Such exquisite work, she admires. She's objective, after having taken the opportunity to study some of the fine jewelry the palace has on display. *And what a gemstone!*

The pendant is suspended on a blue silk ribbon and His Majesty ties it gently around Isabelle's neck, the jewels sparkling in her cleavage.

"It's a locket," he says, and gestures for Isabelle to open it.

Carefully, her fingers shaking both from the love-making and her excitement, she pries open the delicate gold clasp to reveal a miniature portrait of the King wearing a long, black wig and a white jabot blossoming from the neck of a red waistcoat.

"Thank you, Louis," she says, somewhat stunned by the gift, but still making sure to smile at the King. "You are too kind."

He smiles back. "It matches your eyes perfectly, Isabelle."

What a wonderful present, she thinks. *And this is more than just a beautiful locket. It's a totally new status in the King's court. A status which any woman in France would kill for!*

♣

While she is very excited by the new favor bestowed on her by Louis, it is by no means the only gift she receives, although it is by far the most thrilling.

No sooner has the King left than palace servants begin to queue up at her dressing room door with baskets of flowers, perfumed letters and even a pair of star-shaped silver earrings.

Sitting at her dressing table, she opens a couple of the letters to read, more out of curiosity than looking for something special.

As she expects, they are from gentlemen admirers praising her performance and suggesting meetings which are little more than thinly-veiled invitations to their beds.

A year or so ago, this would have been a dream, she thinks, sighing and laying the rest of the letters to one side, unopened. But now I have the favor of the King and a wonderful lover in Albert. These other admirers simply don't interest me.

A knock at the door makes her jump and she calls out, "Not more flowers, surely?!"

"No flowers, I'm afraid," says Babette, opening the door with a smile. "But you'd certainly deserve them if I did. What a show! You were wonderful, my dear."

Isabelle gets up and embraces her friend. "Thank you, Babette."

"The King certainly seemed fascinated by your performance this evening."

"That wasn't the only performance he enjoyed," she says with a sly wink. "He came to visit me in here afterwards."

"Did he now?"

"Yes, he did and he gave me this." She lifts the locket that is still hanging from her neck and flicks it open. Babette leans close to examine the portrait.

"Impressive!" she says, though her smile seems oddly frozen. "A personal picture of His Majesty himself. You truly are favored, my dear. Which reminds me why I came to see you."

"What is it?" Isabelle asks, frowning slightly.

"Only that you are invited *to sit* at the King's table for tonight's Grand Feast. Of course, it's no surprise after your performance. Or should I say, after your performances!" She raises her eyebrows in mock disapproval, but behind the playfulness, Isabelle notices her friend is not looking at her as she usually does.

There is something slightly off in her manner. "Come on. I'll help you get ready."

♣

As Isabelle enters the palace's great hall, adorned in an elegant dress by another of the most innovative designers in Paris, decorated with white swan feathers contrasted with the best black pearls available, the size of the room takes her breath away.

How does such a place exist, she wonders, gazing at the chandeliers and ceiling with its intricate paintings. *I've never seen, or even imagined so vast a room. And where should I go?*

She looks up and down the hall, which has been filled with tables around which hundreds of people stand and chatter with one another.

"You're over there," says Babette, nudging Isabelle and pointing towards a raised dais at the far end of the hall where a long table has been set up. "I'll come with you."

Together they walk up the hall and as she passes each table, the heads of many of the men turn to watch her with admiration.

This pleases Isabelle, though she also is aware of many women observing her, whispering to each other with expressions varying from envy to dislike.

They reach the King's table at the same moment that the King and his entourage enter the room. A courtier sounds a fanfare, signaling everyone to attention.

"You may be *seated*, my lady," a servant whispers in Isabelle's ear. "At the request of His Majesty, King of France."

"Thank you," says Isabelle, sitting down in one of the few chairs as bidden.

This breach of court etiquette raises a few eyebrows from those with the King and they begin to point and gossip.

Babette makes her way to her own table, pausing to share a few words with the queen's lady-in-waiting, a young woman whom Isabelle has met only once before. As Louis takes his seat, only a few spaces apart from her, he claps his hands for the Grand Feast to begin.

The table is beautifully laid out with an emphasis on gold—gold platters, gold cutlery, gold goblets and gold candelabra. Even the tablecloth and napkins are made from gold thread. There are almost as many servants as there are guests again, and the stream of food and drink on each table is decadent.

To start with, there is light soup followed by roast meats of all kinds accompanied with perfectly cooked vegetables and delicious-looking salads, and red, white and rosé wines from the best vineyards across France.

Although Isabelle isn't especially hungry, she eats everything she is served, but in very petite portions, a trick she learned from being invited to many dinners.

For dessert Isabelle is given ice cream, a rare delicacy she has only ever heard about but never actually seen, let alone tasted. As she takes a first spoonful she is stunned by its texture, sweetness and mouth-numbing chill. Her delight is marred, however, as she catches the eye of the queen's lady-in-waiting, who is glaring at her with undisguised aversion.

Oh no! Isabelle thinks, immediately guessing the reason for the women's disfavor. *No! Babette told her about the present, the King's portrait.* Isabelle tries to smile at the lady-in-waiting, but the woman's lip curls into a snarl and she turns away. *This is not a good sign!*

Isabelle finds herself disturbed by this brief encounter and hardly touches the dessert wine, fruits and cheeses that end the feast.

When the meal is over, the King and his guests make their way out of the palace and gather in the gardens, which, although they are still under construction, are breathtaking all the same, lit with huge torches from the palace all the way to the Grand Canal.

Isabelle finds herself on the edge of the crowd when the fireworks begin, bursting in huge glittering fountains of light that are reflected in the water and light up the gardens in red, white and blue.

She senses someone walking up behind her.

"Mademoiselle," says a deep voice, and Isabelle turns to see a man standing close to her, his face shadowed by his large, black hat.

He bows to her. "May I express my great admiration for you? Your performance was a delight, the best I have seen and, of course, heard."

Holding out a hand for him to kiss, she asks. "And who might you be, milord?"

"I am Duke Henri Bernard de Mondo," he says, taking her proffered hand and kissing it gently. As he does, Isabelle catches sight of his snow-white lace cuffs and the elegant fingers with their two beautiful rings, and she knows immediately that she has seen him before.

It's him, she realizes, her heart skipping a beat as she realizes who he is. *The man I dreamt about so much and for so long! The man who kicked off my new life! I know it's him, without a shadow of a doubt!*

"It's a delight to get to meet you, Isabelle," he says as he straightens up. She looks into his eyes for any sign of recognition, but there is nothing. Not even a glimmer.

"You too, your grace," she replies, giving him a flirtatious look and pushing him away. "Though, maybe not so close."

He steps back a little. "Forgive me, mademoiselle. Did you not get my letter?"

"Your letter?" she asks, surprised.

"Indeed. I sent it with the roses this evening."

"Ah. I see." She thinks back to the pile of unopened letters. "But I'm afraid I received so many..."

"Oh." He takes off his hat and fiddles with it, looking embarrassed. "You are so popular, my dear."

She smiles self-confidently. "But of course, your grace." She pauses, enjoying the concern in his face. Then, with her most seductive smile, she continues, "However let's not allow my popularity to get in our way, Henri."

He bows to her again, and when he does, Isabelle looks over his head to see the lady-in-waiting's jealous eye boring into her again.

And not only hers; there are three young women around her, glaring with the same expression.

What's going on? An unpleasant chill runs down her spine. *I wish I knew what the story was with these women. But I know nothing about palace intrigues and the gossip of the King's court. Nothing. I don't even know anyone on the inside, except Babette, and I've had no time to talk about such things with her. Why didn't I make the time to give Babette a present to secure her favor?*

"Let's walk a moment," she encourages, slipping an arm through Henri's in a determined effort to distract herself from this train of thought. "So, how long are you staying here at the palace, milord?"

"Unfortunately not for long," he replies, as they begin to walk around the outside of the crowd. "I have to leave in the morning. I have urgent business with Louis de Maintenon, the King's general. However," he squeezes her hand gently to press his point, "it would be a wonderful pleasure for me to see you again, mademoiselle."

Pretending to stumble, Isabelle grips his arm. "Oh!" adding after a moment, with coquettish smile. "Anything is possible, Henri." She is pleased to notice his cheeks flush and she judges this is the time to leave him... for now.

As Lucie would say: *Once you've got them hooked, let them swim for a bit so you can reel them in all the easier.*

She stops and lets go of his arm. "If you will excuse me, milord," she says curtly. "There are some people I must meet with this evening."

"Of course," he bows and she can feel his eyes still watching her as she turns and walks away; a self-satisfied smile escapes her. *I've got him hooked! And I'm not even sure I really need him anymore.*

"Isabelle!" She turns at the sound of her name and it takes her a moment to spot Babette waving to her a short distance away. "Come here!"

Babette is standing in a company of two other magnificently dressed women.

"I want to introduce you to Lady Aurora de la Maume." Babette indicates the tall, middle-aged woman with large teeth and a face that reminds Isabelle of a short-sighted horse. "And Lady Colette de Dallos."

Isabelle turns to take in the second lady and a chill runs through her again as she finds herself staring into the face of the queen's lady-in-waiting.

"Lady Aurora," says Isabelle, getting a grip on herself and nodding to the horsey woman before turning to the other with another nod. "Lady Colette. We have met before, though only briefly."

"But of course," says Lady Colette with a charming smile that fails to reach her eyes. Isabelle examines her carefully, taking in the pleasant features and her skin as pale as the moon reflected in the canal. "And may I say what a wonderful performance you graced us with in this evening's opera."

"Thank you," Isabelle replies, conscious that both of them are examining her in return, no doubt looking for a point of weakness they can exploit.

"I know His Majesty, the King of France and Navarre, was delighted with it!" says Babette, nodding her agreement.

Isabelle clears her throat, trying her best to ignore the awkwardness of the situation.

"I'm glad you and His Majesty enjoyed it," she says. "It was my pleasure to entertain you. It is wonderful to see how fully Paris has embraced the opera." She fixes Lady Colette with her most ingratiating smile. "The King of France and Navarre seems to have developed quite a taste for opera. A real passion, you might say." A look of concern flitters across Lady Colette's face and her smile begins to falter.

I don't like the look of this, Isabelle thinks, as the women turn to general small talk about life in the court. *What is Babette doing with these horrible people? They clearly don't like me. In fact, this Colette looks at me as though she wishes I was dead or tortured at the very least! Could Babette be part of this?*

She looks around at the faces of the crowd and suddenly they all seem to be unfriendly, full of envy and malice. *It's not a good sign. I am surrounded by enemies,* she thinks, her panic returning. *I need to get out of here! Now! Why won't these wretched women go away so I can have a moment to speak with Babette?*

But none of them show any signs of wishing to depart, so Isabelle is forced to carry on listening to them, nodding occasionally whenever it seems appropriate. She isn't really paying any attention to them, though, but finds herself beginning to suffer with a headache and slight nausea. The wild thoughts that are dizzying her head do not help and finally she cannot take it anymore. *I need to go and rest!*

"Please excuse me, Lady Aurora, Lady Colette, Lady Babette," she says, cutting across the tedious conversation.

"It's been a long day and I must get some rest for fear off collapsing right here."

Babette doesn't offer to accompany her and again Isabelle feels a sickening stab of worry. She finds her way back to her room, though she cannot remember how. A couple of the servants help her on the way and by the time she gets there she feels feverish from anxiety and the sense of impending trouble.

Who can help me with the affairs of the King's court? Her thoughts dart through the faces of all those she knows, but there is no one she can turn to, not Albert, not Henri, not even the King himself. If these women are out to get her, no one can protect her. For a desperate moment she considers going to see Lucie. *After all, it was Lucie who helped me on my climb all the way to the palace. Lucie knows people...*

But not the right people. Lucie isn't involved in the King's Court and palace life herself. No, Lucie can't be of assistance now. Nor do I have time to make new friends of influence. I'm all alone, she thinks, sitting down at her dressing table and staring at nothing. *I'm in a trap like that wretched deer, in the forest, back when I was hunting for Albert.*

Isabelle's head hangs down, face in her hands, as she tries desperately to think of a way out, a way to escape the envy. She knows without any doubt that those envious women want to get rid of her and they will do everything in their power to do it. Raising her head she catches sight of herself in the mirror. *Look at me!* She rubs her eyes and looks again at the large, black circles around them. *How is that even possible in just one night?*

She goes to bed, trying to sleep, but she is shaking from her fever and spends the next hours tossing and turning, unable to settle. So she calls for her maid, Giselle, to make up a bath in her chambers in the hope that it will help stop her shivering and she can get to sleep.

Isabelle looks up to Giselle while the maid fills the tub. She's a small, round woman in her fifties, her face and hands rough from years of hard work. *Surely,* Isabelle thinks, *she must know at least a little about what goes on behind the scenes here at the palace. Maybe I can get some useful piece of information from her.*

"Giselle?" she says, as she lowers herself into the steaming water.

"Yes, milady?" Giselle's voice is as rough as her hands; the sort of voice a crow might have if it could speak.

"You've worked here for a long time, yes? And had many other mistresses before me?"

Giselle smiles, spreading wrinkles across her face. "Oh, indeed, milady. Many years and many mistresses. Before you there was Madame Yvaine de Beaumont, a lovely old dear if I may say so. And Mademoiselle Beatrice Dupont. She *was* a funny one."

"Quite," says Isabelle, interrupting her quickly. "And were any of these ladies objects of envy or intrigue? Did they ever fear for their lives?"

"Why all of them, milady." Giselle looks surprised, as though this is obvious. "I never knew a lady in court who didn't!"

Isabelle considers this before asking, "So what did they do, Giselle? How did they avoid getting taken out by their enemies?"

"Well, many of them didn't, milady."

"Didn't? But they must have tried?"

The maid picks up a lavender scented soap tablet and begins to wash Isabelle's back. "Oh they tried all kinds of things, milady. Some would get servants to taste their food before they ate it or get them to try on their clothes before they put them on, to make sure they hadn't been tampered with. Some of them even used to take a small portion of poison each day to build up immunity, though that didn't work so well for poor Beatrice."

"How do you mean?" Isabelle turns to Giselle with a concerned look. "Was she poisoned?"

"Only by herself! She took too large an amount and ended up killing herself. Sad times, milady."

Isabelle faces away again, hoping her maid doesn't see the look of despair on her face. "So there really is no obvious way to avoid getting killed?"

Giselle stops a moment and thinks about this. "None that I can see, milady," she says, carrying on washing Isabelle's back. "If court people want someone dead, they'll get to them in the end."

Thanks so much for a nice, relaxing bath, thinks Isabelle. *There's nothing for it but to get away from this place. Away from the palace and the ladies in court...* She just sits there as Giselle resumes washing her back. *And where would I go? I won't go back to Jean-Pierre's house... The slums?* She feels giddy at the thought of her filthy, old home and orders Giselle to wash her hair quickly so she can get out.

And if I do that, I'll lose everything, everything I've worked so hard to get, the King, Albert, Henri, all my beautiful clothes and jewelry, the Opera and palace. Everything!

When she is alone and lying on her bed at last, she closes her eyes and is overwhelmed by a sensation that she is falling, deeper and deeper, into a vast, black cavern.

Eyes glare out at her from the darkness. The eyes of the women in Court, Lady Aurora de la Maume and Lady Colette de Dallos, and the eyes of Babette, eyes full of scorn and envy and hatred. She wants to scream and opens her mouth, but she can't make any sound. She feels like all the air has been sucked out of her and she cannot breath.

Suddenly she bursts awake, sitting up in her bed drenched in a cold sweat, her heart beating like galloping hoof beats. Her body shivers as an icy chill envelops her, but all the same, her brief, fitful sleep has helped her.

She has made up her mind. She knows now what she is going to do.

"I'm not leaving!" she resolves, a steely resolve in her voice. "I am staying here in the King's palace, no matter what!" She finds herself finally beginning to feel calmer as the words leave her mouth. She hurries to her desk to write out a list of all her possessions, she decides to bestow to Lucie in case anything happens to her. Once that was done, she returns to her bed and settles, quickly falling back to sleep.

♣

Isabelle's daily routine begins an hour or so after the sun has risen; she emerges from her rooms looking splendid in her favorite dress, her face delicately powdered and rouged, to cover any trace of the dark shadows around her eyes and the anxiety of the previous night.

Hanging from her neck is the locket the King gave her, held in place with the blue silk ribbon.

She has been asked to join Louis' entourage as his guests are shown around the grounds of the Louvres, waited on by a hoard of smartly dressed servants. She makes small talk with other women, smiling and showing an interest in all they have to say.

In the eyes of most of them she sees the same envy that was so evident in those of the queen's lady-in-waiting, so she finds herself just going through the motions in a kind of daze.

So many enemies, she thinks, looking around her at the faces of the crowd. *So much envy built up over the course of one single night. How long before one of these vipers decides they need to strike?*

During one of the brief breaks in the day's activities, Isabelle sees Babette approaching her along the corridor.

"Good morning, Babette," she says, slightly hoping that she was mistaken about her. But Babette nods curtly and carries on her way without looking back. *All right. As I suspected, she is on their side.*

She shakes her head sadly at the thought.

And Babette isn't the only one. As the days go by, more women of Court shun Isabelle, excluding her from their conversations, ignoring her when she tries to speak to them, walking away when she approaches them.

She joins the Kings retine less frequently. This isn't only because of the attitude of the women, but because something strange is happening to her. She loses her appetite, refuse the food and drink brought to her room, and her enjoyment in life begins to wane.

A mere two months after her great performance in the Opera, she sends a message to Giuseppe to cancel her singing lessons and the sound of her beautiful voice is no longer heard in the palace rooms.

Then, a few weeks later, she cannot find the energy and the motivation to get out of bed.

Nothing Giselle does seems to make any difference and, concerned for her mistress, she sends a message to the Royal Chamberlain asking him to inform His Majesty of Isabelle's illness.

Before the sun has reached its zenith, Louis' head physician hurries in to see Isabelle, but despite his best efforts nothing he prescribes can stop her condition deteriorating and she continues to grow weaker and less interested in life.

Both the King and Henri come to visit her in the following days and they are both clearly upset to see her in such a state. Unable to greet them properly, she asks for their forgiveness, but they brush it aside. Their care and concern give her some comfort.

It is good to know that not everyone is against me, she thinks, *and that there are at least some who will miss me.*

There is no sign of Albert, but this comes as no surprise to Isabelle, who assumes he has been poisoned against her by Babette.

Little by little she grows sicker and weaker, until late one afternoon, having slipped the letter with the list of her possessions to Giselle - instructing her to take it to Jean-

Pierre's house and place it only in Lucie's hand - Isabelle feels herself fading and knows her time is over.

With shaking fingers, she undoes the blue silk ribbon tied around her neck and fumbles with the clasp of the locket. It slips from her fingers and drops to the floor. With the last of her reserves of strength, she reaches a hand down to find it, but it has landed somewhere out of reach.

Feeling under the bed, her fingers touch something that feels like the silk ribbon. Clasping it and bringing it up to her face, she sees it is a small doll.

What is most striking is the tiny silk dress it is wearing, an exact replica of the one she wore in the opera. The hair, too, matches hers. So similar is it, in fact, that it could have been taken from her own head.

"It's me!" she whispers, her voice hardly more than a croak, her breathing ragged and shallow.

In the body of the doll, in the place its heart would be if it had one, there is a single needle skewing it through. With shaking fingers, Isabelle reaches up to pull it out, but she has no strength left and her arms drop. The doll slips from lifeless fingers and the darkness closes in.

A single tear glides down her cheek and Isabelle quietly passes away.

Chicago, U.S.A. 2045

Chapter Twenty-two

*A*nn blinked her eyes open, taking a moment for them to adjust to the light of a burning candle. She's completely drained, worse than any of the previous times she had woken on this couch.

"How long was I out?" she asked, turning her head to peer at the psychic.

As before, the old woman was lighting another candle, the black one with the calming scent. "Oh, a couple of hours or so."

"A couple of *hours?*" Ann was surprised.

She felt as though she'd been out more than a year! She rubbed a hand across her weary forehead. Along with the tiredness there was a terrible sadness at witnessing yet another one of her death. She had only just come to terms with the idea that Mi had died for freedom and Ra for love, but Isabelle... why did she have to have such a tragic end? Surely her fate could have been different?

"Do you know what fate is?" Ann asked, sitting up and turning round to face the psychic.

The old woman paused before giving her answer. "Fate is simply a script that is written for you."

"And can I change that script? Can I alter my fate?"

"Of course not!" said the psychic. "No one can *change* their fate. It's written for you and only for you, for your personal way to perfection. But you can make your own choice of how you react to what is written in that script."

Ann looked confused. "You mean fate and freewill are somehow compatible? That they co-exist?"

"Exactly." The psychic beamed, spreading a network of wrinkles across her face. "Now then, dear. Would you care for some tea?"

♣

"Mademoiselle?"

Ann tried to focus on Rob's screen. This third visit to the psychic had really taken a toll on her. Thankfully she didn't have to concentrate on driving, deciding to take the tunnel and leave the directions of the car in the safe hands of her SmartDrive system.

"Mademoiselle?" repeated Rob, who was waving a hand to get her attention, dressed up in a black moustache and white jabot.

"Yes, very funny, Rob," she said. "What is it?"

His pixels rippled and he looked his usual self again. "You have a video message."

Ann sat up in her seat, intrigued. "Well let's see it then!"

Immediately the waterfall graphic on the windshield disintegrated, replaced with a beautiful bouquet of white roses against a pink background. The sound of birdsong and gentle music filled the car as did the gentle smell of flowers.

"Nice!" Ann smiled in appreciation. "Who's this message from?"

As if in answer to her question, Michael's face appeared over the roses, a charming smile lighting up his eyes.

"I wish you a wonderful day, Ann!" said his recorded voice. "Looking forward to seeing you soon!" With that, the waterfalls returned as the message ended and the birdsong and the music faded away. Ann sighed and breathed in deeply, savoring the last fragrance of the flowers before it evaporated.

Closing her eyes she allowed herself to daydream for a little, thinking back to the vision of Isabelle as she toyed with the handsome Albert, though instead of Albert's face she pictured Michael.

We haven't been in touch for quite a long while... Since that dinner and dancing in the nightclub. Ann sighed. *He left me alone then... once again in fact...*

"Who is this guy?" she whispered in irritation. "What are his intentions?" The words fell into a silence without answers as the car continued its journey through the tunnel.

"Well, that was a nice message!" said Rob, now appearing with curly blond hair like Michael's, his voice chirpy and a broad grin on his face.

Opening her eyes, Ann frowned in Rob's direction. "You're no help, Rob! I need to talk to someone who understands about these things!"

"Would you like me to find you a relationship counselor, my lady? According to my database there are twenty-seven in the central Chicago area alone." To demonstrate this, a stream of names and contact details scrolled across the screen of the E-A device.

"Thank you, Rob, but no. I know exactly who I need to talk to."

Rob's face, his hair a mass of unruly curls, reappeared, giving her a knowing look. "I'll put a call through to Nina then, shall I?"

Nina answered on the first ring and her face appeared emblazoned across the windshield.

"Ann, darling, I was just talking about you."

"You were?" said Anne, hunting for the switch to move her seat back so her friend's image was not quite so overwhelming. "Who with?"

"With dear Federico. He's such a love."

"Federico?" Ann looked up in astonishment. "Who's he? What happened to... what's his name? You've only been seeing him for a week or so."

"You mean George? Oh, he's still around, sweetie, don't worry."

"So who's Federico?"

"He's what you might call a comparison. Just a little something to lay alongside George."

Ann laughed. "Laid is right! Your ever-changing line of boyfriends will never end. Could we talk about mine for a moment, please?"

"The lovely Michael?" Nina raised her eyebrows in delight. "I didn't realize he was your boyfriend, darling. Go you!"

"Well, no. He's not. That's the problem."

Nina put on her serious face, which just made her look even more mischievous. "Tell me about it, my sweet."

"One moment," said Ann, disengaging the car from the tunnel's SmartDrive server and taking hold of the wheel. "Just coming up to my exit." Finding herself sitting too far back to reach the pedals, she fumbled around for the button again to make the seat move forward.

"Are you done?" asked Nina, her face shifting from the windshield to the E-A device. "What's the problem?"

"It's just all moving too slowly," said Ann, steering the car up the ramp to join the city traffic.

"Too slowly for what? For sex?"

"I guess," Ann shrugged expressively. "Sex, something tangible, the suggestion that there is a relationship at the end of all this. That we are more than just friends."

"Well, I can't say I'm surprised, darling. He's an archaeologist. Those boys deal in eons and ice ages, and they move about as slow as a glacier. Can't you wait?"

Ann threw up her hands and quickly grabbed the wheel again to avoid hitting a cyclist. "Of course I can wait. I've been waiting for years! And now that I've found a nice guy, waiting is the last thing I want. He's taking forever to make any kind of move. What the hell can be wrong with him?"

"He's an archaeologist, like I said. Glaciers, remember!"

"Point taken." Ann pulled up at a set of traffic lights and looked at her friend's face, still wearing a serious expression. "Tell me, Nina. In your experience how long does the average man take to get going with the physical side of things?"

"It depends, darling," said Nina, considering the question for a moment. "At one end you have guys like Graeme, you remember him don't you? The stock car racer? Unfortunately he wasn't so speedy in the bedroom. It took over a week to get him to take me for a spin! Then at the other end there's Paul."

"Paul?"

Nina smiled at the memory. "Paul the banker. Terrible bore, but thankfully he wasn't interested in conversation. By my reckoning, it was under three minutes from me walking into the bar and him taking me to bed."

Ann stared in surprise. "Three minutes!" A car behind her beeped its horn and she realized the lights had turned green. "He bedded you in three minutes?"

"Well, his hotel room was just above the bar. Classy boy, Paul!"

"So in your experience anywhere between three minutes and a week is how long we should be looking at?"

"Give or take, yes. How long has it been with Michael?"

"More than three months!" Ann shouted, thumping the steering wheel and accidently beeping at the car in front.

Nina's face disappeared from the screen, replaced by what looked like a ceiling light. "Sorry," she said, bobbing back into the picture. "I knocked the phone over. More than three months? Three months! How have you survived, darling? It sounds like torture."

"It does, doesn't it? And yet he keeps leaving me lovey-dovey video messages and wanting to meet up for outdoor activities."

"Outdoor?" Nina says the word as though spitting out something unpleasant. "A lover whose ideas of "activity" happens outdoors is no lover at all, sweetie! Your Michael is a strange one."

"He's not *my* Michael! And since he doesn't seem to want to take this relationship anywhere, I'm wondering what it is that he actually wants... He could be a spy."

"A spy? Like James Bond? Well, darling, that would certainly be something; a proper Hollywood thriller! But I thought such men were supposed to be swift workers when it comes to *indoor* activities!"

"Not that sort of spy. I mean like a competitor. Someone trying to find out what we're up to at A.I.I. and milk me for information."

"Has he tried to... milk you?" Nina laughed at the idea. But she soon went back to the conversation at hand: "Do you talk about business with him?"

"Not at all," said Ann, the frustration clear in her voice. "But I can't see any other reason for him being so damned nice to me all the time. If he doesn't want this," she gestured to her body, though Nina couldn't see most of her, "then what else could he be after? Maybe he's waiting for the right moment to hack into my computer or force valuable insider information out of me."

"But even if he was a corporate spy, he's still a man! And men only really want one thing." Nina winked at her, to make sure her meaning was clear.

"I guess... Unless he's got a girlfriend or a wife back home somewhere, and he doesn't want to cheat on her."

"Seems unlikely to me, darling. All men cheat if they can get away with it. At least, all the men I know!"

Ann sighed, slightly louder than she meant to, and was glad to see that she was nearly back at her apartment building. "I'm exhausted, Nina," she said, and sounded it. "I need to get some rest and forget about all this stuff for a while."

"Come on, darling. It'll all be all right. You'll see." Nina gave Ann a kindly smile. "He could just be a bit crappy at relationships. And let's not forget the ice ages and glaciers. Maybe he's just playing a long game. A really, long game. Whatever it is, it'll all become clear in time

PART FOUR
PEACE

Chapter Twenty-three

*C*orporate spy!"

Ann looked up from her display screen to see Linda halfway along the aisle in front of her, pointing across the office. There was a broad smile on her face and a large orange-yellow giraffe on her dress.

"Quick everyone!" shouted Linda, with a laugh. "It's a corporate spy!"

Ann craned over her desk to see who Linda was talking about, and caught a glimpse of what appeared to be a man on crutches. She stood up to get a better view, but at the same moment the whole floor burst into action with people jumping up from their desks and rushing over to surround the newcomer.

"Let me through," said Ann, weaving her way among the press of bodies. "Let me through, come on."

But she could hardly make herself heard over the buzzing chatter of her colleagues. Suddenly a hand reached out, grabbing her arm and she turned to see John hurrying along behind her.

"What's going on?" he asked. "What's all the excitement about?"

"No idea. That's what I'm trying to find out." She glanced down at John's hand on her arm, her eyebrows raised.

"Sorry," said John, releasing Ann quickly and rushing to follow as she pushed on through the crowd.

At last, she emerged in the center of the throng to find Linda with an arm around the man she had pointed at. Distracted for a moment by Linda's outrageous dress, Ann took a moment to realize that the man next to her, supporting his weight on a pair of crutches, was Peter.

"I don't believe it!" said Ann, staring at her colleague in amazement. "Look at you, out and about."

"Hi Ann," said Peter, inching forward on his crutches. "Good to see you too."

Ann stepped forward, ignoring the hand he was holding out and hugging him instead.

"Ow!" he said, but with a little chuckle, to let her know she hadn't really hurt him.

"Well. I must say you look much better than the last time I saw you, with all those tubes and machines attached."

Peter pretended to frown. "Why did you have tubes and machines attached to you?"

"Funny," said Ann, shaking her head. "I see you managed keep your sense of humor intact. Pity."

John burst through the crowd behind Ann, almost bumping into her, and stared at Peter. "Look at you! You're all out and about," he said, echoing her word for word.

Ann turned to gaze at him. "We've already done that, John."

"Doesn't he look well?" Linda said, stepping forward to stand next to Peter as if claiming ownership.

Ann caught a whiff of Linda's perfume at her approach and she coughed.

Well, whatever she's wearing it isn't French and Louis certainly wouldn't like it!

"So what are you doing here?" asked Ann. "You must only just have got been discharged."

"This morning, yes, but I wanted to let you know that the doc said I could be back at work in a couple of weeks."

Ann looked surprised. "And you couldn't just send me a message?"

"You know me," said Peter, smiling confidently at his boss. "I like to do things in person."

Ann was impressed and, for the first time, she realized that Peter would probably make a good team leader.

"Let's have a chat," she said. "John?"

John jerked to attention at the sound of his name. "Yes?"

"Which Mike is free at the moment?"

After a moment's consideration he said, "Mike-7 is free all day."

"Excellent!" Ann turned to her giraffe-covered colleague. "Linda. Please, could you help Peter into Mike-7 and give him anything he needs? I'll join you in a few minutes. I've just got a report to finish."

"It's okay," said Peter. "I can get there okay. In fact..." He lifted both his crutches off the floor and held them out to Linda. She looked around for somewhere to place the E-Panel that was forever clutched in her hand.

"Ann," said Linda, turning to her and holding out the E-Panel. "Would you mind?"

"Sure."

Having handed the device over, Linda took Peter's crutches, and he began to walk, slowly but steadily, across the office to the applause and cheers of his gathered colleagues.

Ann glanced down at the E-Panel and her eyes were drawn to a single word written on the screen: Michael. Next to this name was a group of numbers and, although she only glimpsed it for a moment, it looked similar to Michael's number at the Field Museum.

Surely not, she thought. *Not Michael and Linda!* Suddenly feeling anxious and confused, she handed the E-Panel to John and made her way through the crowd.

Back at her desk, she tried to focus on the last paragraph of her report, but it was no good. She kept finding herself thinking back to Michael and Linda.

This is crazy! It probably wasn't even his number, or even my Michael. And he's not my Michael, so what am I getting so worked up about? Have I really fallen for him? Is this what unrequited love feels like?

Unable to concentrate, she headed to Mike-7 to talk with Peter.

She was pleased to find Peter alone, with the exception of Mike's ever-smiling face, though the air seemed full of

Linda's terrible perfume, and Ann had to take a moment to compose herself.

"Right then, Peter," she said at last, sitting down on the opposite side of the meeting room table. "A lot can happen in two weeks..."

♣

The following morning, Ann took the tunnel to the supermarket, as a diversion more than anything else, since the SmartHome server sorted all of her delivery needs; she was still troubled by the same obstructive train of thought.

The night of sleep had only managed to make things worse since, once again, her dreams had been disturbed by the same strange images.

What's going on with me, she wondered. *I feel like a ship in a storm being tossed about by the waves of fate.*

"What do you know about fate, Rob?" she asked, as much to distract herself as to get information from him. "The psychic said it's a sort of pre-written script for a person's development, something that cannot be changed."

"Interesting," said Rob, nodding on the screen of the E-A device. "My sources would agree, though it's less like a written script than a program."

"Like a television program?"

"Like a computer program, similar to the one that run me. I cannot change my code, and in that sense I am restricted; I can only do what I have been programmed to do. Yet at the same time, I am constantly growing in knowledge, both through my research and interaction with you. You humans are far more complex, but your individual fate works in the same way."

Ann considered this for a moment. "So, are you saying that the script or program for my life is set? That I cannot change it?"

"Not exactly." Rob's image flickered as he took on the appearance of a professor, complete with mortarboard, gown and glasses. "Let me explain. At present you are Ann, living in twenty-first century America. However, as you have seen, you were not always this person. In former lives you have been Mi, a woman from the Stone Age, and Ra, a priest of Isis in the Roman Empire. And during the reign of Louis XIV, you were Isabelle, a girl from Paris. Correct?"

"Er, yeah," said Ann, impressed. "Nice summary. But what has this to do with fate?"

"You will recall our conversation about Karma?"

"Of course. It's the effect that one life has on the next, yes?"

"Correct!" Rob's hand appeared on the screen and stuck a gold star in the corner. "Now imagine I have a bug in my programming."

Ann smiled. "That's not hard. Especially when you look like that!"

"If I had a bug," he continued, ignoring her, "which I don't, of course, you would get your guys to go into the program and fix the code, yes?"

"I guess so."

"And then you would upgrade me, so I had a new bug-free program; a new life, if you like."

"Are you saying that's what I've done as I've gone from one life to another?" said Ann. "I've been upgraded?"

"Exactly," said Rob, beaming at her and sticking another gold star in the corner of the screen.

But Ann was unconvinced. "So who upgrades me?" she asked. "Who fixes the bugs in my program?"

"Well you do, of course! When you use your Free Will to make correct choices, you are working to upgrade or develop yourself, shaping your own program, your own fate."

Ann thought about this as she disconnected from the tunnel's SmartDrive system and headed towards the exit. Could this really be true? Had her life in twenty-first century America really been shaped by the lives of Mi, Ra and Isabelle? Had there been other lives in more recent history that had also affected her life now?

"So let me just get this straight," she said, merging with the Chicago traffic. "My fate is already set, but it has been shaped by my Free Will, the choices I've made in past lives. Is that it?"

"Exactly," said Rob. "The reason your Creator gave you Free Will in the first place was to make you each different, unique individuals instead of uniform robots produced in some divine mold." He put on a sad face. "Unfortunately I have run out of gold stars."

"Pity," said Ann with a smile. "I was doing rather well! Explain more about the correlation between fate and Free Will. How exactly do they work together?"

Rob seemed to ponder this for a moment, though Ann knew this was just part of his programming; he could analyze many terabytes of data in a fraction of a second.

"Fate and Free Will work together well. You've been given Free Will so you can choose your personal direction, but your choice does not remove the next milestone of your fate. You still have to come that next programmed point." Rob eyed her from the screen, noting the thoughtful look on her face. "Consider this," he continued. "We are on our way to the supermarket, which, if you turn right at the next set of lights, we will approach from the south entrance. However, if you choose to turn left instead, you will end up approaching the same shop from the north. However, your purchases will not be affected by this and you will still end up going to the shop. This is similar to fate and Free Will. You cannot escape your fate, but you can choose *how* you face it."

As he finished, Ann found herself at the traffic lights in question and looked in each direction. "So what difference does it make to me in the course of my life if I choose now to go right or left?"

"Well, as far as your soul is concerned—that being the part of you that goes from life to life throughout your spiritual existence—it's not so much about right or left as it is about good or evil," said Rob. "However," he added, with a wink, "turning right would bring us to the supermarket almost 5 minutes quicker than turning left."

"Thanks," said Ann, pulling away to the right. "Carry on. What difference does good and evil make to my soul, then?"

"This is where Nirvana comes in. By choosing what is good, your soul is enlarged, progressing towards enlightenment and ultimate redemption. But when you choose evil instead, your soul becomes darker, heavier, heading deeper into the gloom of brutality."

Ann turned the car into the parking lot and eased it into a space. Switching off the engine, she picked up the E-A device to give Rob her full attention. "It sounds like we're talking more about *spiritual* choices, rather than deciding which way to head to the shops?"

"Quite," said Rob, his screen rippling as he took on his usual form.

"So what effect do these spiritual choices have on a person in a material sense?"

"My sources tell me that as you progress towards enlightenment, by making choices for good, your eyes are more open, able to see things which you would never have noticed before. You gain a greater understanding, broader insight, a heightened ability to see what is good and evil, and making the right choices become easier. On the other hand, choosing darkness affects every area of a person's life for the worse. Their insight is narrowed, and their capacity for vision and creativity are diminished."

"So making the right choices is pretty important!" said Ann. "How can I ensure I don't end up making the wrong decision?"

"There are various opinions on this matter. Some say the most important thing is to create personal values for yourself. Another is simply to be sensitive to yourself; listen to your true self."

Ann raised her eyebrows. "Well, that may sound simple to you, Rob, but I wouldn't know where to start!"

"My research suggests it may be simpler than you think, my lady. Take the time for solitude and silence, get away from the noise of other people and the constant drone of the media. Then, you can consider your choices more clearly."

Ann considered this, and couldn't remember the last time she was ever really quiet or immobile. "Interesting," she said. "I'll have to give that a shot sometime."

"Not right now though," said Rob, his face fading from the screen. "You have a call."

"Ann!" It was Tomo. "What are you up to?"

"Just shopping," said Ann, pointing to the supermarket, despite the fact Tomo couldn't see it from the camera.

"I need to see you. Come and meet me at Café Sky."

Ann was taken aback slightly by the urgency in his voice. "What, now?"

"Yes, now. I'll be there in fifteen minutes."

"But I'm—" she began, but the screen went blank.

Tomo had gone.

What on earth could be wrong with Tomo? Ann thought to herself as she pulled her car up at the sidewalk and headed towards the Café Sky. *Has something happened to him? Has he been fired? That would be terrible news, indeed, after the amazing work he's done on the 3D imaging for the E-A device.*

Something strange certainly seemed to be going on.

She pushed open the café door and her eyes took a moment to adjust to the subdued lighting inside.

The café's domed roof was emblazoned with a panorama simulating a night sky. Stars twinkled in familiar patterns and, at the center, a full moon glowed a cold white light. The display began to change before her eyes; the black sheet of night shifted through shades of blue, dark to light, until it reached the azure of a summer day, the stars replaced by small, fluffy clouds, the moon by the fierce face of the sun.

A movement across the café caught her eye and Ann dropped her gaze to see Tomo waving at her.

He was dressed in a black, sharp three-piece suit. A smart tie emerged from beneath the conventional white collar of his shirt and he had a dark fedora perched on his head, casting a shadow across his eyes.

Somehow, all these odd items of clothing suited him very well and Ann once again considered how attractive he was.

But the whole effect was pretty bizarre - the sort that Ann had rarely ever seen outside of an old photograph.

"What's this, a fancy dress party?" she said, walking up to his table. "Even lawyers stopped wearing ties years ago. As for that weird hat... did you join an amateur dramatics group or something?"

Tomo looked completely unfazed by her playful sarcasm and leaned back in his chair smiling at her as though he didn't have a care in the world.

"Or something," he said with an easy smile. "I like to dress appropriately for the occasion, and today is a very special day! Please sit down."

Ann took the other seat at the table and looked at him over interlaced fingers. "So what's the big rush?"

"This!" said Tomo, placing what looked to Ann like a slim version of Linda's E-Panel on the table.

"Okay." Ann frowned, unsure what to make of it. "So what?"

In answer to her question, a hologram appeared in the air between them. It was a head and, to Ann's amazement, she realized it was Rob. It smiled at her and it looked so real that she found herself pushing her chair back slightly, finding the head a little creepy.

She peered around it to look at Tomo. "This is... incredible! Is this a holographic version of the E-Assistant? You kept this quiet."

"I wanted to wait until it was just right," he said, his eyes twinkling with excitement. "I was thinking this would make a nice upgrade to our product. Watch this."

He tapped the device on the table and Ann stared in wonder as Rob's head bobbed off across the restaurant, peeping behind the counter where the barista was busy making coffee, then zooming behind a plant before swinging back to hover over the table again.

"It's not tethered to the device," Tomo explained. "In fact, it can move up to a hundred meters from it in any direction."

"Really?" She laughed as she thought of Rob's head bursting through the wall of a dark alley and scaring the people walking along it. "We would have to change the terms and conditions for our users!"

Tomo tapped the device again and the head vanished. "So you like it then?"

"Tomo, I love it!" said Ann, the fascination clear on her face. "You're fantastic."

"Thank you. You're pretty amazing yourself!" he said and leant forward to stare into her eyes. "So, have I made you happy?"

Ann considered this.

She was certainly excited about what this meant for the E-A device and proud of Tomo's work. But, happy? Her thoughts turned again to Michael—to his attentive eyes, his light hair, his gentle touch. She sighed.

"I'm proud of you, Tomo. This is going to be great for our business."

"I reckon so," he said, slipping the device back into his bag and taking out something Ann couldn't quite make out. "Though it's only a prototype at the moment. It hasn't gone through beta testing yet."

"But all the same, it's years ahead of any of our competitors. It was certainly worth rushing here for!"

"But it's not the only reason I asked you to see me, or I would have called you at the office, Ann." He gave her a mysterious look as he opened his hands to reveal a small pretty box, placing it carefully on the table and sliding it towards Ann. "I wanted to give you something else as well."

"What's in here?" she asked with a smile, picking it up. "Another floating head? A real genie, maybe?"

Inside there was a gorgeous ring on which was set a heart-shaped pink ruby encrusted with small diamonds. *Wow,* she thought. *It's gorgeous! It reminds me of the gift from King Louis, and it's probably worth just as much! It doesn't have a portrait hidden inside though.* Ann tore her eyes off it to look back at Tomo. "What is this?"

"A ring," he said, the mysterious look still on his face. Ann felt a blush creeping up her face and was glad to see that the café ceiling was now displaying a sunset, bathing everything in its deep, red glow.

Somehow, Tomo still managed to look cool, even nonchalant, as though they were discussing nothing more than the weather or what they each had for dinner the previous evening.

Ann took a deep breath, pulling herself together, a small frown creasing her forehead. "Yes, I know it's a ring..."

Tomo leaned forward again, his eyes gazing intensely into hers. "It's an engagement ring."

"Wow!" She raised her eyebrows in surprise, sitting further back in her chair. "And it's a beautiful one. Who's the lucky girl?"

"That would be you, Ann."

Ann blinked, completely stunned, unable to take it in.

"Me? But..." She looked at the ring again.

It was so elegant and looked exactly her size, and the temptation to put it on her finger was almost overwhelming.

Nina was right, she thought. *Maybe my haunting dreams are just a side effect of loneliness. And Tomo is a great guy, a genius in his field. It would be so simple to just put the ring on, dissolve in the warmth of Tomo's hand and forget all about this spiritual stuff. That would be nice, like when I'm with Michael... Michael! If I choose Tomo, how can I be with Michael? What was Rob saying about making choices? We have to make a right choice in order not to be robotic?'*

"Try it on, Ann."

Tomo's voice snapped her out of her contemplation.

Watching the ruby heart glistening in the rays of the rising sun, Ann was anxiously thinking.

And how about my own heart? Isn't it fulfilled by love with Michael? Can I accept Tomo, and just throw away my feelings for Michael? No! So long as I have a gleam of hope, even at the expense of my terrible loneliness, I will wait for Michael's love.

"No," said Ann decidedly, looking straight into Tomo's astonished eyes. "No."

Her colleague's face fell and Ann realized she had never seen him looking sad before. She reached out and placed a hand gently on his.

"I'm sorry," she said, as he met her eyes again. "I can't. But thank you. Thank you for everything, Tomo." And with that she stood up and left the cafe.

Back in her car, Ann found all those unhelpful thoughts flooding back, cluttering up her mind and filling her with anxiety.

What do I do? She wondered as she buried her head in her hands. *How has everything gotten so complicated? If only things were clearer with Michael... but I don't know what his intentions are.*

"What should I do?" she said aloud.

"Well, there's still the shopping to do," said Rob helpfully, appearing as normal on the screen of the E-A device.

"Forget the shopping, Rob!" said Ann, sitting up as she made her decision. "We're going back to the psychic's house

Smolensk, Russia. July 1941

Chapter Twenty-Four

She bursts awake as an explosion rips through a nearby building. She's enveloped in a cloud of dust and a shower of stone. Coughing, she brushes the dirt off her clothes and looks around the narrow trench.

Close by, a young woman rocks back and forth on her heels, her arms wrapped around her knees.

"Katya!" she shouts, shaking the woman by the shoulder. "Katya! Are you okay?"

Katya looks up, her face confused for a moment. She tries to focus. "They told us the Germans wouldn't come here today," she says at last. "They told us! Why are they here, Lena? Why are they attacking us today? We aren't prepared at all!"

"I don't know. I guess. . ."

She pauses as another shell lands a street away, tearing through walls and shaking the ground. The echoes die away;

she shakes more dust from her hair and tries not to listen to the screams of the injured.

"I guess the Germans changed their mind. They are ruled by a madman, after all, and unpredictability is his main weapon."

"We have to get a radio transceiver," says Katya. "We need to contact command about the attack."

Lena helps Katya to her feet and together they peer over the edge of the trench. "It should be in there," she says, pointing to a canopy around a hundred meters away. "That's where it's supposed to be kept. Come on!"

They scramble out of the trench together, dirt and blood staining their uniforms.

At their right, the ground is littered with the dead and dying, victims of the bombing that hammered those nearby with a lethal blast of bricks and splintered wood. Scrabbling over the rubble they head towards the canopy.

Katya slips and catches hold of an arm, only to find out there is no body attached to it, and Elena stumbles across a young girl lying on half a door, her face spattered with blood, her breathing quick and shallow.

"Hey, you!" Elena calls, catching sight of a nurse huddling behind a nearby wall. "Get over here and help this girl. She's wounded, damn it!"

Eventually she and Katya reach the canopy where a small trestle table has been set up.

"Here it is!" she says, hurrying over to the radio transceiver sitting on it. Katya joins her and throws the switch to power it up. There is nothing. No sound comes from the radio, not even the faintest crackle of static. Nothing.

"I can't get it to work!" Katya shouts, her voice close to panic.

Elena takes holds of it and shakes it.

"Fuck!" she says at the sound of broken glass rattling inside the machine. "I don't believe it!"

She never would have dreamt of uttering such filthy curses back at home, before this terrible conflict started. Her parents would never have allowed it. But she has been using increasingly worse language in recent months - both in Russian *and* English - as long as no one else is around, since it would be dangerous to reveal knowledge of her native language.

Words have power. These may not be polite, but they help, and war is no place for civility or genteel maidens; just as it is evidently no place for glass tubes!

"This is so bloody typical of the equipment we get dumped with. No wonder the Germans are trampling all over us."

She curses again, under her breath, furious with the Soviet leadership and their cavalier attitude toward their troops.

A young sergeant, barely old enough to shave, hurries into the canopy. When he catches sight of Elena, he stops and salutes.

Oh hell, she thinks, looking at his smooth features. *What is this kid? Sixteen? Seventeen? We're trying fight off the Germans with children and broken glass.*

Another shell strikes, this time only fifteen meters down the street, showering the canopy in stones and dust. They duck for cover, but the canopy holds and the next shell hits several blocks away.

"It's busted!" says the sergeant, pointing at the radio.

"Yes, I'm well aware of that," Elena replies, the anger evident in her voice. "The bloody tubes have blown. Why wasn't this equipment checked and serviced?"

He shrugs and gestures to the carnage around them. "It's the bombing. The glass bulbs can't take the shock. It's the same with the spares. There's not a single one here intact."

"What are we going to do?" asks Katya frantically. "We have to get to a radio! We have to inform command."

"There is another radio," says the sergeant. "Without glass tubes."

Elena looks around at the empty area. "Where the hell is it, then?"

"One kilometer from here, give or take." He turns to point across the city. "That way."

As she turns to see the direction he is indicating, she catches sight of another young soldier running across the square towards the canopy.

Just then, the ground shakes as a bomb rips apart a building to the left, spewing rubble across the square. What appears to be an iron bathtub rockets through the air, striking the runner in the shoulder and knocking him to the ground. Blood pumps from where his head and arm used to be.

Elena stares in horror. *This is a nightmare! Can we possibly survive a thousand-meter-long dash across the city?* Looking back at the broken radio she realizes there is no other option. *We have to try!*

Mercifully, the German artillery shifts its focus and the sound of the bombs grows distant.

She turns to the sergeant. "How long do you reckon we've got before they start shelling us again?"

"Who knows?" he says with a shrug. "Who can predict what these bastards are going to do next?"

"And who knows when we'll get a better chance than this?"

She stops a moment, listening to the sounds of destruction moving steadily away from their position.

"Okay," she says. "We're going to risk it and try to get to that radio. Will you help us, sergeant?"

It isn't so much a request as a command; he follows her and Katya out of the canopy without a word, ducking as they embark on the terrifyingly long kilometer towards their goal.

Fifteen streets separate them from the radio station and each one is littered with rubble, the dying and the dead.

In one of them, Elena sees a small girl, two years old at most, sitting on the steps of a house, crying loudly as she grips the blood-spattered arm of her dead mother.

In another, a wall lies across the thoroughfare and, as she and her companions clamber over it, she notices a single leg sticking out from beneath the broken brickwork.

They scurry through the city, their progress marked by the constant rhythm of the German artillery, some distant, others much closer.

Dear Lord, she thinks, as the windows of a nearby building are blown out, showering the trio with splinters of glass. *Please, dear Lord, save and protect us!*

And then she sees it; only thirty meters away—the bunker that houses the radio. They have made it!

"Leave them!" she shouts, as she turns to see Katya heading towards a group of school children standing around a body; probably their teacher. "There's no time! Come on!"

With a reluctant glance at the children, Katya hurries back to follow Elena down to the bunker.

At one end the ground has collapsed and three bodies lay nearby, bloody and broken.

"Over there!" says the sergeant, pointing with one hand while the other is pressed against a gash in his cheek to stem the flow of blood. "The radio. Do you know how to use it?"

Elena frowns at him. "Of course we do!"

"Thank you, God!" says Katya, pulling out the radio and opening the metal cover. "It's not been damaged."

Elena joins her, making sure not to step on the bodies, and snatches up the headphones.

She pushes in the jack and flicks the power switch, which immediately fills her ears with the crackle and hiss of the radio. *Who would have thought it?* She thinks to herself as she begins to turn the dials. *I've never been so pleased to hear the sound of static! Now to put all that training to good use.*

Eventually, she finds the frequency she is looking for and leans down to the microphone.

"Come in, Eagle," she says, shouting over the sound of the battle. "Come in, Eagle. This is Lynx. Do you read me? Over."

The sergeant joins the two women, leaning close to Elena to try and hear the response. She brushes him away and presses the headphones to her ears. *Why aren't they replying? Why don't they...*

Suddenly, barely audible above the static and the shells, a voice answers her call. It is not clear and Elena can only pick out the words "Eagle" and "Go ahead", but she knows she has made contact with the command center.

"Eagle, this is Lynx," she repeats. "Smolensk is under fire from the south. Repeat, Smolensk is taking fire. Need—"

But whatever she is about to request is cut off as a shell strikes nearby, blasting the roof from the bunker with a deafening explosion.

Elena is sent flying across the bunker, landing heavily across the bodies of the men already lying there. She ends up on her back, the breath knocked out of her, blinking dust and earth out of her eyes as she gazes upwards into the haze.

Trying to catch her breath, she sees a patch of sky appear through the smoke and dust. It is a calm, clear blue.

Here and there small, white clouds float serenely, indifferent to the carnage below, which reminds her of the sky over her homeland in Arizona, so far away. She smiles at the thought as the darkness washes over her.

♣

She was only twenty-two when the war began, fresh out of college and living on her parents' farm in Buckeye, just outside Phoenix.

Of course, she was aware about Hitler's regime and his quest to create a worldwide Aryan race. She'd read about his hatred of the Jews, which she couldn't understand. A number of her close friends were Jews and she always found them interesting and intelligent, great to study with as well as to hang out with.

When she heard about Hitler's plan to rid the earth of Jews, she was incensed, which led her to respond to a government advert in the Phoenix Gazette, looking for young American women who were fluent in Russian and German.

This was her chance to help make a difference!

She had learned to speak Russian thanks to the fact that her grandma - who had immigrated to America with her husband the previous century - could only speak Russian and used to read her fairy tales from the homeland.

Helen's favorites were, "The Little Humpbacked Horse", "The Frog Princess" and "The Snow Maiden." They had a profound impression on the young Helen, and she enjoyed spending time imagining herself in these stories, whether a princess waiting to be swept off her feet by the dashing Tsarevitch Ivan, the frog who finds the prince's arrow and is turned into a beautiful lady or even the Snow Maiden herself, bringing warmth and joy during the long winter months.

Many nights, Helen would drift off to sleep with the sound of her grandma's soothing voice recounting these fables. As she grew older, they still fired her imagination, and her love of the mysterious country of Russia grew, too.

She began to read other stories by Russian writers. Because her parents hated the rise of Communism in the Russian land, Helen continued to study her grandma's language in secret, usually during the night, when she would lock her door and hide under her covers, reading with a small flashlight, a Russian-English dictionary always at hand.

She enjoyed learning the spelling of the words, the way they sounded, how the sentences were constructed, and how the stories flowed. The language was so unlike English, and the stories were of people and places so different from those she had experienced, she couldn't help but delight in her reading. From the fairytales of Pushkin, she moved on to the beautiful sadness of Yesenin's poetry, the powerful, new age rhyme of Mayakovski, and the depth and majesty of Dostoyevsky.

But above all these, was *War and Peace* by Leo Tolstoy; she loved it so much she soon knew some parts of it by heart.

As for German, this was the language she opted for at school due to her love of Johann Goethe.

Her German had been so good that she pursued it all the way to college and emerged as a professional linguist, specializing in this language. Many people assumed she actually *was* German, thanks to her blonde hair and blue eyes, inherited from her father's Scandinavian roots.

As such, when Helen responded to the advertisement and went for an interview, she ended up in a special branch of the U.S. military that was looking to train spies and scouts for missions in both Russia and Germany.

Over the next year and a half, Elena -as she was then known - underwent intensive military training, including skydiving, shooting, map reading, mine detection and clearance, facial recognition, memory skills and especially work with radio transceivers and cipher machines. In addition to this, she had to learn how to behave as a Russian or German officer—how to salute, march, give commands.

She proved to be an exemplary student and she was desperate to put her skills to work in the field.

"Sir?" said Helen, speaking with her instructor after class one morning. "I've heard rumors that Hitler may invade the Soviets. What are your thoughts on that?"

The instructor looked up from his desk, peering at her over his small glasses. "It seems highly likely, Helen. The Nazis and the Russians are hardly good bedfellows and it's only a matter of time before there's an invasion from one side or the other."

"But Stalin and Hitler signed a non-aggression pact; I thought they were allies. Isn't that - I don't know - against the rules or something?"

"Rules?" he let out a bark of laughter. "The Nazis make their own rules and break them as they see fit. As Stalin shot most of the Soviet command a few years back, I wouldn't be surprised if Hitler seizes his chance to attack the headless monster sooner rather than later."

Sure enough, only a few months later – just after Helena's twenty-fifth birthday – Hitler launched an attack on Russia.

There had been no warning, and the Soviets had been caught completely unprepared. Only three days after the attacks began, the Germans seized the city of Minsk. Hundreds of thousands of soldiers of the Red Army were captured.

Finally, Helen's time had come.

"We have to send an agent to Russia," said her instructor, having gathered his students the day after the news came in. "This will be a dangerous mission. This is a real, bloody war that has been started over there, and while we have the basics of a plan, this is still going to be very risky indeed.

We have decided to ask if there is any volunteer among you who is prepared to take on this mission."

Helen's response was immediate, stepping forward, her arm upraised.

"I will go, sir," she said, in perfect Russian. "I have been waiting for this opportunity! I understand the dangers and I am ready. Send me in, sir!"

Her parents were not happy when an excited Helen came home and shared the news that she was being sent to serve in Russia.

"Helen, are you serious about wanting to go to this country infected by the virus of Communism? And at a time when they are at war?" her mother asked, tears welling up in her eyes.

"It's no more dangerous than anywhere else out there, said Helen, disappointed at her parents' reaction. "At least it's not northern Africa. That's the real danger zone at the moment."

Her father, sitting in his armchair by the fire - his usual place when the day of farming was over - cleared his throat. "So what is the army expecting you to do out there? What's the plan exactly?"

"I..." Helen began, longing to share with them the exciting work of gathering intelligence behind enemy lines that she would be doing.

But the mission was top secret. No one outside the military could know, and even there, it was for the eyes of only a handful of personnel. "I can't tell you, dad, I'm sorry. You know how it is. But it's important work. Trust me. I just want you to be pleased to know that I will be involved in vital work for the good of our country."

"You want me to be pleased?" said her mother, her tears flowing freely now. "Pleased that my daughter is being sent off to war? Pleased that she is leaving and may never come back?"

Helen's grandmother, sitting in her rocking chair on the other side of the fire, had been watching this exchange in silence. But now she leant forward and placed her wrinkled hand on Helen's knee and whispered to her in Russian.

"There's no greater thing than to serve, even to die, for your country." The silence that followed these words echoed around the room, broken only by the sobs of Helen's mother.

Barely a week later, Helen parachuted into Russia, a short distance from the city of Smolensk, under the guise of a Russian officer, who had escaped from the German invasion in the Minsk region.

Her mission was to keep the United States military briefed with the strategic and tactical actions of both the Russians and the Germans. Although this was as dangerous a task as her instructor had warned them, Helen was thrilled to find herself in her grandma's homeland and to have this opportunity to serve her own country.

Apart from the uniform, all she had was a Soviet gun, a compass, a three-day ration of stew and bread, and Russian papers with her new name: Elena Mikhailovna Smirnova from Minsk, lieutenant of communications. Most people would call her Lena.

♣

"Lena!" She opens her eyes, her ears ringing, to find herself still gazing up at the patch of blue sky. "Lena!" Turning her head she sees Katya crawling towards her across what is left of the bunker, her face covered with blood.

"Katya?" she says, her voice shaking and oddly distant. "Katya. Are you okay?"

Katya reaches up and wipes some of the blood from beneath her eyes.

"Yes," she says. "This isn't mine. The sergeant was between me and the bomb, which shielded me from the worst of it." A look of sadness flickered across her face. "This is his blood, Elena. He's dead."

Aching all over, Elena clambers slowly to her feet, still dazed from the shock of the blast. *So strange, I'm still alive,* she thinks as she glances across the bunker to the Sergeant's remains. *He was only a boy! And no doubt his mum is waiting for him to come home.*

"Come on!" she says, putting an arm on Katya's shoulder to steady herself. "There's no point staying here and waiting for another bomb to land on our heads. The radio's busted. Let's just hope the message got through."

Yartsevo, Russia. December 1941

Chapter Twenty-five

The message got through. It's over! The Germans have abandoned their attack on Moscow."

Throughout the morning, this news spreads across the town of Yartsevo like wildfire, and that evening, despite the devastation and the ruins around them, the people gather to celebrate.

"Can it really be over?" Elena says while she and Katya try to get themselves as presentable as possible, considering the limited washing facilities. "It seems too good to be true."

Katya looks up at her friend as she runs a broken comb through her hair.

"Hardly *that* good, Elena! Don't forget the hundreds of thousands of our people those Nazi bastards have butchered since June. I wish they'd left sooner!"

"True," says Elena, continuing to brush her clothes. "It's not like it was in the war with France, over a hundred years ago. Kutuzov was the Field Marshal back then and he decided to surrender Moscow to Napoleon to save the Russian army."

Katya stares at her, open mouthed. "How do you know this stuff?"

"From War and Peace. The novel, by Tolstoy. Have you read it?"

"No way! It's far too thick. And to be honest I hate the stories about the tsar and all those aristocrats." Katya spits out the word in disgust.

Interesting, thinks Elena. *Russian aristocrats, the cream of the nation, people with the best education, able to speak several languages, with the best traditions and inheritance... What was left of them now? Most of them have been murdered when the tsar fell, some were forced to escape abroad and the rest were brainwashed by Stalin.*

She doesn't say anything to Katya, keeping the knowledge to herself. As long as she holds silent about such things, she is safe.

She thinks back over the five months since she arrived in the thick of the warfare.

Both she and Katya have nearly been added to the numbers of the dead themselves several times, their near-miss in the radio bunker, their narrow escape from the German's pincer movement around Smolensk and then almost being discovered as they hurried along the road to Yartsevo.

But here I am, she thinks, a smile creeping across her face. *Still alive and well, with my cuts and bruises nearly healed and my undercover status still intact!* She stands up and begins to pull on her uniform. *But let's try and forget about all that, just for tonight, at least. Let's go and enjoy ourselves!*

When they arrive in the town square, several hundred townsfolk and soldiers have gathered for the party. Everyone, from farmers to officials, from privates to officers, join to celebrate and drink to the failure of the Wehrmacht invasion.

There isn't a lot of fancy food - mostly root vegetables and stew - but from somewhere a large stash of home-made vodka has been produced; the party starts to pick up, with plenty of singing and dancing.

At first, Elena hangs on the edge of the crowd, more a spectator than a participant. She sips at the drink she has been handed - the oily liquid burning its way down to her stomach - and watch the people dancing.

Look at them, she thinks, gazing in wonder at the men squatting down and kicking out their legs in time with the music. *How skillful they are! It's just amazing!*

She begins to edge round to get a better view, and then she sees *him.*

He is engaged in conversation with an older, grey-haired officer. Elena admires his Slavic profile from her vantage point a few meters away. His dark hair is cut short beneath an army issue cap, and on his shoulder the epaulets mark him as a captain.

Suddenly he turns his face towards her, and his brown eyes meet hers. Elena's breath catches in her throat.

He looks exactly as I imaged the wonderful Prince Bolkonsky. But Andrei Bolkonsky is not real. He's just a character in War and Peace. This man, however, definitely exists!

She glances down at his chest, where two great medals have been pinned. She recognizes one as the Star Hero of the Soviet Union and the other, a medal of Suvorov II degree.

He's not only a captain, but a hero too!

Looking back up at his face, she notices him smiling at her and she decides to walk over. A few steps away, she stops, hoping that he will come to her and, he does so.

"Good evening," he says, his voice a rich baritone. "I am Konstantin."

Like the great Rokossovsky, she thinks. *Could this guy be any more perfect?*

But aloud, she simply says, "I'm Elena."

"May I have the pleasure of a dance?"

Although her heart is already pounding at the thought of being close to him, she pauses for a moment, as if considering the offer; though in fact she is trying to control her breathing.

"Certainly," she says at last, holding out a hand to him.

He takes it, leading her into the center of the square, where other couples are already dancing to a waltz played by a group of musicians.

The captain draws Elena close to him leads her in the dance; she feels a shiver of thrill run through her body as they move together.

The music draws to a close and she pulls back slightly to look at his face, lit by the flicker of the many fires illuminating the square.

Even in the tasteless dark-green military uniform, he really is handsome; his swarthy features striking, typical

Slavic nose and mouth, thick, black eyelashes and brown eyes.

He exudes confidence and calm and she finds herself being drawn in, sinking into those eyes.

It's almost magical, she thinks, as the music starts again, and they draw closer together. *I wonder if this is how Natasha felt when she first danced with Prince Andrei Bolkonsky. And tonight it is my love story, my world.*

Later that night, as the celebrations subside, Elena and Konstantin walk together, leaving the dying fires and last revelers behind them. Away from the square, the town is silent, ghostlike, and the moonlight sparkles on the frost covered buildings.

"It's not as cold as it has been the last few weeks," says Konstantin, turning to look at Elena.

"Quite," she says, watching her breath drift away on the air. "It feels almost like spring! Look here." She stops, lifting up the lantern she is carrying to better see a tree a short distance from the path. "What a beautiful fir. "

"So peaceful and sturdy," says Konstantin. "It's hard to believe we've been at war for months."

He laughs and leaps off the path, down the slope towards the tree.

"Careful!" Elena says. "It looks pretty steep!"

"Don't worry, Lena. I'm sure I'll be fine, as long as this tree doesn't fight back." He reaches up and, with some effort, twists off a low branch full of large fir cones. He looks up at her, still standing on the path, and smiles. "It's not much, I know. A lady like you deserves a whole garden full of roses, but this will have to do for now." He holds up the branch to her. "Well? Aren't you coming down?"

"I would..." she looks down uncertainly, her lantern still raised. "But I'm not sure I can manage."

"Come on," he raises his arms to her. "Trust me, Lena. I'll keep you safe."

She hesitates for a moment, then steps off the path towards him. It is even steeper than she realized and she finds herself stumbling slightly, slipping on the icy ground.

But Konstantin catches her, wrapping his strong arms around her body. She breathes him in, her face pressed against his body, delighting in his manly smell and the scent of tar soap. Something hard digs into her chin and she realizes it's one of his medals.

"What did you get these for?" she asks, fingering the medals.

"These?" he says, as though he has only just noticed them. "Oh, they're for my role in holding back the German Panzers in a tank battle, just outside Moscow."

"Both of them?"

"Well, this one," he points to the medal, "is for assuming command of the tank division when our battalion leader was killed. This one," he says, tapping the star, "is for taking down twenty-eight of the German tanks."

She looks up at him, her eyes wide and bright. "Really? That's amazing! What happened?"

"When we heard the German Panzers were heading to Moscow, I was put in charge of one of the tanks as we headed out to cut them off at Klimt. It was tough going, but worse for them than for us, I think. On the third day of the combat the commander's tank took a direct hit from one of the German shells. It blew the poor bastards to bits and caused no end of panic across the battalion. Someone had to take control, so I stepped in and tried to get things organized again."

"Just like that? You took charge of the whole division? Thousands of soldiers, hundreds of tanks?"

"Just like that," says Konstantin.

He smiles at Elena, though there is a sadness to it and his eyes have a slightly haunted, far-away look. "Though it was hardly the *whole* division. We were being swiftly whittled away by the Germans. But then we got a lucky break. We managed to ambush a column of their tanks, taking out the front two with one masterful shot each." He mimes shooting with a finger. "Once they were immobilized, the tanks behind got snarled up, with the whole lot bunched up, unable to get past. At this point, we struck the tanks at the rear a couple of devastating blows, leaving the whole column stranded, with no way forward or back. It was like shooting fish in a barrel. My tank alone destroyed twenty-eight of the German machines. It was beautifully done and that's how I got the Star of Hero."

"You hit twenty-eight German tanks?"

"Don't sound so surprised!" he says with a laugh. "It may well have been more. It's hard to concentrate on counting when you're busy looking for the next enemy, while trying to take ground at the same time. Anyway, I can hardly take the credit for it. It's Mikhail Koshkin who should have gotten the medals. He designed the T34s. We just point them at the enemy and pull the trigger! It's simply the best war machine in existence; and it's a Russian one!"

"Better than the German tanks?" she asks, as they make their way back up the slope towards the path.

"They don't even compare!" he says, helping her up. "Look at it like this. The Germans have their Panzer III and IVs. Admittedly they're pretty accurate, but their shells have hardly any effect on our T34s if they get much further away than a pistol shot." He gestures to the gun hanging from his belt then, realizing he is still holding the fir branch, he hands it to Elena with a smile. "Here you are, my lady."

She mirrors his smile. "Thank you, Kostya. You were saying?"

"Yes, so those are the German tanks. Our T34, however, is far superior. Its armor is thicker and stronger, almost impenetrable to enemy shells unless they get right up close, maybe fifty meters or so. But they won't want to get close, since we can penetrate a Panzer at fifteen hundred meters! Not only that, but the T34 can move more easily over the churned up, muddy ground. Like I said, it's superior in every way!"

"Wow!"

"Quite," says Konstantin, taking her arm as they continue their walk through the quiet town. "And when the rounds get there, they hammer straight through the Nazi Panzers. Hence being able to take out twenty-eight of them with a single T34!"

"I guess that's quite impressive," Elena teases, though she finds it hard to conceal her admiration. Thinking back to the years of preparation for her own mission, she asks, "You must have been in training for years to handle a tank so skillfully, yes?"

He laughs at the apparent absurdity of the question. "Years? As if we can afford such a luxury! My training consisted of one week being shouted at, dragged on thirty-kilometer marches and shown which lever and which button in the tanks did what. That was it!"

"One week?!" Now it is Elena's turn to marvel at this absurd idea and almost chokes on the words. "You're kidding!"

"One week for tank training isn't actually that bad! But I got three years of training as an infantry officer at the military academy beforehand. It's better than most. The vast majority of our soldiers were non-military before all this kicked off. Training and mobilizing so many people in such a short space of time is simply an amazing feat! I'm proud to be part of such an army. Our army. The Red Army."

They continue in silence for a while as they are both lost in their own thoughts.

No doubt he's thinking about how wonderful Soviet Russia is, she thinks, *and that the Red Army is unbeatable. I bet he believes every bit of propaganda they spew out. He's blinded to the fact that Stalin, the self-proclaimed "Leader of the People," and his cowardly cronies are using them as cannon fodder. Thousands of men and women, like that poor sergeant in Smolensk, all of them thrown in front of the German Wehrmacht with only a handful of decent weapons in the hope that sheer numbers will make a difference. Moscow was only really saved because Hitler made some mistakes and failed to realize just how bad winter is here, just like Napoleon. But what about next time? What happens if the Germans return when it starts to warm up again? How many good men like Konstantin will be mown down then to protect Stalin?*

She glances up at him, still silent, and imagines him in his full uniform, his strong features framed by the helmet worn by the tank commanders.

Oh, I bet he looks good in one of them!

He notices her watching him and clears his throat.

"So," he says, "what about you? Where did you get this medal for courage?" He reaches out and taps a finger on the medal Elena is wearing. An unexpected thrill of excitement passes through her as his hand brushes against her breast.

"Oh, this?" she says. "I got it here in Yartsevo. After we escaped from the Germans at Smolensk, we eventually circled our way round to this town. By then the Nazis had already settled it, so we took it back from them!"

"Really? You fought here?"

"Yes. And it was a hot fight, too. As you can see..."

Their journey across the town has brought them to an area where the devastation of warfare is only too evident. Although all the bodies have been taken away, the ground is still littered with rubble and other debris and here and there the lantern reveals dark patches, where the dead and dying once lay. Together, hand-in-hand, they pick their way through the ruins, looking around at the devastation that has become an all-too-common site.

Eventually Konstantin breaks the heavy silence.

"I heard that Stalin invited some of the British officers, Montgomery and guys like that, to come here and observe how bravely the Red Army fought. Is it true?"

"Yes. And they came at just the right time, thanks to Rokossovsky. It was under his excellent leadership that we took back the town. Those Nazi bastards didn't have a chance once he stepped in to sort things out!"

She smiles as she thinks of Rokossovsky, whom she has grown to admire and even idolize during her time in Russia. He reminds her of "The Eagle", Prince Pyotr Bagration, one of the great generals of the Imperial Russian Army who fought against Napoleon. Like Rokossovsky, Bagration was hugely popular with the people.

"After Yartsevo was taken back, the British signed an agreement with us to provide material aid in our fight against the Germans."

"Rokossovsky!" Konstantin breathes out the name as though he, too, is in awe of him. "He is one of the best officers we've ever had! And to secure the aid of the British, too. That's amazing. Did you get to see any of the English bigwigs?"

"Unfortunately not. But then, they didn't come here for public relations and I was far too busy fighting like a damn lion!"

Konstantin stops and turns to face her, his eyes wide.

Careful, Helen, she thinks, resisting the urge to close her eyes and relish the feel of his touch. *This guy is no mere foot soldier! I need to be cautious, even with such a lovely man as this.*

But Konstantin smiles, reaching up to her forehead to adjust a strand of hair that has slipped out from beneath her cap. "And I bet you were a very pretty lion, too, full of fury with your flying yellow mane and your icy blue eyes. I wish I'd been there to see it!"

Elena smiles as she closes her eyes, enjoying the feel of his fingers on her skin. "You poor girl," he says, still gently touching her hair. "You're supposed to play with children, not guns." As his fingers brush against her temples and down to caress her neck, she feels dizzy to be so close to her dream man. She gives in and closes her eyes, longing to be lost for a moment, to fly up and away from this endless war. She feels him drawing closer, his voice almost a whisper. "Lena. You are so beautiful." The desire to get closer to him, to kiss him, is almost overwhelming. "Oh Lena, what will tomorrow bring for us?"

"Who can say?" she says breathlessly, her arms wrapping around his neck gently, enjoying this wonderful closeness and giving him a chance to kiss her deeply, properly.

I want to love him, she thinks, her body singing with desire.

"Are we going to have a chance to meet again, Kostya?" she whispers, stroking his dark hair.

He reaches up a hand to twine his fingers into hers. "I'd love to."

"Look." She points towards the horizon where the sun is just beginning to cast a dim glow.

He draws close, clutching her to his chest. "Yes, a new day is coming. And we have to move out towards the southwest."

"Really?" She cannot hide the shock in her voice. "When do you have to leave?"

"This morning."

"This morning?" she says, feeling a stab of pain in her heart at the thought of him leaving.

He nods sadly. "I'm afraid so. Can I write you a letter, Lena?"

♣

"Lena!"

She bursts awake, confused for a moment before remembering where she is.

In her dream she was back on the farm with her family in Arizona, bathing beneath the warm, summer sun. They were all together—her father, her mother and her dear grandma, leaning on her walking stick and smiling toothlessly, wishing *she* was going away to see the land of her birth.

"Lena!" The voice comes again, snapping her out of the reverie. It is closer this time and, a moment later, Katya hurries into the room. "Lena, have you heard the news?"

Elena rubs the tiredness from her eyes and peers at her friend. "I don't know," she says. "What news?"

"The Japanese have invaded America. They've bombed Pearl Harbor."

"What?" she sits up, suddenly wide awake.

"It's in Hawaii," Katya adds helpfully.

"I know where Pearl Harbor is. Is it true? What happened?"

"Word just came through. A load of Japanese planes attacked Pearl Harbor. Which means the Unites States and Britain have now declared war on Japan!"

"That's insane!" she says, hardly able to believe it. "They attack the U.S.? That's suicide!"

"And that's not all. Rokossovsky says that since Germany is allied with Japan, Hitler might declare war on the United States. He can't risk upsetting another important ally!"

Elena struggles not to give herself away to Katya, but she suddenly recalls a conversation with her instructor about the possibility of an attack on U.S. soil by the Germans, some crazy scheme to create a plane that will leave the Earth's atmosphere.

"Leave the Earth's atmosphere?" she had asked. "Is that even possible?"

Her instructor had nodded. "Theoretically, yes, it is. And Hitler's got some of his top scientists and engineers on the case. If anyone can make it happen, they can."

"But why? Why would the Germans want to bomb us?"

"Well, it's not *us* particularly that the Nazis are after," said the instructor, straightening the pencils on his desk absentmindedly. "They're specifically looking to bomb the Jews, and Hitler claims that the epicenter of the Jewish capitalist conspiracy is in New York."

Helen was both shocked and fascinated by this idea. "And how's this... space plane supposed to work?"

"Well, apparently it is supposed to be able to hold its position above the atmosphere as the planet rotates beneath it. It doesn't need much fuel because the Earth does all the work. It just sits there and waits for New York to roll round, and then drops its payload!"

Helen was skeptical about the idea at the time. It had sounded crazy. But now, she is worried. The sooner she can get in touch with her U.S. contacts the better. She gets a grip on herself and simply raises her eyebrows.

"Thanks for telling me, Katya," she says. "This is good news for us."

"You bet it is! Once the Americans get stuck in from the west, the Nazis will have to pull out of Russia to defend themselves. This could be the lucky break we've been waiting for!"

Still excited, Katya rushes back out of the room, and Elena listens for a moment as she shares the news with other women in the barrack.

I guess there's no point worrying about everyone back home, she thinks as she heaves herself out of bed and snatches up her uniform. *At least I'm in a position where I can make a difference. Here, in the strange country of my grandmother, I can fight for my homeland. It makes me feel good and proud of myself. I made the right decision to come out here.*

Kharkov, Ukraine. March 1943

Chapter Twenty-six

*E*lena looks up at a sharp rapping on the dormitory door.

"Yes?" she calls and smiles as her friend, Katya, enters the room. "Is it nearly time?"

"The Captain reckons they'll be here in forty minutes or so." She pauses, giving Elena a meaningful look. "Well? Aren't you going to get ready? You haven't seen him in ages!"

"What do you mean? I *am* ready." With the piece of paper held between her fingers, she gestures to herself dramatically and says with a smile, "Are you saying I don't look beautiful?"

"Hah. As if! Well, some of us need a bit more time to get ourselves presentable." Katya gestures to herself and Elena sees what she means.

Her light hair, which was long when Elena first met her, has been cut short by someone who clearly wasn't skilled at hairdressing. And though Elena has grown to enjoy her friend's twisted sense of humor during their time together, and even her tendency to panic at the slightest provocation, she could not call Katya pretty. Her nose is slightly too long, her eyes just a little too far apart and she has a large, brown birthmark on her forehead.

"Fair point!" says Elena with a wink. "You'd better get to work."

"Very funny! Meet you out front in fifteen minutes." And with that she disappears, the door swinging slowly closed behind her.

Elena looks back at the paper she is holding, torn at the edges and spattered with old mud—her first letter from Konstantin. The second lies across her lap.

Only two, she thinks. *Two! In all the months since I last saw him, since we walked the moonlit streets of Yartsevo together. It seems almost a lifetime ago! Several lifetimes even. So many of those I've got to know since I came to Russia have died, killed in this endless, vicious fighting. Fighting that has kept us so far apart. And all I have are these two letters. They didn't have much information worth passing on to my U.S. contacts, but then these are really meant for my eyes only.*

It had only been days after their first meeting when Elena began the twenty-five day march south to the Ukrainian city of Kharkov, which the Nazis had seized the previous year.

On the journey, Elena became increasingly aware of the change in the season. The ice had long since melted away, replaced by the first flowers pushing their way up to the sunlight, and all around the land was turning from the grey of winter to the green flush of spring.

It seemed strange to think of warfare when life was bursting out all around. Meanwhile, Konstantin had been whisked away with his tank division and swept up in the counterattack to force the Germans out of Russia before turning southeast to defend the city of Stalingrad.

She looks down at his first letter. Its unfolded page so familiar to her, its words almost committed to memory. She picks it up and reads it once again.

"Lenochka," it begins, and Elena smiles at his cute, special name for her. "Lenochka, my little bluet. Words can hardly describe just how much I miss you, my darling. My heart burns for you. My body yearns for you. My every waking thought is of you, and at night I drift into the darkness imagining falling into your gentle embrace. Not that there is much time for sleep here! But at least I don't have to spend my nights in a tank anymore. We abandoned them shortly after getting to Stalingrad, since tanks are pretty useless for city-based warfare. The Germans found that out the hard way, when they tried to barge their way in using their puny Panzers. We've got some guys here who are a crack shot with a bottle of incendiary mixture—what the Finn's call the "Molotov Cocktail"—and a decent number of them make quick work of a Nazi machines! Wish you could have seen it, though no doubt you've witnessed plenty of destruction on your end."

Elena sighs, thinking back to the carnage she has seen since they last met.

Their first attempt to liberate Kharkov had been nothing short of a disaster. After months of preparation and a promising start, the Luftwaffe had muscled in and pummeled the Soviet forces resulting in casualties of over a quarter of a million.

You bet I've witnessed plenty of destruction, she thinks, with a sad shake of her head. *Enough for a thousand lifetimes. How I've survived is a mystery to me!* She looks back at the page and continues to read Konstantin's precise, Cyrillic script.

"Oh, Lenochka, my love. You would not believe the state of Stalingrad now. It's unrecognizable. It's been so badly devastated by the bombing, fires and constant fighting. I remember it before the war, such a beautiful place, a city full of promise and prosperity, with luxurious gardens and bright fountains, great theaters and music halls. I remember coming to hear an orchestral performance with my parents. We had dinner together in a popular little bistro overlooking the Volga, with live music and the best fish for kilometers around. A happy evening. Well, I found the bistro again last week. There's hardly anything left of the place. It's just an empty shell with no music, laughter or life." Elena stops again, this time to blink away a tear.

Although this is not her own land, and there has been no warfare on American soil since the bombing of Pearl Harbor, it is still truly heart-breaking to see the devastation the fighting has caused this country.

"It's day one hundred and twenty eight," Konstantin's letter continues, "and though we are getting help from the locals, it is mostly teenagers, but they know every part of this area—how and where to go, which place is which, even if the damn buildings aren't there anymore. These bastard Nazis are making us fight for every inch of land here. There are even some buildings with each floors occupied by different sides, like some bizarre German-Russian sandwich, you wouldn't believe it, my darling! Still, it means the Nazi airplanes have pulled out as they don't want to risk bombing their own troops. So, it's hardcore fighting, man to man, face to face and the Germans soon learned we've got guts! Most of the European countries; France, Belgium, Denmark; they all fell in a couple of weeks, or so I heard. Well, not us! We're still getting warm food twice a day and have plenty of ammunition. We're going to win soon for sure. I hope this letter finds you well, dear Lenochka. Yours, in love, Kostya."

My Kostya! So brave. Elena smiles again as she carefully folds the letter up and places it back on the bed before picking up the second, still lying open on her knee.

This one was sent not long after the first and Elena had received it by the time the Soviet army had begun their final offensive against the Germans in Kharkov, early the previous month. She shudders as she thinks back to those days, the massive amounts of causalities and the strain of living in constant fear of death. She wasn't as scared as she thought she would be though. *Pretty brave yourself, Helen,* she thinks as she begins to read the letter.

"What a day it's been, my love! One of the luckiest days we've had so far. My team was given an operation to carry out. It was supposed to be hard, going up against a heavily defended outpost, but we won almost without any losses. We just strolled in and took them out! You'll never guess why. Mice! Seriously, Mice. They'd been nibbling away at the electric wire inside the German's reserve Panzers and put the whole stack out of commission. You should have seen the look on the Nazis' faces when they realized. Don't mess with the Russians, even the mice fight for us!"

Elena chuckles, remembering a similar situation in Kharkov when the Soviet troops had finally broken through the enemy lines. Rats! No doubt they had been attracted by the hordes of bodies the Germans had left hanging from balconies around the city, but they had soon found their food supplies too and reduced them to a stinking mess.

The Nazis, trapped inside by the Red Army, had been forced to eat it all the same, she thinks, her nose wrinkling in disgust at the thought. *In fact, probably a step up!* She drops her eyes back to Konstantin's letter.

"As I write this, I am sitting by a nice, warm fire, fresh from a swim in the bathhouse, which was another outpost we managed to seize today. I'm enjoying the brief respite and the chance just to sit and dream about you, my beautiful Lenochka. I wonder how you are doing, my darling. Is everything okay with you? If only I heard just a single word from you. I miss you so much. After the war, when our great land is once again at peace, we shall come here together. I want you to feel the power of the great Volga river and promenade through the streets of Stalingrad. It may be little more than a pile of rubble now, like one of those echoes of ancient Greece and Rome I've heard about, but unlike those ruins, Stalingrad will be rebuilt even greater than it was before! Soon, I will see you and hold you close. Until then, I am still your Kostya, with love."

Elena smiles, a dreamy look creeping slowly across her face.

*Today's the day! Today I shall see my beloved Kostya.
Today we will be together!*

"Are you coming or what?" Katya's voice startles her and
Elena realizes her friend's face is peering around the door.
"Have you even moved?"

"Not really," she says, easing herself up from her bed and
placing the letters carefully into a small shelf. She turns and
looks up at her friend with a mischievous smile. "I'll be
doing *my* moving tonight!"

The two women hurry off to join the crowd waiting to
greet the soldiers of Konstantin's regiment. As the men
head into the city, looking weary from their long journey,
the people wave and cheer, having heard of the great victory
at Stalingrad.

"Amazing, isn't it!" says Elena, shouting to be heard
about the noise of the crowd.

Katya glances at her, still waving. "What is?"

"That these men, our boys, surrounded and captured
over ninety thousand Germans."

"I know. That's Zhukov for you. The man's a military
genius."

Elena frowns at this, not being a fan of the Soviet general.
"Rokossovsky, you mean, surely?"

"What?"

"Never mind," says Elena, whose hard work gathering
information to pass on to her U.S. contacts near Moscow
has given her a clear idea of who the truly great
commanders are in the Red Army. She keeps waving,
searching the faces of the approaching soldiers for the one
she most wants to see. "Say, when do you think they'll be
settled in and ready for visitors?"

"As soon as they can, I reckon!" Katya replies, smoothing her hair back into place as it is caught by a stray gust of wind. "They'll be keen to get welcomed *properly!*"

Sure enough, barely an hour after they walk through the city gates, looking a little less tired after shrugging off their packs and having a quick wash in the river, the heroes of Stalingrad come out to play. Katya and Elena stand in what is left of the main plaza, trying not to think about the bodies they had to cut down from the overhanging balconies.

"Can you see him anywhere?" asks Elena, peering at the faces around her.

"Konstantin? No. But I see a poor, lonely pile of muscle over there who appears to be in need of a little local care. See you!" With a quick wave back at her friend, Katya hurries off and is swallowed immediately by the crowd.

"That's just great!" says Elena, shaking her head.

"What's great?" Her heart leaps at the familiar sound of the man's voice.

"Kostya!" she shouts, throwing her arms around Konstantin's neck and planting a kiss firmly on his lips.

Eventually he comes up for air. "It's great to see you too, my love."

"Come on," she says, grabbing his hand and leading him away from the square. "Let's go somewhere a bit more private!"

He holds her back. "Might I suggest my place? I've got something I want to show you!"

At first, the couple strolls in an almost leisurely fashion, hand gripping hand, arm brushing against arm. But before long, that blissful little contact begins to burn a longing in them that quickens their step, a desire to be away from the noisy streets and watchful eyes; to be together, alone.

Their pace increases to a quick walk, a trot and finally to running along the street, still clutching each other's hand, laughing in delight at being together again.

Back in his barracks, Konstantin slips a record onto a gramophone, and Elena listens to it in amazement. It's the first music she has heard since coming to Kharkov.

"Kostya, it's fantastic! Where on earth did you manage to get a gramophone around here?"

"I brought this little beauty with me from Stalingrad! A company of snipers gave it to me after my division helped them hold back a troop of Nazis for a week."

"Really?" she stares at him in amazement. "And what were they doing with such a machine?"

"Oh, they used it to play Russian music so they could wind up the Germans. Imagine it. Here they are, piled high thanks to Hitler's insane ambitions, hungry, unwashed, frozen half to death and being picked off one by one by our snipers. And on top of all this they're treated to a constant barrage of chirpy Russian songs. Genius!"

Elena laughs, watching Konstantin slip another record out of its sleeve and load it onto the plate. "Oh, I can imagine it all too well! Still, nobody asked the bastards to come to Russia. If they want to come to our country they'd better be prepared to put up with having to listen to our music!" The music starts up again, and she recognizes it immediately. "Kostya! This is *Wearied Sun*, isn't it? By Leonid Utyosov? Oh, it's sublime. My favorite. How did you know?"

"Well," he says, slipping an arm around her waist and pulling her close to him, "it's a favorite of a lot of Russians. Everyone loves Utyosov!"

Elena enjoys the feel of his body against hers. That night in Yartsevo seems like a lifetime ago. "True," she says. "What's not to love? Though his real name's Lazar Vaysbeyn. He's a Jew, from Odessa on the other side of the Ukraine."

"Oh really? And who gave you that information, young lady?"

"One of my Jewish friends from nearby. They've been in hiding since the Germans arrived, but we made sure they had supplies until it was safe to come out again. Nice people."

"Yeah. And some real talented people among them too, like Utyosov or whatever his name really is, and plenty of others. But of course, Hitler and his Nazis think they're the great 'Master Race' and dismiss the entire Jewish race as nothing but 'Untermensch'—subhuman! The same goes for most of us, apparently!"

"And we are continuously proving them wrong!"

A strange look clouds Konstantin's face and he turns away to peer out of the window.

A short distance away the crowds in the square are busy enjoying themselves and the sounds of singing and laughter mingle on the chill evening air.

"I saw this so-called 'Master Race' in Stalingrad. Thousands upon thousands of them, filthy, stinking, covered in lice and not one of them prepared for our Russian winter. Anything they could find, scraps of cloth, dead animals, muddy paper, if they could wrap it around themselves in their desperation to try to get warm, they would. I saw men with noses and ears chewed off by the cold, fingers so frostbitten they had no feeling left in them, and they weren't even capable of undoing their pants to piss in the snow. They just sat there, shivering, with urine spilling unnoticed down their legs. So much for the Nazi dream, huh?"

Elena sighs, picturing the scene. It was not as bad here in Kharkov, since the Germans were concentrated in Stalingrad, but it wasn't much better. The brutality of the Nazis filled her thoughts. Their rotting enemies littered the streets and buildings.

"Animals!" she spits, shaking her head to dispel the images. "They're nothing but animals."

"And yet I remember one guy, after they'd all been captured and were waiting to be marched away, sharing a joke with me and asking for a cigarette like any regular guy back at home. You know we're supposed to hate these people - and there's much there to hate - but strangely I just end up feeling pity for them. I gave him the cigarette; the whole pack, in fact! I kind of liked the guy."

"I guess, when it comes right down to it, there's no 'Master Race' or 'Untermensch'. Just ordinary people. And most of these Nazis are nothing more than puppets dancing on the strings of Hitler's ambitious plans. I heard that Field Marshal Paulus asked him for permission to evacuate Stalingrad with the army while he still had the chance, but Hitler ignored him. He didn't even acknowledge the request! All he wanted was Stalingrad, the city of his worst enemy, and he didn't care how many soldiers' lives it cost."

She walks over and places a hand on Konstantin's shoulder.

"Soon, we'll win this war and there will be peace again. Come on, Kostya, let's drink to our victory!" He turns away from the window and sits on the edge of his bed as she fills two chipped mugs with a bottle from her pocket. "It's not the best," she says, handing him a mug. "But it's as good as it gets around here. To victory!"

"To victory!" he says, throwing the vodka to the back of his throat and swallowing it. He coughs a few times before he tries to speak. "Not bad. It's got a kick like a wounded mule! Fill them up and I'll grab us something to eat."

He soon returns with two metal cans filled with boiled potatoes and stew together with half a loaf of rye bread.

"Well," says Elena, sitting down and taking her share. "We're dining like kings tonight, my love!"

"One king," he corrects her. "And his beautiful queen."

She nods, acknowledging his words. "I'm so happy to see you again."

"You know, Lena, one of the reasons I survived the horrors of Stalingrad was my desire to see you. It was like a beacon guiding me through even the darkest of times. That's what Stalingrad was really about—spiritual strength, rather than military might. The Germans were fighting out of fear of their dictator's wrath, while we were fighting for our homes and the people we love." He reaches out and holds her chin, looking deep into her eyes. "Eat up!"

She blinks and turns her attention to the dinner, skewing a potato on a slightly bent fork. They eat together in silence for a while, enjoying the comfort of being in each other's presence.

"How old are you, Kostya?" she asks, placing her empty tin down on a shelf.

He looks up from his own dinner. "I'll be twenty-seven in July."

Born so far apart, yet we could be twins, Elena thinks. "Where were you born?" she asks.

"Moscow". He waves his fork vaguely as if indicating the direction of the capital city. "But my parents traveled a lot. My father was an officer in the Red Army so I ended up living in many different places."

So he'd have grown up through the horrors of Stalin's repressions and the execution of Soviet officers in the Thirties.

But she makes no comment.

"It was okay, though," he continues, "I just had to put up with a constant stream of different schools and trying to make new friends."

"Girlfriends?" Elena asks with a slight blush.

"Not really. No one serious anyway."

"Really? A handsome guy like you? Why on earth not?"

He laughs and puts down his tin next to hers. "Too busy with studies, work and sports to have any time for that sort of thing. But then I never met such a wonderful girl as you, Lena."

He takes her hands in his and they sit together in silence, enjoying the moment.

Then Kostya gets up and slips another record onto the gramophone.

"Beautiful!" she says, standing up. "I have a little treat for you as well, Kostya." He watches in silence as she lifts her foot and places it on the edge of the bed before easing up her skirt. "Have a feel."

He reaches out a hand and places it gently on her calf. His eyes widen in surprise and he runs his fingers slowly up her leg to the top of the stocking.

"Wow! Is that real nylon? Where did you get a luxury like this, Lena?"

"Oh, I have my sources," she says, thinking, *I can't tell him I brought them with me from America, but at least I can make sure he enjoys them!* "So how long have I got you for, soldier?"

He pauses, his hand resting on the top of her thigh. "Only a couple of days, I'm afraid. This is just a rest stop for me and my guys. We have to head north towards Kursk and meet up with the tanks cutting cross-country."

"Really?" Even now, in the heat of passion, Elena is on the lookout for new intelligence to pass on to her U.S. contacts. "What's the plan?"

"Who knows? General Zhukov doesn't invite me into his war cabinet. I just get told where to go and who to point the tanks at!"

"Fair enough," she shrugs, but is disappointed not to have more information to pass on. "Come on, let's dance."

As they turn around the small room, the scent of *Red Moscow,* perfume borrowed from Katya, mingling with the smell of their bodies as they press close to each other, Elena finally feels at peace, as though she and Konstantin are the only two people in the whole universe.

She looks up into his eyes. "I just want to make you happy, Kostya."

"I *am* happy, Lena," he says, his face serious. "I am truly happy now I'm with you, my little bluet."

He bends down, kissing her deeply before dancing her slowly towards the bed and gently lowering her onto it.

As he bends down to join her, she reaches up a hand to hold him back, to keep him standing, watching. She can hear the excitement in his breathing, the pounding of his heart against her palm. With almost painful slowness, she loosens the hooks on her skirt to reveal the white lace-trimmed slip underneath, a luxury she got for the price of a tin of stew from a woman who had lost her daughter.

Konstantin's eyes widen in surprise and desire as he runs a hand down the lace until it reaches her knee. She shivers with delight as his fingers begin to slide beneath the slip and she pulls him down to her at last.

"Kostya," she whispers, stroking the hair in the nape of his neck. "I want to be with you tonight. I've longed for this since the moment I saw you in Yartsevo."

"Oh Lena." He flicks open the buttons of her top, and his breath catches in his throat as he sees the smooth pinkness of her skin beneath. He bends down, kissing her eyes, her cheek, her neck, lower and lower with each touch of his lips. "I wish I could be with you forever." He pauses, pulling back his head to look deep into her eyes. "I love you, Lena."

With a hand on each side of his head, she pulls him into a kiss, and as his strong body pushes against hers all the worries and horrors of the war begin to dissolve as the pleasure wipes out everything else.

This is what she has been dreaming about all her life—the delight of being with her prince, her Kostya.

♣

In the morning, Elena wakes to find Konstantin already up. He bustles into the room carrying mess tins and a couple of chunks of bread.

"Breakfast!" he says, handing her one of the tins and perching on the edge of the bed. She takes it and looks, unimpressed, at yet another portion of stew. *That's one thing I really miss about being back home,* she thinks. *A proper breakfast with pancakes, maple syrup and bacon. God, I hate this war!*

"Did you know," she asks, setting her tin to one side, "that the Bolsheviks, under the leadership of Lenin, stripped Russia of its riches? They took the great works of art and treasures from our nation's public buildings and palaces, even looting churches, to sell what they took on the international market, all so they could fill their coffers?"

He frowns, swallowing his food quickly before speaking in a harsh whisper. "Lena, you shouldn't talk like that. I don't know what you think you've heard, but if anything like that ever really happened it was no doubt done for the good of the country, for the Party."

"Really?" says Elena, feeling irritated at this typical, close-minded way of thinking that seems so pervasive in this country. She is desperate to tell him all the things she's been thinking about, all the concerns about the Soviet leader that have plagued her day and night.

"So what about the terrorist actions carried out by Stalin? Your beloved hero bombed people to help finance the Bolsheviks, did you know that? His damaged right arm is a reminder—proof—of his part in the Bolsheviks' terrorism!"

Konstantin jumps to his feet, his bread falling to the floor uneaten. "Lena, enough! Please do not talk about Comrade Stalin in such a way! He is the Master, the Father of Russia. Anything he did for our Party he did out of love for his people! Whatever it might have been."

"Oh Kostya!" says Elena, shaking her head sadly. "I am sorry for you. Truly I am."

Chapter Twenty-seven

W ho are you, and what have you done with Elena?" Katya stands in the doorway of the Kiev Restaurant, an amused smile on her face.

Elena looks up from the murky tub, her hair dripping with inky water. "What do you think? Definitely my color, wouldn't you say?"

"Black? It'll take me a while to get used to it. What on earth made you want to dye your hair now? You do realize the Germans are pushing us out of the city?"

"Of course I'm aware," says Elena, rubbing her hair dry with a dusty sheet. "That's why I'm going black. I need to fit in here when the Germans settle back in."

Katya frowns, the smile quickly fading. "I don't understand. What do you mean 'Fit in'? Don't tell me you're staying here."

Elena lets out a short, humorless laugh. "Okay, I won't tell you."

"No! What's going on, Elena?"

"It's quite simple. I've been asked if I will remain in Kharkov and report back to command on what the Germans are up to here and any plans I can get hold of."

"A spy?" Katya's mouth, which was already wide with disbelief, somehow manages to widen even more. "You're going to spy on the Germans?"

"Of course!" says Elena, thinking back to the eagerness of her U.S. contacts when they heard that the Soviets had come to her with this request.

The Russians had clearly seen something in her that the instructor back in the States had also seen—smartness, courage, and, probably most important of all, a desire to make a real difference. A shiver of excitement passes through her at the thought of what she is doing.

"And where exactly are you going to be doing your spying?"

"Right here," she says, gesturing to the restaurant. "The Petrenko family who own this place have already been through one Nazi occupation and they're keen to do anything they can to help us. I'm going to work for them, posing as a waitress. Don't you see? It's perfect! When the Nazi officers come in to dine together, loosening their tongues with beer and vodka, I'll be right next to them, listening to their conversations."

Katya shakes her head as though trying to clear her thoughts. "But how will you get messages out to us? We'll be on the other side of the German defenses."

"Come and see," says Elena, dumping the blackened, wet cloth on a table and heading towards the rear of the restaurant. Together the two women enter the storeroom behind the kitchens, where the elderly Missus Petrenko is busy gathering supplies for the evening, and make their way down into the basement. As they do so, the sound of gunfire, which has been slowly increasing in the main restaurant, becomes muffled and distant. There, behind a stack of old crates, Elena pulls aside a pile of canvas sacks.

Katya breathes in sharply in surprise. "They gave you a cipher machine?"

"They sure did!" says Elena, pulling off the top cover to reveal the series of rotors that would enable her to send coded messages not only to the Russian command but also to her U.S. contacts. "Look at it! All this complex machinery and yet it's fully mobile, so I can move it around the city to ensure the Germans can't trace the signal. It's perfect."

Without speaking, Katya peers into the machine and runs a finger over the components inside. A look of sadness mars her usually cheerful face and, for a moment, she seems lost in her own thoughts. Suddenly she straightens up and takes a deep breath, turning to look at Elena.

"So you reckon you've got it all covered? You're ready for life in an occupied city?"

"Of course."

"I'm not so sure." Katya reaches out a hand and lifts some of Elena's blackened hair in her fingers, an unimpressed look on her face.

"What?" Elena looks around, wondering if there's something she hasn't thought of, some concern that hasn't already been thrashed out with her superiors. "What is it, Katya?"

"Your eyebrows. They're still blond!"

"Get out of here!" says Elena, laughing at her friend. "Go on! Before the Germans get any closer and you end up stuck here working as a scrubber in the kitchen!"

They both rush up the stairs and Katya hugs her friend before she leaves. "Keep safe," she says. "I'll be listening with interest to see what happens."

"Don't worry, Katya. I'll be fine. Just make sure you get out of the city alive."

Katya turns to leave and, as she pushes the restaurant door open, the sound of gunfire grows suddenly louder. Elena listens, trying to judge the distance.

They're close, she thinks, her heart jumping excitedly at the thought. *Barely a kilometer away by the sound of it. Better take care of my eyebrows and get ready!*

♣

The following morning, less than one month after the Soviets reclaimed the city, the Germans force the last of the remnants of the Red Army out of Kharkov and seize occupation once again. Missus Petrenko receives this news with a stoic lack of concern.

"Forwards and backwards they go," she says with a shrug, pausing in the act of cutting up potatoes. "First it's the Germans, then it's the Russians. Now it's the Germans again... but no doubt the Russians will be back. All this to-ing and fro-ing doesn't make life any easier, my dear, but then when has it ever been easy?"

With that she turns back to her preparations for the day, putting together a stew for customers that may never even appear. Elena watches her, amazed at the old woman's attitude.

"So you don't mind having Germans in the city?" she asks.

"It's not a case of whether I mind or not," says Missus Petrenko, waving her knife towards the front of the restaurant. "It's a case of making do. They might be evil bastards, but we've got our fair share of them whether we're at war or whether we ain't. As long as they like good, wholesome Ukrainian food and are happy to pay for it and not trash the place, I don't care who the hell they are."

Elena watches the knife slicing through the air, fascinated. "You think they'll come here, then? As customers?"

"Don't see why not," the old woman brought the knife down suddenly, slicing cleanly through a potato before flinging the two halves into a large pot of water. "They did the last time they were here and no doubt, they will again."

And she is right.

Once the Germans have settled into the city and set up their barracks in the many deserted houses around the main square, the soldiers begin to arrive—the common soldiers during the day, officers in the evenings.

For most of them, the restaurant is a place to come and escape the pressures and the reality of war. They sit together in twos and threes, enjoying Missus Petrenko's cooking, while knocking back their shots of home-made vodka or downing glasses of beer chatting about life back home and their plans for the future.

And all the while, the dark-haired waitress moves amongst them, always listening, always smiling, always ready to serve.

Everything that might prove valuable, Elena relays not only to the Russians camped behind their defenses beyond the city wall, but also to her U.S. contacts.

Despite the constant fear of discovery, she delights in her new role as a double-agent.

This is what all those months of training were for, she thinks, as she heads back from a table where two officers - beer loosening their tongues and raising their voices - are discussing news of what they call "Operation Citadel", clearly a reference to their plans for a forthcoming attack on Kursk.

It may be dangerous, and I may have to keep dying my hair with that horrible black mess, but I'm really making a difference here. Serving my country and saving lives, that's what it's all about!

Later one evening, a month or so into the German occupation, Elena is busy wiping down the bar when she notices one customer still slumped over a table in the back corner, his head resting on the table.

His hat lies nearby, its skull and crossbones clearly visible—the insignia of the Gestapo.

"I'm locking up in a minute, Herr Officer," says Elena, effortlessly slipping into German as she approaches the table. "I'm going to have to ask you to leave now, please."

There is no answer from the man except for a slightly muffled snoring.

"Sir?" she says, giving his a shoulder a gentle shake, her fingernail catching on his armband, bright red emblazoned with a large, black swastika. "Time to leave!"

The man mumbles something in a drunken slur, but Elena can't make out any of the words. She returns to her cleaning up, stacking the chairs and mopping the floor, occasionally glancing back at the man, but he doesn't show any signs of waking up.

Right, she thinks, when her chores are at last complete. *Guess I'd better help get this guy back to his rooms.*

With some difficulty, she manages to rouse the man and get him to stumble, leaning against her, out of the restaurant and to the restaurant's delivery wagon, parked at the side of the building.

She loads him into the passenger seat, an envelope falls from inside his coat and she catches it, slipping it back into his pocket, but not before she has read the name, Kriminalsekretär Hans Schmidt, written across it in neat German script.

Kriminalsekretär, she thinks. *I'm not very familiar with the ranks of the secret police, but that's a fairly senior role, isn't it?*

Once they are both in, Elena drives him across the town to the where the German officers are housed. One of the soldiers standing outside recognizes her and waves towards a building along the street, where the Gestapo have stationed themselves.

"Here we are, Mein Herr," says Elena, opening the passenger door. "All home and safe."

Hans blinks up at her, his eyes bleary from sleep.

"Ah," he grunts, gathering himself together slowly before wrenching his weary body out of the wagon.

Elena watches him straighten up, getting a bearing on him. He looks like the German ideal: tall, blond and, despite his current state, clearly very fit. She smiles.

"Go and get some sleep. It's got to be more comfortable in your own bed than on that table!"

"Ah, yes," he says, waking up slightly and rubbing the red mark on his forehead from where it had rested on the hard, wooden surface. "My apologies, fraulein."

"Not at all! You're welcome to nod off in the restaurant any time."

"You are too kind," he says, looking her up and down and slowly breaking into a smile. He hiccups suddenly and breathes strong alcohol fumes at her. "Let me show you my appreciation. How about I take you to the movies tomorrow afternoon? It's my day off."

Elena raises her dark eyebrows as she considers this. The U.S. military want me to recruit a German spy, she thinks. This is my opportunity for sure.

"Certainly," she says. "Tomorrow at the movies it is. For now, though, go and get some rest."

"Until tomorrow," Hans replies, clicking his heels and delivering a crisp salute, only slightly spoiled by knocking off his hat. He gropes for it drunkenly and shoves it back on his head. "Good night, fraulein." He turns on his heels and walks towards the doorway, stumbling as he does so.

♣

A sparse crowd of viewers files out of the hall as the movie draws to a close, mostly a few lone officers and a group of soldiers. This last group makes their way noisily along the road towards the lights of a nearby restaurant.

Elena emerges in the street and Hans offers her his arm.

"Come, Elena," he says, pointing in the opposite way to that taken by the soldiers. "I know a small café in the east of the city. Will you join me for a cup of tea with cake?"

"Thank you," says Elena, taking his arm. "That sounds lovely."

They don't attract the attention of Germans. Elena and Hans look like a couple; she a pretty, slim brunette and he a tall, blonde officer in the striking black uniform of the Gestapo. "So tell me, Hans, do you have any family back home?"

"My wife and our two children, Heinrich and Karin."

"Really? You must miss them terribly."

He nods and steers their course down a narrow side street. "Of course. But it is better they are home in Berlin rather than being here. They are safe there."

"So tell me," she says, watching him out of the corner of her eyes. "Why do you drink so much?"

Hans stops and looks at her, his eyebrows raised, and for a moment Elena worries she has offended him. But then he sighs and starts walking again.

"To help me sleep. I find it almost impossible to settle at night and drift off unless I'm drunk."

"How come?"

"No... it's a long story."

Elena laughs.

"I've just sat through a two-hour-long film about Frederick the Great. I reckon I can handle any long story you've got after watching that!"

"Fair enough," he says, but he doesn't share her laughter. Instead, his face takes on a haunted look. "I was just a kid really when I joined the Nazi party, almost ten years ago. At the time I believed we were doing what was right, both for our homeland and for our people, making Germany great again! When an opening came up with the Gestapo I leapt at the chance to serve my country, desperate to help in the fight against partisans who were killing our men out here in the east. I was told Russia was a land filled with foul smelling barbarians, thanks to their homemade vodka and cheap tobacco, nothing more than animals that needed to be put down for their own good."

"Well," says Elena, as they emerge into a large, cobbled street. "I hope you don't have the same opinion of Ukrainians!"

"No. I don't even think that about Russians anymore. Not after Bolotino."

"Bolotino?"

Hans clears his throat before he continues.

"It's just a small Russian village near Pskov, barely thirty or forty houses clustered together around a narrow strip of river. Or rather, it *was*... not any more. The few men that lived there were farmers from the kolkhoz, struggling to provide a little bread for their wives and children. There were Russian partisans holed up in a nearby forest. My team, with an SS division, was headed through the region and these partisans opened fire on us, killing a number of our men. We tried to flush them out, but nothing seemed to work. Our commanding officer, the gruppenführer, insisted we interrogate the Bolotino villagers to find out where partisans were hiding."

"Why?" asks Elena. "Were partisans in touch with the villagers?"

"I don't know, but the gruppenführer certainly thought so." Hans sighs, recalling the painful memory.

"What happened?"

"We interrogated the village leader, who was the head of the Bolotino kolkhoz, but he refused to tell us anything about the partisans."

"That's understandable."

"Quite. We promised him rewards. Then we threatened him, but when he still refused to give us any information, the gruppenführer shot the man in the head. Right there, in front of his family!"

Hans pauses, shaking his head as if to shake off the ghosts of the memory. "Then he ordered us to gather up all the villagers, including the women and children, and lock them in one of the barns. I helped, assuming this was nothing more than an attempt to scare them into giving away information about the partisans."

"I'm guessing it wasn't."

"Oh, Elena," says Hans, his voice breaking slightly as he tries to share what happened. "It was awful. Such horror! Once the barn doors were boarded shut, we were ordered to pour gasoline around the base of the walls, all of which were made of wood. And again, in my naivety, I thought this was all part of some trick to get them to tell us what they knew. But then the gruppenführer barked out the order to set fire to the barn." He turns to look at Elena, the pain of the memory evident in his face. "I couldn't do it. I couldn't even move. I just stood there staring in disbelief. And then he walked over and thrust a flaming stick in my hand and pushed me towards the barn. I still couldn't do it, though, it was so inhuman! Even with the gruppenführer screaming in my face, I didn't move. In the end, he grabbed my arm and lifted it up so the fire licked over the straw of the roof. It burst into flames immediately, and all around me men were busy lighting the petrol covered walls. In minutes the whole barn was on fire. That was when the banging began. Those poor villagers tried the break through the door, throwing themselves at it, but there was no way they could get out. It was nailed shut. I can still hear it now, the desperate prayers of the men, the screaming of the women, the terrible crying of the children. Before long it all mingled in a single frenzy of screaming as the fire engulfed them. Awful screaming, beyond anything you could imagine. That's the screaming that keeps me awake at night."

Elena realizes that they have stopped walking, both of them consumed with the horror of Hans' story. She places a hand on his, hoping to bring some sort of comfort.

"Eventually that barn door burned through and collapsed in a heap of smoldering embers. Two figures ran out from the inferno, both of them already on fire and so badly burned that I couldn't tell if they were men or women. But there was no escape. The gruppenführer gave an order to mow them down with automatic guns before they got ten paces from the barn. I couldn't do it, and had to run and throw up in the bushes. Then we gathered up the farm animals, food and the very few valuables they had before burning the whole village to the ground." He sighs, and starts walking again, heading towards the light of the café at the end of the street. "Slavic blood may not be as good or as acceptable as that of us Germans, but they are still humans all the same. They still bleed like us, feel pain like us and die like us. And sometimes, because of us, they die screaming like the people of Bolotino. And only vodka can silence them in my head. That's why I drink!"

He pulls open the door to the café, holding it for Elena to enter first. The room inside is filled with smoke, lit by the warm glow of paraffin lamps. A handful of soldiers sit in a huddle near the window, sipping tea or beer and talking in hushed voices.

"Your usual table?" says a voice through the haze, and Elena spots a short man looking up at them from behind his enormous gray moustache.

Hans nods. "Thank you, Tolya." The little man leads them through to the back of the café, which Elena is pleased to see is almost entirely deserted. One old lady, whom Elena assumes is Tolya's wife, sits at a table by the kitchen, sifting through a pile of papers. *This is the perfect place,* thinks Elena, as she takes her seat at a table against the opposite wall. *And I reckon poor Hans is ripe for signing up. I've never seen anyone so disillusioned.*

"Two teas and two cakes, please," says Hans and, as Tolya hurries off back to his counter, he leans forward in his chair, and continues in a low whisper. "I don't know about you, Elena, but I just want this war to be over, so I can go home to my wife and children and try to forget about the screams of those wretched families we butchered in Bolotino."

"So would I, Hans," says Elena, leaning forward and keeping her voice low as well. "Wouldn't you like to play your part in doing that?"

Hans frowns. "Doing what?"

"Speeding up the end of this horror."

"How?" says Hans, looking back towards the front of the café to make sure no one can hear them. "What do you mean, Elena?"

"It may come as a surprise, Hans, but I am not really a waitress. Well, I am... but I'm more than that. I play an important role in helping to stop this nightmare that Hitler started. But I can't do it alone. I need other people, people like you, to help me bring about an end to this inhuman war."

Hans takes off his hat, holding it in both of his hands, his fingers running over the insignia as he considers Elena's words. She holds her breath, suddenly anxious about her decision to approach him.

With a word, he could unmask her, destroying her work and putting her contacts at risk. She clenches her fists, praying silently under her breath.

At last, Hans looks up at her and nods. "Yes, Elena. Please tell me more."

Chapter Twenty-eight

*D*ammit!" says Elena, leaning over the small sink and gripping the edge with white knuckles. "It's been sixteen weeks and I just can't shake off this morning sickness."

She retches again, but brings nothing up.

"It will be over soon," says Missus Petrenko. In one hand she holds Elena's hair back from her face, while the other gently rubs her back. "It was just the same for me, my dear. I was sick with every one of my six children, sometimes up to the twentieth week."

Elena straightens up and wipes a flannel across her face. "That's not very reassuring, but thanks all the same."

"Well, if you're done, I'll go and make you up some breakfast." And with that the old lady shuffles out, leaving Elena with another wave of nausea to cope with.

Thank goodness I'm here with Missus Petrenko and not out on the front lines, she thinks, as she heads to her room to get dressed. *I doubt there'd be anyone there to hold my hair for me or offer me salted cucumber to get rid of this awful nausea. And this little fellow is really starting to show.*

She pulls a night dress on and looks down at her naked belly. It's not large, but the baby bump is clearly noticeable and Elena smiles as she runs a hand over the unfamiliar bulge. *If only I had some way of getting a message to Kostya. He has no idea that he is going to be a father! But what can I do? The Germans have this place sewn up; no messages get in, no messages get out. Except for my coded messages of course!*

She climbs into the usual working clothes and, pausing briefly to make sure that her blond roots aren't growing through, heads down to the restaurant. The thought of the cipher machine, which is currently hidden in a house on the other side of the city, reminds her that Hans is supposed to be dropping in soon.

Since he agreed to work as her agent, he has provided invaluable information about the German strategic and tactical decisions. Her mission is working exactly as planned.

I just wish he didn't always have that haunted look, she thinks as she begins setting out the chairs and preparing for the day's business. *I'm always worried he's about to burst into tears at any moment. After what he went through in that village, I'm not surprised he finds it hard, but he just seems a little... unstable.*

They usually meet at the restaurant early in the day, and today, when Hans arrives an hour after opening, he is almost glowing with eagerness to share his news.

"What is it, Hans?" asks Elena, having made sure that there are no other customers in. "You look like you're going to burst!"

"I have information about Operation Citadel," he says, his voice an excited whisper. "Information, and an idea!"

"The forthcoming invasion of Kursk? What's happened? Hitler hasn't decided to change the date again has he?"

"No, no. Nothing like that." Hans leans forward over his cup of tea. "We received word today of an airstrike to prepare the way for the invasion. In two weeks' time, the Luftwaffe will carry out a series of bombing raids to destroy as many of the Soviet tanks as possible, paving the way for our new, improved Panzer forces."

"Improved?" Elena raises her eyebrows in surprise and concern. "What do you mean? How have they been improved?"

"After the devastating effect of the T34s, our mechanic and designers have been working to make something better. The latest intel is that the new Panzers have much thicker armor. They are almost impenetrable, apparently. And their guns have been upgraded so they're accurate to six thousand feet, far further than the range of the T34s."

Elena breathes in sharply, her thoughts immediately turning to Konstantin. "Are you sure, Hans? The improved Panzers and the airstrike?"

"Absolutely. The Gestapo is always kept informed of the latest directives. The airstrike's definitely going to happen, Elena. In two weeks."

As she considers the implications of this news, Elena slumps down in the opposite seat, a hand on her forehead, her hair falling across her face. "Is the date already fixed?"

"Yes. It's going to start on July fifth," says Hans, still wearing his eager expression. "And remember I said I had a suggestion?"

"Yes?" Elena looks up at him, pushing her hair out of her eyes.

"Well, our intel on the Kursk region is scant at best. As far as I can tell we have no detailed maps or descriptions of the area, which means we don't know where the Soviet tanks are based."

"Okay. But I don't see what difference that makes. Once your planes are over Kursk, they'll soon spot the tanks. Those T34s aren't small!"

"They may not be small, but they can be camouflaged to hide them from the Luftwaffe." Hans looks over his shoulder to make sure it is still safe to talk before continuing. "Once that's done, the Soviets can create dummy tanks elsewhere to draw away the bombers. Simple."

"It doesn't sound *that* simple," says Elena, as she considers this plan. "But I'll definitely pass it to my contacts. Thank you, Hans." She places a hand on his for just the briefest of moments. Then, noticing some customers entering the restaurant, she gets quickly to her feet and, speaking in a louder voice, says, "More tea, Herr Officer?"

Hans sits back and looks up at her, matching her tone for the benefit of the restaurant's other customers. "Thank you, fraulein. And maybe one of your delicious pastries?"

Twenty minutes later, leaving the restaurant in the care of Missus Petrenko, Elena slips through the front door and heads to a building across the square, where her cipher machine is currently located. She turns the rotors to the setting that ensures only her U.S. military contacts near Moscow can decrypt her message and begins to type, sharing this latest intelligence from Hans; both his information *and* his suggestion.

She waits to hear confirmation that her message has arrived, expecting the door to burst open at any moment as the Germans trace her signal. Eventually the confirmation arrives, only this time it comes with a reply.

Using her codebook, as she has been trained to do, she painstakingly pieces together the message, which reads, "Extraction plan in progress. Return to Eagle in two months. Await instructions."

Extraction plan? She frowns at the message. *They're pulling me out? But I've only just got everything set up here. It's all working so perfectly.* She runs a hand across her belly. *It's the baby. Wouldn't look good back home to let an American women give birth out here.* Elena switches off the cipher machine, pulls the cover back over it and heads back to the restaurant in a daze. *Home. I'm going home. Back to the States, back to my family and my friends! I can't believe it!*

♣

"I can't believe it!" says Hans as he sits in the restaurant late one evening. "The plan worked even better than I expected."

Having slipped the lock on the door, Elena brings over a single candle to the table and joins Hans. "Tell me," she says. "What's happened?"

"As we anticipated, the invasion began on July fifth, five days ago. But when our new Panzers came rolling in, certain of finding the Soviet tanks all but wiped out by the Luftwaffe over the last few weeks, they were surprised to find the T34s in full force. Your guys have more than double the number of tanks we have, if not more! Those dummies worked perfectly!"

Elena breathes a sigh of relief. Over the last few weeks, reports of the devastation wreaked by the German bombers and the destructive power of the upgraded Panzers have made her increasingly concerned for Konstantin, her beloved man and the father of the coming child. To hear that the ruse with the fake tanks paid off almost overwhelms her.

"That's wonderful news, Hans! Does this mean the battle will be over swiftly?"

Hans shrugs. "Not necessarily, I'm afraid. It could still be a number of days or, who knows? Maybe even weeks yet before the Soviet tanks really start to make their presence felt. After all, those upgraded Panzers are real heavyweights. They're going to make life very hard for the T34s. But I'm sure it's only a matter of time. This could be one of the key battles that brings this war to an end, thanks to—"

He stops at the sound of footsteps approaching and they turn to see Missus Petrenko shuffling in from the kitchen.

"Don't mind me," says the old woman. "I just found something I think belongs to you, Elena."

"What did she say?" asks Hans, unable to understand Missus Petrenko. "Can she understand German?"

Elena shakes her head. "Not even a little." Then, speaking in Russian, she turns to Missus Petrenko. "What is it? What have you found?"

"A letter," says the old woman, holding out an envelope. "It was hidden in among the groceries. Thankfully they rarely ever get searched by this lot." She jabs a finger towards Hans, dressed as always in his Gestapo uniform.

"What was that?" he says as Missus Petrenko shuffles back into the kitchen.

"Nothing. Don't mind her. Look," she says, her eyes flicking over the words on the envelope excitedly, "I'm going to have to go. This is important. Thanks again for the update. Please do keep me posted."

Having let Hans out and bolted the door shut again, Elena hurries back to her room, one hand clutching the large bulge of her belly as she heads up the stairs.

Kostya! She thinks. *At last! I don't know how you managed it, but this is definitely your handwriting.* Once in the seclusion of her room, she sits on the bed and tears open the envelope. She straightens it out on her lap, revealing Konstantin's familiar handwriting across the back of a torn poster.

"Lenochka, my darling," she reads, her eyes hungrily devouring the words. "Here we are on the eve of battle and it's looking like a big one! We're ready for it though, thanks to all the information we've received from our agents and allies in recent months. Even the British have been helping us, the enemy of our enemy and all that! We also extracted information from the German officers we captured at

Stalingrad, so we not only know the "surprise" attack is coming, but the forces we're going to face: at least a million soldiers of the Wehrmacht and three thousand German tanks. But we're the ones with the surprise! We've had months to prepare our defenses and they're ready at last. With the help of the locals, we've dug enough trenches to reach from Moscow to the Far East together with thousands of tank traps. You wouldn't believe how much hard work it's taken, Lena, even just to shift the earth for a single tank trap! Last night, our guys caught a couple of German snipers, still busy building a nest for themselves, and we squeezed them for information on the time they were due to launch the offensive and from which direction. Not long now, and our artillery has got a nasty treat for the Nazis when they make their move. Should all be over in fairly short order." Elena shakes her head at Konstantin's words. *It must be six days since he penned this letter,* she thinks. *And Hans reckons there could still be another week of fighting. Hardly what I'd call "fairly short order"!* She turns her attention back to the closing lines.

"Lenochka, my love, I am worried about you. I have not heard from you since we parted over all those months ago. I do hope the little misunderstanding of our last discussion has not played a part in your silence. I miss you and I look forward so much to seeing you again soon. Very soon! With all my love and kisses, Kostya."

Elena sighs as she folds up the letter. Although delighted at receiving word from Konstantin, she is disappointed that she cannot reply, cannot tell him how she feels, cannot tell him how concerned she is for him. And she cannot tell him about their baby.

She undresses for bed and slips into the covers, but finds it impossible to sleep. Her head is buzzing with questions about the future.

Is Kostya going to be alright? Is he going to survive the Germans' attack on Kursk, what with the improvements Hans says they've made to their tanks? And if he does, will I be able to get word to him about the baby before I am whisked off back to America? And what happens when I get back there? Will I be able to return after I give birth? Will I even want to?

Round and round her thoughts go, alternately anxious for Konstantin and for the child growing inside her. At last, Elena drifts into a fitful sleep, but even here there is no rest. Instead she finds herself caught up in a nightmare.

In her dream, she turns and there behind her is a towering furnace, its flames fiercely licking at molten steel, casting a deep orange glow into the darkness around. She tries to back away, to escape from the searing heat of the furnace, but she cannot move.

"Lena." She looks up at the sound of her name and peers into the fire, shielding her eyes from the blinding light. There in the flames is Konstantin, in the helmet and uniform of the tank leader. His handsome face is its usual calm, though his eyes are sad and there are a few soot marks on his cheeks. "Lena," he says again. "You are such a wonderful woman. It has been my greatest joy to meet you and get to know you. I shall never forget those beautiful moments we've had together." He pauses, as he gazes at her from the flames with sorrowful eyes. "I have come to say farewell, Lena, my darling. Please do well and remember that I love you. And I always will."

She reaches out to touch him, to hold him, to stop him from leaving her and finds herself lying in her bed, one arm outstretched, her body drenched in sweat.

What was that all about, she wonders, as she gasps for her breath.

What can this dream mean? And then her blood runs cold as she realizes what this must have been—a final farewell from Konstantin. She lets her head drop back onto her pillow and, unable to get to sleep again, she lies there until morning, her arms wrapped around her swollen belly in an attempt to comfort herself.

"Not long now before takeoff."

Helen looks up at the man who has addressed her. *Another Gestapo officer,* she thinks, noting his black uniform with the usual insignia. *This plane must be full of them!*

"I hope not," she says, turning back to peer out of the window at the runway.

She only boarded the plane a few minutes earlier, but already she feels much of the anxiety and pressure of her life in Kharkov slipping away as the aircraft slowly fills up with the passengers for its flight to Berlin.

So far the extraction plan has worked perfectly. Helen's hair is once again its usual blond, though cut much shorter than before, and her restaurant clothes have been replaced with the uniform of the SS-Helferinnen—black coat, skirt, cap and boots. Her U.S. contacts managed to smuggle her a set of papers to go with her disguise, and when she came to board the plane as Liesel Schneider the guards ushered her straight on.

This flight to Berlin, however, is only the first leg. Once she has landed, she is to board a plane to Stockholm and then another to Egypt, which is now allied territory. From there, the United States Air Force will get her safely back home to Phoenix, Arizona.

Helen glances back at the man who addressed her, but he is in conversation with another officer. Looking over the heads of those seated in front of her, she counts merely twenty people. She is just over a third of the way down the aircraft, so she reckons there are around fifty people in all and only a few stragglers making their way on board.

Barely half full, she thinks. *And every one of them officers of the Wehrmacht or the Gestapo. What a gathering!*

The sound of laughter catches her attention and she sees a group of men talking in cheerful tones, clearly pleased to be returning to Germany and their friends and families.

I know how they feel! I can't wait to see mine. How long has it been since I last saw them? Two years at least.

She leans back in her seat, gazing, unseeing, out of the window as she imagines the look on her mom and dad's faces when they see her again, and how wonderful it will be to talk with her grandmother about the adventures she's had here in the old woman's homeland.

They had been the only ones who were allowed to know she was coming out here, and even they did not know the details of her mission.

My poor mom, she thinks, remembering her reaction to the news. *She really didn't want me to come here. Even my dad seemed close to tears! They're going to be happy to have me back home again. Grandma will make one of her famous apple pies. And no doubt mom will cook up that Korean stuffed duck she knows I love, with dad plying me with rum and cokes, his special mix!*

She smiles at this thought, while a wave of excitement mixed with homesickness washes over her, and pats her belly, enjoying again the thrill of how much it has grown in the past few weeks.

Here's one surprise they certainly won't be expecting! A grandson for my parents, great grandson for my granny.

And, although she can't explain why, Helen is certain that the baby *is* a boy. So certain, in fact, that she has already settled on naming him Konstantin—the best name in the world—after his heroic father and the great Rokossovsky.

I hope you look like your dad. Those light brown eyes, that dark hair, those soft Slavic features, a daily reminder of the man I came to love. Helen sighs, saddened again at the thought of her nightmare and the death of Konstantin. *But it was just a dream,* she thinks, hope flickering in her chest. *He may not be dead at all. Maybe one day we will see each other again.*

Feeling the tears welling up in her eyes, Helen quickly thinks about her journey home to distract her from the grief that threatens to overwhelm her.

Come on, girl! This is no time to for self-pity. There's too much at stake.

She goes through the details of the extraction plan in her head, the agent she is to meet in Berlin, who is taking over her role in Russia, and to whom she needs to pass on vital information; the contact in Stockholm, who will furnish her with a new passport and disguise.

Not long now and this whole nightmare will be a thing of the past!

With a smile once again spreading across her face, Helen peers back out of the window just in time to see a black car pulling up on the runway outside. As she watches, a number of men, all in the uniform of the Gestapo, emerge from the vehicle and she glances at them briefly without really looking. But as she turns away, Elena's blood seems to freeze in her veins and her breath catches in her throat.

It can't be, she thinks desperately, as she looks back at one of the men. *Hans! He's not supposed to be here!*

The men disappear from view, but soon reappear, making their way onto the plane. As they begin to head down the aisle, she sees the look of despair on Hans's face with the angry, purple bruise on his cheek. His hands are held behind him a curious, unnatural fashion. *He's been handcuffed,* she thinks, her panic growing. Fixing her gaze straight ahead, she works out for few seconds what is going on. And no matter how she looks at it, she always comes to the same conclusion: *Hans has failed! He's been broken... And now these men have come for me.*

During their time working together, Hans explained some of the methods the Gestapo employ to extract information from people.

"They always break in the end," he had told her. "Whatever you do, don't let yourself be caught by the Gestapo, that's for sure. It's better to take your own life!"

It's better to take your own life. These words keep going round and round in Elena's head. *There's too much at stake, too many contacts that could be exposed, too much information that she could be forced to divulge. As could I, when the Gestapo discover my role in Kharkov and my Russian and U.S. networks, which they inevitably will.*

She runs her hand across her belly once again, but not feeling the bulge of the baby this time. Instead her hand moves higher to another bulge, one that will bring death rather than life.

Ever since she was a young schoolgirl, Helen has always made sure she is prepared for every eventuality, and though she hoped the bomb hidden beneath her thick coat was an unnecessary precaution, she suddenly realizes that this has just become the only option. In only a few moments the future that stretched out before her has been snatched away, snuffed out by that one brief glimpse of Hans' bruised face.

Her hand slips into the coat, carefully drawing out a trigger switch. Concealing the device in her palm, she rests her hand on her belly and takes a deep breath. Beneath her fingers, Elena feels the push of tiny legs as her baby moves inside her. She smiles sadly and turns to peer over her shoulder.

There, several rows back, between his two Gestapo guards, Hans looks wretched and afraid. For a moment their eyes meet.

Then, knowing it is the right thing to do, she opens her hand and presses the trigger.

Chicago, U.S.A. 2045

Chapter Twenty-nine

nn's eyes snapped open. She was breathing heavily and staring at the ceiling in confusion. Lifting her arm from the couch, she ran her hand across her belly, feeling for the child that seemed to be there only moments before.

"What?" She struggles to collect her thoughts. "Where am I?"

"It's okay, my dear," a voice said nearby. Ann couldn't immediately place it, but it sounded old and somehow familiar.

"You'll feel unsettled for a few minutes, but that's okay. You've been out for three hours now."

"What do you mean three hours?" She turned her head to see an old lady striking a match and holding the flame to a strange-looking candle, which immediately began producing great plumes of dark smoke.

The psychic smiled across at her.

"Just that, three hours. Your longest session yet... and your last. Your friend, Nina has been waiting for you."

"Nina?" Ann racked her brains, trying to make sense of this and, as she breathed in the candle fumes, her mind began to clear at last. "Nina! She's here?"

"I certainly am, sweetie." Ann's friend swept into the room on her high heels. "Gods, I've been waiting in that damned room forever. I notice you ignored my advice to get in some decent entertainment for your guests." She cast an accusing glare at the psychic. "I've spent the last thirty minutes boring myself to death with a magazine on pig rearing. Anyway, darling," she said, perching on the arm of Ann's couch and addressing her. "I just had to come and see you, so here I am."

"How did you know I'd be here?" asked Ann, shuffling backwards so she could sit up.

"Well, Rob told me of course. But that's not important. A little bird told me you've got another guy fighting for your attention. A certain *Japanese* man?"

"How the hell do you..." Ann stopped, a frown creasing her forehead as she turned to look at the psychic. "Sorry, did you say this was our *last* session?"

"That's right," said the old woman. "You have seen all that I can show you, my dear. And all that you needed to see."

"So that's it? There are no more past lives to revisit?"

"No more that you *need* to revisit, no."

"So, what am I supposed to do now?" said Ann, still looking confused. "I still don't have any concrete answer about what I'm doing or where I'm going!"

"Ah." The psychic smiled at her, showing off her lack of teeth. "That, my dear, is the beauty of life!"

"She's a funny old stick, isn't she?" said Nina, as she and Ann made their way along the alleyway towards their cars. "So what were you this time? An astronaut? Or the guy who discovered America?"

"You mean Christopher Columbus?"

"That's the guy, yeah."

"I wasn't him. I was a young woman in Russia during the Second World War. In the end I blew myself up and destroyed a plane full of Nazis."

"Wow!" Nina raised her eyebrows in astonishment and flicked her hair out of her face. "You sure get plenty of excitement, don't you!"

"But it's all so sad," said Ann, stopping as she reached her car and turning to look at her friend. "In every one of these past lives I've died young, in my prime. Have you heard of Natasha Rostova?"

"No. It sounds Russian, though. Is that who you were in the Second World War?"

Ann shakes her head.

"Hardly. She's the heroine in *War and Peace,* my favorite novel back when I was... in that life. Why couldn't I be more like her? She used to be beautiful in her youth, attracting the greatest men in Russian high society. But she wasn't cut off in her prime. She went on to have a family of four children, though she also ended up losing her figure, becoming fat and a bit of a whiny old hen."

"That's the way of the world, darling. We all have to sacrifice for our dreams in the end."

"But I sacrificed myself when I was still young. I never had the chance to grow old and have my own happy family."

"So you had no kids in that past life?"

"Oh, Nina," she said, her face mirroring her misery and the tears welling up in her eyes. "I... I was going to have a child. A boy. But I was still pregnant when I died. I never even got to hold him in my arms."

"Ann, my love," said Nina, throwing her arms around her friend. "There's still time in *this* life. You have years ahead of you! You can have a child if you want to."

Ann pulled away slightly. "I don't know, Nina. Who with?"

"Well, by the sound of it, you've got a choice. There's Michael, your glacier-like archaeologist, or Tomo, your Japanese admirer. I'm sure either of them would leap at the chance to do their part in the whole baby-making process!"

"I don't know," said Ann, still looking dejected. "I have to figure out what's going on with Michael."

Nina stepped back, placing her hands on Ann's shoulders and looking into her eyes. "Yes, that's right, sweetie. You've got men fighting over you. And there's plenty more when they came from. If you want to get what you want, all you have to do is make the right choice. It's all in your hands, darling!"

"Is it?"

"Of course it is." Nina let go of Ann and glanced down at her watch. "Anyway, I've got to dash off and see Roger now, but I just wanted to catch you and ask if you'd like to meet up later for a drink at the Tower. Just me and you, and we can forget about all our cares for the evening. Eight o'clock work for you, sweetie?"

"Sure," said Ann, opening the car door and stepping inside. "Sounds good. Thank you, Nina."

"Where to, my lady?" asked Rob, his face appearing on the E-A device, a blue flower tucked behind one ear. "It's not too late to get to the shops if you still want to."

Ann looked at him a moment as she pulled away from the sidewalk. "Sure," she said. "Let's go shopping. Doing something normal might help clear my head."

"Are you okay?"

"I think so," Ann replied, a wistful note in her tone. "Or at least I'm trying to be. You know what really bugs me, though, having experienced life on the front line?"

"What's that, my lady?"

"How come monsters like Stalin and Hitler appear throughout history, when fate is controlled by our Creator? What's that all about?"

"It's a fair question, my lady, and one that has plagued many over the years. And it's a difficult one to answer. Do you remember what happened to the two monsters you mentioned?"

"They ended up tearing each other apart."

"Exactly! And in the end one evil destroyed the other."

Ann considered this as she turned the car round, heading back into the city.

"That's true," she admitted. "But they weren't the only ones caught up in that fight. Thousands upon thousands of people were killed in that war; not just soldiers, but civilians too, even children! Over and over again, monsters rise up and innocent people die."

"Innocent?" said Rob, raising an eyebrow at this claim. "It's these so-called innocent people who create these monsters. They only rose to power because people allowed them to, because people raised them up and gave them that authority!"

"I suppose so. But it seems such a waste of life. What possible purpose could such tragedy serve?"

Rob shrugged in his screen and said, "We can only hope that it will provide a lesson for humanity and stop people from giving power to such monsters."

"Huh," said Ann, unconvinced. "We're not so good at learning from history!"

"What about you, my lady? Can *you* learn from history?"

"Well, sure, I guess," said Ann, taken aback by the directness of the question. "But I'm only one person, Rob. What difference can I make?"

"What difference can anyone make? Every choice, every action, every decision, no matter how small, makes a difference for better or for worse. It's true for monsters. It's true for saints. And it's true for you, my dear Ann."

"I guess. Though I'm still not sure *every* choice makes a difference."

"Well, here's an opportunity to put it to the test," said Rob, smiling once again. "You've just got a message from Michael asking you to meet him in the Japanese Botanical Gardens."

Ann blinked in surprise. "Oh! When?"

"Now. He says he'll be waiting you there." Rob paused, allowing this to sink in, the blue flower behind his eye slowly morphing into the pink blossom of a cherry tree. "So what's it going to be? The choice is yours."

Why does Michael want to meet me suddenly? Ann wondered. *He's lovely, charming and everything, but I still have no idea what this guy actually wants from me. Could he really be from a competitor company looking to steal our ideas? Or does he want to buy me out for his own business? Or... something else?*

"If only it was easier to know which choice is the right one," she said. "But I must see him, if only to try and find out what's going on between us. Plot me a route to the Botanical Gardens, Rob. I'll never get my shopping done at this rate!"

The parking lot was almost deserted as Ann pulled into a space next to Michael's distinctive car.

She switched off her E-A device and slipped it into her bag, hurrying off to get into the Japanese Garden. After several minutes, many of which were spent wandering in the wrong direction, she found it and there, sitting on a bench beneath a maple tree, was Michael.

Dressed in a white shirt with rolled up sleeves and casual dark blue pants, his tanned face a picture of peace, he didn't look at all treacherous.

He turned to gaze at her as she approached, a smile spreading easily across his face.

"Ann," he said, getting to his feet and holding out his hands to her. "Thank you for coming to see me. You made the right choice."

She stopped, her eyes widening in surprise at this mention of choice.

Does he know what I've been talking about? she wondered. *Has he been spying on me this whole time?*

"Come," he said, stepping forward to take her hand. "I have some people I want you to meet."

People? What people? A shiver of anxiety shot through her as Michael began to lead her away through the trees. *Who could he want me to meet? His parents? His work colleagues?* She looked around, but couldn't make out any other figures in the garden.

"Where are they?" she asked.

"They're not right here, exactly, Ann," said Michael, turning to give her a reassuring smile. "We have to travel a little to meet them, but it will be short trip. Trust me."

Trust you? How can I trust you, when I don't really know who you are? If this is some attempt to get me to sell out A.I.I.'s innovations or something, I can't get involved. I can't betray my team, my guys, and everything we've worked for. These thoughts flashed through Ann's mind, but she kept on walking and all she said was: "A short trip where?"

"You'll see," said Michael, stopping outside what appeared to be a small cabin, which Ann assumed was used by the gardeners. He turned the handle and opened the door, gesturing for her to enter. "Everything will be fine, my dear."

Finding herself unable to refuse him, Ann forced a smile as she stepped nervously into the darkness of the cabin. Michael followed her and pulled the door closed behind him.

"What's going on?" asked Ann, feeling her panic rising. "What is this place?"

"Hush," said Michael and, in the dim glow from the cabin's one window, Ann watched him reach out his hand and placed his palm gently onto her forehead.

Her eyelids grew suddenly heavy and she felt for a moment as if she was falling, falling into a void that would swallow her up, yet somehow she felt as though that was okay, as though that really was the right thing to be doing and she embraced the darkness.

HEAVEN

Heaven. No Time Place

Chapter Thirty

W hen she opened her eyes again, she was surprised to find herself still on her feet. Michael dropped his hand and Ann gasped in surprise. The cabin, which only moments before had been dark and gloomy, was now bathed with white light streaming through its window.

"Welcome," Michael said, pushing open the door to reveal, not the gardens, but a vast room whose walls and ceiling seemed to glow from within. "Welcome to Heaven."

"Heaven?" Ann stared out through the open doorway trying to make sense of what she saw.

The maples and Japanese cherry trees that had been there when she walked in were gone. Instead there was this vast, cathedral-like room, glowing with its strange white light. She looked up to see a vaulted ceiling, beautifully carved from what looked like glass or crystal, towering far above them.

A movement caught her eye and she realized that there were amazing constructions of glass and crystal visible beyond the room she stood in, visible through vast windows stretching away to the right and left. These objects were spinning around their axis, sparkling in all the colors of the rainbow.

Awesome, she thought. *It reminds me of the kaleidoscope I had as a child with its rotating patterns and colors. I wonder what those things are. They're just hanging in space like - well - spaceships!*

Glancing around the room, she caught sight of several people standing next to desks with sleek computer-like screens, their faces bathed in the soft, white light.

She turned to Michael. "Is this some sort of trick?"

"It's an impressive trick, if it is!" he said with a smile. "But no, this is Heaven. Come on, let me introduce you to some people." He headed out of the cabin and, after a brief moment of hesitation, Ann followed.

She tentatively stepped onto the softly glowing floor and was surprised to find it firm, her feet cushioned as though by a deep carpet. As she entered the large room a woman, wearing a loose, light robe, which Ann somehow associated with Ancient Greece, approached her.

She looked around fifty years old, her face friendly, her body slim and athletic.

"Welcome, Ann," she said. "We've been expecting you."

Ann's eyes widened in amazement as she realized the woman's smile did not move as she spoke. Instead the greeting seemed to make its way directly into Ann's mind, as though it was a cloud of thought instead of speech. *She's speaking straight into my head,* she thought.

"That's right!" said the woman, and again no actual sounds came out of her mouth. "This is how we communicate here."

Here? thought Ann. *Could this really be Heaven?*

"That is correct." Again the cloud of thought. "Welcome. My name is Elizabeth, or Beth for short."

"I—" Ann began, thinking the word instead of speaking it. Beth nodded, encouraging her to continue. "I am pleased to meet you, Beth."

It was a strange sensation to be communicating in this way; though, far from being uncomfortable in any way, Ann felt a sense of peace and belonging as she did so.

Michael's hand, which rested on her shoulder, added to this feeling of safety.

"And we are pleased to meet you too, Ann," said Beth. "Let me introduce the team to you." She turned and gestured towards the others gathered around their screens. "We are God's front line, a part of God's taskforce. We are the supervisors of the humans on the Earth. We oversee the human beings, helping nations and shaping events as required in accordance with the Great Plan. This is Eva.'

A young woman emerged from behind a desk, her chocolate-colored skin covered with fine white cloth, her hair long and dark. She glided across the floor, her hand outstretched, and Ann noticed that she really *did* glide. Her feet did not touch the ground and her legs made no walking movements.

"Nice to meet you," she said, using the same thought cloud as Beth.

Ann almost jumped as Eva gripped her hand, shaking it firmly.

She had almost expected her to be like a ghost, with no tangible, physical presence. Instead of replying, Ann just stood there with her mouth open as Eva released her hand and glided back to her desk.

"It's okay, Ann," said Michael's voice in her head. She turned to look at him, her eyes wide. "I know this is all very strange and new, but trust me. There is no trickery here. You will do all these things too, with a little training."

One by one, the members of the team were introduced, each one gliding forward to greet Ann and shake her hand before drifting back to whatever it was they were working on.

They were all very good looking and friendly, but there was something else about them. Something that Ann could not quite fathom at first, but which they all had in common and which set them apart from the normal, everyday people that Ann knew, like Nina, Peter, Tomo and others. It was not only the way they moved and smiled and communicated with each other, but it also had to do with the way they made Ann feel, somehow at peace as though surrounded by friends, as well as the light that seemed to emanate from each of them.

Their faces, their arms and every other parts of them that were not covered, seemed to shine from within, which, in addition to each of their other characteristics,, created an overwhelming sense of belonging, of being at home, somewhere you would always be welcome.

This is all so surreal, thought Ann, as the last member of the team, a tall man called Julian, completed his greeting and floated back behind his screen. *I must be dreaming or something. Maybe I'm still on the psychic's couch in some kind of trance.*

"It's all very real," Michael's thoughts assured her as he wrapped her hand in his very real fingers. "In fact, you might say this place is even more real that the world you have lived in until now."

"But—" said Ann, again, concentrating as she tried to communicate with her mind instead of her mouth. "But why me? What am I doing in this place? Why am I in..." she paused as she considered the word she was about to say, then realized it must be true, "...in Heaven?"

"Ann." Ann turned, recognizing the feel of Beth's thoughts. "As you know, as we have allowed you to see, you sacrificed four of your physical lives for what we call the Highest Intangible Values."

Ann frowned. "What are they?"

"In your case," Beth continued, "they were Freedom, Love, Courage and Peace. You achieved Hope in your fifth - your current life - when you declined the engagement proposal from Tomo, keeping your hope for true love alive. As a result of that karma, you have achieved freedom from the reincarnation chain. You no longer have to go from life to life, in an attempt to attain Redemption—you've done it, Ann. No more pain. No more struggle. No more risk. Instead you have been granted *Immortality*, a single life without death."

Michael gave a light handshake to Ann. "In your last, fifth life, you have also acquired knowledge of high-technology as well as the ability to achieve your goals and targets, which along with the gain of spiritual awareness have made you a very desirable asset here in Heaven. Now you can stay with us, helping to oversee the humans and increase their knowledge of higher things, should you wish to."

"Should I wish to?" Ann looked from Beth to Michael and back again. "You mean that's what the last few months of struggling with the spiral, discovering my past lives and meeting Michael have been for? To get a deeper understanding of myself? Preparing me for... this?"

She waved around at the sparkling room and up towards the enchanting dome far above her. And as she did so, she realized that the cabin she had arrived in had disappeared.

"Exactly!" said Michael. "The Spiral of Evolution was given to you to show your own sacred path within Spiritual Eternity. The sense of unease was coming from the reincarnation chain, which was trapping you for unresolved karma. But not anymore."

"And if I had accepted Tomo? What would have happened then?" Ann asked hesitantly.

"You would be given another chance to break the chain, but perhaps not in this current life."

Ann nodded, assimilating the awesome information. "So, what do you do in here?" she turned to Michael.

"We have tasked Michael with taking on the role of overseeing your training and partnering with you in the work you will be doing here. He will be your guide and will help you through every aspect of your job here," Beth replied.

"And what is this job, exactly? What work will I be doing here? I won't have to sit staring at a computer screen for the rest of eternity, will I?"

Across the room, Eva's head popped up from behind her screen and for a moment Ann was concerned she had said something wrong.

"Sorry," she said. "No offense meant."

In her mind, Ann heard Eva laugh, a pleasant sound that filled her with a feeling of reassurance. "None taken," she replied before returning to her work.

"A lot of your time will be spent time-space traveling and learning on the job. Our equipment is pretty complicated. You aren't supposed to just use it, but also to know how and why it works," Beth said, turning to point at an empty desk. "But we also have a workstation here all ready for you."

Ann looked around again at the others in the room. "So who exactly are you? You don't really seem like humans. After all, this is supposed to be Heaven, right? I thought angels lived there."

"From the human point of view, we are angels." Beth paused for a moment and looked at Ann thoughtfully. At last, as though having made up her mind about something, she said, "I can see this is all a lot to take in, and this is not an easy decision to make. However, I would like to offer you an incentive to join us."

"An incentive? Like what?"

"That is up to you, Ann. Is there anything from your lives that would make your transition here easier? Anything you wish us to give you?"

"Anything?" said Ann, after some thought. "From any of my past lives?"

"Indeed."

"When I was in the Stone Age, I had a son." Ann looked nervously at Michael, who smiled and nodded encouragingly. "Can I... Can I get my baby boy back?"

"Yes, you can," said Beth, a smile spreading across her face.

"Really?" Ann's eyes widened in delight.

"Sure. And don't worry, we will adjust his physique and intellectual capacity to the current moment. It will be as though you gave birth to him in your current life."

"Ah." Ann sighed.

"So, would you like to join us, Ann?"

Beth held out her hands towards her and, for a moment, Ann stared at them as though unsure what they were. Then, with a burst of joyful laughter, she took them in her own hands.

"Would I ever!" Ann said, and she felt the wave of delight from the others in the room wash over her.

Michael drew Ann into a hug.

"It's great to have you on the team," he said. "You're going to love it here. Come on. Let me show you around."

Epilogue

A while later - though exactly how long, it was hard to tell as the passage of time seemed somehow hard to measure here - Ann found herself standing in what appeared to be a room without walls.

The softly glowing floor stretched away in every direction and she could see tall towers of white marble in the distance as well as great palaces made of crystal. Far to her right, there was the shimmering sparkle of a waterfall, which must have been hundreds of meters high.

As she gazed around in wonder, she heard Beth's thoughts nearby. "I have someone to see you, Ann."

Ann turned round to see Beth entering through the archway and she gasped in amazement. There, in the woman's arms, was a young boy; not much more than a year old.

"Ann," said Beth. "This is. . ."

"Wu!"

Ann knelt on the floor, holding her arms out to her son as Beth lowered him to the floor. He smiled at Ann from beneath his brown curls and she realized that, although she had never actually met him, or at least not in this life, he recognized her.

"Mommy!" he said, as he walked towards her, more surefooted than she expected.

She felt a lump in her throat and blinked away the tears as she wrapped her arms around Wu, overwhelmed to be reunited with him.

She kissed him on the head and whispered in his ear, "My special boy. Mommy's here for you. Always!"

She got back to her feet, sweeping Wu up in her arms and turning back to the magnificent vista around them.

"Look at this place, Wu," she said, stroking his head, her son's head, affectionately. "I wonder where we are!"

"This is the Portal," said Michael, standing by her shoulder. "It is here that we will do most of our work."

He stepped forwards and pressed his hand against something which shimmered beneath his touch. Ann realized that, although the room seemed to stretch out to the distant horizon in every direction, it was in fact contained within four walls, though, except for a slight shimmer to indicate their presence, they were almost entirely invisible. From one of the walls, Michael drew out a huge pair of white wings - bigger that those she had seen on a swan.

"Angel wings?" she said, her thoughts laced with incredulity. "Really?"

Michael laughed. "I guess you could call them that, yes. Actually this is a very simple and convenient way to travel around in the past."

"Travel? In the past?" said Ann, even more incredulous.

"Sure. These wings are non-expensive and ecologically friendly."

"So are you saying you have time-machines to go back in time?"

Michael nodded. "Yes. We have developed a number of methods to travel both to the past and the future. We shall start our training from the simplest one."

"Wait. Are you saying that I, that *we*," she gestured to herself and Wu, "are going travel to the past?"

"Yes, you are. We have all of human history to oversee. And since you have a sound knowledge of Russian language and culture, we have decided to give you responsibility for the country of Russia from the six to the twentieth century."

"Six to the twentieth century Russia?" said Ann, hefting Wu onto her hip.

Immediately the young boy reached out to the wings, still clutched in Michael's hand, and began to play with the snow white feathers. "But Russia's huge, and, well, it's a long time! Hundreds of years. That seems a lot to oversee."

"Well, you've got plenty of time," said Michael, with a reassuring smile. "And you don't have to do it all at once. Our work is intimate and personal. We deal with one situation, one person, at a time."

"And should I wear these?" asked Ann, pointing to the wings.

"Not yet. They're going to take a bit of training to use; although it's actually quite similar to hang gliding. You remember that don't you?" said Michael with a wink.

Ann smiled and nodded as Michael slid the wings back into the wall, which swallowed them into invisibility. "I just want you to get a feel of the equipment we'll be using. For now, though," he continued, pulling something else from the wall, "We'll be using this." The object that he drew out was a cube, its sides roughly a foot long, fashioned from what looked like pearl.

From one side a large glass eye stared out unblinking.

"What is it? "

"We call it the Projector. This is a simple tool that will enable us to travel through time without ever leaving this room. It's all very safe and keeps us out of harm's way."

"Out of harm's way?" Ann frowned and hugged Wu tighter. "You mean we're going somewhere dangerous?"

"Well, this is medieval Russia we're dealing with here. Times were pretty cruel back then, so you never know." Michael looked her in the eye, his face serious. "Are you scared?"

"No," said Ann, and realized this was true.

Ever since she had stepped out of that cabin and into this new world she had felt somehow serene. Not just because it was a calm place, but for the first time since she was a five-year-old girl, back when her parents were alive, she felt completely at peace.

There was no more fear, no more worry, no more struggles. She was perfectly content.

"No," she repeated. "I feel great."

"Well, even if you were worried, your days of risk and worldly troubles are over now that you're with us. You are safe, trust me." Michael reached into the wall again, pulling out a bundle of clothes and handing them to Ann.

"You'll need to put these on," he said. "There's some for you and your son."

They were soon dressed in medieval attire, with Ann wearing a long dress, her head covered with a veil, while Wu wore a simple woolen tunic. As Michael made a few adjustments to the Projector, she picked Wu up, enjoying being close to him again.

"I'll never leave you alone again, my love," she whispered in his ear.

Suddenly, one of the invisible walls burst into bright light as the Projector fired up.

"All right," said Michael. "Is everybody ready?"

"We're ready!" said Ann.

"Ready," said Wu, copying the word and making Ann laugh.

Michael ran a hand over the Projector and Ann was amazed to find herself looking out across a sunlit field.

Wild grass stretched away before her eyes, where a small cluster of wooden houses huddled together at the end of a narrow path.

Along this path, his gray head bent down under the weight of a bundle of sticks, his short pants and tattered shirt held in place with a knot of rope, was an old man making his way slowly from the houses.

"I don't understand," said Ann. "Is this like a film, or is it actually happening?"

Michael glanced at her. "Oh, it's happening. The year is 1217, but by using the Projector, we're able to see and be seen, to hear and be heard."

"So this old guy here can actually see us?" asked Ann, hoping that he couldn't also hear her thoughts in the way Michael could.

"Sure. Wait a moment... Ann and Wu, get ready. I'm switching it on.... now!"

The man stopped and craned his neck to look up at them just as Michael thought the words.

Ann watched as his eyes widened and he suddenly dropped to his knees on the stony path, reaching out a hand towards her.

"It's the blessed Virgin!" he cried, and though his Russian was archaic, Ann understood him well enough. "See! She is holding the Christ child! God has blessed me!"

And with that he bowed his head down to the ground.

Michael passed a hand over the Projector and the image faded, the old man, the field and the houses vanishing to be replaced by the softly lit room and the distant columns and towers.

"What was that all about?" said Ann. "Did he think we were Mary and Jesus?" She nodded to her son, still snuggled in her arms.

"Mommy," he said, looking up at her, and she kissed him gently on his curly hair.

"It looks that way," said Michael.

"But shouldn't I have said something to him? Do we even know who this guy is?"

Michael smiled up at her. "He's someone who needed a little nudge; something to help him on his spiritual path. That's what our job is here, to develop people's spiritual awareness. And I reckon you did just fine on that score. Perfect in fact! Do you want to see?'

"Er, sure." Ann bent down to watch as Michael began to fiddle with the Projector again. He was turning a small wheel that was set into the pearl casing. "What are you doing?" she asked.

"Just tuning it, that's all. It's quite simple, a bit to the right and we move into the future, a bit to the left, into the past. Difficult?"

"Piece of cake!" said Ann with a smile. "Especially after Rob."

"Great! And now we're shifting forwards a few days ahead and moving to the church in the nearby village."

He ran his hand across the surface again and an image burst into life across the wall.

Ann stared out into the inside of a small church, its wall covered in icons of Jesus, the Blessed Virgin and various saints, the air full of the sound of the choir. There was a large crowd of people, kneeling before the altar, their lips moving in silent prayer as a priest, dressed in his immaculate robes, a black hat perched on his head, spoke blessings over them.

"It's alright," said Michael. "They can't see us this time. I've set it to project one-way only." But Ann wasn't worried about that.

She was busy studying one of the icons.

"Michael," she said at last. "The handsome guy in the icon, with the long, blond hair, thrusting a sword in that dragon-like creature... is that you, by any chance?"

He walked across to stand next to her, taking her hand in his, their fingers intertwining.

"Yes, that's me all right," he said, peering at the icon. "'And there was war in heaven: Michael and his angels fought against the dragon.' Not a bad likeness either! That was painted a few hundred years ago though, back when I had my own mission to Russia. Good times! You're going to enjoy working here."

Suddenly the door of the church flew open and, for a moment, the choir faltered in their singing.

"Ah!" said Michael. "Here's our old friend, right on schedule."

Ann watched in amazement as the old man, still in his short trousers and shirt, though without the bundle of sticks, hurried towards the priest.

"Father!" he shouted. "Father! It's a miracle, a miracle, I tell you. The Lord has blessed me with a vision. I saw her. The Blessed Virgin and the Lord. I saw them both as clear as I see you now."

The priest had made his way through the crowd towards the old man.

"Is this true, Ivan?" he asked, holding the man by the shoulder and looking him in the eyes. "God has granted you a sacred vision?"

"O Father! You should have seen it. Such a blessing!" Tears were welling up in the old man's eyes.

"Come," said the priest, placing an arm around him as they walked together. "Let us talk about this great wonder, and pray together."

The image faded once again and Michael turned to face Ann.

"That old guy, Ivan, hadn't been into a church since his wife died seventeen years ago. As I told you, our work is close-up and personal, helping, guiding and shaping one individual at a time. And you made a real difference for that fellow. That vision of you and Wu will last him for the rest of his life, and he is only forty-five now; without a doubt, his story will spread. There will be icons of you two, encouraging people to believe that God watches over them and blesses them, reminding them of the importance of the Blessed Virgin and the power of motherhood and of woman. This has been a great start, Ann. Congratulations!"

She took a step closer to him. "Come on, Michael. All I did was stand there. You were the one who did all the, whatever it was you did with the Projector. You were the master here."

"Let's say it was both of us," said Michael. "The three of us, even. Wu played his part, after all."

"Yeah, he did pretty well, didn't he?"

She let her son down so he could stand next to her and ruffled his hair with her fingers, while he seemed quite content waving around an angel's feather, which Ann realized he had pulled out of the wings.

"It's wonderful to be reunited with Wu. I love him."

"Oh?" said Michael, slipping a hand around her waist and drawing her closer. "And what about me?"

Ann turned her face up towards his, enjoying the warmth of his body pressed against hers.

In the distance the waterfall sparkled, its light reflecting in her eyes, and from somewhere the sound of gentle birdsong could be heard.

She smiled as a wave of deep contentment and joy washed over her.

"Let me show you," she said.

.

"Ask, and it will be given to you;

Seek, and you will find;

Knock, and it will be opened to you."

—Holy Bible

Thank You

for the reading my novel Redemption!
I would appreciate to get Your valuable
review on Amazon.com.

Most Sincerely,

Jacky

www.ingramcontent.com/pod-product-compliance
Lightning Source LLC
Chambersburg PA
CBHW070832260626
47170CB00007B/2336